Praise for *The Wild Colonial Boy*

"A well-plotted thriller...What sets *The Wild Colonial Boy* apart from other books of its kind is Mr. Hynes's clear compassion for everyone who suffers in the Irish predicament." —*The Wall Street Journal*

"A suspenseful novel written with commitment and clarity." —*Chicago Tribune*

"Tautly plotted...strongly and elegantly written...Hynes is a wonderfully adept writer....This immediacy...provides much of the book's narrative strength. It is the characters, however, that truly engage attention. All are vivid, drawn clearly enough to reveal the logic behind their actions, yet, like real people, they never become entirely predictable." —*The Philadelphia Inquirer*

"Compelling...James Hynes delineates his characters' motivations in broad, credible strokes; each is arrestingly believable." —*New York Newsday*

"One of the most exciting first novels of the season, a literate, beautifully managed tale that manages to make the almost impenetrable complexities of the Irish troubles unusually clear...Combines an intricately detailed story with writing worthy of any fine novel, for a quality thriller." —*Anniston* (Alabama) *Star*

"With narrative skill, a vivid sense of place, a facility for incisive descriptions of people and emotions, and a flair for dramatic scenes, James Hynes takes us...on this thrilling adventure. Hynes is a masterful storyteller, able to hypnotize his readers with spellbinding narrative." —*Grand Rapids Press*

the WILD COLONIAL BOY

tHe WILD COLONIaL BOY

JAMES HYNES

Picador USA
New York

ACKNOWLEDGMENT

*The author is grateful to James Michener and the
Copernicus Society of America for their generous support.*

For information on Picador USA Reading Group Guides, as well as ordering,
please contact the Trade Marketing department at St. Martin's Press.
Phone: 1-800-221-7945 extension 763
Fax: 212-677-7456
E-mail: trademarketing@stmartins.com

Book Design: Barbara Marks Graphic Design

Library of Congress Cataloging-in-Publication Data

Hynes, James.
    The wild colonial boy / James Hynes.
        p. cm.
    ISBN 0-312-20442-6
    I. Title.
    PS3558.Y55W5 1990
    813'.54—dc20   89-39246
                                                                     CIP

First published in the United States by Atheneum, a division of Macmillan
Publishing Company

First Picador USA Edition: January 2001

10 9 8 7 6 5 4 3 2 1

For my mother and father
and for Dean Garrison, Jr.

The Irish are not philosophers as a rule, they proceed too rapidly from thought to action.

JAMES CONNOLLY

"Surrender now, Jack Duggan, for you see we're three to one.
Surrender in the Queen's high name, for you're a plundering son."
Jack drew two pistols from his belt and proudly waved them high.
"I'll fight, but not surrender," said the Wild Colonial Boy.

TRADITIONAL IRISH SONG

J immy Coogan kept his eye on the road behind him all the way out of Belfast, watching the blue-black ribbon raveling away in the rearview mirror as he drove up the valley of the River Main. He was aware of his own caution, and that annoyed him, for after fifteen years as a guerrilla his watchfulness ought to have come as easily to him as walking or breathing. In town, in the gray and crumbling streets off the Falls Road, he knew when the Brits were looking and when they were not, and he could watch his back and mind the edges of his peripheral vision without thinking, all the while doing something else—talking, eating, whistling up a tune—as if it were the only thing on his mind. Out here, though, driving past flinty Protestant farms under a scrubbed blue October sky, there was no telling who might be watching him, unseen, from the broad, brown hills on either side. The tight warren of lanes and secret border crossings in South Armagh were as familiar to him as the cramped streets of the Falls, but here, north of Belfast in open moorland, he didn't know the signs, and that rattled him. Glancing again in the mirror at the empty road behind, he caught himself thinking what he never thought in Belfast, wondering what it would be like to visit, say, America, where he wouldn't have to watch his back all day and night. A dangerous thought, and he nearly smiled, as if at the naïveté of a child: he was as liable to see America as he was the dark side of the moon.

1

Until he left the city he had even felt calmed by the routine of evasion. Maire had rented the car for him, a nearly new Ford Escort smelling of cigarette smoke, and had dropped the keys at their safe house. He had carried the plastique himself, wrapped tight in an old gray blanket and stuffed into a leather Adidas carryall, from the arms dump in Turf Lodge to the safe house, then across town with the keys to the car that had been parked in Ormeau Road. It was breaking the rules for a battalion commander to do his own fetching and carrying—moving the stuff himself in broad daylight, renting a car instead of hijacking one—but he was a commander without any men, the members of his Active Service Unit shot to death at the border three months ago by a suspiciously lucky Brit patrol. But even that, Coogan thought bitterly, worked to his advantage. At least he didn't have to worry about the rest of Belfast Brigade; they would not miss the plastique for several days. And by then, he thought, it would be too late.

All he had to worry about were the Brits, and God knows he was used to that. Still, he had a bit of a fright just outside of Ballymoney, when an army lorry loomed up suddenly behind him, arousing for an instant something as close to panic as Jimmy Coogan ever knew. But he resisted the urge to floor the accelerator and did his best to ignore the canvas-covered grille of the lorry in the rearview mirror. He tried not to think of the Adidas carryall on the floor behind his seat, as though thinking could give him away. Beyond the town he pulled into a lay-by and watched as the lorry, full of bored and gaunt-faced squaddies, turned north up the road he'd intended to take. He waited a moment, gripping the wheel tightly and taking deep breaths; then he started off again, twenty miles out of his way, through Coleraine and then back northeast to the coast.

In Portballintrae he drove to the carpark at one end of the village and stopped the Escort. There were no other cars in the carpark, but even so he reached over the seat and fussed with the carryall for a moment, wishing that he had at least a blanket to throw over it. Then he glanced at his watch and saw that he was late, and he opened his door and turned sideways in the seat, wondering if he ought to move the bag into the boot. But if anyone was watching, that would arouse even more suspicion, so he simply got out of the car and closed the door, locking it and slipping the keys into the pocket of his mac.

He started east along the beach through a fine mist of sea spray, and he pulled the wide lapel of the mackintosh all the way across and buttoned it. The mac was an expensive one, a Burberry. He had tried it on in a posh men's store in Bond Street, turning this way and that in front of the tall mirrors like a woman while the clerk fussed around him and tugged at his cuffs. Coogan'd had no intention of taking it until he realized how Maire would scold him for it—and she did, telling him that it was his business to remain inconspicuous, that the mac made him look like a bloody television correspondent—and even then he'd had no intention of *paying* for it; he'd sent the clerk into the back for a box, and when the man was gone he had slipped out the door as someone else came in, disappearing skillfully into the crowd along Oxford Street, feeling an uncommon pleasure at using the arts he'd cultivated as a guerrilla to do something for himself.

Now he was glad he had the mac as he left the beach and started climbing the headland; he flipped up the collar with both hands as he came onto a narrow path between a rusty barbed-wire fence and the crumbling edge of the cliff. The coat was warm in the stiff, salty wind blowing off the sea, and it made him look, he decided, not like a journalist, who were pretty seedy as a rule, but like some up-and-coming Sinn Fein politician. Just the sort of thing you'd wear at an Easter rally, Coogan thought with contempt, or if you were running for Parliament. Or, he thought with even more contempt, to a secret negotiating session with a British minister. Which was what it would come to eventually if Joe Brody and his lot had their way. It never failed: let a man of action go public, let him turn political, and the next thing you know he's chatting up the Brits and shopping his comrades to Special Branch.

Not that Brody had ever really been a man of action. His

family was Republican all the way back for three generations, true enough, but Joe was always more likely to have his nose in a book than his finger around a trigger. He'd spent his internment in the Kesh reading a lot of bollocks, socialist theory and all that; whatever Republican fervor he owned up to was strictly to please his elders. On the other hand Coogan had learned his politics at the age of sixteen in a harder school than Long Kesh, in the streets of the Lower Falls in the summer of '69. He didn't have Joe's head start, either: Jimmy's own mother had offered tea to British soldiers when they'd first arrived; six months later she was on her knees on her doorstep, banging a dustbin lid to warn the street of a Brit patrol, her husband in the Crum, her Jimmy on the run. Coogan himself remembered his first taste of CS gas, the way it burned his eyes and nostrils and scalded his tongue, the way his windpipe constricted as though someone had him murderously by the throat. Fuck socialism, let Brody read Fanon and Debray and Guevara if he wanted: Jimmy had joined up to drive the Brits out of his country, his city, his street.

Yet Coogan had never had any cause to doubt Joe Brody's commitment to the armed struggle. He could accept the lip service paid to the political side, could accept Brody's dual role as, secretly, Chief of Staff of the Army Council, and publicly as president of Sinn Fein and abstentionist Member of Parliament. He could even accept Brody's overtures to the militant British left, but only grudgingly: as far as Jimmy was concerned, a Brit was a Brit was a Brit. But at the end of the day, Brody's bookish socialism had clearly got the better of him. Something happened to men when they got to the top: they lost sight of the goal. It had happened with Michael Collins in 1921, it had happened with de Valera ten years later. And now it was happening again: there was talk that at the Ard Fheis, the annual Sinn Fein party conference, in Dublin next week Joe Brody would propose actually taking the seat he had won in the Irish Dail, throwing in the sponge on sixty years of abstentionism. Coogan tucked his chin down between the raised collars of his mac and tightened his fist around the car keys in his pocket. He had ten pounds of Czech plastic explosives in the Escort behind him that said that Brody had no more chance of taking a seat in the Dail than he did. Vincent Brennan of London Brigade and his ASU were with Coogan in this; get us the plastique, he'd said, and my lads'll arrange something spectacular, just in time for Brody's opening address. Mind you, Coogan had told Maire, we don't want to cause a split. All we want to do is light a fire under Joe Brody's arse to help him remember what it's all about.

Coogan paused on the clifftop to look at his watch again. He'd been late getting to Portballintrae; that meant that Billy Fogerty should have been waiting for him in the carpark, or at least should have met him on the beach just beyond it. The plan was for Billy to drive another rented car to the carpark at Giant's Causeway, two miles up the coast from Portballintrae; the two men were to walk toward each other along the coast, exchange keys in passing, and continue on. Then, as Coogan drove Billy's car back to Belfast, Billy Fogerty would drive the rental over the border into Donegal and deliver the plastique in Donegal Town to Desmond Cusack, who would take it the next leg of the trip.

Unless, of course, Billy had lost his way. He hadn't been waiting in Portballintrae, nor had Coogan met him on the beach. Pausing in the wind on the clifftop, waves rumbling against the rocks below, Coogan looked ahead to see a single car in the carpark of the Causeway visitors' center. Below that he saw someone in a dark green anorak walking down the paved pathway that led around the base of the cliffs ahead toward Giant's Causeway. He recognized the anorak: it was Billy, apparently late as well. Coogan could hardly fault him for that, but now the boy was walking the wrong way, away from Coogan, east along the base of the cliffs. Which meant either that he was confused, which wasn't likely, or that something was wrong. Coogan watched Billy disappear around a bend in the pathway, and he considered turning back. But if Billy knew he was being followed he wouldn't have come here. It was obvious that he wanted to talk, that he was nervous and needed encouragement. Coogan drew a breath and cursed the boy for an idiot, but he started down the slope toward the pathway.

Billy was waiting for him on the Causeway itself, a low, uneven tongue of gray basalt columns, fitted together like a honeycomb, that descended gradually into the sea like a ramp. Coogan left the asphalt walkway and stepped from column to column toward where Billy stood facing out to sea. Not far beyond him the sea rolled in long, booming waves into the curve of the Causeway, each wave giving up too soon, hissing back into the sea without really trying. Coogan stopped a few paces behind Billy, his hands in the pockets of his mackintosh, the wind driving the skirts of the mac between his legs.

"What's the crack, Billy?" he said, watching the boy's back.

Billy glanced over his shoulder without surprise, then looked back out at the sharp horizon.

"I have to talk to you," he said, just loud enough to be heard over the rumble of the waves.

"Good bloody place for it." Coogan hunched his shoulders against the damp wind. "Very dramatic. Perhaps I should have brought a film crew."

Billy twisted his shoulders and looked pleadingly at Coogan, a child begging not to be teased.

"I can't do it," he said. He watched Coogan uncertainly and looked away again.

"Stage fright, Billy?" What an appalling place to meet; there was nowhere to run. "Want me to hold your wee hand for you?"

Billy turned around to face the tall basalt columns of the cliffs above the Causeway, his arms crossed tight over his chest. Coogan looked the boy critically up and down; he was eighteen or nineteen years old, of the generation that had grown up since '69; unlike Coogan he couldn't remember anything other than war in the streets of Belfast. He was thin, sunken-eyed, jumpy; he smoked too much. But Coogan had picked him for this particular job because he wasn't the sullen sort of incorrigible you saw hanging about on street corners in the

Falls. He was no hood, as far as Coogan knew; he had no history of petty thievery or joyriding. He kept himself neat; his hair didn't hang slack the way some boys' did, like unwashed curtains over their gaunt cheeks. Right now, though, he was shivering and red-faced, and even in the new jeans and sweater and anorak Coogan had bought him he looked small and guilt-stricken, as if he had put on an older brother's clothes in the dark by mistake. He snuffled back some snot, and Coogan realized that it wasn't entirely because of the chill.

"They know," Billy said in a husky voice, as if he was about to cry.

Coogan felt the first tremors of alarm again, and he stiffened, resisting the temptation to look around and see the lorry load of soldiers lining the clifftop like red Indians.

"You were followed," he said, narrowing his eyes against the wind.

The boy looked away, shuddering.

"I don't mean the Brits." He looked at Coogan, his eyes wide and red-rimmed. "You know who I mean."

"Who, then?" Coogan held himself very still, propped up against the wind with his feet apart.

"The Provos."

Coogan felt a freezing cold spreading under his coat that had nothing to do with the wind, but he smiled as if at a child and said, "Idjit, I *am* a Provo."

"Maybe, maybe not." Billy stared hard at Coogan and sniffed.

"Quit fuckin' me about." Coogan was finding it harder and harder to maintain his bemused grin. He felt colder by the minute.

"Look, you know what I'm talking about," Billy said. He took a step toward Coogan, his cheeks red, as much with anger as with fear or the cold. "Joe Brody says, bring the plastique back and he'll let it go this once."

Coogan hated to show it in front of Billy Fogerty, but for a moment he couldn't speak, and he opened and closed his mouth and made no sound.

Billy watched him, and his look seemed to soften, so that he just looked cold.

"Christ, it's starvin' out here," he muttered in the country fashion, hugging himself. Then he looked at Coogan and said, "Look, he says bring it back and there's no harm done. That's what he said."

"You came alone?" Coogan said in a tight voice.

"Christ, I wouldn't tell him where, all right?" Billy stood very close and peered at Coogan, half pleading, half angry. "I told him I wouldn't tout on a mate. He didn't like it much, but I walked out on my own two legs, didn't I? He told me he'd let me alone if I told you that, that there's no harm done. I fuckin' risked my life to tell you that, so carry your own fuckin' bomb."

Coogan stared blankly at Billy for a long moment, his mind stuttering uselessly while Billy looked nervously away and then back again to see if Coogan was still watching him. Somebody had seen Jimmy leave the arms dump; it was as simple and as stupid as that. He felt frozen through and unsteady; a good strong gust of seawind could blow him over and shatter him on the rocks like a block of ice. He was scarcely out of the gate and Brody already knew. He felt anger bloom in his chest like a flower, but it was a cold emotion, calculated for maximum effect. He raised his hands.

"You useless little shit." Coogan grabbed for the front of Billy's anorak. "You fucking told him!" he shouted, but Billy threw up his arms and knocked Coogan's hands away. His face was red; in a street-corner reflex he shoved Coogan in the chest with both hands.

"I didn't have to tell him, did I!" he shouted. "He fucking knew already!"

Coogan was going numb all over. He couldn't feel his hands and feet, but he felt a kind of euphoria, like a freezing man in his last moments. Without thinking he swung at the boy, missing him by inches. Billy staggered and fell anyway. Coogan checked himself and took a step back. He pushed his trembling fingers back through his hair, the boy at his feet scrambling away crabwise across the damp, uneven stone.

"Hang on, Billy, I'm sorry." He squeezed his eyes shut, opened them again.

"You *lied* to me!" Billy shouted, his voice shaking. "You said this was Provo business and it's not. You *lied*, you fucker."

Coogan stepped unsteadily toward him, only the wind holding him up, and Billy jumped to his feet and skipped sideways from column to column, a few feet away from the soughing green water.

"That's what you *said*," he shouted, red faced. He stopped with his back to the cliff, shivering in his too-large clothes, dancing on the toes of his new white running shoes, ready to bolt at Coogan's slightest move.

"You didn't tell me you'd gone off on your own." He was crying now. "I don't want no part of your family squabble. I'm lucky now if they don't kneecap me."

You're lucky if I don't, Coogan almost said, but he caught himself. It wouldn't do any good; the boy was more scared of Brody than of him. He lifted his palms to the boy, to show he meant no harm.

"Joe Brody's not your friend, Billy." His voice sounded thin and high against the rumble and hiss of the waves behind him; he felt numb with the wind at his back, pressing the collar of his mackintosh along his chin. "I know you didn't tell him anything, and that's good. He's not fighting for Ireland anymore."

He stepped toward the boy, but Billy started to run. Coogan felt his knees weaken at the sight. He wanted to fall down and plead with the boy, he wanted to run after him and break his arm, but all he could do was muster his voice and cry, "Wait!"

"Fuck off!" Billy shouted, skipping backward now over the broken columns. He turned and leaped onto the asphalt pathway, running for all he was worth back up toward the carpark.

Coogan jammed his hands in his coat pockets and watched him go, his mind blank and cold. It was pointless to go after him. When the boy disappeared around the bend Jimmy started back, stepping unsteadily from column to column, his mind unable to work, grinding uselessly like a cold engine on a winter's day. At the top of the path he found the visitors' carpark empty, a crescent cut in the gravel where Billy had spun the wheels of the car in his haste. Coogan shivered and turned away, starting back up the headland toward Portballintrae. He didn't feel warm again until he was stumping along the clifftop. For a moment he wondered if the boy would tout on him now; then he decided that Billy was too scared and too smart to do anything that stupid. Even Joe Brody would disapprove. Then he wondered if Brody had had the boy followed, and he stiffened at the thought of a bullet coming out of the tufted grass around him. But then, walking faster, he decided that Brody wouldn't do that, that it pleased Joe's vanity to sit back and wait for Jimmy Coogan to come back on his own, all humble and contrite, on his knees, bearing the parcel of plastique in his arms like a bastard child he was owning up to. Bless me, Father, for I have sinned. Coogan jogged down the slope of the headland toward the little curve of beach below the carpark, and he started to laugh. St. Joe would love that, surely, the opportunity to soften his steely idealogue's demeanor and slip into the stern compassion of the confessor, shepherd to his flock. Christ, what a priest he'd have made! First he'd forgive me, then he'd bless me, then he'd break my legs. Then he'd kill me. Coogan smiled and opened the front of his mackintosh, and he started to run along the beach, spitting sand after his feet like clods of turf at the racetrack.

"Fuck Joe Brody," he said out loud, and he laughed, thinking, Billy Fogerty's not the only fish in the sea. I'll find someone else.

On the way to his cousin's wedding, Brian Donovan's car dropped its drive shaft on the Ford Freeway and rolled to a stop in the center lane. It was a '68 Chevy Impala station wagon with 240,000 miles on it—enough miles, Brian liked to point out to nervous passengers, to have driven to the moon. Brian had known that it was liable to die on him at any moment, but even so it made him queasy and frightened to floor the accelerator and hear the engine roar while the car rolled slower and slower, as if in a dream. He sat in shock for a moment with his hands on the wheel while cars in the fast lane blared their horns and swerved around him, and he remembered how in a fit of chivalry he had let Molly take the Volvo without argument two days ago. He started to laugh. Flooring the accelerator and going nowhere seemed to be the story of his life lately.

Waiting for the tow truck he took his cigarettes out of the glove compartment and put the pack in the pocket of his suit jacket, and when the guy came Brian gave him the registration and told him he could have the car. At the gas station he called a cab and spent twelve of his last twenty dollars getting to the church, tying his tie in the back seat of the cab and asking the driver how he looked. He showed up in time to join the reception line in the corridor between the church and the banquet hall; his father glanced at his watch and scowled at Brian before he'd shake his hand, and as his mother kissed him she brushed his cheek with her knuckles to see if he'd shaved.

"Okay?" he said, stepping back and opening the jacket of his thrift-shop suit so that she could see the red suspenders that went with his red hightops.

"Are those appropriate for your cousin's wedding?" she asked, pursing her lips at the sneakers.

"Gee, maybe they are a little dressy, Mom," he said, starting down the reception line. He shook hands with his enormous, red-faced uncle, who murmured something unintelligible and covered Brian's hand with two large, damp palms. He kissed the bride and stopped at his strapping, loutish cousin, who widened his already dilated eyes and gave a slow, stoned smile. He insisted on giving Brian the whole elaborate handshake he had learned in his fraternity, and Brian endured it with a crooked grin.

"Let's get together later, okay, dude?" the cousin mumbled, fumbling with Brian's fingers. His expression implied the possibility of further substance abuse in the parking lot.

"Sure," Brian said, with no intention of doing anything of the sort.

An hour and a half later the groom was still trapped at the head table, his high having worn off, his eyes dilated now with sheer animal fear, and it was Brian's father who clutched his arm and steered him away from a beautiful cousin in a green dress, saying, "Come with me, Brian. We have to talk."

He held Brian's arm all the way into the rectory, as though he were marching him in to see the priest.

"I didn't see your car outside," he said.

"It died," Brian said, gently pulling his arm free. "That's why I was late."

"Well, goddamnit, why didn't you call me? I'd have come got you."

"I know."

His father stopped at the heavy oaken door of the priest's study, and he looked his son up and down. For a moment Brian felt like apologizing. Perhaps it was because he felt as if he were being hauled up before Father Garrison to make an accounting of his wasted life, but he found himself reflecting on the sin of pride, which made him give a perfectly good car away to an ex-girlfriend and spend the last of his money on a cab to keep from calling his father for help.

"We got a certain situation in here," his father said, his hand on the doorknob.

"I never laid a hand on her, Officer."

"What?"

"It's a joke," Brian sighed.

"You can start by knocking off the smart-ass crap." His father turned the knob and pushed the door with his shoulder. "Maybe you just better be quiet for once and listen."

He waved Brian in, following him and pushing the heavy door shut behind them. After the fluorescent bright of the reception hall, Brian paused on the thick carpet of the study and let his eyes adjust to the dim light. Only the brass desk lamp was lit, its yellow light gleaming in the dark paneling. His two uncles were there, Uncle Martin leaning against a bookcase, and Uncle Matt, the florid-faced father of the groom, propped in the padded window seat with his cummerbund loosened and an iced drink clutched on his knee. Brian's cousin Mike, the groom's younger brother, sat in a deep, red-leather chair, his leg in a long white cast propped up on an ottoman. A pair of aluminum crutches leaned against the bookcase next to Uncle Martin. Mike looked up wide-eyed at Brian and smiled uncertainly, and Brian smiled back in anticipation of another complicated handshake.

"Hey, Brian," Mike said.

"Mike." Brian nodded. "Don't get up."

Mike laughed nervously and rubbed his cast, and as Brian's father eased himself behind the priest's desk Brian saw his grandfather seated in the other deep, wing-backed chair, looking withered and dry in his old tuxedo, his frail hands propped on the cane between his knees. The shadow of one of the chair's wings fell across his face, but as Brian's eyes adjusted to the light he could see how the left side of his grandfather's face drooped, as though someone had kicked out the supports. Brian's father settled in the priest's creaking chair and squeezed his nose between two fingers. Brian noticed that only Mike and Uncle Martin were watching him; his father sorted some envelopes on the desktop, while Uncle Matt stared into the middle distance in a haze of Scotch whisky. Grandfather Donovan probably didn't even know where he was.

"Well," Brian said, looking around unsuccessfully for someplace to sit, "I suppose you're all wondering why I called you here today."

His cousin Mike snickered and looked around to see if anybody else was going to laugh. Brian's father ignored it and lifted a travel agency folder, holding it across the desk toward Brian.

"What's this?" Brian took the folder and tilted it toward the desk lamp to read it.

"It's a round-trip ticket," his father said. "To London."

Brian raised his eyebrows at his father and tried to read the smudged computer print on the invoice.

"Gosh, I dunno," he said. "Can I pass and go straight to the bonus round?"

Mike tried to laugh again, circling the room with his frightened eyes. Brian set the ticket on the edge of the desk and spread his hands.

"What is this?"

"We need you to go to Ireland for us," his father said, pinching his nose again. "On an errand for your grandfather. Mike was supposed to go ..." He nodded at Brian's cousin, and Brian turned to him.

"Broke it playin' football," Mike said. The yellow light gleamed on his skin and Brian saw that he was sweating.

"Tackle?"

"Touch." Mike shrugged.

"You're an idiot, Mike."

Brian was certain that he already knew what this was about. In this light, if you didn't know better, you might think the focus of the meeting was Grandfather Donovan, sitting very still in the shadows with his hands on his cane and his chin lifted like the family patriarch everyone pretended he still was. But Brian knew that if he lifted the lapels of his grandfather's tuxedo jacket he'd find nothing there but cobwebs and empty space, like a room left locked for fifty years. Yet he was moved in spite of himself. Once upon a time, when he was younger than Brian was now, Grandfather Donovan had been a real revolutionary, had killed a policeman in Ulster, and then had paid for it by a lifetime away from his country.

"Does this have to do with Grandfather's gun money?" Brian asked.

"Your cousin was supposed to take it," Uncle Martin said.

"I was *gonna* take it," Mike protested, looking at Brian but pleading with the older men in the room. "I *wanted* to do it."

Brian met his father's eye in the silence that followed, while Mike fidgeted in his chair, trying to get his leg comfortable. Brian knew that his cousin had no interest or even knowledge of Irish politics, that, contrary to his protest, he was going because he had no choice, and everybody in the room knew it. Mike used to sell dope out of a house in Ann Arbor when he went to school there a few years after Brian, fairly harmless amounts, but then in the summer before his senior year he was busted, caught with a virtual pharmacy in the trunk of his father's BMW in the parking lot of Cobo Hall on the night of a Bob Seger concert. Mike's father and his two brothers called in some favors and laid out a little hard cash—more than the little prick is worth, Mike's father had said—and the police dropped the charges, secure in the knowledge, perhaps, that a couple of years in Jackson Prison were nothing compared to what Mike was going to suffer from his family for the rest of his life. Which, as it happened, dovetailed neatly with Grandfather Donovan's periodic fits of Irish Republicanism, since if they had to send the money with someone, it might as well be a family member who couldn't afford to screw up. Or who was expendable, for that matter. Consequently Cousin Mike was doing his sweaty best at the moment to convince everyone that he wasn't enormously relieved to have broken his leg.

"I thought Grandfather didn't do this anymore." Brian brushed the edge of the desk with his fingertips and lowered his voice out of deference to the old man. From the window seat Uncle Matt snorted loudly over his drink.

"He don't know what he does anymore," he said, lifting the drink halfway to his lips and lowering it again. "Why don't we just tell him we sent the goddamn money and spend it on something serious."

"It's still his money, Matt." Brian's father swiveled in the creaking chair to face his brother.

"Jesus H. Christ," mumbled Uncle Matt, lifting his drink with a clatter of ice.

"How much money is it?" Brian asked.

"Ten thousand dollars," said Uncle Martin. "In cash."

"And you want me to go instead of Knute Rockne here?"

"I could do it in six weeks," Mike piped up. "Maybe eight."

"The thing is, it has to go now." Brian's father leaned back, his hands resting lightly on the arms of the chair. "For one thing, the Provos are expecting it. There's a relative of your grandfather's in the old country who expects to see an American cousin the day after tomorrow. It's all set up."

"Isn't he your relative too?" Brian said to his father, lifting the corner of his mouth.

"The other thing is your grandfather thinks he's going to die soon." Uncle Martin spoke from the shadows behind Grandfather's chair without lowering his voice, while Brian's father glared at his son. "He wants this money to go to the Provos and he doesn't trust us to take care of it after he's dead."

"He's right too, the old bastard," Uncle Matt muttered.

"Goddamnit, don't talk about him like he wasn't here," Brian snapped, surprising even himself. He glared at Uncle Matt in the sudden silence, half expecting his father to bark at him for being disrespectful, but nobody said anything.

"You don't have to do this if you don't want to," his father said after a moment, almost gently, staring at the desktop. "Nobody's pressuring you."

"I'll go."

"Part of the reason we asked you is because you're not on a fixed schedule like the rest of us," his father went on, as if he hadn't heard. "You can take a week off."

"I think the word you're looking for is 'unemployed,' Dad." Brian picked up the ticket and rapped the edge of it against the desk. He wondered if he was considered expendable too, the next best thing after Mike. "I said I'll go."

"Tell him about the money," Uncle Martin said.

"Aw, for Chrissakes," Uncle Matt complained. "He already said he'd do it."

"There's a thousand dollars for you when you get back," his father said hoarsely, ignoring Matt, not looking at Brian. He pushed an envelope across the desk. "Here's five hundred in traveler's checks for expenses. You can keep what's left over on top of the thousand."

Brian slipped the plane ticket into the pocket of his suit jacket, and he drew a deep breath, looking down at his father.

"I'll do it for nothing," he said, and his father glanced up at him with a withering look of paternal exasperation. Brian half expected him to reach across the desk and yank Brian over his knee. Instead he leaned back in the desk chair and sighed.

"Nobody'll think less of you for taking the money," he said wearily. "And it's not like you don't need it."

"Jesus H. Christ," Matt exploded. "He said he'll do it for nothin'."

"Shut *up*, Matt," roared Brian's father, nearly upsetting himself in the priest's chair. "If your idiot son hadn't broken his leg, we wouldn't be asking my boy to do this."

Brian blinked in surprise, and he glanced back to see his cousin Mike shrinking into his chair, looking as though he was about to cry. He turned back to see his father lean forward and fold his hands on the desk to keep them from shaking.

"I think we can talk about this when Brian gets back," Uncle Martin suggested from behind Grandfather's chair.

"Right," Brian's father said, glancing up at Brian, then twisting his face away as he pushed himself up. Without a word it was clear the conference was over, and Uncle Martin lifted the crutches and came around Mike's chair to help him up. Uncle Matt, red-faced, drained his drink and stood, staring hard at nothing in the middle of the room. Silence seemed to swell out to the corners of the study, and while no one was looking Brian picked up the envelope of traveler's checks and slipped it into his pocket with the ticket.

Then, in the middle of all the masculine throat clearing and moving about, Brian saw his grandfather shift in his seat and lift one pale, shaking hand off his cane to reach toward him. Everyone stopped as if the corpse at the wake had come to life, Mike half raised out of his chair with Uncle Martin at his elbow, his father frozen in the act of hiking up his trousers. Brian stepped up to his grandfather as if they were the only two people in the room and took his hand, smiling down at him, tipping his head down to hear what the old man had to say. But his grandfather's grasp was weak and papery and cold, and as he looked up at his grandson with his watery eyes he moved his lips with no sound. Brian gave the old man's hand a gentle squeeze, and he bent over the chair, at first surprised then unashamed at the tears in his own eyes, and he laid his other hand on Grandfather Donovan's shoulder and whispered in his ear, so that no one else could hear, "Up the Republic, huh, Grampa?"

Brian's father drove him back to Ann Arbor that night, and in the padded quiet of the Cadillac they put off speaking as long as they could. His father drove one-handed, hunched against his door, his face green in the dash light, and Brian watched out the window past his pale reflection at the dark October countryside.

"You got a passport, right?" his father said at one point.

"Yeah."

Ten miles farther, the joints of the old highway thumping under the wheels of the car, Brian said, "Why am I flying to London? Why not fly me straight to Ireland?"

His father shifted in his seat, settling himself more comfortably, and he spoke without looking at Brian.

"It's safer," he said. "You're less liable to be searched coming into Ulster from Scotland than you are from the Republic."

Brian thought for a moment, and said, "So what if they search me? I'm not carrying weapons."

"They're liable to be a little suspicious of anyone coming into the province carrying ten thousand dollars in cash. Especially if they dress like you do."

"There's nothing wrong with the way I dress."

"You dress like a fucking workman."

"Dad, I *am* a fucking workman."

His father groaned and twisted in his seat.

"Brian, don't give me your bullshit Marxism," he said, and when Brian protested his father cut him off with a sharp movement of his hand.

"You're drifting," he said, and when Brian tried to speak again he nailed him with a stare and said even more emphatically, "You're drifting."

There was silence again for a moment; then his father cleared his throat.

"The police there can hold you for seven days for no reason," he said. "American passport or not. And during those seven days, believe me, Brian, they can find out anything they want to know."

Brian looked across the seat at his father.

"You sound like you've done this," he said, trying to make his voice as even as possible.

"Maybe I have," his father said with sudden vehemence, glancing back at Brian.

"It's nothing to be ashamed of."

"Brian, listen, I don't give a rat's ass for the IRA." He lifted his hand briefly off the wheel. "They're a bunch of street punks playing at being revolutionaries."

"That's what they say about every revolution. That's what they said about Grandfather's generation."

"Maybe they were right."

Brian gazed in deliberate amazement at his father.

"This is your *father* we're talking about, remember?" It wasn't what he wanted to say, but there was something about arguing with your parents that reduced everything to the level of a dinner table shouting match, something that stripped the argument of all subtlety and wit. Suddenly you were sixteen again.

"And I love him," his father said. "Which doesn't mean I can't see him for what he is."

"Which is what?"

"I don't know." His father was silent for a moment, and Brian tried to marshal arguments in his head. But they all faded as he looked at his father's face in the dim green light, and the bottom dropped out of his stomach as he saw how old his father had become.

"I don't know what he was like in the old country," his father said at last, quietly. "Just a kid, okay, whatever that was like back then. Maybe even a revolutionary. But I'll tell you what he is now. He's a frightened old man who thinks he's going to die." He smiled to himself. "Maybe he thinks that after all these years he's going to meet up with the ghost of that constable he shot, ever think of that?" He glanced at Brian and chuckled, and Brian smiled indulgently. "I swear to God, when

I was growing up that goddamn policeman got bigger and nastier every time he told us about it, until I finally began to wonder if the old bastard ever actually shot anybody. Hell, I wouldn't be surprised he knocked some girl up and just hightailed it to America. Either way you look at it, what he's sending back is guilt money."

Brian sighed and looked away. He wondered if the children of revolutionaries were born cynics, if whatever passion had driven his grandfather as a young man was doomed to be swept aside in the inevitable war between father and son.

"Speaking of knocking someone up," his father went on after a moment, "don't tell that girlfriend of yours about this. Just tell her you're coming home for a week."

Now here, Brian thought, was tinder for an argument, but he answered matter-of-factly, all his anger burned up in arguing with Molly herself.

"That's not a problem," he said. "We're not speaking anyway."

"What, you guys break up again?"

"I think she means it this time. She moved in with another guy."

Brian turned to look out the window, his face suddenly hot, and he resigned himself to another outburst from his father; it would end, he knew, with an argument over money, especially when it came out that Brian couldn't afford the apartment without Molly's income, that he would probably have to move back into the half-finished apartment over Mark's woodshop, that Mark still owed him three months' back wages.

But there was a long silence as Brian silently ran down the inevitable progression leading back to his decision to quit school, and as they slowed for the Ann Arbor exit his father shifted in his seat and put both hands on the wheel, sighing as if he agreed with Brian how futile another argument would be.

"Well," he said, "it's probably just as well."

Jimmy Coogan liked to call it the bridal suite, but it was really only a damp back bedroom in a crumbling old terraced house two streets off the Falls Road, two up, two down, with a bog out back. Still, when he and Maire lay together all flushed and sweating after making love in their whining, sway-backed bed, he liked to imagine that it was the top floor of the Europa, or even—he smiled at the thought—a suite in the Grand Hotel in Brighton, where they'd tried to blow up Maggie Thatcher. Maire would hear none of it, though, neither his daydreaming nor even the suggestion of a real honeymoon. She wouldn't even let him knock the spider web out of the window; it's good luck, she said, it keeps the soldiers out.

Right now she lay across him with her breath hot against his chest, her heart still beating hard, the moistness between her legs pressed against his thigh. The thin blanket was pulled up to her ears, with only the top of her head showing. Outside the narrow house, a British helicopter thudded overhead.

"So what are we to do now?" she said against his chest.

He smiled at the dark ceiling and lifted his arm outside the blanket to stroke her hair. The cold air of the room tightened his bare skin.

"I could think of one or two things," he whispered, pressing his cheek against her forehead.

Under the blanket she squeezed the soft flesh at his waist.

"Ow." He twisted a little under her. "Bitch."

"You know what I'm talking about," she said. She lifted her head to dig her chin uncomfortably into his shoulder. "And don't call me a bitch."

"Is it a cigarette you want? I give up." Christ, just once couldn't she be playful or tender afterward. All sharp edges, Maire was, but the first time they'd met he had kissed her, even before they had spoken a word to each other. He'd been on the blanket then, serving two years in the Kesh for possession of a pistol, refusing to shave or bathe or wear a prison uniform. She was only just out of her teens then, one of the girls the Republican movement relied upon to smuggle communications in and out of the prison, the comms written on cigarette pa-

21

pers, rolled tight, and hidden in their vaginas. They'd met on visitors' day, Maire posing as a friend of his sister's, and he'd had to pick her out of a crowd even as he pretended to recognize her. Then, with a wary screw leaning over the partition of their cubicle, she'd kissed him, pushing the comm from her mouth to his with her tongue. Sure it was no pleasure kissing a gaunt, shaggy blanketman, but to his surprise she'd held the kiss a moment longer than was necessary, twining her fingers through the lank hair at the back of his neck. Then they'd talked, about what Jimmy no longer recalled, but he always remembered the kiss, remembered the look on her face as she leaned back, her bright eyes and her thin-lipped, self-satisfied smile. He'd kissed other girls under these circumstances, but none of the others seemed to find any pleasure in it. Walking back to his filthy cell, the comm spirited up his anus at the first opportunity, Jimmy realized that the light in her eyes was not for him but for the thrill of getting away with it. Imagine that, he thought. He was in love.

"Jimmy, this is serious." She lifted her head off his chest to scowl at him.

"I know."

Either the helicopter veered away outside, or the wind caught the sound and carried it off, leaving the entry silent beyond the window.

"Give it back," she said.

Jimmy sighed and rolled his head away from her on the pillow. She'd come a long way since the days of the blanket protest; she'd gone active on her own, working her way up the Sinn Fein ladder during the hunger strikes and after, giving herself notions beyond her experience.

"Ah, Christ, Maire, you know I can't do that."

"Why not?" She tipped his face back toward her with the tips of her fingers.

"It wouldn't make a difference, would it? As far as Joe Brody's concerned, I'm good as dead. Bringing the plastique back wouldn't change anything."

"Maybe it has already." She lifted her head, freeing her hair from the edge of the blanket. "You've made your point with Joe. Maybe you don't actually have to carry on with the rest of it."

She folded her hands on his chest and rested her sharp chin on her fingers. He looked up at the ceiling and sighed again. Ah, women, he would like to have said, or, You wouldn't understand, love, but she'd just brush that aside like a cobweb. Somehow Maire had come out of convent school tougher than a Jesuit, an admirable quality in a Belfast city councillor, but not so admirable in a wife. *My* wife, Jimmy thought, and he wanted to laugh. Somebody should do a feature on us for *Fortnight*; we're a bloody two-career family.

"Well?" She was waiting for an answer.

"All right, then." He pushed himself up, the bed groaning as he slid out from under her to lean against the cold iron of the bedstead. "Even if I take it back, Joe'll kill me as an example."

"If you don't take it back, he'll kill you for certain." She curled against his knees and leaned on one elbow, pulling the blanket around her.

"Only if he catches me." The cold air of the room was nothing to the chill he felt inside, talking with his wife about the chances of his surviving the next week or so. "If he doesn't, and my lads go through with the action in London—"

"*Unauthorized* action."

"—then it's not just between him and me anymore," he finished, ignoring her. "The whole bloody world'll know that there are some Provos who don't approve of their Chief of Staff giving up the struggle to run for fucking Parliament, who don't approve of him playing footsie under the table with the Brits."

"With the Militants, Jimmy," she said. "It's not like he's talking to Thatcher."

"They're all fucking Brits from where I sit. The IRA's not a fucking negotiating unit."

"Here, here," Maire said dryly.

"Christ, woman, I'm just after trying to explain—"

"Easy," she said, touching his shoulder to calm him. "What if I went to him, as a sort of intermediary—"

"Fucking hell!" Jimmy exploded.

"Let me finish—" she protested, but Jimmy brushed her hand away.

"Nobody knows about you and me," he said angrily. "It's for your own bloody good."

"I know, but—"

"Look, love, it's dead easy." He sat up straight and lifted her up with him, his hands under her arms. "Joe Brody's selling us out. He's practically handing us over to the Brits. He's using the liberation of his country as a stepping stone to his political career. He's got his eye on the main chance instead of on where he came from."

He held her tightly by her upper arms, her breasts pressed up against him, and she watched him wide-eyed like a girl.

"Well, that makes me bloody angry, and some others as well. Half the lads in London are with me on this, if I can only get the plastique to them. It's the only way I know to either topple the bastard or bring him down to earth again. As far as he's concerned I'm dead already, so all I can do is take it as far as I can and put him in a position where he's got to deal with me. We've got everything to lose by going back, and everything to gain by going ahead with it."

He paused, closing his eyes and relaxing his grip on Maire. He settled back against the creaking bedstead and sighed.

"All I've got to do is get the bloody parcel across the border to Desmond Cusack, and the rest takes care of itself. Then keep low till it goes off."

He felt spent suddenly, and tired. He opened his eyes to see Maire gazing at him, her eyes shining in the dim light, the way they had the first time, in Long Kesh.

"I'll take it," she said.

"No." He shook his head. "I can't allow you to take the risk."

"It's not up to you to allow me to do anything," she snapped. "I'm not your wee housewife."

"That's not what I meant," he said, though it was. "You're much more valuable away from the military side of things. We can't afford to lose you."

"Well, then, what *are* you going to do?" Her anger flared and she struck him hard on the chest. He looked away, at the gray curtain across the window at the foot of the bed. In this light the spider web was invisible.

"What about your cousin?" he said quietly, surprising even himself. "The American."

"You're mad." Her glare turned to disbelief, and she swayed toward him. "You can't be serious."

"Why not?"

"Christ, I . . . I've never met him," she sputtered, her eyes searching his face, looking for a hint that he was joking. "He's just a lad. He's an *American*."

"Exactly," Jimmy said, meeting her gaze, warming to the idea. "He'll probably have a rented car. Christ, they'll carry his bags over the border for him. He doesn't even have to know what it is he's carrying."

In the gray light Maire looked pained, as if struggling with indigestion, trying to think of an objection.

"I don't know anything about him," she said finally.

"So?" Outside he could hear the helicopter again, the thud of its blades echoing down the hard streets and rattling the windowpane.

"Americans are like children," she said with sudden venom, clutching her arms against the chill. "They come here like tourists to see a bit of aggro, get their thrill, and go home. It's like fucking Disneyland to them. Ulsterworld."

"Just talk to him, then." Jimmy Coogan reached for his wife and started to massage the stiffness out of her shoulders. "Sound him out without telling him anything, and if he seems up to it, ring me up and I'll come have a wee chat with him myself. That's all I ask."

He rubbed her shoulders and peered at her in the dark. The rattle and whine of the helicopter was quite loud now, and its searchlight slid across the window and filled the room like a photoflash, making strands of the spider web glisten. Suddenly Maire pressed against him and kissed him hard. The search-light glided away, the room reverberating to the beat of the rotor in the sudden dark. He started to roll her over, and as she stroked him he shivered and laughed and murmured in her ear, "You little whore." She rolled with him, but in a sudden movement she had him by the balls, tightly enough to make him freeze and hold his breath.

"I'm not your whore," she said into his shoulder. He swallowed and did not move, unable to see her eyes.

"When we've done with the Brits, we're going to work on Irishmen. There's going to be some changes." She rolled back to look at his taut face, still clutching him tightly. "Just so you know."

Under a low and drizzling sky, the bus left Larne and ground north up a road that wound carefully between brown hills on the left and a black, turbulent sea on the right. With his backpack propped in the aisle seat, Brian fought to keep his eyes open, watching the moorland beyond the smudged and scratched window; last night, landing in Ireland for the first time in his life, all he had seen beyond the harsh blue floodlights of Larne harbor were a row of houses and random lights scattered like stars across the dark. He had hoped to see more today, but after a few miles, the breath of the handful of people on the bus was enough to steam up the window, so he turned to a newspaper he found on an empty seat. There was a possible buyer for the idled De Lorean plant; three policemen were killed when their car was blown up by a culvert bomb; two Protestant men tied a Catholic to his chair and sawed his right hand off. He put the paper aside.

He was still jet lagged, but he could not sleep. After landing at Heathrow yesterday, he had tried to sleep on the train north. Once, in the middle of an erotic dream about Molly, he had awakened to find a broad-shouldered young Canadian sitting across the tea table from him. Brian knew the boy was Canadian because he wore a blue baseball cap with an orange maple leaf stitched across the front.

"Are you an American?" the Canadian said.

"Born and brewed in the U.S.A.," Brian yawned.

The Canadian squinted at him.

"Are you afraid to be an American overseas?"

Brian laughed and said, "Not until just now."

"That's why they told me to wear this," the boy went on, pointing to the maple leaf on his cap. "So nobody would mistake me for an American."

"God forbid." He did not ask who "they" were.

"Listen," the boy said with sudden vehemence, leaning across the table. "My sister was *spat* upon in London because someone thought she was an American."

"I apologize," Brian had said, closing his eyes again.

The bus only went as far as a village called Cushendun, and after that Brian hitchhiked. Even that, his father had said, was safer than going into Belfast to catch a bus that would take him all the way to his grandfather's village. But no one picked him up, and Brian walked through the rain up into the brown moorland, his knees aching with the unaccustomed weight of the backpack. There were few cars going his way, and every time he heard one coming he spun clumsily about, swinging the pack around and sticking out his thumb. Each time, though, the driver shook his head or made an indecipherable hand signal, and Brian wondered if he'd have to walk all the way to the next town and call someone to come get him.

As the light began to fade he found himself trudging through a misting rain along a narrow blue-black road, with nothing to see but the lowering sky and dying bracken and, in the distance, the dim gray sea. He tried to sing, but after a spiritless rendition of "The City of New Orleans" he ended up cursing everyone responsible for his being here in the fucking rain, shouting out loud the names of his father, his ex-girlfriend, his clumsy cousin, even his grandfather. Stopping to rest he dumped his pack on the ground and angrily stripped off his anorak. The fat money belt he wore had gotten twisted around to his side as he walked, and he reached up under his sweater to twist it roughly back into place. In the bed and breakfast in Larne last night he had hung the belt in the stall with him while he took a shower, and he had tried to sleep with it on, the thick packet of hundred dollar bills cutting into his back so that he was finally forced to turn over on his side. Now, as he wrestled his anorak back on and heaved the pack up off the soggy ground, he thought how ironic it would be to come all this way only to get hit by a car in the rain fifteen miles from his grandfather's village. He saw himself as a headline in tomorrow's paper: RICH DETROITER RUN OVER IN ULSTER. DOLLARS SCATTERED FOR MILES.

At last he got a ride from a soft-spoken man and his mother, and Brian squeezed into the back seat of the car with the man's two shy little girls and answered polite questions from behind the backpack on his lap.

"Pity it's rained on your holiday," said the man from the front, "but it's the time of year."

"Don't I know it," Brian said. "Next time I'm going to the Bahamas."

The man dropped him in the town square of Bushmills, in front of a World War I memorial, the soldier on top silhouetted against a gray sky fading to black. Brian walked the last mile to his grandfather's village. In Patrick Donovan's day Ballywatt had been a cluster of thatched cottages on a tiny, scalloped inlet, but the cottages had long since been replaced by two-story pebble-dash houses in a single row around the edge of the inlet. Dark had fallen by the time Brian came to the village's only intersection, and Ballywatt was only dimly visible in the amber streetlights, the sea hissing invisibly against the rocks at the narrow entrance of the inlet. Apart from a tiny grocer's shop, the only other public establishment was a pub occupying the ground floor of a tall, roughly plastered house, all its windows lit with the same yellow, dollhouse glow. A sign in fading red letters announced Donovan's, the pub run by Brian's cousin. Turn right and keep going, his father said, it's the only three-story house in the village.

Wet and exhausted, Brian paused in the yellow light on the step to read a hand-lettered sign on a piece of gray cardboard that said WELCOME COUSIN MICHAEL. He blew out a sigh and shouldered his way through the door, pausing in the vestibule to push back the hood of his anorak and gasp in the humid warmth like a beached swimmer. Through the next door he heard the low susurrus of voices, as of a crowd waiting politely for a meeting to begin. He took a breath and went into the warm, smoky bar, swinging his pack heavily to the floor as the room fell silent and the pale faces of all the people crowding the tables and lining the walls turned to him. With his pack off Brian felt unbalanced and unsteady, and before he said a word the barman, a broad-chested man with a thick, pushed-in face, lifted the trap door and came out smiling from behind the bar.

"Michael," he declared, offering his meaty palm. "I'm your cousin John."

Brian sensed the crowd collectively breaking into smiles as he met his cousin's firm, callused grip.

"Actually, I'm not Michael," he said, feeling John's grip loosen and the crowd catch its breath.

"Are you not?" John's face went blank.

Brian glanced around at all the puzzled faces, pushing his wet hair back from his forehead.

"Michael broke his leg," he said. "So they gave me his ticket and pushed me out the door." After a moment he added, "I'm his cousin Brian Donovan . . . son of Thomas, son of Patrick."

His cousin blinked at him, still confused, and the rest of the people glanced covertly at each other or covered their embarrassment with a sip of beer.

"Sorry, folks." Brian gave them his best smile. "I'm the best they could do on short notice."

But then, with his arm around Brian's shoulders, John announced that here was a cousin from America, Patrick Donovan's grandson *Brian*, and Brian found himself immersed in the crowd as if in a warm bath, shaking hands moist from clutching pints, accepting thumps on the back, and returning soft-spoken welcomes. Then a plump, pretty woman in a sweater and jeans pushed her away into the crowd like a teacher breaking up a schoolyard brawl and pulled Brian away to give him a hug and a dry peck on his cold cheek.

"The boy is half drowned, John," she scolded her husband. "Sure it wouldn't occur to you to send him upstairs first to dry off and have his tea away from all these terrible people."

There were cries of protest, but the woman—his cousin's wife, Ann—hooked her arm through Brian's and hauled him away, smiling and shrugging, while John mugged husbandly contrition behind her back and followed with Brian's pack tucked under his arm like a sleeping child.

"Have you eaten, Michael?" she asked, and before Brian could say anything her husband called out, "He's not Michael."

"I'll hear nothing out of you," she snapped over her shoulder. "You're in trouble as it is."

An hour later the guest of honor sat on a bench against a white plastered wall at the rear of the pub, crowded in by distant relatives and friends of the family, his glass of warm Guinness set atop a gas heater shoved in the corner to keep him warm. The glass was carried off periodically and refilled without his ever having to get up, and after a while he lost count. An old man in baggy clothes and a cloth cap who remembered his grandfather sat thigh to thigh with Brian on the bench, his pint on the heater next to Brian's, his hand paternally on Brian's knee, and he asked repeatedly after old Pat in a voice eroded by years of hard drinking. Cousin John came and lifted several empty glasses to a round tray, replacing only Brian's with a full one, and as he set it among the sticky rings of drying beer on the heater top, several of the men noisily cleared their throats and looked wide-eyed at each other in mock concern, wondering loudly when their free pints were coming.

"Next time you visit me from America," John said, pausing waist-deep in laughter from the pale, upturned faces, the tray held expertly on the tips of his fingers. "If I tried to keep you lot in drink, I'd be on the dole in no time."

"Better us than you, is it?" one of the men said, and John shook his head and twisted away through the crowd to more derisive hooting, holding the tray over his head. The old man squeezed Brian's knee and opened his mouth to speak, but then waved his hand dismissively and reached for his glass, as if overcome by emotion. Brian's head was light, and he felt as if he were watching himself from above. He looked at the faces around him, wondering which one of them was going to take him aside later and ask for the money. Then he thought, Maybe it isn't just one. Maybe it's all of them. He wondered if they all knew, if they would have thrown a ceilidh had he simply shown up on a visit. Grampa should be here, he thought with a boozy pang. Except for the money I don't mean a thing to these people.

He excused himself and got up to piss, stepping high over men's knees and squeezing past thin women who sat with their coats on as if they expected to leave any moment. When he came out of the gents', John reached across the bar and without a word handed him another pint. Brian nodded and snaked aimlessly through the crowd, holding the damp glass close to his chest, coming finally to a crowded table under a slowly churning pall of cigarette smoke, where a group of young men sat drinking with a couple of girls wedged in among them. Brian shook hands all around and let himself be pulled into a seat at the end of the table. For a change he tried to divert attention from himself, asking the men nearest him where they were from, trying to look as though he had heard the rolling, alliterative place-names before. Then someone asked him what part of America he came from, and he said, "Detroit."

"Is that where the cars come from?" someone asked.

"They used to," Brian said, lifting his beer. "Not so much anymore."

"Yeah," said someone else. "My da used to work at the De Lorean plant. Before he got arrested."

Brian swallowed hard and lowered his glass, wondering whose arrest the man meant, his dad's or De Lorean's, but before he could ask he found himself the center of attention again as they began to ask about life in Detroit, listening with serious faces to the answers he tried to give. He wished he hadn't drunk so much; he felt like a sodden undergraduate at a fraternity mixer, glass in hand and a trace of foam on his upper lip. But his mouth got drier the more he talked in the heat and the cigarette smoke, and he kept sipping at his beer for relief. The intent faces floated before him, and slowly he became aware of one a few faces down, a slender, yellow-haired woman who smoked a cigarette and watched him with a severe gaze. Maybe it was only the drink, but Brian began to wonder if she was making eyes at him, turning away from him only to sip from her beer.

A man with a round, sorrowful face propped up in both hands asked him what it was like to travel.

"Great," Brian said, forcing down a mouthful of beer. "Nothing like it. I recommend it."

"Been quite a few places, have you?" The man's voice was slurred by the weight of his head in his hands.

Brian shrugged, glancing at the woman with the cigarette. She had a long, narrow face and a pinched nose, but she was very pretty for all that.

"Been to Ireland before?" asked someone else.

"First time."

"How do you like it?"

Brian picked up his glass and smiled broadly.

"It's grand," he said, and everybody laughed; even the yellow-haired woman gave a tight, thin-lipped smile. Brian glanced around the table over the rim of his glass.

"What's the best place you've been?" The sorrowful man raised his voice over the dwindling laughter.

Brian sighed and ran his hand back over his hair. He felt numb from drink, and it was hard to concentrate with the woman watching him like that all the time.

"Mexico," he said finally. "It was warm, the sun was always shining, and it was really cheap."

"Cheap?" the man said, and all around the table Brian saw eyebrows go up.

"Um, the cost of living." He shifted in his seat, unable to recall how he'd gotten onto this topic. "It's relatively low. You can live a long time on a small amount of money."

"How small?" Everyone watched Brian raptly, and in spite of himself it made him feel flushed and happy.

"Say you had five hundred pounds," somebody else said.

"Christ," someone muttered, and Brian blinked and said, "How much is that?"

Somebody translated it into dollars, and Brian laughed.

"You could live like a king on that kind of money."

"Really?" The sorrowful man's eyes were as wide as a child's.

"For months," Brian laughed.

Around the table men looked at each other and shook their heads.

"And where are you going to get five hundred quid?" someone said, and the man with his face in his hands looked as if he was about to cry.

"That's nothing." Brian leaned forward, vaguely aware of his reserve crumbling like a rain-weakened dike. "Right after high school a buddy of mine and I took all the money we had between us and spent the whole summer in Costa Rica." He leaned heavily on his elbows, his hands out in front of him, his voice lowered for emphasis. "We rented a house on the beach, on the *beach*, mind you, for seventy-five dollars a month." He held up his hand and ticked off items on his fingers. "Two bedrooms. A veranda. A cook, a maid, and a gardener." He laughed. "Seventy-five dollars a month."

Nearly everybody had leaned forward; a couple of the men shook their heads. Brian couldn't keep from smiling; he was overflowing.

"The best time I ever had in my life," he said. "The best. Listen." He lowered his voice again and everybody leaned a tiny increment forward. "Food was almost nothing. The local whiskey was seventy-five cents a bottle."

Somebody moaned, and there was an undercurrent of restrained laughter.

"Women," Brian went on, instantly silencing the table. He

saw before him the thin faces of the women at the table as if they were glowing through the haze, but he apologized to them silently and said, "Women were four dollars a night." He leaned back against the wall and reached for his glass, smiling at the wide-eyed faces leaning forward around the table.

"Costa Rica," murmured the sorrowful man. "Is that near Hawaii?"

Brian gagged on his beer and lurched forward. The man next to him slapped him on the back, and when he looked up again the whole table was laughing, the sorrowful man slumped in his chair with his arms crossed, blinking sheepishly around at the others.

"Geography's not my strong suit," he protested weakly.

"I'm sorry," Brian gasped. "I didn't mean to . . ."

"Yes, you did," said the man next to him, and everyone laughed again. As he laughed with them through a tight throat Brian saw the yellow-haired woman grind her cigarette out against the tabletop, push her chair back with both hands, and walk away without a word to anyone.

"Excuse me," Brian said, and he got up to follow her. But by the time he got away from the table he'd lost her, so he went to piss again, propping his hand against the damp wall over the urinal to keep from swaying. Then he tugged his anorak on and went outside alone. He leaned on both arms on the low stone wall around the little inlet and sucked in deep, cold breaths like a drowning man suddenly pulled out of the water. He pushed away from the wall and stood up, the sharp, salt air driving the cigarette haze out of his head like the wind through a fog. The moon was nearly full in a black sky, surrounded by a wide, frosty ring, and the white houses across the inlet stood out in the pale blue glow, one or two windows in each house full of warm yellow light, wraiths of coalsmoke rising at the same angle out of each chimney. In the streak of moonlight in the water, waves ran in wide, black serrations to slap against the gravel beach, and he heard the sea rushing against the rocks at the mouth of the inlet. Behind him, amid the mingled talk and laughter of the pub, he heard the full, fruity wheeze of an accordion, and he smiled to himself, thinking of his grandfather's raspy, unsteady tenor renditions of "Carrickfergus" and "The Wild Colonial Boy" and even, God forbid, "Did Your Mother Come from Ireland?" Brian laughed out loud, remembering how much he used to love to hear that old bastard sing.

He felt a little woozy as his laughter subsided, though, and he steadied himself against the wall. People are wondering where I am, he decided, and he pushed away and turned back toward the pub, his hands in his pockets against the cold. He hoped he'd cleared his head enough not to embarrass himself any further. Perhaps he was jet lagged still, but he usually handled his liquor better than this; dancing until two in the morning with Molly in some sweaty bar in Ann Arbor, he'd never felt so loose and out of control. He squeezed his eyes shut at the thought of her, and opening them again he saw the door of the pub open, letting out a gust of singing as the yellow-haired woman came out onto the step. She tied the belt of her raincoat around her narrow waist and looked both ways up the empty street as if to make sure it was safe. Brian almost stopped, his hands half out of his pockets, but then he walked on, lifting a scarf out of his pocket to loop it over his neck. She saw him now, and she pulled her cigarettes out of her coat pocket and tugged one out of the pack with her lips.

"A bit close in there," she said evenly, the cigarette wobbling up and down in her mouth.

"Yes, it is." Brian smiled and rocked back on his heels, hoping he wouldn't fall over.

Her face was lit by the cupped flare of the match. She could be very beautiful, Brian thought, if she weren't wound so tight. Perhaps I could help her unwind. She let the breeze blow the match out and dropped it in the street, and she pushed her hair back to one side.

"I'm your cousin Maire, Brian," she said, holding out her hand. "From Belfast."

Brian's wounded, drunken heart sank, and he smiled brilliantly to cover his disappointment. He took her hand and she

35

shook it briskly, taking her cigarette with her other and blowing a stream of smoke to the side.

"Come for a walk?" she said.

"Sure."

Maire walked with her chin tucked down, her heels clicking against the pavement, her cigarette trailing smoke in the wind. They stopped at a stone wall overlooking a narrow beach, where glowing breakers fell against the sand and left a haze of sea spray glowing in the moonlight. Just below the wall the dark water seethed over rocks, trailing phosphorescence through every crack as it subsided. A few bright lights shone like stars against a dark headland, and above that a handful of real stars were scattered across a deep velvet sky.

"So," Brian said, emboldened by drink, "I'll be honest with you."

Maire raised an eyebrow at him, her hands folded on the wall with the cigarette stuck between her fingers, her hair blown away from the side of her face.

"I thought you were coming on to me in the pub back there." He smiled, hoping to embarrass his pretty cousin a little, but she drew her eyebrows together and gazed out over the beach.

"Um, making eyes at me," Brian explained. "Flirting."

For the first time he saw a look of chilly bemusement cross her face.

"Is that what I looked like." She drew on the cigarette and blew the smoke away. "I must be losing my touch."

Brian smiled, feeling embarrassed himself now, and said, "I'm sorry, I didn't—"

"What you were doing, Brian," she said in her flat Ulster singsong, "was making me furious."

"Pardon me?" Brian blinked at her.

"How do they say it in America?" she said with a narrow smile. "Angry? Mad? Pissed off?"

Brian opened his mouth, couldn't think of anything to say, and closed it again. He cleared his throat.

"It's just that I'm not like those poor lads back there." She turned away from the beach to watch him with clear, bright eyes, her hair lifted off her shoulders by the wind. "I know where Costa Rica is, and I know it's just a wee small country that suffers mainly from being too close to the United States. That's all."

Brian raised his hands and smiled ruefully in surrender, but Maire wasn't finished.

"Tell me," she said, dropping her cigarette and grinding it out under the sharp toe of her shoe, "when you were down there on the beach, paying seventy-five dollars a month for a house and the services of three people, not to mention four dollars for the use of a woman, did it ever occur to you—"

"You're absolutely right." He leaned forward, not smiling. He did not want to argue politics with a beautiful woman on a moonlit night. "You're absolutely right, and I apologize. It was incredibly callow of me to talk about it like that, let alone to do it in the first place, and I have no excuses. I know better than that now."

"Do you." She watched him coolly.

"Yes, I do." Brian leaned back from her and nodded.

"How might that be?" She pulled the cigarette pack out of her pocket and skillfully lit another in the wind.

"I've been around a bit since then, worked for a living." Even drunk he knew how feeble he sounded. "I've worked with my hands, worked in a factory." He tightened his smile and ran his hand back over his head. "I was just out of high school when I went to Costa Rica. I was just a spoiled rich kid."

"And what are you now?" She drew on her cigarette and let the smoke out in a brief, open-mouthed gasp.

Brian swallowed and gazed wide-eyed without seeing her.

"A socialist," he said.

She twisted her head away as if in embarrassment and laughed.

"A fine bloody socialist you are," she said, "buying your women by the pound."

"Fucking Christ, lady, give me a break." Brian heard himself shouting. "I was eighteen years old."

"When I was thirteen," Maire snapped, silencing him, "the

British army tore the floorboards out of my bedroom looking for guns. When I was fourteen they came and took my father and my brother away. I can't say about you, but I got my political education by just looking around me."

Brian watched her, his head reeling. He couldn't think of anything to say.

"I want you to come to Belfast with me tomorrow," Maire said in a low voice, her eyes suddenly withdrawn. It was almost as if he weren't there, as if she were talking to herself.

"What for?" Brian steadied himself with a hand on the wall; he was afraid he was going to be sick.

"To deliver the money you're carrying." Maire looked away across the beach.

Brian blinked at her, surprised at himself for not being surprised. I should have known, he almost said, but instead he said, "Why don't you take it now?"

"Because I want you to take it." Her voice was firm, her eyes bright again. "You're the great socialist," she said with a crooked smile. "You should see what the money's for. It's my impression that you are a frivolous person, but I don't mean that personally. I imagine that most Americans of your class are frivolous people." She turned her face to Brian without seeing him. "You can afford to be. I can't."

Maire was silent now, gazing at God knew what, and Brian backed away from her. He tore his scarf away from his throat and unzipped his anorak, and he reached up under his sweater to fumble at the buckle of his money belt. Maire's eyes narrowed and she stepped back and hunched her shoulders. He wondered if she thought he was going to lunge for her, and he lifted his chin and laughed. Maybe I should, he thought, but instead he jerked the money belt free and twirled it, making Maire flinch and twining the strap once around his hand.

"Is that frivolous?" he said, holding the belt up like a dead snake. "Ten thousand American dollars. Is that a fucking joke to you, lady?"

He swung his arm over the wall as if to throw the belt away. The strap tightened around his hand, the belt snapping out over the waves booming against the rocks. Maire watched the belt as if hypnotized, the ragged clouds of spray hanging for an instant in the air before hissing back into the sea.

"For Jesus' sake," she muttered.

"For two cents, I'd let your money go," Brian said, the belt twisting in the wind. "Then we'd see who's frivolous."

"Don't be an idjit," Maire said, trying to recover command of the situation and not quite succeeding. "It's not your money."

"But it's not quite yours yet, is it?" He watched her face carefully, his anger draining away.

"If you let that money go," she said, her calm returned with a cold, even stare, "you'll be in worse trouble than you can possibly imagine."

Brian swung the money belt back over the wall and held it out to her with a smile, his arm stiff.

"Then you take it."

Maire watched him with something approaching a smile, and she looked down at her cigarette, which had gone out. She flicked it over the wall, and turned back to him, her hair blowing about her face.

"No. Tomorrow."

"Beg pardon?" He leaned toward her, the money belt hanging between them.

"You keep it. I trust you."

Brian shook his woozy head to clear it. Maire let out a breath that could have been a sigh, and she turned away from the wall, holding her hair out of her face with the back of her hand.

"You're drunk," she said calmly, "and I'm angry. We'd best talk about this in the morning. Good night, Brian."

She started to walk away, her heels clicking, her chin tucked into her coat. Brian stumbled a few steps after her and stopped.

"Hey, Joan of Arc, wait a minute," he called out, shaking the belt in the air like an empty rattle. "I think this entitles me to say a few things."

Maire turned and walked backward a step or two, with a

smile that left Brian unnerved, whether by her beauty or by something else he couldn't tell.

"See you in the morrow," she said, and she turned smartly on her sharp heel and walked back up the street toward the pub.

"It's on. He'll do it."

"Ah, that's brilliant. What'd he say?"

"I haven't asked him yet."

Over the phone Jimmy Coogan sputtered in exasperation; it sounded like a burst of static on the line.

"Christ's sake," was all Maire got out of it.

"He'll do it," she repeated, peering around the corner from the vestibule into the pub, where John Donovan and one of his sons were collecting empty and half-empty pints from the deserted tables. "All I have to do is ask."

"Then *ask* him!" Jimmy exploded.

"Not now. He's asleep." She leaned wearily against the dirty wall with its penciled numbers and smudged imprecations. "I'm bringing him down tomorrow. You can ask him yourself."

There was silence on the other end and Maire waited with her eyes lifted to the ceiling. There was a hiss that could have been his sigh, or a sigh of the line itself.

"Shall I bring him to the room?" she said after a moment, meaning the safe house where they met.

"Christ, no," Jimmy muttered. "Not there."

There was another long, hissing silence, and Maire listened to the scrape of tables and chairs from the other room. She wondered why he didn't want her to bring Brian there, if he thought it was unsafe or if he just didn't want a stranger in their room. He was just sentimental enough for that.

"All right," Jimmy said at last. "Bring him to the Plough and Stars."

"It's all closed up," she said. "How will we get in?"

"Don't you worry about that," he snapped. "It'll be private, won't it? Just be there by noon."

"You didn't answer my question," Maire said, but she was wondering why he needed privacy so badly. Two weeks ago Jimmy Coogan could almost have conducted his business in broad daylight on any street corner in West Belfast.

"Bring him round the back door at noon," Jimmy said, ignoring her.

"It's a risk."

"Christ." Jimmy's voice sounded suddenly very close, as if he wanted to shout but didn't dare. "You don't know what it's like for me right now."

He trailed off, letting the line crackle and hiss. Then he started to say something, and Maire interrupted him.

"*A chroí*," she said, lowering her voice. "You were right and I was wrong. It's a good idea."

She lifted the receiver gently to its hook, and in a cold phone box in Belfast Jimmy Coogan stared in astonishment at the handset as he hung it up, and he said to himself, "Well, thank God for that."

In a narrow bedroom above the pub, Brian closed his eyes and felt for the money belt under his pillow. He wondered if it was a mortal sin to lust after your cousin, and he smiled in the dark at what Maire would think of that. But then it came to him that she was only a distant cousin after all, and wondering just how far removed she might be, he drifted into an erotic fantasy that wavered unsteadily between Maire and Molly, and finally, in the unreal tangle of limbs and shifting faces, he dreamed of the sea and of tall, rocky cliffs and of falling very, very slowly. He was not afraid, for it felt as if he might fall for his whole life, as if this was what his life was for, and when someone caught him at the last moment before impact he pulled his arm away, preferring to fall. But whoever it was caught him by both wrists, and he twisted angrily in the rushing air, ready to shout.

"Up you get." Maire jerked him into a sitting position. "It's time to go, Brian."

She released him and he sank back onto his elbows, the bedclothes in his lap. He rubbed the heels of his hands into his eyes and pushed his fingers back through his hair. His mouth felt parched and sour.

"What time is it?"

"Half nine. You've missed your breakfast." Maire stood before the window in her raincoat; beyond her the headland tilted flat and green against a gray, overcast sky. She lifted his pants off the chair and tossed them across his lap.

"Get dressed and packed. We'll find you something to eat in Belfast."

He grunted and sat up, his bladder aching.

"What about Cousin John and . . ." He couldn't remember John's wife's name just at the moment and he paused to think about it.

"They understand." She leaned over the bed again. "*Now*, Brian."

He clutched at the covers, afraid she was going to throw them back.

"We've not much time. I want you downstairs in ten minutes."

Brian carried his pack heavily down the narrow stairs to find the pub empty, the air stale with last night's cigarette smoke. His head ached and his eyes were still gummy, but he humped the pack through the outside door, which seemed to have gotten heavier since last night, and stood blinking in the chill morning air. John's wife, Ann, and Maire stood not speaking to each other on opposite sides of a battered little blue Morris Minor, Maire hunched into her raincoat smoking a cigarette,

Ann scowling and hugging her elbows. When she saw Brian standing there squinting in the gray light, Ann hustled toward him with her arms wide.

"Do you have to be away so soon?" she said, clutching his upper arms and shaking him gently. "We were hoping to have you for a day or two."

Brian grinned and looked over the car at Maire, who dropped her cigarette and furiously ground it out with her toe. Brian shrugged and said, "I'll be back."

Maire got in and slammed her door, and Ann took Brian's arm and walked him to the car.

"Well, be sure that you do. The wee ones were so disappointed not to see you this morning before school."

Maire leaned across the tiny car and pushed open the door, and Brian swung his pack over the passenger seat and into the back. As he turned to Ann he saw John appear in the pub doorway, barefoot and tangle-haired, blinking the sleep out of his eyes.

"Michael," he called out hoarsely.

"*Brian*," his wife scolded.

"Christ yes, *Brian*," John scolded himself, padding across the cold pavement. He shook Brian's hand, blushing and speechless with embarrassment. Maire started the car as Brian bent to hug Ann.

"Don't let her wear you out with politics," Ann said, loud enough for Maire to hear. "She's a good lass, really."

"Brian," Maire called out, and Brian stooped into the car. Maire ground the gears and took off even before he had the door closed.

"She's one of your peace movement types," she snapped as Brian twisted awkwardly in the narrow seat and waved goodbye. "A bloody Malone Road liberal. She's all for freedom as long as nobody has to die for it."

She fell silent as the little car buzzed out of the village, driving crouched over the wheel like an old woman, gazing warily down her nose at the blue-black road. They rattled out into low farmland, passing between wide, treeless fields separated by nearly leafless hedgerows. As they turned off the main road into a narrow, blacktopped lane, Brian said, "They know about you?"

"Of course they do." She slowed the car and watched the ditch and hedge on either side, as if for a signpost. "I'm a Sinn Fein city councillor for West Belfast. So far, that's not against the law."

Maire noisily shifted down and let the car coast to a stop at a curve in the lane, where all they could see ahead and behind were road and hedge and gray sky. She turned to Brian in her seat, her raincoat rustling.

"It was right here, Brian," she said, "that your grandfather shot a B-Special in 1922."

Brian looked through the scratched and dirty windshield at the road. The leaves were off the hedges and clotted in the weeds and tall grass of the ditch, but the bare branches were still thick and tangled enough to block the view. Brian tried to muster a reaction, but with his head aching and his mouth dry all he could think was that there must be thousands of miles of road like this all over Ireland.

"Did you know about that, Brian?" She peered at him, the car idling unevenly.

"Sure I know about it." He was irritated at her for putting him on the spot, angry at himself for feeling nothing.

"Doesn't it mean anything to you?"

"You want me to get out and lay a wreath or something?"

Maire put the car in gear, and they drove in silence out of the lane.

Jimmy Coogan was running out of favors. All day yesterday doors that used to open for him—if not always welcomingly, at least without question—were now closed in his face. Old friends refused to see him, or looked the other way on the street. Faces turned from him in unison the moment he walked into a pub or a shop, and even the old woman who lived in the safe house had scowled at him as he left by the back door this morning. The word was out about him, and he had the queasy sensation of having woken up into a world that had been turned upside down overnight, a foreign country where no one spoke his language and he couldn't read the street signs. What made it worse was that everyone knew him. It unnerved him to think that he'd be safer carrying the tricolor up the Shankill Road than he was walking the streets where he had grown up.

At the moment he stood just inside Katie Donnelly's front door in a narrow terraced house off Grosvenor Road only because he had bullied his way past her seven-year-old daughter, sending the wee girl squalling into the kitchen, screaming for her mam. Jimmy sagged back against the door and inhaled the aroma of soaking nappies and burnt sausage, thankful at least that his back was protected for the moment. He pushed himself up when he saw Katie boiling out of her kitchen, half angry and half terrified, and before she could say a word Jimmy stopped her with a hand on her bony shoulder and said, "I need the keys to the Plough and Stars."

Katie twitched her shoulder away and stood with her arms akimbo.

"You've got a nerve coming here . . ." she began in a low voice.

"Give me the keys and I'm away."

Behind her there was an eruption of shrieks and bangs and hard, flat laughter from the kitchen, and as she turned, her voice already rising, Jimmy stepped around her and took hold of her wrist. She started at his touch and tried to twist away, her warning to her children halted in mid-sentence, but he twisted her arm nearly straight up between her shoulder blades, pushing her up against the peeling wallpaper of the hall. She groped blindly behind her with her other hand for a moment, but then splayed it against the faded yellow flowers on the wall.

"Paul would give them to me," he said quietly. "No hesitation."

Her face was turned toward him, her cheek pushed up against the wall, and in her eyes he saw her searching for the courage to refuse. Paul Donnelly was in Crumlin Road jail for something that Jimmy and everyone else knew he'd had no hand in. For the time being his pub was shut down with no one to run it, and Christ only knew how Katie was managing.

"The 'Rah would like a word with you," she whispered, her voice slurred and shaking, and it occurred to Jimmy that Katie was likely managing on a combination of the broo and a little something every week from Belfast Brigade, in recognition of Paul Donnelly's unwilling sacrifice. Which meant she was probably doubly unwilling to turn over the keys to her husband's pub to a renegade Provo.

Jimmy swallowed and tightened his hand around Katie's wrist, ratcheting her arm a notch higher and making her squeeze her eyes shut. He looked from her toward the kitchen, which had become unusually quiet, and he saw three of her children standing in the doorway, the two younger girls huddled behind her son, a hollow-cheeked, skinhead boy of ten in a threadbare sweater. The boy stood with his hands in the pockets of his jeans, gravely watching his mother flattened against the wall by a tall, unshaven stranger in a mackintosh.

"Where are the keys to your dad's pub?" Coogan asked him.

"Don't you move!" Katie's voice was surprisingly loud for a woman in her position, and she cracked one watering eye open to gauge Coogan's reaction.

"Go you and fetch them to me." Watching the boy, Coogan twisted Katie's wrist an inch higher, and she cried out sharply and cut it short, squeezing her lips together, tears trailing down her cheek. She made a fist of her other hand and pounded the wall, once. The boy watched them with a slight frown, his eyes narrowed, as if he found the sight of his mother shaking and weeping distasteful. Then he turned, his hands still in his pockets, and shouldered his way past the two young ones and disappeared into the kitchen. Coogan lowered Katie's arm slightly and relaxed his grip; he didn't want to be thought cruel. Katie gasped and shuddered, her eyes still shut. Through the doorway, past the two wee girls clutching each other, Coogan saw the youngest child, of indeterminate sex, grinning stupidly and hammering the tray before it with its palms, spattering itself with strained peas.

The boy reappeared and came into the hall, where he stopped as close as he dared to come and held out a small ring of keys at arm's length to Coogan.

"Good lad," Jimmy said, and he took the keys with his free hand and slipped them into the pocket of his mac. He released Katie and backed away, watching the boy, who gazed back with something approaching hatred. Katie turned slowly around, her face turned away from Coogan, and sagged against the wall, rubbing her shoulder. Then she lowered her hand, drew a breath, and slapped the boy hard enough to knock him down. The two little girls in the doorway flinched and disappeared like frightened deer, and Katie stood over the boy, who lay on the worn lino without a sound, his knees pulled up, his hands raised over his face. Katie half turned her head to Coogan, without looking at him.

"Get out, you fucker," she said.

"I'll bring the keys back," he said, turning to the door.

Just outside of Belfast the sun came out, and the light gleamed in the scratches in the windscreen as they descended Crumlin Road. Here and there sharp spires rose from the dark coils of terraced houses below, and beyond them, amidst the silvery glare of the River Lagan, Maire saw the articulated silhouettes of the cranes and gantries at Harland and Wolff. Then the narrow, redbrick terraces of the Ardoyne were flashing by like rows of grain, and Maire glanced at Brian, wondering what he was thinking, but his face was turned away. Neither of them had said much for most of the ride, and Brian had spent most of the last hour acting as if she wasn't there, gazing silently out his window at fields and distant woods and hummocks of brown moorland. Now she smiled to herself, wishing she could see the expression on his face. Surely he couldn't help but notice that most of the shops were either burned out or bricked up and that those that weren't were barricaded behind corrugated iron and wire mesh. Surely he had never seen anything in America like the defiant whitewashed slogans on the iron barriers and dark brick walls, their letters bright in the harsh sunlight slanting into the narrow street: BRIT THUGS OUT. UP THE PROVOS. SMASH H-BLOCK.

At the center of town she managed to find a parking space not far from City Hall, and she took Brian to an American-style fast food takeaway, a harshly bright place with red plastic seats and wobbly little tables. All the entrées on the plastic menu board were named after Snow White and the Seven Dwarfs, and Maire caught a smile from Brian as he read the list.

"Know what you'd like, then?" she said.

"Gee, I can't decide. A Sneezyburger sure sounds appetizing."

"Two Snow Whites, two Cokes, and a large chips," Maire said to the countergirl, and she led Brian to a booth in the corner. She sat with her back to the wall, where she could see both the door and the counter, a precaution she'd picked up from Jimmy. Brian sat across from her, turning sideways in the seat with his legs stretched out on the stiff red plastic. Maire unbuttoned her coat but did not take it off, and she rooted in a pocket for her cigarettes. This time she offered the pack to Brian, and he shook his head.

"I'm trying to quit," he said.

"Too bloody right," she mumbled as she lit one for herself. "Filthy habit."

"So where are we going?"

"To drop off your money." She glanced around the small shop as she waved the match out; they were the only customers this early, and the countergirl was busy chatting up the teenage cook.

"All right." Brian gazed past her with his chin propped in his hand.

"So, Brian." Maire blew out a stream of smoke and lifted her chin. "What *do* you think of your grandfather?"

Brian laughed, and Maire smiled, wondering what was so funny.

"We back to that?" he said, and she shrugged.

"Is he a good man so?"

"Sure, he is." He smiled at her as if he hadn't understood the question. "I mean, yes." He crossed his arms, his anorak crackling in the narrow seat. "He is a good man."

"A hero, is he?"

"For shooting a cop?" Brian tightened his arms and smiled, and Maire felt a brief, uncharacteristic rush of alarm. This wasn't the sort of young man she was used to dealing with; he was too calm, too well-fed, too satisfied with himself. He was nothing like the gaunt, anxious, chain-smoking boys she had grown up with. There was nothing to hook him with; there was no rage in him. In her experience, the most Americans were capable of was an innocent, earnest solidarity, the sort of overeager enthusiasm women sometimes displayed for their new boyfriend's favorite sport. She'd shown the sights to her fair share of well-intentioned American leftists, who had followed her as closely as ducklings and agreed with everything she said. And as far as she could tell, she couldn't even count on that much from Brian; whatever identification he felt with her struggle was a sentimental one, based as much on nostalgia for the Ould Sod as on any political sophistication he pretended to. How did Jimmy expect her to reach someone like that? He seemed less a foreigner than someone from another planet entirely. The man who fell to Ulster.

"He did his part," Brian said, still smiling.

"I'm not so certain." Maire leaned forward across the unsteady table, her hands clasped around her cigarette. What made it harder was that her cousin was a handsome boy, good-looking enough to have turned the heads of some of the young women the night before in John Donovan's pub. Much of his self-satisfaction was no doubt vanity—over his clear blue eyes and his scrubbed, clean-shaven cherub's features, over his curly blond hair, fashionably cut with a little crest like a breaking wave over his forehead and a tightly woven pigtail down the back of his neck—and Maire wondered if she was recruiting her cousin or chatting him up.

"I think your grandfather strayed," she said, hunching her shoulders and gazing down at the tabletop.

"Strayed? From what?"

"His duty." She lifted her eyes to him.

"Bullshit." Brian laughed, and Maire had to admit to herself that he had a smile to make a girl weak at the knees.

"Many's the man who stayed behind," she said. "Many's the man who died or went to prison."

"I forgot. The Irish prefer dead failures to live successes. Better Bobby Sands than de Valera."

Maire felt her face tighten, and she straightened in her seat. Without realizing it—how could he know?—he had stung her heart. She had been fired in the heat of the H-block protests, a political education she had acquired at no small risk to herself, addressing meetings, organizing marches, smuggling comms inside her own body. She had wept when Bobby Sands died, something she hadn't allowed herself even when her father died. But she was determined not to be baited, and she looked past her cousin at the menu board over the counter and tried to calm herself by remembering as many names of the Seven

Dwarfs as she could, glaring wide-eyed at their bright cartoon faces painted across the top of the board: Happy, Sleepy, Grumpy, Doc . . .

"Sometimes," she heard herself say, "sacrifice is worth more than growing old and fat in America."

Sneezy, Dopey: she'd seen the film when she was a girl, but what she remembered best was a dog-eared book of the Disney version, handed down from somebody.

"And rich," said Brian. He gave her that charming smile again—a bedroom smile—and patted the thick money belt at his waist.

Cultural imperialism they called it, and they were right, but Christ, she'd loved that book, with its big type and its vivid, colorful pictures. Whenever her father had read it to her he'd sing her the song in his impossibly deep voice, "Heigh-ho, heigh-ho, it's off to work we go . . ."

She smiled back at Brian and said, "Guilt money."

"You don't have to take it."

"That's right. We don't."

He blinked back at her, momentarily speechless, and she silently congratulated herself. That got him. Then Brian swung his feet to the floor and pressed his palms to the table, half rising out of his seat.

"I can't give this money away." He smiled at her, but without the control he'd had before. "Maybe I'll go back to Costa Rica. I could buy a lot of Latin pussy with ten thousand dollars."

He was sliding out of the booth, prideful, vain, and angry, and suddenly Maire reached out and caught his wrist, pinning it gently to the table.

"Bashful." She blinked up at him.

"What?" He was tensed to go, half out of the booth.

"Bashful." She gave him the most charming smile she could muster in broad daylight. "I've been sitting here trying to remember all the dwarfs, and I've only just come up with the last one."

Brian looked down at her, puzzled, and shook his head.

"Brian, sit down. Please."

He lowered himself slowly back into his seat, his palms on the table.

"All I wanted you to see is that your grandfather's sacrifice wasn't enough. I meant no disrespect. It's just that he walked away leaving the job undone behind him."

"So why are you telling me?"

"I want you to understand."

"Great. I understand. I brought your money, okay? What else do you want me to do? Shoot another cop?"

Maire ground her cigarette out in the little foil ashtray and drew a deep breath, surprised to find that her heart was pounding, as if she were about to ask Brian to become her lover. This was Jimmy's job; he should be doing this. She looked up and leveled her gaze at Brian. If she didn't ask him now she never would.

"Two Snow Whites, chips, two Cokes." The girl at the counter raised her voice as if the place were full of people.

Brian searched Maire's face almost as if he knew what she was going to ask, but then he pushed himself up and said, "I'll get it," and walked away toward the counter. Maire let her breath out in a long sigh and sagged back in her seat. Let Jimmy ask him.

Somewhere Brian had read that more people died of traffic accidents in Northern Ireland every year than of political violence, and he wondered now which list Maire was liable to make first. In the country she had driven like an old woman, squinting warily over the wheel, but in Belfast she drove like his father on the Ford Freeway, trying to avoid rush hour. After lunch she roared out of her parking space like a getaway driver and wrenched the little car through a violent U-turn that left Brian clutching the dashboard.

"You, um, angry or something?" he said.

"No more than usual," she said with a crooked smile. The smiled faded, though, as she fell in behind an armored Land Rover with fat black tires, its rear doors latched open to reveal several tired-looking young soldiers sitting on benches with assault rifles across their laps. Her knuckles white on the steering wheel, Maire followed close upon the Rover's rear bumper as it moved at will among the cars and buses and black taxis; together they circled once around an ornate, gaudily imperial building with a ribbed green dome and flak-jacketed officers at every entrance. The floor of the Rover was right at Brian's eye level, and he watched a Pepsi can only a few feet away rolling between the soldiers' black boots; he dug his fingers into the edge of his seat and stole a glance at Maire, wondering half seriously if she was trying to make both lists of statistics at once. But at the last moment before a near-certain collision she twisted the wheel violently and glided out of the Rover's slipstream and across two lanes of traffic, ricocheting up a wide side street.

By now Brian had passed through anger and indifference and back to curiosity. He was a little exasperated with his secretive cousin, but he presumed secretiveness was a survival skill for someone in her situation, and he was willing to forgive her for it. Still, he wondered if she wasn't being a bit too melodramatic; surely she could just take the money herself. Beyond the window of the car the buildings abruptly fell away and they came into a no man's land of weeds and rubble, where the bright sunlight lay heavy and unwelcome, a spotlight on a disfigured face. On the far side of the waste ground stood the blunt ends of rows of narrow houses, with here and there a spine of broken wall pointing toward where the row used to continue, the cauterized stump of an amputation. The gray walls were painted with huge white slogans: UP THE PROVOS. SMASH STORMONT! BRITS OUT. As he looked up the gritty side streets Brian saw that several houses in each row were burned out, with black crescents of soot over the bricked-up doors and windows. Some of the houses were gone entirely, leaving a gap like a missing tooth. He thought of the boarded-up factories and empty lots along Woodward in Detroit, but this was different. At home the devastation was spread out, giving the worst parts of the city an empty, ghost town feel, but here the destruction was impacted and ingrown like a tumor, living cells sharing a wall with dead ones.

They waited for the light at a busy intersection, the car buzzing angrily as it idled, as impatient as his cousin. Aging, dented black taxis rattled by carrying five or six passengers each, and on the sidewalk across the wide street middle-aged women in overcoats and scarves passed skinny young mothers pushing strollers or tugging bawling children along by the hand. In front of a burned-out shop whose owner had moved back in—the plastic letters spelling Newsagent were shriveled and twisted by the heat—there were whitewashed boulders at intervals along the sidewalk to keep car bombs from being parked too close to the building. As the light changed and Maire turned, Brian watched a group of skinny teen-age boys in tight jeans and heavy, scuffed boots coalesce out of nowhere on the corner by the newsagent, looking about as if they expected something to happen.

"This is the Falls Road," Maire said. "Perhaps you've heard of it."

She drove along a long, high redbrick wall. The wall was covered with enormous whitewashed slogans celebrating the Provos and their revolution, and there were long, uneven lines of weathered and fading Sinn Fein election posters, some, Brian noticed, with his cousin's name on them.

"Maire," he said, "you're a star."

"This is my constituency," she said simply, and she turned again, past a pub on a corner, its walls blank and window-less, its doorway protected by a cage of dull metal strips and wire mesh. She let the car coast around the pub and into a narrow, dead-end alley where another cage protected the back door.

"Get out and knock on the door," Maire said. "I'll follow you in a moment."

"What do I say?" Brian asked. "Swordfish?"

But she ignored him, and he climbed out of the little car with a sigh and pushed gingerly at the wire mesh door of the cage. It shrieked on rusty hinges and then shrieked again as it banged shut on its spring after him. He glanced back at the car as Maire backed it out of the alley and turned around, and he turned back and knocked on the scratched and splintered service door of the pub. He heard a muffled shout and, with another glance back at the car, tried the latch and pushed the heavy door open. He was struck by the stench of stale, dried beer, and in the light from the alley he saw a rough wooden floor and, on one side, stacks of dark, empty bottles in battered wooden crates and, on the other, dull, dented metal kegs perched precariously on top of each other, three high. Straight ahead he saw an open doorway and the rear of a dark counter with two tap handles stuck up against the gloom beyond.

"Anybody home?" He stepped in cautiously, crunching grit underfoot, his hand still on the latch. "Hello?"

Brian took another gritty step into the storeroom.

"Can I interest you in a magazine subscription?" he said, and behind him the door swung shut with a thump, the light sliding shut with it. He felt something hard and cold pressed behind his ear and heard a voice close behind him saying, "Hands up, lad."

Brian gasped involuntarily.

"You don't read much, huh. I can understand that."

He started to turn around, but the man behind him jammed the gun harder against his ear and said, "I mean it, Michael. Hands up."

Brian slowly lifted his hands, his anorak crackling, and the man started to pat him down one side with his free hand.

"Um, my name is Brian." He managed to keep his voice steady.

The man's hand stopped and he said, "What was that?"

"I said, my name is Brian."

The end of the gun barrel shifted behind Brian's ear.

"You're not Michael?"

Brian closed his eyes and sighed.

"Michael's my cousin. He broke his leg and couldn't come, so they sent me. Maire sent me in."

The man grunted and finished patting Brian down, reaching around under Brian's arm to pat his chest.

"Right." The man stepped back, the gun still pressed against Brian's head. "Now walk straight ahead."

Brian stumbled a step or two forward in the dark, his heart pounding, and the man reached up and pulled his arms down, taking one at the elbow.

"Don't worry, Brian," he said, close enough for Brian to feel the warmth of his breath. "I won't let you run into anything."

The man guided Brian through the doorway, out of the smell of old beer, and around to the front of the bar. He left Brian there with his hands on the counter and walked back behind the bar to turn on the lights. The light was not even enough to make Brian squint, only dim bulbs in conical metal shades, just bright enough to show an empty pub with unmatched chairs stacked on round tables, and a few booths along the warped and buckled paneling. It was a lot like any number of neighborhood bars along Woodward in downtown Detroit, but instead of smelling of cigarettes and disinfectant, this one smelled only of cold and damp and sweating walls, like someone's basement. On the wall behind the counter, where a mirror would be in an American bar, there were political posters: a blurry photo of Bobby Sands with one of his crude poems printed beneath his face, a facsimile of the rebels' proclamation from the Easter Rising, and a couple of old Sinn Fein campaign posters. Below the posters were two shelves lined with dusty bottles and pint glasses, and when Brian lifted his hands from the counter his palms were coated with a thick, gray, clinging dust.

"Business is slow," the man said. He stood near the storeroom door with his hand still on the light switch, his other hand holding a large, nickel-plated revolver tilted toward the ceiling.

"I'm not surprised." Brian smacked his hands together, a flat sound in the dead air of the empty pub. "You welcome every-one like that, they're bound to take their business elsewhere."

"I'm sorry about the name."

"Well, that makes all the difference."

The man smiled and lowered the gun. He looked to be in his thirties, with an angular, deeply lined face, his hair receding from his steep forehead, fastidiously cut. He wore a broad-shouldered, voluminous raincoat that hung unbuttoned around him like a tent, and it rustled as he walked around the bar with the gun dangling at his side. As he came closer, Brian could see even in the dim light that the man needed a shave, that there were bags under his eyes. Even so, his eyes were bright, as if he were saving up a joke for Brian, and he smiled as he laid the .44 on the countertop with a clunk.

"The most powerful handgun in the world," he said, giving the revolver a little spin. "Just like in the movies."

"Right." Brian nodded and smiled, watching the gun as it wobbled to a stop.

"So, Brian," the man said, holding out his flat hand. "Now that I've got your name right."

Brian took his hand, and the man said, "That's a grip. You must work for a living."

"I'm a carpenter. Sometimes."

"Ah." The man smiled, his eyes widening. "Like Our Savior."

"Right," Brian laughed, and they both turned as they heard the screech of the metal door of the cage, and then the thump of the wooden back door. Very quickly but calmly, the man picked up the gun and stepped back out of sight of the store-room door, leveling the gun with both hands at the dark door-way. He lowered it again as Maire came out of the storeroom with a cigarette in her mouth, its end glowing red in the gloom. She paused and looked at both of them, plucking the cigarette out of her mouth and blowing a stream of smoke out to one side.

"You've met?"

"Yes." The man smiled as he came back down the bar. He reached out a long arm to tap Brian on the shoulder with his fingertips. "This is the American cousin you've been telling me about."

"Different cousin, same arrangement," Brian said, smiling. "And you are . . . ?"

"It's best if you don't know his name," Maire said.

"I'm with the Provisionals," the man said, making it sound like an insurance company. He lay the gun down again. "Do you know who we are?"

"Yes."

"Good. Are you interested in helping us, then?"

Brian looked from one to the other. Maire leaned in the doorway with one hand in her coat pocket, watching him without expression. Brian felt like a schoolboy whose teacher had hauled him up in front of the principal.

"I'm not sure what you mean," he said. "I thought I already was."

"Already was what?"

"Helping you."

The Provo looked at Maire and said, "She said nothing to you?"

"About what?" Brian shrugged and stuck his hands in his pockets. "She didn't say anything about doing something else."

"Something else?" The Provo looked blankly at Brian.

"I think he means the money," Maire said.

"Ah." The Provo nodded, watching his fingers as he brushed something on the countertop.

"What we got here," Brian sighed, "is a failure to communicate. She didn't tell you my name, and she didn't tell *me* you wanted another favor. Maybe we should let the lady explain."

The smoke from Maire's cigarette drifted across the bar as she and the Provo exchanged a long look, each seeming to accuse the other of something. Brian wondered if there was something more between them than their professional relationship; they looked less like urban guerrillas than a pair of newlyweds blaming each other for leaving the water running at home. Brian forced a laugh and leaned against the bar, his anorak rustling noisily in the empty pub.

"Somebody want to tell me what this is about? Or should I try and guess?"

"I need to know where you stand first," the Provo said at last, turning away from Maire. "If you've no intention of helping us, tell me now and we won't waste anyone's time."

"How can I tell you if I don't know what it is?"

"And I can't tell you anything until I know I can trust you." The man leveled his gaze at Brian as if he were taking aim. "I need to know if you're with us or against us."

"I'm carrying your money, aren't I?"

"Brian, answer his question." Maire stepped up to the bar. "This is an important man. He hasn't got time to waste."

"What about my time?" Brian snapped at her. "All this cloak-and-dagger shit, I don't know what the hell's going on."

"I only wanted you to see that your grandfather's sacrifice wasn't enough."

"Send him a postcard."

"That's not the point," Maire said angrily.

"This is condescending bullshit," Brian laughed. "I'm just a poor bourgeois Yank who wouldn't know real suffering if he stepped in it."

Maire groaned and said, "Your self-pity disgusts me," and they both started shouting at once, their voices rebounding off the hard walls.

"Hey!" The Provo's cry silenced both of them. They glared at each other like angry siblings, their words lost already in the dead air. The Provo leaned on the bar and smiled like a forbearing parent.

"Brian," he said, "I love your grandfather."

"I'm sure he'd be glad to hear it," Brian said, scowling at Maire.

"I'm sure he would too." The Provo watched Brian with a ferocious, feral grin. "The question is, what would you do to prove you're as good a man as he was?"

"I don't know. We could arm wrestle?"

For the first time this morning Brian felt wide awake, as alert and attentive to every word and gesture as if he were in the middle of a seduction. Although who was seducing whom was a little vague at the moment.

"Look, I won't be lying to you, Brian," the Provo said. "We're in a tight spot or I wouldn't even be asking for your help. I know you're sympathetic to our struggle, you wouldn't be here if you weren't, but we do not ask outsiders to do our work for us." He looked down at his hand on the bar as if puzzled to find it there. "But at the moment we've no choice."

He glanced at Maire, and then looked at Brian again.

"Do you know what a supergrass is, Brian?"

Brian shook his head, and he looked at Maire, who had tossed her cigarette away and stood with her arms crossed, her face a blank.

"It's an informer," the Provo said. "It's somebody in our organization who the Brits have turned, by torture or by blackmail. They give him a list of names they want, and he gives them enough information to put them in jail, without a jury. They go away on his word alone. D'you understand?"

"All right."

The Provo licked his lips and his eyes shifted momentarily toward Maire, and Brian wondered if he was being told the truth. Brian looked at Maire too, but she scowled at the floor and poked at her cigarette with the toe of her shoe.

"I'd be a liar if I said it wasn't hurting us," the Provo went on, his eyes dull now. "It's crippling us, Brian. These are trusted men, and they know enough to put whole brigades out of action." He drew a breath and said, "I'm in danger of being lifted myself."

Maire seemed to be averting her face, and Brian wanted to know why. What was going on here? The Provo moved closer to him, laying his hand on Brian's arm.

"There are some who want us to lie low for a while." He seemed to be almost pleading now, peering at Brian as if through a haze, the light coming back into his eyes. "They want us to run *candidates* in *elections*; they want us to show our *political* strength."

Maire glanced up sharply at this, and Brian resisted the urge to look at her.

"But our *political* strength, Brian," the Provo said vehemently, "depends on ours being an armed struggle." He lifted his hand away from Brian's arm and tightened his fist. "It's our *only* strength. There is no other way. The only thing the Brits understand is violence. The only way they will realize that we cannot be defeated is to hit back now."

He banged his fist on the bar, startling Brian.

"When they think they have us on the run." He pounded the bar again. "Hit them in their own country."

He uncurled his fist and laid his hand again on Brian's arm.

"D'you understand?" He squeezed Brian's arm, his eyes shining. "Until now all you've done is talk politics with a stranger. If I go on you're implicated."

"Don't fucking plead with him!" Maire's voice was harsh and unrecognizable. She glared furiously at the Provo, her hands on her hips. "Just tell him what you want and he'll do it!"

The Provo turned slowly toward her, relaxing his grip on Brian's arm.

"You've got no bloody choice," she raged at Brian, her eyes alight. "You're fucking implicated already. All I have to do is call the Confidential Phone and they'll lift you off the street like a bloody puppet, American fucking passport or no!"

"What the hell is she talking about?" Brian looked at the Provo, who closed his eyes and drew a breath to calm himself.

"We're not here to threaten you," he said in a low voice.

"You'll do it all right," Maire said, losing steam, her eyes wide.

"I tell you what." Brian pushed back his anorak like a gunfighter and reached under his sweater. "You guys get your act straight and give me a call sometime."

The Provo opened his eyes and watched Brian unbuckle the money belt and lift it onto the bartop. He stood very still with his hand on the bar, his eyes blank and lifeless and dead, and for the first time Brian was frightened.

"I'm just a tourist, okay?" Brian lifted his hands and stepped gingerly around the Provo, who made no move toward the money on the bar, did not even turn to watch Brian go. "Here today and gone tomorrow."

As he started away from the Provo, Maire stormed to the end of the bar and blocked his way, her eyes wild.

"You're not going anywhere!" she said.

"Be cool, Maire," Brian said, lifting his hands again, but she clutched his arm painfully with both hands, saying, "I've still got your rucksack in the car."

Brian wrenched his arm free and tried to step around her, but she skipped in front of him again. Behind him he heard a foot scrape against the floor and he started to turn, but a powerful arm clamped around his neck and lifted him off his feet, while the Provo hissed in his ear.

"You Americans are all alike." His voice was full of disgust; he shook Brian violently, rattling his head. "Not a bloody one of you'll take a stand on anything."

Brian clutched at the man's arm and tried to twist free; his toes only brushed the floor. Somewhere at the edge of his vision Maire was dancing on her toes, her hair swinging, and she was shouting something that Brian couldn't hear over the blood pounding in his ears. He started to see stars, and he jerked his knees up to his chest and heaved his shoulders forward, pulling the Provo off balance and bringing them both down onto the cold, gritty linoleum. The Provo released his hold on Brian to break his fall, and Brian rolled away into a table, sending a chair clattering across the floor. The Provo was on his hands and knees, scrambling to get up, and Brian snatched his wrist out from under him and twisted it against his back in a wrestling hold, splaying himself across the Provo's back. Brian bore down, his toes bent back against the worn floor, and pressed the Provo's cheek against the linoleum. The Provo groped wildly with his other hand, and Brian snared it and pinned it against the man's back, the two of them grunting and hissing hot breath in each other's faces. In an old reflex Brian looked up for the referee and saw Maire instead, dancing from toe to toe,

her face blotched with red, loose hair flying about her forehead, the revolver held unsteadily in both hands.

"All right!" she shouted shrill and girlish. "Enough!"

Brian watched her, the Provo still straining beneath him,
and suddenly he let the man go and pushed back, scrambling
to his feet away from Maire and out of the Provo's reach. He
backed into a table and knocked over another chair, and as
Maire wobbled the gun in his direction he raised his palms and
stood shaking, his heart beating hard, the sweat on his face chill
in the damp, close air.

With his face twisted away from Brian the Provo rolled onto
his side and slowly levered himself up; Maire skipped forward
and caught him under his elbow, letting the gun droop in her
other hand. When he was on his feet she peered up into his face,
turning it gently from side to side with her hand on his chin.
When Brian started to lower his hands she shook the gun at him
one-handed, so he sighed and raised them again. She said something to the Provo in a low voice and he nodded. She let him go,
but as she started to back away he reached for the gun, and she let
it go only reluctantly, glaring across the pub at Brian. The man
slid the gun out of sight under his coat and slowly turned to Brian,
fussily brushing off the sleeves and lapels of his raincoat. He
looked up, a bruise already forming along his narrow cheekbone.

"Best two out of three?" Brian offered, his own breath still
coming hard.

A long moment passed. Maire stood at the end of the bar
with her arms crossed, watching them both sullenly. The Provo
fussed with his coat, and Brian looked from one to the other,
feeling flushed and dizzy. Then the Provo lifted his chin and
smiled crookedly, and he held out his hand.

"I lost my temper," he said. "I apologize."

With a glance at Maire, who looked away, Brian came up
and took his hand.

"Me too," he said.

"You're free to leave, Brian," the Provo said as they released
hands. "Maire will take you wherever you want to go."

Maire started to say something, but the Provo looked sharply at her.

"You never told me what you wanted me to do," Brian said, scarcely recognizing the sound of his own voice.

The Provo looked slowly up from straightening his cuffs, his eyes brightening. Brian drew a deep breath and let it out in a sigh. He smiled.

"Well, I'm just standing here," he said, "trying to think what Grampa would do, you know?"

"Are you certain?" the Provo said, smiling brilliantly.

Brian opened his mouth, but in his astonishment at himself nothing came, and he simply lifted his hands and let them drop.

"Brian," said the Provo, leaning back against the bar, "do you know what Semtex plastique is?"

"This should be the least of your worries," Jimmy was saying. He reached into the Adidas carryall with both hands and lifted out the bundle of plastique, wrapped in an old gray blanket and tied with twine. This was the first time Maire had actually seen the parcel, but she resisted the urge to move away from the wall behind the bar and take a closer look. Instead she reached into her pocket for a cigarette and turned away from the two men on the other side of the bar to light it, hoping that neither of them saw how her hands were still shaking.

When she turned back to them, smoke curling around her head, Jimmy was holding the parcel out to Brian. The American took it gingerly, holding it away from his body and gazing at it with dull, dazed eyes. Maire felt a jolt of alarm up her spine, and she widened her eyes at Jimmy across the bar. Couldn't he see that the boy was nearly in shock? He looked like a rubber-bullet victim, unsure of where he was, uncertain where the pain was coming from. But Jimmy ignored her, refusing to look in her direction. He smiled instead at Brian.

"You can drop it, you can hit it with a hammer, you can set a bloody match to it, and it won't do a thing. It's safe as milk without a detonator." Jimmy took the parcel back from Brian. He spun it once in the air like a football and caught it. "It's brilliant stuff, courtesy of Colonel Qaddafi."

"Right," Brian said. "Okay." His eyes shifted blankly from Jimmy to Maire, but she looked away. She wanted no part of it now: Jimmy had lied shamelessly to the boy about the supergrass business—that was three years ago—and if Brian was half as savvy as he thought he was, he'd have known it was ancient history. If he knew the truth he'd run like a hare.

"Now, what's in this bottom compartment here?" Jimmy dipped his chin at the American's rucksack. It lay flat on its back on the bar, like a last patron sleeping it off.

"Um, my sleeping bag."

"Take it out."

Brian unzipped the compartment and pulled the sleeping bag in its blue nylon cover out of the backpack. Jimmy set the plastique down on the dusty bartop and took the nylon bag, grabbing a fistful of Brian's expensive sleeping bag and hauling it out of the cover with a long hiss.

"Now, listen carefully, Brian." He glanced over the bar at Maire, and she wanted to say, I'm bloody furious with you; this boy will get us both killed or caught. But instead she withdrew her eyes and blew a stream of smoke to one side. Let him wonder.

"The train will put you in Derry by two." Jimmy tugged the blue sleeping bag cover over the end of the bundle of plastique. "You take the first bus you can get to Donegal Town. You'll have no trouble at the border. They only look for things coming in."

He looked up at the boy, who gazed at the bundle on the bartop without seeing it. Maire licked her lips and drew a breath to speak; Brian was going to panic, he was going to run like a scared bloody rabbit, he was going to tout on them all and put them in prison for the rest of their lives.

"D'you understand?" Jimmy said, raising his voice slightly,

and Brian started and nodded. He slid his hands into the pockets of his anorak.

"All right." Jimmy jerked the bundle up into the air by the drawstring of the bag to pull it tight; then he set it down on the bar and started to stuff Brian's sleeping bag a handful at a time into his carryall.

"Find yourself a bed and breakfast in Donegal Town," he said. "Then at nine o'clock you go up to a pub called O'Connor's. Leave the plastique in your room, don't for God's sake take it with you. In the pub you look for a man reading a book in a booth." He looked up at the American. "You go up to that man and you say, 'Ireland unfree shall never be at peace.'"

Maire loudly exhaled a cloud of smoke and rolled her eyes. Why not dress the boy up in fatigues and a balaclava and pin an Easter lily to his lapel? But if Jimmy knew what she was thinking, he ignored her.

"Can you remember that?"

Brian cleared his throat and said, "Donegal Town, a guy reading at O'Connor's at nine tonight, Ireland unfree shall never be at peace."

"Good." Jimmy zipped the carryall shut and lifted the plastique, dangling it by the drawstring of the nylon bag. "Give us a hand here, Brian."

Brian stepped up to the bar and held the lower compartment of the rucksack open with both hands.

"What if the guy doesn't show up?" he said as Jimmy twisted the bundle into the compartment.

Jimmy glanced up at Brian, and then at Maire. She smiled back at him, thinking, You didn't think of that, did you? That should put paid to the whole business. If Cusack doesn't show up, Brian will run straight to the Gardai, or try to bring it back over the border.

"Then you ring me," Jimmy said, zipping up the flap of the compartment. He gave Brian the phone number of the safe house, and Maire felt her jaw slacken in astonishment. He made the boy repeat it twice, and she widened her eyes at him, barely able to contain herself. That was it, Jimmy had gone mad, he'd gone completely daft.

"Who do I ask for?" Brian said.

Jimmy thought a moment and then said, "Jack Duggan."

Maire looked away and dropped her cigarette, grinding it out against the floor.

"Jack Duggan," Brian said dully.

"Don't worry, though. Your man will be there," Jimmy said. "Any questions?"

Brian drew a deep breath and let it out slowly, and he laid his hands gently on the rucksack, one hand resting lightly on the bottom compartment.

"Do you have something in another color?" he said.

Jimmy laughed, loud and long and too heartily, obviously humoring the boy, crinkling the deep lines around his eyes. He laid his hand on Brian's shoulder and gave him a paternal squeeze.

"That's magic, Brian," he said. "Another color. That's great crack."

She hated him like this, she'd decided a long time ago. When he was in the middle of something, when his blood was up, he was insufferable, as full of himself as some arrogant British squaddie kicking in a door or feeling up some wee girl at a P-check. And it was worse when he was successful: one time, only hours after he had blown up a Royal Ulster Constabulary captain and his wife in their car, he had broken every rule they had made for each other and had shown up at her flat, climbing up the drainpipe and coming in the rear window, his breath reeking of Bushmills, his hands still trembling with adrenaline. That night she had hit him, not any coquettish slap, either, but with her fist, as hard as she could, the way she used to fend off her loutish brothers. What he'd wanted that night, or so she tried to explain to him afterward, was to rape her, to top off his adrenaline high with a brutal fuck. But that was afterward, when he was sober; at the time he wasn't ready for criticism, and she wasn't interested in reasoning with him. She had raged at him, hitting him again and again, shouting, "I'm not your fuckhole!" until he backed away.

Jimmy and Brian were still laughing together, and she turned sharply on her heel and walked away into the dark storeroom and out through the back door. What worried her was that he was coming to love the struggle more than the goal, that it was becoming a great game to him, that he loved the adolescent cloak-and-dagger bollocks of cover stories and aliases and safe houses. She pushed through the shrieking door of the cage and went to her car, sliding in behind the wheel and leaning across to the glovebox. Worst of all, she was afraid that he loved the violence more than he loved his country, more than he loved her. She rooted through the maps and pens and tissue packets in the glovebox and pulled out a flat Polaroid camera. Just minutes ago Jimmy and the American had rolled about on the filthy floor of the pub like a couple of lads in a schoolyard, and now they seemed to love each other for it. With the camera in one hand she climbed out of the car and pushed through the cage and the back door and stalked into the pub, where the two men turned to her as she came through the storeroom door. Because of their juvenile punch-up Jimmy seemed to think he could trust the boy implicitly now, that they understood each other in a way that Maire could not, that they belonged to some brotherhood of bruises and testosterone. But she wanted something a little more concrete to ensure Brian's complicity, something she could hold over his pretty head, and if it made Jimmy angry, so much the better.

"How about a photograph to commemorate the occasion?" she said, popping the camera open and lifting it to her eye.

Once, in the middle of an argument, Molly had told Brian that he was a master of the uselessly quixotic gesture.

That's redundant, was the only thing Brian had said at the time.

He sighed at the memory and pushed himself up in his seat, letting his boots drop heavily from the facing seat to the floor.

His backpack was propped next to him in the window seat, and he peered around it to look out the window, where a wide, glassy river ran amid low sand dunes mottled with stiff tufts of grass. Bright noonday sunlight glistened in the broad tidal flats; a fishing boat with blistered yellow paint sat half keeled over in the mud. The backpack rocked gently in its seat to the galloping rhythm of the train, and Brian pushed at it for a moment, trying to get it settled. Another useless gesture, he thought. Nothing to lose by refusing, nothing to gain by doing it.

He looked at his watch; the train was an hour out of Belfast. Maire's bad cop routine had continued right up to the door of the train station. As her car idled noisily at the curb, and as Brian sat with his door open and one foot on the pavement, Maire had threatened him with the snapshot, but without showing it to him. He had wondered in the pub why she'd taken it, if she was keeping a scrapbook or what, but now he knew that she'd meant it as blackmail. A photo of Brian with his arm around the shoulders of a known terrorist, she'd said, was all the police needed to put him away for a long, long time. It's in your interest to keep this all to yourself and just do the job. As she talked she reached into her coat pocket, and for a moment he thought she was going to pull the picture out and wave it threateningly under his nose, but instead she stammered a final warning not to screw up and told him to get going. The Provo, on the other hand, had shaken his hand one more time at the back door of the empty pub, gripping Brian's elbow with his other hand like a salesman and giving him a manly, avuncular wink.

Brian looked out the window across the aisle and saw that the train was clattering along the coast now, a line of houses flashing between the track and the slow waves curling onto the beach. Beyond his own window the faceted surface of a tall cliff rolled by only inches from the streaked glass, and he thought of a song he and Molly used to dance to at Rick's back in Ann Arbor, or at Joe's Star Bar before they tore it down, a bar band original, in which the singer laid out a really hopeless situation in each verse and then sang, What would Brando do?

"I coulda been somebody," Brian muttered to himself, thinking of his grandfather. What would Grampa do?

Two boys in stiff jeans and heavy woolen jackets came boisterously into the car, banging the door after them. One of them was tearing open a packet of cigarettes, and swaying with the motion of the train he paused in the aisle over Brian and asked for a light. Brian slouched down to get into his pocket, and he handed the boy his lighter. The two boys sat across the aisle and lit up, and Brian looked at them openly, at their taut, narrow faces and stiff, unkempt hair, and he tried to see his grandfather at that age, firing a gun in a dark lane and then sprinting away over muddy fields, running finally as far away as Detroit. But no matter how hard he stared, he couldn't see his grandfather in these young men, let alone a revolutionary in his grandfather. Too many memories got in the way: his old-man smell of strong soap and tobacco as he lifted little Brian onto his lap. His dry, papery hands guiding Brian's around a baseball bat or over the keys of a piano. His ragged tenor as he sang along with his Clancy Brothers records. The moistness in his eye when he'd had a few and the accent crept back into his voice.

"Yo, bro," said the boy across the aisle in his best, booming Sylvester Stallone, and both boys laughed at the American's startlement. Brian grinned and took back his lighter and the cigarette the boy offered him. He lit up and sucked the bitter smoke in deeply, turning to look out the window. The cliff had curved away from the track to reveal a mountain with a steep north face, its upper tier of rock bared against the blue sky like teeth, the land below marshy and scored with ditches. He tried to picture his grandfather fighting side by side with his grim, beautiful cousin, and he couldn't do it, not even if he imagined Grampa as a young man. Maire's revolution stood a better chance of success, but it was a more ruthless revolution than Grampa's, a revolution without sentiment, with no flair for the grand gesture. The uselessly quixotic gesture, he heard Molly say.

As he watched, half-asleep, a thick mist climbed out of the marsh beyond the window and brushed against the glass like a cat, leaving the low sun shining weakly out of a pearly sky, its pale reflection flickering alongside the train in the silvery water of a wide ditch beside the track. A one-way ticket to Palookaville, he thought, mouthing the words, letting his head roll against the headrest. He lifted the cigarette, his other hand resting against the side of the pack in the other seat, steadying it against the motion of the train.

Jimmy Coogan pushed the keys to the Plough and Stars through the letter slot of Katie Donnelly's door and listened to them tap against the lino on the other side. He straightened and paused with his ear close to the scuffed wooden door, like a doctor listening for a pulse. Folded through the key ring were five American one hundred dollar bills from the money Maire's cousin had brought, ten times the weekly amount from Belfast Brigade. Rent, Jimmy intended it to be, for the use of the pub, and for Katie's trouble. But he heard nothing; either no one was home or they had seen him coming up the empty street, so he picked up the Adidas bag with the American's sleeping bag in it and started up toward the Falls Road, smiling to himself in spite of the silence behind the door. Let Brody top that.

It was noon, when the street should have been wild with children too young for school running in packs like stray dogs, when housewives should have been fiercely scrubbing their front steps or gossiping hands on hips in doorways. But instead he was alone in the incongruous quiet of the narrow street, the last man in one of those end-of-the-world films, able to walk into any house he saw and help himself to the pantry, draw himself a bath, stretch out on the bed. He lifted a corner of his mouth at the empty street; he knew where they all were, all the people on whose behalf he had offered up his life. He knew that if he whirled about, he'd see parlor curtains twitching shut all down the street, behind every gray window.

He put his hand in the inside pocket of his mackintosh and felt the thick envelope of American money and the still tacky surface of the snap Maire had taken in the Plough and Stars. She had disappeared while he had been smoothing the American's ruffled feathers, and he'd thought that she was leaving him to it. He wiped the dust off one of Paul Donnelly's bottles and offered Brian a drink, and as the boy dutifully swallowed a painful mouthful, Jimmy helped himself to the money, flicking through the stack of bills with his thumb and then shoving the envelope out of sight. And then, just as he was getting the American to smile and laugh again, Maire reappeared with her fucking Polaroid, snapping it open and aiming it like a gunsight.

"How about a photograph?" she said, and both Coogan and the American turned to her in surprise. Bloody bitch, he thought, smiling ferociously at his wife across the bar, trying to communicate to her that it was a tricky moment just now, that the slightest misstep could panic the lad and send him running back to America. You could threaten someone like Billy Fogerty, you could threaten Katie Donnelly, you could even threaten Joe Brody and get some sort of result, but how could you threaten someone who had no stake in it, who could get on a plane and be safe home in eight hours, well out of reach? He heard the whirr of the automatic lens as she tried to find her focus in the dim light, and he glanced at Brian. He saw the doubt gathering in the lad's eyes, saw that he was only now realizing what he had agreed to do.

"How about it, Brian? One for the scrapbook." Coogan put his arm around Brian's shoulders and felt the boy wince. Better to bluff it out, Coogan thought. He tried to look daggers at Maire, but one eye was squeezed shut and the other hidden behind the eyepiece as she pointed the camera at the two men standing there like old schoolmates. Maire's problem, Coogan had decided at moments like this, was that she fancied herself the radical feminist, but most of it was pure, pigheaded, convent school bitchery. Coogan smiled, and the flash blinded him.

"There," he said, dropping his arm from Brian's shoulders. "Something to look at in my old age."

But as Maire ushered Brian out the back door, Coogan came up behind her, caught her elbow with one hand, and handed her the empty money belt. She stopped dead, waiting just long enough for Brian to get out the door before she whirled and said, "Where the hell's the money?" She held up the limp money belt like evidence of Jimmy's infidelity.

"Does Joe know it's coming?" he said, still clutching her elbow, trying to pull her toward him.

"No, but that's not the point." She pulled free and glared at him anew, hissing at him as if to keep from waking a child in the next room. "That's ten thousand dollars."

"And it's in good hands," he said, clutching her around the waist and nuzzling her at the nape of her neck. She didn't struggle, but she didn't move against him either, holding herself rigid as he plucked the damp snapshot from her coat pocket as skillfully as a pickpocket. Then he had let her go and she had pushed out the door, the money belt flying. Her last word to him had been, "Bastard," muttered through clenched teeth.

Coogan pulled his hand out of his pocket as he came around the dog's leg bend in the empty street. He noted the numbers of the houses and remembered that his uncle used to live there, in number 12; he'd lost his job when the mills shut down after the war, then he drank himself to death. Coogan didn't know who lived there now, some young lad who'd lived all his life on the broo, probably, and who was hiding now as Coogan came up the street, watching from an upstairs window. Coogan pushed gently at the bruise the American had given him and hefted the Adidas bag in his other hand. It's like one of those Western films, he told himself, one with the sheriff all alone. They're all waiting in terror for Joe Brody to show up on the noon train from Tombstone or Tucson or wherever it was, and only when it was all over and the smoke had cleared would they come rushing out from under the stairs to congratulate the winner and slap him on the back. Coogan smiled and rubbed his stiff, two-day beard and put a little more Gary Cooper in his walk.

But then he slowed as he saw the real reason for the noontime quiet. Up ahead he saw people lining the Falls Road, and over the heads of the people on the pavement he saw a blond coffin float slowly by on the shoulders of six young men, its pale wood gleaming in the angled sunlight. Coogan slipped to the side of the street, under the lee of the houses there, and came quietly up behind the line of people on the pavement, craning his neck to see over their heads. Ahead of the coffin some undertaker's long black hearse crawled up the road, while behind the coffin walked a line of young women in black dresses, their arms linked together like peace marchers. The woman in the middle was older and shorter than the others, a fussy black hat pinned to her gray hair, her face hidden by a black veil; she seemed to be held up by the two younger women on either side, and her unsteady feet set the dragging pace for the whole procession.

He recognized a couple of the women, not enough to put a name to them, but he knew the priest right enough, Father McClain, a terrible, womanish liberal who moved slowly in his skirts beside them, the pale eggshell of his head bowed, his hands joined over a worn black Bible, his nervous fingers threaded with a blue rosary. As the priest passed where he stood, Coogan tipped his face down, in case the priest looked up and saw him. But he didn't, and after the line of women Coogan watched the silent procession, first the older men and women, his father's generation, all bundled up against the chill in overcoats and sweaters; then the younger ones, the women in cheap Sunday dresses, the men in their best trousers and Sunday shoes, ties knotted uncomfortably over the V necks of their sweaters, all of them scraping up the street in the self-conscious shuffle of public grief.

Who is it, Coogan wanted to know. It had to be a civilian;

Coogan would have heard if a member of the Brigade had been lost, and anyway there was no honor guard, just the self-righteous old priest. All along the curb old men removed their caps, and housewives in scarves and girls in jeans crossed themselves, the gesture rippling down either side of the street like a wave front. A few people glanced back as Coogan moved behind them, and a man who recognized him snapped his head forward when he saw who it was. Coogan shook his head; he wanted to laugh. If he'd had a mind to, he could have nicked the pocketbooks and handbags of every man and woman on the street, and at the moment he had more money in his coat than all of them put together.

Then, abruptly, from overhead, came the percussive roar of a helicopter, and without thinking he looked up to see an olive green Lynx dangling itself high over the street, twisting slowly on its own axis as it beat the air over the long lines of terrace chimneys. The walls around him reverberated to the rhythm of the blades, and Coogan twisted his face away from the copter and shouldered through the line of people on the curb. He waded into the funeral procession, hunching his shoulders and dropping his chin between the lapels of his mackintosh. The people around him in the procession averted their faces and flinched away from him, but instead of following the procession Coogan drifted across it like a fish across a stream, keeping his eyes on the shuffling feet of the funeral marchers and the gritty surface of the Falls Road, the tattoo of the British machine beating against his bare head.

But he stopped short as he stepped up onto the curb on the other side, and he halted in the middle of the pavement, resting the Adidas bag on a whitewashed boulder. Next to a rough wooden bin of red and green apples, Billy Fogerty slouched on the scalloped front step of a greengrocer's shop, his hands in the pockets of the jeans Coogan had bought him last week, the new anorak unzipped and pushed back. Coogan glanced up at the Lynx as it drifted slowly away from him, hovering over the procession as it crawled toward Milltown. He loosened his shoulders and looked at Billy, who stared back at Coogan without emotion, a different person from the frightened boy on Giant's Causeway three days ago. He seemed to have reverted to type, with the stony and unreadable gaze of every other useless boyo in the Falls. Even his new clothes looked duller and shabby in the shadow of the grocer's tattered awning. A hood, Coogan thought, that's what Billy Fogerty's become. I offered him a chance at something better, and he threw himself back into the dung heap, head and shoulders.

"Billy," Coogan said, and he smiled. But the boy didn't flinch as the others had done in the procession scraping along behind him. Instead he lifted his chin up the road toward the gleaming coffin and said, "Eamonn Loftus."

When Coogan didn't say anything, Billy added, in a monotone, "Fuckin' UVF pulled him off the street Monday last and hacked him to death with a hatchet, fuckin' bastards."

Coogan glanced down the street at the coffin, only the lid of it visible now above the heads of the crowd; he hadn't heard, what with his own problems. He vaguely recognized the name; the man had not been politically active, just another poor bastard plucked at random off the street and murdered by Shankill Road thugs. He felt the first flush of cold rage, but he turned and directed it at Billy.

'What are you going to do about it?" he said. "I gave you a chance to make a difference—"

"Joe Brody's already seen to it," Billy interrupted him, with a bit of a smirk. "We stiffed two of their bastards last night."

"We, Billy? You and Joe in charge of everything now, is it?" Coogan felt the coldness spreading as he watched Billy's insufferable smirk widen.

"Yeah. Joe says to tell you there's some of us who haven't forgotten who the real enemy is," Billy said. "He says—"

But he swallowed the rest of it and gave a very satisfying jump as Coogan jerked the carryall off the boulder and started toward him. Billy whisked his hands out of his pockets and glanced both ways up the street for help, but everyone along the pavement made a point of looking the other way. Then

Coogan was forcing him back into the gloom of the grocer's shop; just inside the door the lad behind the counter turned his face away as Coogan pushed Billy through the narrow doorway. The grocer squinted instead at the quiet procession beyond his dusty window, as if comparing it critically with other funerals he had seen, and Coogan reached under the anorak and yanked up Billy's jeans by the rear.

"Come with me," he whispered, and he frog-marched the stumbling boy the length of the dim, sweet-smelling shop, through the dark back room, and bang through the door into the entry at the rear of the shop. He let go of Billy, and Billy half spun, half fell against a stack of greasy cardboard boxes leaning against the wall. The boxes teetered but did not fall, and Billy stood up panting and twisted his rucked-up jeans with both hands.

"Jesus," Billy said, his voice shaking, "I'm just after telling you what he said."

"I've heard that one already, Billy," Coogan said. "Tell me another."

The entry smelled of rot, the ground smeared with lettuce leaves and crushed tomato. Behind the stack of boxes a corroded drainpipe snaked up the wall into the eaves. Billy shuffled his feet in the muck and twisted this way and that, looking everywhere but at Coogan.

"I'm just, I'm just saying," he stammered, "that I'm just passing the message on, that's all . . ."

Coogan backhanded the boy, not quite hard enough to raise a bruise, just a clout along the boy's downy jaw to move him up a groove. Billy's head snapped back and he rocked back on his heels for a moment. Then he steadied himself and brought his head forward very slowly, his eyes cloudy.

"Now," Coogan said.

"He says," Billy began, his face still half averted.

"Who says?"

"Brody says." Billy's wounded eyes met Coogan's. "He says he knows about your man in Donegal. I think he said his name is Cusack."

Coogan took a step forward, and Billy started violently, lifting his hands.

"I didn't tell him, Jesus God, I didn't." His hands trembled like leaves. "I didn't even know the man's name until Brody told me, did I?"

Coogan dropped the Adidas bag and grabbed Billy by his sweater, shoving him up against the damp wall.

"Have you touted on me?" he hissed, pushing the boy hard. "Are you a fucking tout?"

The stack of boxes tumbled over like a child's blocks, and Coogan pushed the squirming boy onto the sharp angles of the jumble, pinning Billy's leg with his knee, grabbing the boy's wrist.

"Jesus, no." Billy's voice was high-pitched and girlish, his eyes wide. "How could I know?"

"You told him where, didn't you, Billy?" Coogan tipped the boy even farther back, crushing the boxes under the weight of both of them, pushing Billy's head down into the filthy joint of wall and pavement.

"You told him where you were to meet, you wee bastard," Coogan rasped. Billy tried to avert his face, looking up the drainpipe as if for a handhold. "And that's all he needed to know. Joe's just bright enough for that."

"Jesus." Billy's face reddened in spite of his fear as the blood rushed to his head. Coogan felt his control weakening, and he freed a hand to pull the .44 out of his coat.

"Oh, Jesus," Billy whimpered, squeezing his eyes shut and twisting his face to the wall as Coogan screwed the barrel of the revolver into his ear.

"Don't," Billy whispered. "He said . . ."

"He said what?" Coogan let himself down full length against the boy like a lover and thumbed back the hammer on the gun, his face close enough to Billy's to kiss him. "I can't hear you, Billy."

"He said . . ." Billy swallowed, his eyes still squeezed shut, his nose bent against the wall. "It was about your wife . . ."

Coogan pulled back in surprise. In the same instant he smelled the ammoniac tang of Billy's fear and heard the flat, rhythmic chopping of the Lynx coming back. At the slight release of the pressure of the gun barrel Billy cracked one eye open, but Coogan was looking up at the Lynx rocking in the breeze overhead, just beyond the eaves of the shop. They couldn't see him, not at this angle, and it didn't worry him, but he thought about Brody's knowledge of his marriage, thought about the stammering fool of a priest who had shopped the secret to Brody, or shopped it to someone who shopped it to Brody, thought about Maire driving that pretty American with his ponce's haircut through the middle of Belfast, as naïve and undefended as a school outing, and he indulged himself in the bright, fulsome image of the copter flowering in orange flame and gleaming shards of metal, a slow-motion roar out of one of those space war films. He pushed himself up with a grunt, propping himself over Billy with a hand on the cold wall, and he peered down at the boy through the skirts of his mackintosh, as if at a stunned small animal he had hit with his car. There was a dark stain at Billy's crotch where he had pissed himself, but he lay very still, making no move to cover it. Billy looked back at Coogan, his eyes wide and white, searching Coogan's face for permission to speak. Coogan frowned down at the boy as if trying to place his genus and species, and Billy licked his lips and said, "He said, take care for your wife." He drew a breath and nodded hopefully. "Jesus, I didn't even know you were married, Jimmy."

"Here's a message for Joe," Coogan said quietly, not hearing the boy. "See that you pass it on."

He bent as if to help Billy up, and Billy struggled up onto his elbows. But Coogan pressed the end of the gun barrel against Billy's leg and fired through the boy's kneecap into the boxes underneath. There was that hollow bang that Coogan always felt rather than heard, like the thump of a drum. Billy's elbows jerked out from under him and he arched his back and howled, climbing into a high, keening whine like an animal's. Blood soaked around the leg of his jeans like a tourniquet. He twisted back against the stiff edges and corners of the boxes as if trying to make himself comfortable, his shattered leg bent in the middle at a cruel and unnatural angle.

Coogan stepped back and sighed. He was shaking all over, his hand with the gun in it trembling. He looked up and saw an empty sky, the helicopter gone, as though it had been only a dream or an omen. Billy's cry was something distant, like the screech of a tire against pavement many streets away, and Coogan picked up the Adidas bag and started to jog unsteadily down the entry toward the street, the .44 hanging dead from his other hand. A colder part of his mind began to work again, slowly, and he thought, Cusack's still at work now, it's still possible to reach him before Brody does. Coogan started to run faster. But the American's on his own, he thought, and he pulled up short where the entry came into the street, looking at the revolver in his hand as if surprised to find it there. Then he shoved it away out of sight and trotted up the street away from the Falls Road, thinking with every beat of his heart *Maire Maire Maire.*

In front of the railway station Maire wanted to get out of the idling car and yank the seat out to look for the damn photograph, but some fool behind her was sounding his horn, so she cursed and put the Morris in gear. As she started up Donegall Road she took first one hand off the wheel and then the other, rooting in the pockets of her coat for the snap; if she couldn't find it in the car she'd have to go back and see if she'd dropped it behind the Plough and Stars. But all she found in her pockets was rubbish: a dried-up pen; a crumpled, empty cigarette packet; a lint-encrusted Chapstick. She dumped the stuff on the empty seat next to her and saw, poking out from under the seat onto the gritty floor mat, the end of the strap of Brian's money belt. She tried to remember if she had mentioned the money to Joe Brody. She didn't think she had, but she couldn't be sure.

Wasn't it just like that bastard husband of hers to have his own way and leave her to explain things to Joe, if it came to that. For now, though, forget it. There was a women's meeting in Armagh she'd promised to attend a fortnight ago, and she was already late. She twisted her wrist to look at her watch and cursed again. In spite of everything, she was still angry at him: one of these days Jimmy was going to have to learn that her work was as important as his.

Still, when she came to the roundabout at the start of the M1, she circled it twice, wondering if the bloody photograph was lying in the entry behind the pub for anyone to pick up. She didn't curse again but only groaned at herself: after all, it was her own damned fault, taking the picture in the first place, trying to one-up Jimmy at his own schoolboy game of cloak and dagger. Better to go look than let it prey on her mind all bloody day. She turned off the roundabout up Broadway, toward the Falls Road and the pub.

When she saw the VCP ahead, her breath caught in her throat and she took her foot off the accelerator, instinctively twisting around in her seat to see if she could turn off somewhere or reverse without calling attention to herself. Normally a roadblock was only an annoyance, though once in a while they placed her license number and she'd be ordered out of the car with barely disguised glee to be felt up by some thick-fingered, nineteen-year-old Birmingham yobbo while the others stood about and laughed.

But it was too late to avoid it now: another car had already come up behind her, and a soldier was waving her forward into the queue. She pulled up behind the last car and the squaddie, a lean, bony boy in brown camouflage fatigues and a flak jacket, cradled his SLR and blinked at her through her window as if trying to think of an opening line, the red-and-white plume quivering nervously at the front of his beret. The Royal Highland Fusiliers: Jimmy had taught her the cap badges. She snapped her eyes forward, alarm beginning to throb in a vein at her throat; two cars up a lance corporal stooped to the driver's window while another soldier stood off to one side, all his weight canted on one leg, and leveled his Sterling at the windscreen. Behind them two more squaddies crouched in the bricked-up doorways of an abandoned terrace, while another lay flat behind a concrete plug and watched the street over the dull barrel of his machine gun. Across the street another two squaddies in jump boots and flak jackets stood well apart against a high brick wall.

The squaddie outside her window rapped on the glass with his red knuckles, and Maire started. She gave him as level a gaze as she could muster, and, still blinking, the boy raised his voice to stammer, "P-please switch off the engine, m-miss." Maire nodded curtly and fumbled for the ignition, and as clear as a sound track in her head she heard her father's voice in falsetto, mimicking a lilting, sugary voice: "Why, you must be Bashful!" She looked away from the squaddie and gripped the steering wheel with both hands; in the rearview mirror she saw that there were now two cars behind her.

She glanced down at the wayward money belt strap and wondered if she dared lean over and tuck it out of sight. There was nothing in it now, but if some sharp-eyed squaddie saw it, it was enough to bring her in for four hours and ask her a lot of embarrassing questions, not to mention tearing the car apart. In the mirror she saw Bashful edge into view behind her car. She averted her eyes as if afraid he might look back at her in the mirror, and she started to negotiate her left foot over the transmission hump past the stick. If the photo was in the car, down between the seats where she hadn't had a chance to look yet, they'd match it up with Jimmy's prison photo, and they'd want to know who the other lad was, the one with the posh hair.

A snatch of song began to play in her head, and she was unable to silence it as she scraped at the end of the strap with the toe of her shoe. In her father's deep, long dead voice she heard, over and over, "Heigh-ho, heigh-ho, it's off to work we go . . ." Up ahead she saw the squaddie with the Sterling shift the gun in his hands and yawn, and in spite of herself she thought, Sleepy.

She glanced down; her foot hadn't been anywhere near the strap. She licked her lips and tried again, her shoe poking at the floor mat, her leg trembling with the awkward stretch. "Heigh-ho, heigh-ho, heigh-ho, heigh-ho." Her father's voice had been joined by others now, and over the drone of the song she heard Bashful stammering the letters and digits of her number plate, calling them out to one of the squaddies in a doorway up the road, who repeated them in turn into a radio. Her toe caught the strap and jerked another six inches of it out from under the seat.

"Shit," she hissed, while at the front of the line the lance corporal waved on the first car and gestured the rest of the queue forward. Maire dragged her foot back over to her side of the car and tugged at her rucked-up skirt, reaching for the ignition with her other hand. She took a deep, unsteady breath and let it out slowly, and the queue lurched up one space like a snake, the Morris whining in first gear. If they asked her out of the car she'd chat them up a bit, let them cop a feel, turn it into a joke; maybe then they wouldn't search the car. There was a whole chorus of dwarfs in her head now, and she stopped the car and left the motor running, second in line. Maybe she'd get through before the computer came up with her name.

But now the lance corporal had turned away from the driver of the car ahead of hers and was listening to the squaddie with the radio; now he was turning to shout something to Bashful, and for the first time she got a good look at the corporal, a deathly pale Northern English boy with a weak mustache and ears that stuck out under his beret like Prince Charles's. Prince Charming, she couldn't help thinking as he waved the first car away. Her heart began to pound, and she thought, I've done it, I've made it through, but as she fumbled the Morris into gear the Prince trotted toward her unholstering his pistol, and Sleepy stepped in front of the car with his legs spread and pointed the Sterling through the windscreen at her face. She twisted around, her head full of the idiot singing of dwarfs; Bashful was gesturing the cars behind her back toward the roundabout, and they were backing and turning around, scrambling like roaches exposed to the light.

"Stop the engine!" the Prince shouted through the glass, and Maire tried to roll down her window, stumbling over her first words of protest. But the corporal crouched with his 9 mm Browning poised at his shoulder, and he wrenched open her door.

"I said stop the fucking engine!" His voice was suddenly loud inside the car, and he reached roughly past her to twist the key out of the ignition.

"Wait a bloody minute!" The engine shuddered to a stop and Maire grabbed for her keys, but Prince Charming grasped her by the wrist and dragged her out of the car into the October chill.

"Fucking bastard!" she shouted, half walking, half dragging away from the Morris. The Prince twisted her arm behind her, forcing her upright and marching her straight toward the wall.

"I want an ATO and a search dog down here," the Prince shouted in a trembling voice, practically in her ear. "I want a Wheelbarrow and a pig and the whole fucking kit!"

"Right!" someone shouted, and as the wall rushed up to meet her Prince Charming tripped Maire, hooking her shin with the toe of his boot so that she fell forward and caught herself with her free hand against the gritty wall. The song in her head was a seamless, dissonant bass roar, as if the dwarfs had forgotten the words. The Prince wrenched her hand from behind her back and splayed it against the wall, well apart from her other hand; he kicked her feet farther apart with his heavy boot.

"There's s-something st-sticking out from under the s-seat," she heard Bashful say, and she felt Prince Charming turn away from her, his boots scraping against the pavement.

"Stay away from the fucking car, Warner," he shouted. "Let the ATO worry about that."

Maire felt her arms shaking and she tried to hold them still, focusing her eyes on the gray wall just beyond her nose. She tried to force her thoughts around what was happening, struggling through the deafening roar in her head. This was more than routine harassment; the Brits' computer had heaved up something more than her name and her political affiliation, the Prince had called for a bomb disposal officer, did they think . . . ?

"Am I under arrest?" She tried to lift her chin over her shoulder, but the Prince whirled and pressed the freezing muzzle of his 9 mm into her cheek, nudging her face back to the wall.

"Shut your fucking mouth, sunshine." His voice shook, as if he was in the grip of some powerful emotion. "Baxter, watch this cunt while I search her."

He grabbed both her wrists and wrenched her arms back just long enough to strip off her coat; then he pushed her back up against the wall as he rifled through her coat pockets. The dwarfs were moaning like monks now, a long, sustained groan dampening her thoughts like white noise. Even if they'd caught him coming out of the pub Jimmy wouldn't tell them anything, at least not right away, and Brian was on the train, safely out of reach, but in spite of it all they thought *she* had the parcel.

"They say go ahead and arrest her," somebody shouted from up the street, probably the radioman. "Before we get a crowd. They'll sort it out later."

"Hear that, sunshine?" Prince Charming was right behind her now. "It's your lucky day. You're under arrest."

Boots scuffed on the pavement, and she felt his hands push up under her arms and slide heavily down her sides. She went rigid, gritting her teeth to keep from swinging around with her fists clenched.

"What am I charged with?" she managed to say, her voice barely under control.

Prince Charming stood right up against her from behind, pressing himself outrageously against her buttocks, his breath warm in her ear.

"Northern Ireland Emergency Provisions Act, sunshine. I arrest you under my authority as a member of Her Majesty's forces." His voice was hard and too loud, as if he was as frightened as she was. He ran his hands heavily over her breasts, and she wasn't able to keep from jerking her breath in with a girlish little gasp. She'd thought she could handle this, she had before, but today was different, today they weren't laughing and larking about and sizing her up, today they knew something was on, today the boy feeling her up was all business. The Prince let his hands drop and stepped back. Maire tried to draw a deep breath, but she couldn't; her diaphragm was too tight.

"You can't do this." Her voice shook, and she swallowed dryly and mustered her best Queen Victoria. "I am a Belfast city councillor."

"Bobby Sands was a Member of Parliament, sunshine." The Prince grunted as he squatted down behind her. "See where it got him."

A hand jerked one ankle and then the other, pulling her feet out farther and forcing her face closer to the wall, and then his cold, enormous hands slid up her legs under her skirt. A vacuum opened up in Maire and sucked all the breath out of her, and she squeezed her eyes shut, trying to think over the deafening roar of dwarfs, thinking, Who could have known, who could have touted on her, but against the red glow at the back of her eyelids all she could see was herself kneeing the lance corporal in the balls, shooting him between the eyes with his own pistol; she saw herself rage-tautened in the ragged front line of an aggro, flinging bottles and pieces of brick down the littered street at a line of squaddies behind riot shields; saw herself crouched in a dark doorway with a mask over her face and an Armalite clutched to her chest.

And then she came out the other side of the rage into silence, and she thought, Brody knows. This is nothing to do with the money belt or my license number. Brody knows about Jimmy, and he knows about the two of us. Brody did this.

The Prince stood up behind her and stepped back, and she opened her eyes to the pitted moonscape of brick before her. If Joe was desperate to stop Jimmy, and if he couldn't lay his hands on Jimmy himself, what would he do? All it took was a call to the Confidential Phone with her name, and Joe wouldn't even have to leave his chair. Brody *knows*.

The roar had died in her head, and in the ringing silence she heard the singsong wail of a siren coming. She wanted to laugh, but she felt enervated and giddy, every limb weak as if after a long illness. She lowered her head between her upraised arms and closed her eyes again, while behind her Prince Charming shouted incomprehensible orders up and down the street.

After six days of hitchhiking, Clare Delaney allowed herself the luxury of a bus ride. She had taken herself as far north in Ireland as it is possible to go, and now that she had decided to head south again, the proprietress of the bed and breakfast in Malin told her that she'd have a hard time getting a ride anywhere but Derry, and what would a sweet young girl like her want to go there for?

Clare let that pass, and said, "I'd really like to get to Donegal by tonight."

"Then you should get the bus down the road at half twelve to Derry," the old woman said, contradicting herself. "There's a bus there that'll take you to Donegal Town."

The bus was a half hour late, and as it rattled and groaned down the narrow roads, Clare let herself be drawn into conversation with a tiny, ancient, birdlike nun, who noted Clare's American accent right away and asked her all the usual questions: What was her name? Ah, she was Irish. Where was she from in America? Bless me, I had a cousin in Philadelphia once, but he's dead now, God rest his soul. Did she have people in Ireland?

Clare smiled and answered all the questions, though she half expected the sister to know her answers already, through the network of elderly nuns and lonely old bachelors that Clare drew like a magnet. It seemed to her that she had already answered all these questions sufficiently. It was one of the reasons she had started hitchhiking finally. Then the sister asked how long Clare had been away from home, and she raised her bushy eyebrows when Clare said a year.

"I was going to school in London," Clare said by way of explanation.

"Oh, you must miss your home terrible," the sister said, and for the first time in a long while Clare did, looking out the greasy window at the bald, brown hills of Inishowen.

"I do," she heard herself say. "I miss the colors this time of year." She smiled at the sister's puzzlement. "You know, when the trees change."

"Ah, yes." The sister nodded sadly. "Ireland used to be covered with trees, you know. The Sassenach cut them all down."

Now it was her turn to smile at Clare's puzzlement.

"The Brits," she said crisply, as if to a child.

The bus depot in Derry consisted of a pair of battered prefab huts standing at the edge of a cracked and pitted and nearly empty parking lot overlooking the river, like a pair of abandoned survival huts at the edge of an Antarctic plain. Coming down off the bus into the diesel stink, Clare saw long rows of houses across the river, marching like ranks of infantry up the hill under a pale blue sky. On this side of the river gray buildings crowded together on the slope under the Derry city walls; narrow streets cut through the buildings like ravines. The blocks around the depot seemed abandoned, a desolate landscape of empty, rubbled lots in which the houses left standing were like dried skulls, bricked and boarded up and half demolished. Clare felt a pang of fear and pity, thinking of herself for a moment in the same way as the B&B proprietress had that morning, an innocent abroad, wide-eyed and all alone in the Irish Beirut.

Then she shook it off, and hitching her backpack farther up on her shoulders she marched twice around the huts looking in vain for a bus schedule. The scuffed and dented doors at either end were locked, and nothing was visible in the darkness through the filthy windows. Finally she stopped a uniformed bus inspector and asked for the next bus to Donegal, and the man pointed down the line of buses at the curb to a battered red-and-white coach at the end and said that it was leaving at half past three.

Clare carried her pack down the line of buses, and as she came along the dusty side of the Donegal bus she saw the driver sitting behind the wheel with his head down as if he was reading. But looking up through the door she saw that he was sleeping sitting up, his head tilted forward through his loosened collar, his belly tipped like a load of sand over his belt buckle, his hands curled palm up in his lap like two dead leaves. She lifted her hand to rap on the door, but lowered it again, thinking of the man's embarrassment at being awakened on the job. She knew she could smooth it over and smile her way onto the bus—you have such a lovely smile, her mother always said, lately in a tone that implied that she never expected to see it again—but more than anything else Clare Delaney hated to be thought of as sweet. There had been times in college when she was almost willing to try anything short of catching a social disease to prove that she wasn't. At parties she used her smile like a weapon against the tepid boys who tried to pick her up; she went with a butch girlfriend to working-class bars, where she'd get sloppy drunk and flirt dangerously with musky young men in T-shirts, counting on the girlfriend to fend them off. But finally she wasn't able to master the side effects of the wild life: she couldn't hold her liquor, marijuana put her to sleep, and cocaine gave her a ferocious headache and two days of depression. Worst of all, she suspected that nobody believed her for a minute, for at crucial moments she found herself betrayed by her mother's expletives—darn, son of a gun, gosh—and saw the eyes of her companion light up with amusement. So in the interest of anti-sweetness Clare moved in the other direction, into a kind of stubborn, narrow-eyed earnestness that allowed her to champion charity, compassion, and commitment with a severity that belied any trace of her mother. It also led her wry and gentle English boyfriend to start calling her St. Clare, first behind her back, then to her face, and finally as an almost affectionate parting shot. So that now she traveled alone, standing biting her lip outside a bus in Northern Ireland.

"To heck with it," she said, and she stepped back and looked both ways down the line of buses. Across the street on her left was a small, stylish new brick building with a sign out front that said Tourist Office, and she started toward it. Perhaps they'd watch her pack until the bus left.

"People are a little wary of unattended packages," said the nervous woman behind the desk, and Clare sighed. Right, she wanted to say, I came all the way from Ardmore, Pennsylvania, to blow up the tourist office in Londonderry. But instead she nodded and turned to go.

"Perhaps they'll take it at the bus station," the woman suggested, in a tone that admitted that they probably wouldn't.

Outside the office Clare looked at her watch and wondered how she could pass the next hour and a half without dragging her pack every step of the way. It should have occurred to her that it might be a problem here, but it hadn't; it had never been a problem in England or the Republic. As she stood on the curb, a jeep ground noisily by with three soldiers huddled in the back, their weapons each pointing in a different direction, and Clare felt a gust of self-reproach: if not finding a place to leave her backpack was the worst hardship she suffered during her ninety minutes in Northern Ireland, she had nothing to complain about, did she? The jeep took the corner too fast, and the soldiers in the back shouted and clutched each other and the sides of the jeep to keep from tumbling out. One of the soldiers reached up to clout the driver on the back of the head as the jeep disappeared from sight behind the line of buses, and Clare saw another backpacker pounding on the door of the Donegal bus. As she started to trot her backpack across the street, she saw the bus driver raise his head, shake the sleep out of it, and push himself up out of his seat.

"Is this the bus for Donegal?" the guy in the backpack was saying as the door clattered open and Clare came up behind him. He was an American.

The driver cleared his throat and said, "Aye, but not till half three."

"Aha." The backpacker pushed back the cuff of his anorak to look at his watch. He looked up at the driver again.

"Could I just sit on the bus till it's time to go?" He lifted one boot to the first step. "I've been up since six this morning and I'm dead on my feet."

The driver scratched the back of his neck and blew out a sigh, and he glanced wearily over the backpacker's head at Clare, afraid that she had a question too. The American glanced around his pack to see what the driver was looking at, and Clare glimpsed a square face with broad cheekbones and curly blond hair, a good-looking guy.

"Listen," she said, "I don't want to stay. I'd just like to leave my pack while I go get something to eat."

The driver frowned and sniffed and grunted skeptically, and he lifted a hand to the metal pole beside him, blocking the way. Immediately Clare was annoyed at herself for seeming to cut the ground out from under the other backpacker. She tried to maneuver next to him in the narrow doorway, hoping to present a united front, but the guy looked at her as if she was trying to crowd him out. Then he looked back up at the driver and started to say something.

"You could look in our packs if you want," Clare said quickly, glancing hopefully at the backpacker, but he looked back at her wide-eyed as though astonished to discover that they spoke the same language. He put a hand on the door to keep it from closing and looked up at the driver.

"Look, she can leave her pack with me," he said. "I'll keep an eye on it." He glanced at Clare and gave both her and the driver a crooked but charming smile. "If it blows up, we'll all go together."

The driver sighed loudly and waved his hands dismissively.

"Ah, it's all right," he said. "Come on up, then."

Clare hung back as the backpacker stepped up into the bus and squeezed past the driver. Then the driver waved her up, saying, "You too, lass. Bring your rucksack up. We'll keep an eye on it."

She smiled at the driver and climbed up the steps, wriggling out of the straps and pushing the pack down the aisle ahead of her. She stopped where the American was lifting his own pack into the luggage rack.

"Thanks," she said, smiling.

"You bet." The guy smiled back at her, and for a moment she thought he was offering to lift her pack into the rack as well, but he stooped past her and sagged back into a seat with his eyes closed, his hiking boots set wide apart and his hands on his knees. He did seem tired, but he was uncommonly good-looking nevertheless. She watched him through her arms as she hefted her red pack into the rack next to his blue one; she didn't like the way he wore his hair, with its curls hanging loose over his smooth forehead, but his choirboy's face and full lips gave him a Billy Budd look of bruised innocence. Even his day-old stubble looked downy and golden, and when he caught her looking at him, she was startled by the autumnal blue of his eyes, and she stepped back from the luggage rack, leaving one of the black straps of her pack swinging.

"Um," she stammered, "you look really beat."

The guy surprised her by laughing.

"Thanks," he said.

"Don't mention it." She blushed and smiled and hugged her elbows.

"Did I hear you say you were going to get something to eat?"

Clare let go of her elbows and shoved her hands into the back pockets of her jeans.

"Can I bring you something?" she said, overly solicitous.

The guy stretched in his seat like a cat and said, "Well, I'm not real hungry." Then he relaxed again and said, "But if you come across an apple or an orange . . ."

"No prob." Clare cringed at her own heartiness, but she managed a smile and turned back down the aisle.

"Have a nice nap," she called back over her shoulder. The guy made no reply, but she glimpsed the top of his head over the back of the seat in front of him, the loose curls glowing in the afternoon sunlight slanting through the bus window. The driver winked at her as she dropped down the steps to the sidewalk.

There were other passengers on the bus by the time the girl came back, a few thick, middle-aged women all bundled up in overcoats and scarves, and two or three unshaven men who sat with their coats unbuttoned and their collars loosened. Several uniformed schoolchildren sat together without talking near the front of the bus, their bookbags held neatly on their laps. Brian had jerked awake each time someone else got on, lifting his head out of a hot, fitful, uncomfortable sleep at some subliminal cue, blinking in the speckled sunlight coming through the window as each newcomer paid his fare and exchanged a few words with the driver. Each time Brian had looked at his watch and found that only a few more minutes had crawled by, and he would close his eyes and try with little success to find a different, more comfortable way to sleep in the stiff seat.

When the girl returned, with only a few minutes to spare, Brian had given up trying. She bounded up the steps breathless and flushed, and she balanced a paper bag on her knee as she paid her fare. While the driver made change from a soft wad of colored bills, she glanced down the aisle toward Brian, glancing away again when she saw him looking back. Then she came down the aisle holding the bag in front of her and, in spite of her breathlessness, sat lightly on the edge of the seat next to Brian, as if she didn't expect to stay.

"Almost didn't make it," she said, rooting in the paper bag, not looking at Brian.

"Relax." He edged forward into her line of sight. "Have a seat."

"Thanks." She fell back against the seat and smiled sidelong at him. It was a very pretty smile, and if her cheeks hadn't already been bright red from running, Brian would have sworn she blushed a little.

"Hold this?" She handed Brian the bag, and he held it on his lap while she pulled off her bulky sweater and pushed up the sleeves of her red flannel shirt. She had a narrow face with high cheekbones and thin lips and a long, graceful neck, and when she had rolled her shirtsleeves tight enough for her satisfaction, she pushed her slender fingers back through her short, curly brown hair.

"Help yourself." She nodded toward the bag and leaned forward to unlace her hiking boots. "Half of that's yours."

"Great." Brian reached into the bag, pulling out a hard roll, an apple, and a warm Pepsi. "How much was it?"

"Oh, it's on me." She glanced at him over her shoulder. "For watching my pack."

"I dunno, I didn't watch it very carefully." He set his food between his legs on the seat and rolled the bag shut. "I was asleep most of the time. Maybe it's not there anymore."

She twisted away from her boots and glanced up at the luggage rack, and he admired the pull of her shirt across her back. Then she pushed her boots under her seat and sat up, curling one long leg under her and then the other.

"It's okay." She smiled and took the bag from Brian, pulling out a fat red apple and polishing it against the thigh of her jeans. "It's still there." She took a huge bite out of the apple and said with her mouth full, "Yours is gone, though."

It took him a moment to understand what she had said, and then he started, half rising to his feet, knocking his food onto the floor between his boots. The girl froze and watched him wide-eyed with her mouth full of apple, and she forced it down half chewed and reached out to touch him lightly on the arm, jerking her hand away again almost immediately.

"I was joking," she said, patting the corner of her lips for a stray bit of apple. She narrowed her eyes at him as if he were hurt, and he sat tensed in his seat, wondering if he should clamber over her into the aisle to see for himself.

"I'm sorry," she began, peering at him, her hands clutched around the apple in her lap. The bus shuddered as the engine rumbled to life, and up the aisle the driver pulled the clattering door shut.

"No, *I'm* sorry." Brian settled slowly back into his seat, bending over to retrieve his own apple and roll and Pepsi from the floor. He sat up and smiled at her. "I've been on the road too long. I'm just a little paranoid."

"Okay?" She started to lift the apple to her mouth again, watching him sidelong.

"Really. It's okay."

"Okay." She took another hearty bite of apple, and after a moment she held out her hand in two short, hesitant jerks.

"Clare Delaney," she mumbled through the apple. "From Philadelphia."

Her hand was cool and strong and sticky with apple juice.

"Brian Donovan. From Detroit." He held on to her hand a moment longer than necessary.

The bus nosed laboriously around a block of ruined buildings and then climbed a road high above the wide River Foyle. Even this late in the year the sides of the valley were grassy and green behind a gray scrim of bare branches, the river shining in the late afternoon light. On the other side of the road, though, out Brian's window, was a long, wintry rampart of bricked-up houses, like an outgrowth of the city walls.

The girl ate as if she hadn't seen food in days, finishing the apple and prying apart one of the hard rolls, spraying crumbs all over her lap and the seat. Brian turned away from the window to watch her. He popped open his warm Pepsi and took an acid sip.

"You been here long?"

"In Northern Ireland?" Clare looked at him with a ragged piece of roll poised near her lips. When Brian nodded she said, "Only a couple of hours. I only came through Londonderry for the bus connection. I was up in Inishowen this morning. What about you?" She put the bread in her mouth.

"Just a few days."

Clare frowned and nodded.

"I was going to spend some time here, originally. But my relatives down south—in Cork?—they talked me out of it." She tore off another piece of roll, looking past Brian out the window. He turned and saw blackened walls rising out of rubbled lots; high up in one shattered wall he saw a single window with its glass intact and its white trim looking new.

"I guess I thought I'd get too depressed," he heard her say. "Is that a terrible thing to say?"

"Beats me." He sipped at his Pepsi and watched her over the rim of the can. "I just came to visit family. I'm a stranger here myself."

"You have family here? Where?"

Brian told her about the reunion at John Donovan's pub, and the bus turned away from the river, passing tidy new brick houses with the initials IRA or INLA already daubed in white spraypaint on their walls, like trees marked for cutting. There was no one on the streets, and it seemed to Brian as he talked that the new houses beyond the city walls had already been emptied by a plague; their inhabitants slept now in the huge cemetery he saw high up on the steep, round hill over the town, its ranks of stones marching up the slope toward a row of massive Celtic crosses silhouetted against the sky.

"Did your relatives talk about, you know . . ." Clare chewed the last of her roll and circled her hand to indicate the Troubles.

"Actually," he said, "it never came up."

"I want to know more about it." She looked past him out the window again. "You just wish there were something you could do."

Brian nodded and cleared his throat, and he looked at the hard roll in his hand, wondering just how hungry he was. The bus slowed, and up the aisle the schoolchildren got quietly out of their seats and crowded up next to the driver, who stopped the bus and let them out. Outside they erupted into shouting and laughter, and they ran past the nose of the bus into the new housing estate. As the bus started up again Brian brushed off the roll and took a bite out of it.

"Here we are," Clare said.

"What's that?" Brian looked up, his mouth full of sour bread.

"The border." She craned her long neck to look down the aisle.

The piece of roll stuck dry and hard in Brian's throat, and he had to force it down with an acid swallow of Pepsi. Suddenly the view outside the window was gone, and there were only tall gray barriers of corrugated iron on either side. The bus slowed to crawl over a pair of speed bumps. On the left side of the bus a steel watchtower stood on a low, grassy mound, a matte black, narrow-slitted blockhouse on top of it, the mound surrounded by a wire fence threaded like ivy with barbed wire. Clare sat up straight in her seat with one leg tensed under her for better elevation, and with her hand on the back of the seat in front of her she bit her lip and looked all around the bus. Brian tried to speak, but his mouth was dry. He forced down another mouthful of pop and said, "Do we have to get out here, or what?"

"I don't know." The girl didn't look at Brian, but instead up toward the front of the bus. "When I came through the other way this morning a guy just got on and walked up the aisle."

"Uh-huh." What did the guy do, Brian wanted to ask. Did he ask questions? Did he look in anybody's bags? Did he have a dog sniffing for explosives? You'll have no trouble at the border, the Provo had said, but if it was so fucking easy why didn't he do it himself? Why didn't Maire do it? Maybe he was as expendable as Cousin Mike had been meant to be.

He wished the girl would sit down. Beyond the window across the aisle a soldier with his arms crossed leaned in the doorway of a tiny wooden guardbooth, and another officer in a dark uniform stood just before the booth with his hand stuck in his overcoat like Napoleon. The bus crept to a stop, vibrating as it idled, the driver tapping his fingers on the steering wheel. The soldier in the guardbooth yawned and nodded, and the bus heaved wearily forward, its engine grumbling. It crept over more speed bumps past an armored personnel carrier in a barbed-wire corral and into a bare corridor of dull corrugated steel. Clare lifted her chin to see what was coming next, but Brian stared at the back of the seat ahead, his stomach tightening to the size of a walnut.

"I think they're more worried about things coming in," he managed to say, his throat tight, "than about things going out."

He drew a deep breath and looked at the girl. It almost didn't matter if she'd heard him, he'd said it as much to reassure himself as to add to the conversation, but the girl sank back slightly, as if disappointed.

"You're probably right," she said.

The bus stopped again at a guardbooth right outside Brian's window. There was yet another officer in a black overcoat, and a soldier in crisp combat fatigues and a black beret standing jauntily at ease. Brian tried not to look at the soldier, but he couldn't look away. Clare leaned toward him to get a better view, and he wanted to push her back. The officer and the soldier each glanced down the length of the bus, and they nodded simultaneously, the soldier laughing and rocking back on his heels at something the officer had said. The driver lazily lifted his hand to them and guided the bus slowly over a final pair of speed bumps, then he turned to the left, away from the checkpoint, the engine grinding up in pitch as he accelerated down a narrow blacktopped road lined with bare trees.

The girl turned in her seat to watch the little maze of corrugated iron and barbed wire disappear behind, and while she wasn't looking Brian squeezed his eyes shut and shuddered and let all his breath out very slowly and silently through his nostrils. His shoulders were jammed up tight against the back of the seat, and he relaxed them and opened his eyes. Clare turned around and sat down with a sigh. Outside his window Brian saw an old couple walking along the road, the man, no taller than the woman, pulling a child's rusty wagon full of parcels and sacks. As they fell away behind he saw, standing above the weeds beside the road, a sign displaying a faded green shamrock and the words Good-bye, Come Again. A few seconds later another, newer sign appeared, saying Welcome to Donegal in Gaelic and English.

Brian felt drained and happy, as if he had just finished a run. For the first time the low sun shone directly down the aisle in a wide, dusty shaft, filling the bus with a warm glow and making Brian squint in the welcome glare. He arched his back and yawned like a cat, rolling his shoulders and stretching his legs out as far as he could under the seat in front of him. Outside his window the trees glided by at regular intervals like telephone poles, their bare branches gilded with sunlight, and beyond the trees he saw a golden field of grass, and beyond that a long, low ridge turned almost red by the sun. He wanted to laugh out loud, but instead he only smiled at Clare, who smiled back, her eyebrows drawn together, as if she was puzzled.

"Too long on the road, huh?"

"You bet." Brian laughed. "And miles to go before I sleep." He tore off a piece of hard roll and popped it in his mouth. He felt like singing.

The bus began to slow again, and Clare squinted up the aisle into the light.

"Are we stopping again already?"

"It's a stopping bus," Brian explained happily, and the bus rolled off the pavement, the sun wheeling to slant through Brian's window. The engine ground down as the bus lumbered over an uneven, unpaved turnoff and stopped in front of a long gray building of concrete blocks, where two men in blue overcoats stood on the steps out front. The letters of a sign threw vivid, distended shadows along the side of the building:

THE REPUBLIC OF IRELAND

CUSTOMS

Brian was breathless suddenly, as if the cabin of the bus had been depressurized, emptying it of all that warm air, sucking the breath out of him, leaving him gasping in a bright vacuum. The older of the two customs officers walked down the steps and approached the idling bus, while the younger one stood hatless on the top step, swinging his arms and bouncing on the balls of his feet as he looked both ways up the road.

Clare looked at Brian with her eyebrows raised as the door of the bus rattled open. The driver nodded as the customs man climbed the steps and leaned against the metal upright at the front of the bus.

"Do you want your apple?" Clare said, and Brian snapped his face to her. Up the aisle the door thumped shut, and the bus crunched over gravel and back toward the road.

"Sure." He fumbled with the apple in his lap. "I mean, no. Here." He handed her the apple and she began to polish it against her thigh.

Brian was afraid he was breathing too fast, using up precious oxygen. His clothes pulled tight around him, binding him in all the wrong places. In an instant the warm light had curdled and warped, becoming pale and cold, throwing the customs officer's shadow all the way down the aisle like a carpet, darkening the bus as if he blocked the entire windshield. The officer spoke to no one, not even the driver a foot or two away; he stood with his arm hooked around the metal post, rocking from side to side with the motion of the bus, staring severely down the aisle.

Clare crunched on the apple, making soft smacking noises, and she delicately sucked the juice off her fingers. She offered a bite to Brian.

"We ought to finish this before we have to declare it," she whispered, smiling.

Brian shook his head. He lifted the Pepsi and drained it, watching the customs man over the end of the can, silently daring him to walk down the aisle and yank Brian's pack out of the luggage rack. The backlit officer scowled back and lifted his cap to rub his bald head. Brian lowered the can and held the stare, his stomach tight again, the blood roaring in his ears, the glare of the sun like needles in his eyes.

The bus was slowing again, the narrow, compacted white houses of a village gliding more and more slowly by, crowded up to the edge of the road like the curious at an accident. This is it, Brian thought; the checkpoint at the border had been only a dress rehearsal, a prelude to the real thing. Everybody out for customs, that's a good lad, those with explosives to declare please move to the left.

Brian crushed the empty Pepsi can between both hands, and Clare lowered her half-eaten apple and looked at him. The bus stopped in front of a tiny grocer's shop, and the customs officer stood away from the pole and leveled his cap with a sharp tug on the brim. Brian twisted around in his seat and saw that there was no rear door on the bus. Maybe one of the windows popped out, an emergency exit, the way they did on Greyhounds back home. He twisted back to look out his window at the wall of narrow houses all jammed together, leaving no way between them. Grampa ran all the way to America, he thought. Where would I run to?

He turned to the front again. The officer should have been halfway up the aisle, but he was gone, and the driver was pulling the door shut. A couple of old women, newcomers, were whispering with each other and smoothing their coats over their bottoms as they settled into their seats. As Clare finished her apple and stuffed the core into the crumpled paper bag, Brian sagged in his seat and watched the customs officer walk past the front of the bus and across the road to a stout woman waiting on the other side. The bus began to roll forward, and Brian, nearly numb, watched the officer pick up the basket at the woman's feet and start up the road with her, his hand affectionately at the small of her back.

"Why don't these buses have bathrooms?" Clare said almost to herself. "My hands are all sticky."

Brian felt too tired to speak, or even to close his eyes. The bus passed the old couple and rolled around a tight curve away from the village. There was no endorphin rush this time, just a cold, aching, bowel-loosening relief, as if after a near miss on the freeway. He felt clammy and chilled with sweat, and he rolled his head against the seat to look at the girl next to him. She blinked back at him for a moment and then looked away.

"So," she said, her cheeks reddening, "how far are you going tonight?"

The light was draining quickly from the sky, and in the electric blue of twilight Sean Boylan sat on a reasonably dry patch of ground behind a rocky outcrop and waited for Desmond Cusack to come home. He had pulled off the Wellingtons he'd worn coming up over the hill from the car, and he sat cross-legged in his warm woolen socks, his muffler wrapped twice around his neck, his gloves pulled up over the cuffs of his field jacket. In the fading light the hills around him seemed to swell and darken and take on a substance they didn't have in daylight. Off to his left he watched the long shoulder of Crownarad seem to lift itself slowly up against the deepening blue like the back of a great beast. Straight ahead, across the valley from him, rose the twin bald domes of Tawny Hill and Croaghbeg, their features fading as they took on weight and stature, while down the valley to his right he saw the orange and yellow lights of Kilcar come on one at a time, like candle flames. Beyond them, through a gap in the hills over the bay, he saw the swelling sea turning darker under the still luminous sky, while above the sea the heights at Slieve League were already black in silhouette against the brilliant orange clouds in the west. Sitting here waiting he felt like a wee lad again, lying in bed alone and watching the shadows swell out from the corners of the room into monster shapes; he was almost afraid to turn around and look up at the darkening bulk of the tall hill behind him.

Instead Boylan turned and pulled the rifle away from the rock where he had leaned it, and he lifted it to his shoulder to look down the hill through the scope. The gun was an old Lee-Enfield No. 4 sniper's rifle, a relic from his father's days during the Border Campaign, a simpler time when there were no Provos or Stickies or space cadets from the INLA, no Brit soldiers patrolling the streets of Belfast and Derry, and no little Sean Boylan. Just one IRA, more or less, his da and a handful of other diehards creeping about the border blowing up RUC barracks and customs huts and engaging in picturesque gangster-movie shoot-outs with the B-Specials and the Gardai. When his father had appropriated it from a British armory, the rifle had been a .303, but Boylan had refitted it to 7.62 NATO standard, bringing it all the way up to date with a modern nightscope, a great bucket of a thing that was bloody murder to zero in but scooped up light like a steam shovel. About fifty meters down the slope he saw the dark gash where the Glenaddragh River ran swollen with October rain, and then twenty-five meters beyond that he saw Cusack's back garden and his darkened house. He swung the scope along the narrow road that ran up the valley. A few houses in the distance were lit already, and it was a quiet enough evening for him to hear a dog barking somewhere far off, and even the rush of the river below. He brought the cross hairs back to the rear of Cusack's house, creeping them across his back door and his kitchen window.

There was a bit of a breeze coming up the valley from the bay, but it wasn't much to worry about. The cold it brought was more annoying than anything else, a damp, wintry chill that numbed his nose and cheeks and threatened to stiffen his fingers. Boylan lowered the Lee-Enfield and laid it across his lap, and he lifted his chin to rewind the muffler around his throat. High overhead a jet gleamed in the last of the sunlight, scoring a luminous vapor trail against the sky like a diamond against deep blue crystal. Boylan supposed that the more comfortable way to go about this would be to creep down the hill in the dusk and break in Cusack's back door and wait in the dark parlor, but for his own sake he preferred to sit up the hill in the cold. He'd managed to overcome most of his reservations about this on the drive up, and after he'd left the car in the trees up Croaghcullin way, he'd had a long tramp through the dying bracken to think about what Joe Brody—Brody himself—had told him on the phone: that Desmond Cusack was a traitor and possibly a tout, that he was helping to smuggle out explosives stolen from Belfast Brigade for his own profit, that he was meeting with someone tonight at O'Connor's in Donegal Town to clinch the deal.

Boylan pulled off his gloves and breathed into his cupped hands to warm his stiff fingers. He could still scarcely believe it, but the word came from Joe himself. *I want him stiffed,* Brody had said, *and I want it done tonight. Then I want you to take his place at O'Connor's; chances are whoever he's meeting doesn't know him. All you have to do is sit alone in a booth reading a book and answer to the password.*

The headlights of a car glided into view around the bend at the east end of the valley, and Boylan lifted the Lee-Enfield and sighted through the scope. In the gloom it was hard to tell, especially with the glare of the lights going before, but it looked like Cusack's battered old Cortina. Then he heard the uneven buzz of the little engine rising up the valley like the distant sound of a chain saw, and he knew it was Des, coming home from the fishery in Killybegs. He lowered the gun slightly and watched down the long barrel as the car crawled up the road pushing its lights ahead of it, and then turned off, disappearing behind the house below, the nimbus of its lights rising around the house like the moon coming up over a mountain.

Boylan's stomach tightened as the buzzing of the engine stopped and the lights went out, and he felt one last pang of regret. Des was a mate, which was why Boylan sat up the hill and not in the parlor: at the end of the day, he wasn't sure he could do it face to face like that, with Des standing just inside the door blinking in surprise and reeking of fish. But then, on the other side of the coin, friend or no, Des had betrayed his comrades, and keeping his mind on that Boylan smoothly and nearly silently drew back the bolt on the Lee-Enfield and chambered a round. Down the hill he saw a glow through the kitchen window as Des turned on a light in another room, and in spite of everything Boylan felt annoyed. *What if the bugger draws a bath first,* he thought. *I'll be up here all bloody night.* In which case he'd be late getting to O'Connor's himself. What was that fucking password, anyway?

But then he had a bit of luck as Des switched on the overhead light in the kitchen and flashed by the window in the yellow glare. Boylan twisted onto one buttock and lifted his knee, steadying the Lee-Enfield on it, a practiced balance of hand and elbow and shoulder. The wood of the stock was cold, but there was no heat left in his numbed cheek to warm it; indeed, he could barely feel the stock against his cheek at all. Des passed the window again, only his feet and his legs visible from this sharp angle, and just for an instant Boylan remembered sitting on a hillside during a dry summer when he was a boy, lifting this very same rifle when it was a .303, pointing it downhill at a line of empty Guinness bottles in a parched streambed. The gun had been without a scope then, but even without the extra weight it had been nearly too heavy for him to lift, let alone aim. He had emptied the first magazine into the dirt below, miles from any of the bottles, his wee bony arms shaking with the effort of holding the rifle up. He remembered being almost too terrified to pull the trigger and asking his da why the bullets didn't roll out of the barrel when he pointed the gun down the hill. His da had cuffed him, but what was worse than that was his father's bitter, unforgiving laughter, which after a moment, because of his prison-ruined constitution and in spite of the dry heat, became a hacking, consumptive cough.

"Come on, Desmond," Boylan muttered against the stock, angry now, "show us your bloody face."

Then, as if he'd heard his name called, Cusack appeared at the kitchen window carrying a teakettle, framing himself neatly in silhouette between the curtains as he filled the kettle at the tap. Boylan could almost hear the rattle of those old pipes as he centered the cross hairs on Cusack's forehead and thumbed the focus on the scope. Des just stood there and Boylan squeezed the trigger, the gun jumping in his hands like a live thing, lifting his elbow right off his knee. He steadied it again to see Cusack still there in the window, scratching the back of his neck. Then all the way up the hill Boylan heard the thwack of the bullet against the side of Cusack's house, probably a few inches to the left of the window.

Fucking wind, Boylan thought, chambering another round and dropping the gun to his knee and sighting down the scope. There was Desmond, thick as they came, pulling aside the curtain and peering out into the dark, wondering what that thump and crack had been. Boylan pulled to the right, centering the cross hairs nearly at the window sill, thinking, Poor Des, he never did have the sense God gave him.

He fired, clutching the Lee-Enfield more tightly this time, watching the left hemisphere of the scope as the top of Cusack's head burst and he tipped back, teakettle flying, his arms in the air as if he were leading a cheer.

On the way back to the car, Boylan kept to the lee of the hill, staying away from the top where he might be seen against the rising moon. He went as fast as he could, stumbling over the dark, uneven ground in his Wellingtons, hoping to get back in time for a shower before he had to go down to O'Connor's. He kept his mind a blank, careful not to think of what he had just seen, but it was hard. Think of the uniform, not the man, was the sniper's motto, but Des hadn't been in uniform. Still, Boylan managed to let his thoughts drift, wondering what he might wear to the pub, as if it was only a night out, wondering what book he might take, so that when he remembered the password it came to him unbidden like a snatch of an old song: Ireland unfree shall never be at peace.

"I am Detective Inspector Glassie," the policeman said. "You are not required to say anything unless you wish to. Whatever you say may be written down and given in evidence. Do you understand?"

Maire said nothing, but only lifted her cigarette to her lips. She sat across from the detective inspector in a chrome and plastic chair, in a small, brightly lit room of thickly overpainted

white. The chair was carefully contoured for the human backside, but it was comfortable only if you sat upright in it like a
convent girl, with your back straight and your knees together,
and Maire slouched down in it with her arms crossed and one
leg thrown over the other at the knee, her own backside pressed
precariously against the molded ridge at the front of the seat.

"You are Mary Cathleen Donovan?"

She held herself up in the chair only by the heel of one shoe,
all of her weight on it like a buttress; she could feel her calf
trembling under the strain. If she released the pressure on her
heel, she would slither out of the chair to the smooth, scuffed
gray lino like a bored child at Sunday dinner. Her calf was
beginning to ache, but that was what she wanted: the pain was
palpable and reassuring in a way that the tiny red light under
the lens of the video camera over the door was not. It was
private, a pain of her own making, something inside her that
she could cling to without having to rely on anything the
inspector might offer.

"You are obliged to identify yourself, miss." The detective
spoke without looking up from the open dossier in front of him,
smoothing the top sheet with the side of his hand as if brushing
away crumbs.

Maire turned her head to one side and blew out a stream of
smoke. The pack of Players the uniformed constable had left
with her lay on the unpainted wooden table between her and
the inspector. Everything about the room—the glossy white
walls still smelling of paint; the shadowless, silent fluorescent
lighting; the gleaming green door with its electronic lock and
Perspex peephole—appeared new except for the table, which
had seemed at first, in the brief moment she'd been alone in
the room, to be a mistake, an afterthought, a leftover from the
simpler, unvarnished time when interrogation rooms were dank
and chilly and dim. She had found herself wondering which of
the dents and gouges in the gray wood had been made by
cheerfully battered Republican heads. Now, with the detective
inspector seated across from her, his thick features sagging
under the weight of years and disappointments, she realized

that the presence of the table was not a mistake but a subtle, deliberate reminder that the good old days weren't over yet, that the video camera didn't intimidate her interrogator in the slightest. The red light under the lens was meant to remind him that someone was watching all the time, but the fact of the table, blunt and weathered like the inspector's face, reminded her instead that the tiny red light might as well be a distant and unsympathetic star.

"First of all, I refuse to recognize the authority of the British army in the Six Counties." Maire leaned forward suddenly and stubbed the cigarette out against the tabletop. "You've no right to detain me."

Detective Inspector Glassie looked up a little too quickly from her dossier, his jowls quivering, and she wanted to smile. A goal for the side.

"Second, you've got to have a woman constable in the room with us." She settled back against the chair, but with her shoulders hunched forward and her elbows pressed to her sides as she ticked the points of contention off her fingers. "Third, I was never informed of the charge against me—"

"You were arrested," interrupted the inspector, leaning back in his chair, "under Section 14 of the Northern Ireland Emergency Provisions Act. The arresting officer is not obliged—"

"Then why was I strip searched?" Maire leaned forward again, resting her hands tensely on the edge of the table. "Why were my hands swabbed for explosives? You can't do that under Section 14."

She shivered, goose flesh prickling all over at the memory of the search, but she glared across at the inspector, hoping that he wouldn't notice. But how could he help noticing, she wondered, when her flesh still burned coldly from the rubbery touch of the two policewomen, when her outraged nerves still vibrated from the search, how could he not hear that in the tiny room, her whole body humming with rage like a tuning fork.

"*Did* you have explosives?" The inspector leaned forward, his eyes hard and bright in the dead flesh of his face, his thick fingers tented over her file.

But that was the point, wasn't it, to the whole ritual of her arrest, to jolt her nerves like an overloaded circuit, to humiliate her, to simultaneously isolate her and destroy her privacy, to take away her control over her own body. She could understand that intellectually and dismiss it, but it was hard to convince the flesh to take it so dispassionately, not when the search was her worst nightmare of a gynecological exam gone suddenly brutal—no backless gown, no stirrups, no shred of a bedside manner, just two ham-handed Protestant policewomen who examined her naked and standing up in a bare, freezing room lit like an abattoir. It was worse than anything the screws had ever done to her when she'd gone to visit Jimmy in the Kesh. As Glassie waited for his answer she could still hear the crepitation of rubber gloves being peeled on, could hear the hard, flat voice of one of the women saying, "Lift your arms, miss" or "Turn around, please," still felt the clammy hands turning her about like a side of beef on a hook or forcing her to squat over a mirror so they could see up her anus, still felt the blunt rubber fingers prying her apart as they peered up her vagina with a penlight. For a brief, foolish moment she had struggled, shouting, unable to believe that one woman could do this to another, but one of the officers had twisted Maire's arm behind her and shoved her up against the bright tiled wall and said in her ear, intimately, like a lover, "Please cooperate, miss." After that Maire had let her muscles go limp while they searched her for what they knew they weren't going to find. In the end they had stood her in her bare feet on the cold tile floor and helped her on with her clothes in the reverse order of their removal, like a film run backward.

"As a matter of fact, you've got to let me go." Glassie was breaking the rules by not having one of the women officers present, but Maire was secretly relieved. This was a little easier without one of those dour women looking on. She drew a deep breath to calm herself and fixed her eyes on the inspector across the table. The trick from her side, she told herself, was to give him nothing, to say as little as possible, to place no trust in him whatsoever. And when she did speak, to answer his questions with demands, with questions of her own.

"Do I indeed?" Glassie almost smiled, his jowls lifting under his narrow mouth.

"You can only hold me for four hours under Section 14." She reached for the pack of Players and tapped it one-handed against the table so that three or four cigarettes fell out. "You may even have already had me for longer than that, though of course no one's bothered to return my watch yet."

The inspector watched her silently across the table for a long moment, and Maire began to worry that she'd gone too far, talked too much. Whatever you say, say nothing, she scolded herself, and she pushed the cigarettes on the table away from her.

"I'm afraid the situation's changed." Glassie spoke in the tone of a doctor about to give his patient the bad news. He lifted his voice and said, "Constable, will you come in here, please?"

The uniformed officer stuck his head in the door, his eyebrows raised solicitously like a waiter's.

"Light the young lady's cigarette, will you?"

The constable came around the table, his black shoes squeaking on the lino, the noise and bulk of his presence making the room seem crowded suddenly, and he fished in the pocket of his stiff green tunic for his lighter. Maire glared across the table at Glassie as the constable bent over her and clicked his lighter, and she ignored the little blue flame at the edge of her vision, debating with herself the value of not picking up another cigarette. She could smell the constable's after-shave. Then, as he started to pull the lighter away, she picked up a cigarette and lifted it to her lips.

"Good." Glassie nodded, and the constable lit the cigarette, both he and Maire careful not to touch each other. When it was lit she looked away, and he stepped back.

"Now please be a witness, Constable," Glassie said. "I am rearresting Miss Donovan here under Sections 11 and 12 of the Prevention of Terrorism Act. Got that, have you?"

"Sections 11 and 12, sir." The constable lifted his elbow to slide the lighter back into his pocket. He straightened his tunic with a sharp tug on the hem.

"Very good. Now please wait outside."

The constable squeaked back around the table and shut the door silently. Maire drew on the cigarette and slipped down in the chair again, reinforcing the ache in her calf, concentrating on it. Now they had her for seven days, without a lawyer or even a visitor. She had expected it, but when he actually said it she was alarmed to discover how much she had hoped to be out in four hours. She blew out a cloud of smoke and watched it twist away in the harsh light, suddenly furious with herself. Section 12 was suspicion of violating another section of the PTA; that covered the money belt. And if they'd found the photograph, that was . . . what? She couldn't remember. But Section 11 was the giveaway: failing to disclose information about an act of terrorism. They'd have lifted her for Section 11 only if somebody had whispered in their ear about Jimmy, and only Joe could have done that. She ground her heel into the floor, tightening the bands of pain around her leg, cursing herself for not preparing for this, for not bolstering herself for the long haul, for seven *days*.

"Now." The detective pushed the dossier with a blunt finger. "You are Mary Cathleen Donovan?"

"I refuse to recognize the jurisdiction of British law over the Six Counties." She lifted her chin, watching the gray smoke hanging in a thin, flat cloud just above her head. "I am a political prisoner."

"Are you Mary Cathleen Donovan?" Glassie raised his voice to be heard over hers.

"Furthermore, I was physically abused," she went on, raising hers, "in public, by a British soldier—"

"Are you Mary Cathleen Donovan?" He leaned forward, wide-eyed.

"—not to mention strip searched illegally before I was charged—"

"*Are you Mary Cathleen Donovan?*" Glassie roared, the wattles at his throat pulled nearly taut.

Maire jerked bolt upright in the chair and slammed her palm down on the table, making the cigarettes jump.

"I am an elected official!" she bellowed. *"I won't be treated this way!"*

Her shout was lost immediately in the dead air of the small room; the door swung open and the constable stuck his head in. Glassie shook his head and waved a hand, and the constable withdrew, closing the door.

"Then you are Mary Cathleen Donovan? Sinn Fein city councillor for West Belfast?" Glassie said it in a low voice, breathing hard.

Maire looked away, her own breath coming hard, her heart racing in spite of herself, and she thought, Fuck fuck fuck, that was a mistake, for Jesus' sake, woman, calm down . . .

"The Sinn Fein councillor for West Belfast," she said, leveling her voice at him like a weapon, "is *Maire* Donovan."

"I'll take that as a yes." Glassie picked up his pen from the fold of the dossier and wrote something down. Then he laid down the pen and looked up at her, folding his hands again.

"I don't care if you're queen of the fucking Irish," he said. "I've got you, lassie, dead to rights. I've got a witness says you know the location of ten pounds of Semtex *and* that you know what it's for. That's five years, guaranteed, in Armagh. You're going to prison, love, make no mistake about it."

Glassie's voice was still a little breathless, and for the first time since her arrest Maire felt as if she had wrested a little control back for herself. He was bluffing, and she knew it. His "witness" was Joe Brody's anonymous voice over the Confidential Phone. Watching Glassie across the table she nearly smiled; get him angry enough, she thought, and perhaps his tight Orange heart would seize up like a rusty joint and leave him gasping and convulsed on the floor.

"Let's be realistic for a moment, shall we?" Inspector Glassie drew a deep breath and hitched himself forward in his chair, resting his forearms on the table on either side of her open file. "I know who you are, miss, and I won't insult your intelligence. I'm well aware that you're miles more intelligent and sophisticated than ninety-nine percent of the lads we get in here. Tougher too, I shouldn't wonder." He gave a wince of a smile, an unlovely thing. "A regular Bernadette Devlin, am I right?"

He was coming over all fatherly all of a sudden, but it didn't wash; his eyes gave him away. The man was old school RUC, she could see it: his first instinct with a prisoner was to batter her off the walls, no matter what the new rules were.

"We know about Jimmy Coogan," he was saying, his tone that of a stern but forbearing priest with a sullen child. "We know about the explosives. We didn't know about the money belt, that was just a bit of luck on our part. Now, we didn't find the Semtex, but that doesn't matter now, Mary, because as I say, we've got a witness."

She caught herself from correcting him again on her name, thinking, Relax, he's doing it deliberately, he's just trying to provoke you. She searched for the pain in her leg and felt an instant of panic when it wasn't there, and she realized that in moving in her chair a moment ago she had taken the pressure off her calf. Her cigarette had nearly gone out; she lifted it and let the ash fall to the floor.

"Either way," Glassie said, spreading his ham hands, "explosives or no, city councillor or no, you're going to prison. So the question is, Mary, how do you want it to go?"

"I want a solicitor." She drew on the cigarette, making the end glow. If it came to that, she could put her hands under the table and burn herself.

"I'm offering you a deal, Mary." Glassie smiled, wholly insincere. "Tell me about the explosives and perhaps we can come to an accommodation."

She said nothing. She'd nearly gone too far before, let herself get overexcited, but now she had found her center of calm again, though she wasn't sure how long she could hang on to it. She needed something else to hang on to, to worry over like a sore tooth, and she thought, Take what they give you, turn it against them.

"Tell me where the explosives are now, Mary." Glassie spoke

in a confidential tone, as if it was a secret just between the two of them. "Does Jimmy Coogan have them?"

And she thought of that moment in the Falls when Prince Charming had pulled her arms behind her back and hand-cuffed her. Then they had blindfolded her and handed her up like a sack of potatoes into the back of an armored Land Rover. With her arms behind her the only way she could balance on the narrow bench was to bend forward and spread her legs with her feet flat on the floor.

"It's up to you, Mary," Glassie said. "Talk to me or meet your constituents on visitors' day for the next five years. Longer, Mary, if that bomb goes off."

Then the squaddies had come thundering on, grunting and snuffling and jostling each other like cattle, treading on her feet, filling the rear of the Rover with the steam of their breath and the humid stink of their unwashed bodies. One sat on each side of her, pressing in close and forcing her knees together. In her private dark between the two soldiers she felt small and frail, as if she were a girl again wedged in between two pungent uncles in the back of a black taxi. Then the doors squealed shut on their hinges and they were off, swaying against one another without apology like passengers on a crowded bus, the squaddies silent except for coughs and sniffles and throat clearings.

"Tell us about the money, then, if you like," Glassie was saying, trying another tack. "How much was there, altogether?"

And outside she heard a singsong siren, and she tried to count the corners right and left, but coming around one too fast she had to throw out a foot to keep from falling, and the squaddie on her right lifted his arm around her shoulders like an overfriendly drunk. Her stomach knotted up in rage and frustration, and she wanted to pull away from him and cry out and stamp on his feet, but in that tiny metal room full of men there was nowhere to run, and she couldn't shrink any smaller than she already had. Then somebody let go a great canvas rip of a fart, and there were groans and stifled laughter among the soldiers. "Beans for tea again?" somebody said, and amid the laughter the squaddie on her right had shifted his hand companionably on her arm, and Maire had squeezed back tears of rage, but now, in memory, those swallowed tears ignited and burned and became a cold, hard flame cupped in her heart like the constable's lighter, a flame that lit Maire's eyes from within.

"What money is that, Detective Inspector?" she said sweetly.

The inspector seemed a little taken aback, but he leaned forward over the table to cover it.

"In the money belt, Mary." He gave her a lewd, insinuating smile, a filthy thing. "Unless you want me to believe it was your chastity belt."

"Oh, no, sure it's a money belt." She smiled brilliantly at Glassie.

"Then what was in it?" he whispered. In another moment he'd be winking at her.

"My bride price."

Glassie froze, and the flame in Maire's heart soared.

"What's that?" he said, as if he hadn't heard her properly. He fumbled thick-fingered for his pen.

"I said, it was my bride price." Her cigarette had gone out, so she dropped it to the floor and crushed it into the lino with the toe of her shoe. She gave Glassie a heartbreaking smile, something he would see in his dreams. "It's the prize for the man who can tame my wild Celtic ways and win my lusty heart."

The front of O'Connor's stood nearly at the curb, and it looked to Brian as if the wall of chipped white plaster leaned out over the narrow sidewalk of Donegal Town. But when he looked up at the two stories of dark brick above the façade of the pub, he saw that the building rose straight as a plumb line into the night sky. Somebody edged past Brian with a glance and pushed through the heavy wooden door, and Brian stepped back off the curb for a moment, drew a breath to clear his head, and went in.

He stepped down through the low doorway into a chilly vestibule with a battered pay phone on the wall, and he stopped next to the phone, in the narrow doorway to the main room. It wasn't like his cousin's pub in Ballywatt, which looked the way an Irish pub ought to, all old stone and low beams; here the room was high-ceilinged and square and lit by a sickly yellow light that reminded Brian of bingo night at the Knights of Columbus. The bar ran along one side of the room and low-backed booths along the other, and in between, facing a tiny wooden stage at the far end, were several rows of low, black leatherette couches better suited for a doctor's waiting room than a pub; between the couches were shin-high Formica tables upon which Brian half expected to see six-month-old copies of *National Geographic* and *Highlights for Children*.

A few young men in jeans and sweaters sat at the bar, watching the door and talking in low voices, and they turned back to their drinks as Brian stepped in and unzipped his anorak. The booths were all empty—no book readers yet—so Brian slid into one facing the door, his back to the stage, and folded his anorak into the corner of the seat. A girl in jeans and a cotton apron came, and Brian ordered a Guinness; he watched her walk away, her heart-shaped ass switching between the couches. As she slipped behind the bar, a man moved away from the jukebox in the corner just inside the door; the machine whirred and clicked, and a moment later Whitney Houston began to sing about a boy she knew, the bass line thumping loud enough to drown out the voices of the men at the bar.

"Are you interested in traditional music?" The proprietress of the bed and breakfast had asked him, a tall woman in a yellow smock, her courtesy practiced and offhand, as though she had something else on her mind. "Americans usually are."

He had glanced at Clare and stammered something, but the proprietress was operating on automatic.

"There's traditional music every night at O'Connor's. It's just

116

up the way you came, through the Diamond, then up the street on the left."

At the mention of O'Connor's Brian had lifted his head, but the proprietress had already turned back up the stairs, saying, "This way, sir."

She let him into his room, told him that there were no baths in the morning, and left him there while she showed the girl to her room. He set his pack gently in the corner and sat on the edge of the unsteady bed, blowing all his breath out slowly. He stared at the pack propped in the corner, especially at the bulge in the bottom compartment, thinking, O'Connor's, nine o'clock, man reading in a booth. He flopped back onto the bed and felt it shake under him, his stomach tightening as if at the prospect of a blind date, and he mouthed the words of the goofy password at the ceiling. Ireland unfree shall never be at peace.

The bed wheezed as he sat up straight again, thinking of the girl. She'd found him the room, sticking her head out of the phone booth after they'd gotten off the bus and asking him if he was interested in a single room at six pounds, the woman had two left.

"Sure," he'd said, and they'd helped each other on with their packs and walked together to the bed and breakfast, continuing the conversation they'd had on the bus, trading travel stories, laughing tentatively at each other's jokes. Now he pushed off the bed and opened the door wide enough to peer into the dim hall. It was empty, and he patted his anorak for the keys the proprietress had given him and then slipped out the door, pulling it quietly shut behind him. He tiptoed down the stairs and out the front door, feeling like a jerk; the girl was charming and very pretty, and if she was also nervous and talkative, you could chalk that up to the loneliness of travel. But as he walked up the dark road back toward town, zipping up his anorak and pulling on his gloves, he reminded himself that this wasn't a social occasion, that the Provo hadn't told him to bring a date. Just once, he scolded himself, tugging his scarf roughly around his neck, just once, try not to think with your dick.

The barmaid brought Brian's Guinness, and he lifted it right away, taking a long pull of the smoky, bitter beer, wiping the foam off his upper lip with the back of his hand. He lowered the pint and looked at his watch: it was twenty to nine. He had eaten fish and chips in a café by the bus depot, and then walked a couple of times around the empty town square under the frosty haze that hung beneath the orange streetlights. Now he leaned back in the booth with his arm along the back of the seat and looked around the pub as casually as he could manage. There were more guys at the bar now, smoking cigarettes and whispering to one another, checking out the young women who came in groups of two or three and sat on the couches in the middle of the pub with their coats on, ignoring the men at the bar. But as Whitney Houston faded out on the jukebox, the men along the bar looked up as one, and Brian turned to see Clare standing in the doorway, slowly pulling off her gloves and squinting down the room as if she'd forgotten her glasses. The jukebox segued, grinding and whirring, to the Pet Shop Boys, and Clare's gaze drifted across Brian and immediately whisked away again. He sighed and let his own gaze fall to the tabletop. It should have occurred to him that she might show up here, or, who knows, perhaps even have come looking for him. He could ignore her, he supposed, but as he glanced up again she was looking straight at him, her expression on the cusp between recognition and disappointment, and he felt a pang of guilt at even the thought of ignoring her this time, at the image of her pretty face shutting down in hurt. He smiled and lifted a hand to her, and she blinked and then smiled back, acting out surprise a little too broadly. Before he could think again he had waved for her to join him, and she looked around once more as if to make sure there wasn't someone else she knew, and then started up the line of booths.

"Hi." She stood at the end of the table, flopping her woolen gloves back and forth in her fist, her high cheeks still red from the cold outside.

"Have a seat." He motioned to the seat across the booth from him. Surely the Provo would want him to act naturally, and what was more natural than this?

"Are you sure?" She narrowed her eyes at him, the way she had on the bus when she'd asked him a question.

"Yes, absolutely." He leaned out of his seat and touched her elbow. "C'mon, sit down."

She smiled and shrugged and slid into the booth, uncoiling the scarf from around her neck. Brian signaled the waitress and sat back down. All the lads at the bar turned back to their pints.

"I knocked on your door before I left," Brian lied, "to see if you wanted to come."

"I fell asleep in the bath." Clare rolled her eyes at her own absent-mindedness.

"You're not clear on the concept, Clare." Brian reached for his beer. "Baths are for bathing, beds are for sleeping."

Clare snapped her fingers and shook her head, laughing. The barmaid arrived, and Clare ordered a Harp.

"So this is traditional music," she said when the barmaid went away. In their droning West End drawl, the Pet Shop Boys were extolling the virtues of money.

"What were you expecting?"

"I don't know. The Irish Rovers?" She wrapped her gloves in the scarf and set them on the table.

"Right. Lusty, red-bearded men in cableknit sweaters."

"Yeah." She started to strip her sweater off over her head.

"It's the march of progress."

"I guess." She had changed her clothes since the bus, and now she wore a man's blue button-down shirt. "It's kind of a shock to hear the same old music on the jukebox."

"Yeah, I was expecting little thatched cottages myself."

"And leprechauns." She smiled and settled back in her seat, her face still glowing from the cold. The barmaid came back with a pint and waited while Clare fumbled in her jeans for a pound. Brian checked his impulse to pay, but he was glad she had come. After all, he decided, what was the harm? Better to sit talking with her than to sit alone with his stomach in knots, his heart pounding every time someone new appeared in the doorway. He could always excuse himself when the time came. And after all, he decided, what was the point of playing at intrigue without a beautiful girl? He sipped at his beer, watching her over the glass. Maybe he should have ordered a martini, shaken, not stirred; he wondered what she'd look like standing across from him at a gaming table in a strapless black evening gown. Perhaps O'Connor's had a baccarat table in the back.

"I know what you mean," Clare was saying, leaning forward over the table, her long fingers wrapped around her Harp. "It drives my cousins crazy, in Cork? I made the mistake of going on too long about how nice my cousin's stereo was, and she got all defensive and said, 'Clare, we're not the edge of the known world anymore.' I mean, every night at ten we watched 'Lou Grant.'"

"What does your cousin do?"

"The father is a doctor. The oldest daughter is about my age." She lifted her glass with both hands and sipped a little off the top. "But tell me about your cousin's pub. I'm curious to know what you thought of Northern Ireland. Do you mind talking about it?"

She watched him across the table with a clear and intent gaze, nothing like the smoldering look of a femme fatale, and Brian looked away across the smoky pub. One of the men had finally peeled away from the bar to sit on a couch with two of the women, turned toward them with a hand on the backrest and one haunch balanced on the edge of the seat, while the two women glanced at each other and smiled. Brian reached for his glass.

"John's pub is a lot funkier than this one."

"Gosh, I never thought of an Irish pub as funky."

"I mean, it's more what you would expect." He paused to drink. "They're pretty far away from Belfast and Derry, so they're not very political."

"Yeah, I remember that's what you said before." Clare slowly rotated the glass between her hands. "I think that's really interesting, though. I mean, that life goes on for people in spite of, you know."

Brian nodded with the glass up to his lips, wishing she'd talk about something else. He glanced past her down the row of booths; a couple of them were occupied now, but no one was sitting alone, reading a book. He tipped the glass up for another swallow.

"I just think it's ironic," Clare was saying, "that your relatives probably think less about the IRA than I did all last summer."

"How's that?" So where was the guy? Caught in traffic?

"I shouldn't bring it up." She sighed and looked down at her glass. "It sounds like I'm bragging."

"Oh, go ahead, brag."

She gave a little laugh and leaned back in her seat.

"You know the bombs that went off in London last summer?"

"Uh-huh."

"I was across the street when one of them went off."

Beyond Clare Brian saw a heavy, dark-bearded man in a long tweed overcoat come into the doorway of the pub. He was carrying a hardcover book.

"Another few minutes and I would have been right there." Clare gazed off across the pub as if embarrassed. "I stopped at a bank to change some money, and when I came out I heard this bang, it was like, I don't know . . ."

The man walked down the row of booths, pulling out his scarf by one end from under the collar of his coat. By its tattered cover Brian saw that the book was *Trinity*, and he wanted to laugh, thinking, Are these guys subtle or what? The man slid into the booth behind Clare, facing Brian.

"I didn't know what it was at first, but people started running and saying, 'Oh, God, not again.' "

The barmaid came to the man's booth, and he looked up to order; Brian flicked his eyes away.

"I mean, you could hear people screaming all the way across

the road, even with all the traffic." Clare shuddered at the memory.

Brian risked another look past her shoulder; he could feel the pulse beating in his throat. The bearded man shrugged out of his overcoat, and then opened the book and leaned forward on one elbow, propping his cheek against the heel of his palm, holding the book flat with his other hand.

Brian drew a breath to calm himself, and he noticed that Clare had stopped talking; she sat staring into her drink.

"You, uh, must've been pretty upset," he managed to say, forcing his gaze at the girl across the table.

Clare sighed and then smiled sheepishly, embarrassed at herself.

"My summer vacation." She lifted her glass to drink.

Behind her the bearded man slowly turned a page, and Brian thought he saw the man's lips moving under his mustache. Brian put his hands on the edge of the table to get up, but even without rising he felt a touch of vertigo, of giddy airlessness, and he sank back against the seat. No need to be rude to Clare, he thought. Why not let the guy finish the chapter? Instead he lifted his glass, his throat suddenly parched; it wouldn't hurt to have another beer first. The barmaid was bringing the bearded man's whiskey across the room, and Brian lifted his finger to her for one more.

"Hey, what's this?" Clare set down her glass and sat up straight. "We may be in luck."

Brian turned in his seat to see three men climbing the steps to the stage, one of them carrying an accordion, another an electric bass, while the third man eased himself behind a drum kit already on stage. The jukebox died in mid-song, leaving a hollow silence full of murmurs and cigarette smoke. The accordion player pulled a stool up to the microphone, while the bass player plugged his instrument into an amp.

"Doesn't look too promising, does it?" Clare said in a low voice. Brian glanced back at her over his shoulder, and then turned back toward the stage; from the corner of his eye he saw that the man in the booth immediately behind him was sitting alone. Brian twisted farther in his seat, his heart beginning to pound, and saw that the man, narrow faced with close-cropped, receding, straw-colored hair, held a well-thumbed paperback tightly in both hands, as if afraid that the book might jump up and snap at his pointed nose. A half-empty pint sat on the table in front of him, dripping foam down the side of the glass onto a napkin.

"Another Guinness, is it?"

Brian whirled around in his seat, knocking his empty glass with his hand, and found the barmaid bent over the table with a fresh pint in her hand. She pulled her face back at Brian's sudden movement, but she didn't spill a drop, reaching out with her other hand to steady the empty glass.

"Didn't mean to startle you," she said with a trace of a smile, and Brian blew out a sigh and sagged back into the seat.

"S'all right," he said. Across the table Clare dipped her head and pressed her lips together to keep from smiling.

"Uh, how much." He leaned forward to pull his wallet out of his pocket.

"A pound twenty, sir."

"Yes, right, sorry." Behind him, without a word of introduction, the band began playing something vaguely Celtic, the accordion wheezing, the bass and drums thumping, the band lurching along as if it had started the song in the middle.

"I think I'm going to be disappointed," Clare said, frowning. The waitress shot her a glance as she took Brian's money; then she whisked the empty away and left. The bearded man behind Clare sipped from his whiskey and turned a page of his book, and Brian had the absurd idea that the man behind him was doing the same, the two men drinking at the same time, moving their lips in unison to the same book, mirror images of each other. It was all he could do not to turn around and look; instead he leaned across the table and said to Clare, "Maybe they're just warming up."

"I hope so," Clare said glumly, and Brian leaned back and lifted his glass for a long, thick drink of Guinness. His head pounded with the beat of the band. Maybe he could try the password on both of the men and give the parcel to the one who answered quickest. But what if they both recognized it, what if one of them was a cop or something? He repressed a hot belch and cursed the band, cursed his greasy dinner, cursed his goddamn cousin, cursed himself for drinking too much beer. Then the phone number came to him unbidden, the number the Provo had given him to call in case of trouble, and Brian felt steadier for a moment. Call the number, ask for Jack Duggan, get him to describe the man he was supposed to meet.

Suddenly the song ended, as abruptly as it had begun, as if the band simply decided to stop rather than play all the way to the end. Somebody out front clapped, and somebody on stage said thank you. Across the table Brian realized that Clare was watching him, and when he let his eyes focus on her she glanced away. Over his whining PA, the accordion player mentioned hopelessly that people could dance if they wanted to. Then the band started up again, thumping listlessly away at a reel.

"Did you spend much time in England?" Clare leaned forward, raising her voice to be heard over the music.

"Just a day." Brian tried to smile, and he pushed himself up from the table. "Excuse me a second."

"Oh, sure." Her face went blank and she sat back, and Brian slid out into the aisle and walked past the bearded man, steeling himself not to look at him. His heart beating hard, he walked up the aisle toward the vestibule where he'd seen the pay phone. At the door he paused by the silent jukebox and glanced back through the cigarette haze at the two men sitting alone, drinking and reading, facing each other down the row of booths, while Clare sat between them, her hands joined around her glass, watching as the band played and nobody danced. He thought of the number one more time; then he turned around the corner to the phone, digging in his pocket for change.

Coogan heard the burr of the phone in the hall, but it took a long, groggy moment for him to realize what it was. He had lain in the parlor since dark with all the lights out and the curtains drawn, tucked up on the sofa under the Sacred Heart, fully clothed with his head on one armrest and his mackintosh pulled up to his chin like a counterpane. His only concession to the old woman's furniture had been to take off his shoes, which he had lined up neatly on the floor next to his .44. His stocking feet stuck out beyond the hem of his mac and hung over the other armrest, and as he struggled up out of an exhausted and dreamless sleep, he thought, My feet are cold.

He lifted his head and blinked, gazing down the length of himself as he wiggled his toes in the darkness. He couldn't burn turf in the grate, couldn't risk the smoke; perhaps he'd buy an electric fire for the house. The phone rang again and he let his head back down on the armrest, thinking, The old woman will get it. But dimly, like a piece of a dream imperfectly grasped, it came to him that she wasn't here, that he had given her two American hundreds and sent her away to her sister's in Larne. He couldn't quite remember why, and he shook his head once, feeling dizzy and queasy and uncomfortable, as if he had just stepped off a whirling carousel. He tried to recall what he was doing here on the sofa, what had happened before, and he remembered coming up the entry behind the house and scrabbling over the wooden fence into the tiny square of back garden, remembered the gun in his coat pocket thumping against his leg as he ran along the fence to the back door, remembered the old woman's seamed and bony face as she looked up accusingly from her tea, and it all came back to him in a sour tide, the weight of it pressing his head and sickening him like a hangover.

The phone was still ringing in the hall. He sat up convulsively, like an electroshock patient, jerking his knees nearly up to his chest and swinging his feet to the floor, crumpling the mackintosh and shoving it aside into a corner of the sofa. He pushed himself up and stumbled into the hall, bumping into the little table with the phone on it. He fumbled with the handset, turning it over in his hands to get the proper end up to his ear.

"Yes," he said, cotton-mouthed. "Hullo."

Over the hiss of the wire he heard the pipping of a pay phone, and he closed his eyes and waited, trying to place himself, trying to remember everything that had happened, trying to put it all in order.

"Hello?" A voice drifted down the wire.

"Yes, hullo?"

"Jack Duggan, please." It was Brian. He'd made it through, he hadn't been caught with Maire.

"Where are you?" Coogan dipped his head, as if bending to hear.

"Listen, Jack." Brian was trying to sound casual. "This isn't really an emergency, but there's sort of a problem here."

In his drawling, American way, Brian sounded nervous. There was music in the background, some pub band banging away, and Coogan pressed his finger to his other ear, concentrating on the earpiece of the phone.

"I can't hear you," he said.

"I said, I've got a problem." Brian raised his voice. "There's two guys here reading."

"Where are you?" Coogan demanded. He wished he had time to clear his head, to wake up.

"Where I'm supposed to be, okay?"

Coogan felt a flash of anger, but at least the lad was cool enough not to mention the name of the pub over the phone.

"Listen," Brian went on, "it's like a library in here. What does your guy look like? There's two guys reading."

"Listen to me." Coogan raised his voice. "Are you listening? Get out of there."

"What's that?" Brian's voice faded, and the music swelled and faded as he evidently switched the receiver from one ear to the other. "It's hard to hear with the fucking band, okay? What did—"

The phone began to pip suddenly for more change, and Coogan cursed aloud and spun halfway about on his stockinged heel in frustration. There were two readers in the pub, apparently; no doubt neither of them was Cusack, who had almost certainly been lifted by now, or killed. Coogan listened to the bloody pips and squeezed the sleep out of his eyes with his thumb and forefinger. Dead was more likely. Which meant that one of the readers was one of Brody's men, and the other, possibly, Garda Special Branch. Or both were Brody's. Or both Special Branch.

The maddening pips stopped and Brian came back on in mid-sentence.

"—did you say before? I didn't catch—"

"What's the number there?"

"The number?"

"Yes, the fucking number!" Coogan shouted. "Give me the phone number where you are and I'll ring you back."

"Okay, right."

Coogan stuffed his free hand up under his sweater and twisted his felt-tip pen out of his shirt pocket. Saying the number was as good as saying the name of the pub if anyone was listening, but Coogan had no choice but to hope that no one was. There were precious few telephones in the Falls, but not so few that the Brits could listen to them all at once. It was a slim hope, all right, but it was all he had to cling to at the moment, and as Brian recited the number, Coogan pulled the cap off the pen with his teeth and in the dark wrote the number on the damp wallpaper over the phone.

"Now ring off," he said, the pen cap still in his teeth.

"What?"

He spit the cap into his hand and said, "Hang up. I'll ring you right back."

Coogan was awake now, and he broke the connection and began to dial without having to refer to the number on the wall, without turning on the light. He hadn't turned on any lights since he'd sent the old woman away. As the sun had gone down he'd sat in the darkening kitchen and listened to the radio report of Maire's arrest.

"In Northern Ireland today," the reader had said, bland as pudding, "a Sinn Fein city councillor for West Belfast, Maire Donovan, was arrested at an army roadblock in the Falls Road district of Belfast and taken to the RUC Interrogation Center at Castlereagh. In a brief statement, an RUC spokesperson said that Miss Donovan is being held under the provisions of the Prevention of Terrorism Act."

Coogan had gone straight round to Maire's flat after leaving Billy Fogerty, and he had come around the corner to see her street full of Saracens and police Rovers, soldiers and RUC trooping in and out of her front door like ants in and out of a piece of cake. He'd managed to keep walking without missing a step, turning the next corner to snake back through the streets toward the safe house, but he was moving only on instinct by then, a rat in a maze. For once it was almost too much for him, beyond his ability to make sense of it. Brody had touted on Maire, there was no way round it, and Coogan was forced into the helpless position of hoping that Maire had seen the peelers at her door before they saw her and had gotten away. But that wasn't likely, he knew, and he'd found himself hoping that she'd at least gotten her cousin on the train before she'd been picked up. But with that thought came uncontrollable tides of contradictory emotion that were nearly as paralyzing as his fear and worry, and as he'd run up the entry behind the old woman's house like a frightened child, the tides threatened to carry his heart in several directions at once—he felt guilt at putting his wife in this situation in the first place, a stupid rage at Brian for perhaps getting away, even gratitude to Joe Brody for not simply having Maire killed.

"The president of Sinn Fein, Joe Brody," the reader had said, "issued a statement about Miss Donovan's arrest late this afternoon. 'The illegal detention of Maire Donovan,' Mr. Brody said, 'is another example of British state terrorism in the Six Counties, and we will fight it with every means at our disposal.'"

Now, standing in the dark hall, Coogan could hear the switches clicking down the phone line, like doors falling open one at a time toward Donegal Town, like his own synapses as he tried to put what was happening into some sort of order. Even now, Coogan had to admire Joe Brody's shrewdness and his coolness under fire. He didn't dare kill Maire—there'd be too many questions raised, both inside and outside the movement; the fact of Coogan's dissatisfaction would become common knowledge less than a week before the opening of the Ard Fheis in Dublin, and even Brody couldn't deal with that, not yet. But, thinking that she had the plastique, or knew where it was, Brody had to do something, so he did the next best thing to killing her, he touted on her, he shopped her to the RUC, assuming that she'd know nothing of Provo affairs, that she'd have nothing she could betray to the police, counting on Coogan to have kept her in the dark for her own good. And he was right: the only Provo Maire could give to the RUC was Coogan, and nothing would make Brody happier than that, unless it was Coogan himself with a bullet in the back of his head, his body wrapped in black plastic and dumped on a bit of waste ground. Let her squirm in Castlereagh like a gaffed fish for the next seven days while he, Brody, made pious noises at the Ard Fheis next week and vented his righteous outrage at her arrest on the BBC.

The phone in the pub rang only once before someone picked it up.

"Jack Duggan?" Brian's voice sounded timorous and faint, the band still banging away in the background.

"Listen carefully," Coogan said. "The two men reading, what do they look like?"

"Um, one's a big guy, kinda heavy, with a beard . . ."

"That's not him. Tell me about the other one."

"Thin, real short blond hair." There was a pause as Brian cleared his throat away from the phone. "He's got a long nose."

Boylan, thought Coogan. That wraps it up. Cusack was dead, he had to be. Coogan had tried calling him from the safe house, first at the fishery in Killybegs, where they said he was out with a lorry, then at home, where Coogan let it ring long enough to wake the dead. Which probably wasn't the case, under the circumstances, since Des almost certainly was dead, face down in a bog somewhere, or slumped over the wheel of his Cortina in a ditch. He knew too much Provo business; Brody would have no qualms about having him killed like some joyriding hood. Coogan closed his eyes and pressed his forehead against the cool, damp wallpaper, his stomach dropping as if down a lift shaft. There was no way around it: Joe was a professional at figuring the angles, as cool as a champion snooker player on the television.

"One's reading a paperback, the other's reading *Trinity*," Brian said, and Coogan cut him off.

"Listen to me," he said, and when Brian started to stammer something, he said again, *"Listen to me."* All he could hear was the thump and whine of the band coming down the wire, the tune unrecognizable. "I want you to do two things. Can you hear me?"

"Yes."

"First thing I want you to do, as soon as you ring off, I want you to get out of there, right away. Your man has been arrested, d'you understand?"

There was no need to put the wind up the lad, to tell him the truth about Cusack. Even so Brian's voice was suddenly querulous.

"Arrested?" he said, loud enough for anyone around him to hear.

"Shut up and listen!" Coogan put his hand on the wall at arm's length, propping himself up. "You've nothing to worry about. He didn't know who was coming. As long as you don't say anything to either of the men there, you're safe as milk." And as long as the RUC don't crack Maire, Coogan thought, but there was no need to tell the lad about that at all.

"What the fuck is going on?"

"We're going to have to change the arrangement." Coogan tried to brush past the boy's anger, but Brian interrupted him.

"Look, I'm bringing it back."

"Don't be fucking stupid!" Coogan barked. "They *look* for things coming in. It's too risky."

"This isn't?" There was a note of defiance in the boy's voice now, and Coogan cursed himself for shouting at him.

"I'll leave it someplace," Brian went on. "A bus locker, okay? I'll mail you the key."

"No." Coogan mastered his voice. "I need you to hang on to it a day or two more. There are lives at stake here—"

"What's to keep me from throwing it in the river and taking off?"

"That's desertion," Coogan snapped. "Do you know what happens to deserters?"

"I'm not in your fucking army," Brian interrupted, his voice low but pulled tight as wire. "I'm doing you a fucking favor, so don't you *fucking* threaten me."

"All right, all right, all right." Coogan squeezed his eyes shut. "I'm sorry. But there isn't an alternative. If you do as I tell you, it'll all be over the day after tomorrow."

There was a long silence down the line; the band had stopped playing, and all Coogan could hear was the hiss of the wire. His heart began to pound: what if the lad hung up on him?

"Lives are at stake," he began to say, stalling.

"Yeah, yeah, what about mine?" Brian's voice was weary.

"Just listen. This is what you do." There was nothing again for a moment, and Coogan wanted to pray, hang on hang on hang on. "Are you listening?"

"Yes."

Coogan cupped his hand over the mouthpiece and blew out a sigh; he had him, at least for the moment.

"Whoever turned in your man doesn't know who you are. All you have to do is leave the pub as soon as you ring off, all right?"

"All right."

"Then the first thing tomorrow you go south, d'you understand? You go south, anywhere you like, so long as you leave where you are now and don't cross the border again. Then you ring me here tomorrow night at nine. Have you got that?"

Coogan heard another voice talking to Brian and he caught his breath, pressing the heel of his hand against his other ear, straining to hear.

"What's going on?" he said.

Brian came back, saying, "Someone wants to use the phone."

"For Christ's sake, *listen*," Coogan said, speaking slowly, as if to an idiot. "Go south tomorrow. Call me tomorrow night at nine. Can you hear me?"

"Yeah."

"Just use your head and there'll be nothing to worry about."

Brian rang off without saying anything more, but Coogan listened to the angry burr of the line a moment longer. Even he didn't know what Cusack had planned to do next, whether he'd meant to take the parcel all the way to London himself, or if there'd been a step in between. Now Coogan had twenty-four hours to find a way to get the parcel across the water himself. He placed the handset down gently in its cradle, as if afraid of breaking it, and pushed away from the wall. There was the money, of course, but he couldn't use that. In fact, he'd used too much of it already; from now on every American hundred he threw away was like a flare showing the Brits where he'd been. Best to bury the rest of it in the garden, where he could get it when all this was over.

He went round the corner and sagged back onto the couch, his head tipped back against the wall with his throat bared as if for the knife. In spite of the couple of hours of sleep he'd had, he felt drained and bone-weary. Christ, there was so much to be done and all he wanted to do was sleep. Then he thought of Maire and where she was and what she might be going through right at this moment, and he pushed the thought away and jerked himself forward to the edge of the couch, bending to reach for his shoes.

In the morning, Clare came down to find herself alone in the dining room of the bed and breakfast. She took a seat at a table set for two along the wall, under a bright expanse of blue floral wallpaper, and she glanced around once in case there was some nook or alcove she hadn't seen from the door where he might be sitting. But she saw no one else, only, across the room, a large, hagiographical color portrait of John and Jacqueline Kennedy. A skinny girl with short, spiky hair and an oversize blue smock hurried out of the kitchen and stood silently at Clare's table, clutching the cuffs of her smock and blinking the sleep out of her eyes, while Clare consulted the typed menu and ordered a breakfast. She tried to catch the girl's eye, hoping to think of a way to ask if anyone else had come down yet, but the girl gazed blankly down at the place settings on the linen tablecloth—the tented napkins, the soap-spotted silverware, the teacups upturned on their saucers—and nodded once without saying anything, hustling back through the swinging door as if she had a room full of patrons instead of just one woman without much of an appetite.

Clare folded her hands on the tablecloth and looked down the room at the weak light falling through the windows and across the place settings at the empty tables. She'd almost brought a book down with her, had weighed it in her hand, and had left it on the bed finally, afraid that it would kill the conversation over breakfast. Now she felt like pinching herself, thinking, What conversation? and she gazed across the room at the portrait of the Kennedys. John was in the foreground, filling half the frame, his intense but hopeful features lifted toward a heavenly light. Jackie sat in the background looking up at him in his reflected glow, her eyes lit from within with love and admiration and even, perhaps, a little wholesome passion, and Clare lifted her shoulders and shivered at the picture of herself in the pub last night, wondering just how big a jerk she'd made of herself. Across the room Jackie looked as if she wanted to reach for the president, but wasn't sure she should disturb him; last night Brian had gotten up to go to the bathroom and had come back to the booth pale and a little sweaty, and Clare had been tempted to reach across the table and put her palm on his forehead.

"I think my dinner's coming back to haunt me," he'd said, smiling weakly. "I think I better take off."

"Are you okay?" she'd said, reaching for her sweater. "Listen, do you want me to walk you back?" But by time she'd pulled on her sweater Brian was already standing in the aisle wrapping his scarf around his neck, smiling and stammering excuses.

"Don't let me spoil your evening," he'd said. "You came to hear the band. Stay and finish your beer or I'll feel bad."

"I really don't mind," she'd said, without getting up.

"I'll be fine. Really. It's okay."

She had nodded without looking at him and reached for her beer. But looking up, he was still there, gazing down at her as if he couldn't make up his mind whether to leave or not.

"I'll see you at breakfast tomorrow, okay?"

"Okay." She'd managed a little smile, turning the pint between her palms. "I hope you feel better."

Now the gaudy portrait across the room was getting the better of her. She couldn't decide if it was a photograph or a painting or a little of both. She was about to get up to take a closer look when the kitchen door banged open, and she snapped her eyes away as if she'd been caught at something. The girl trotted up to the table with a tray and set before Clare a bowl of cornflakes, a little pitcher of milk, and a pot of tea.

"Thank you," Clare said, turning over a teacup, but the girl didn't go away, and as Clare looked up, seeing her opportunity to ask about Brian, the girl spoke for the first time.

"Will you be wanting a fry, sir?" she said to someone behind Clare.

"Please," Brian said, and the girl spun on her toe and hurried off, clutching the empty tray to her breast.

Clare resisted the urge to turn around, and Brian came around the table and laid his hand on the back of the chair across from Clare, pausing to raise his eyebrows at her.

"Please. Sit." She gestured at the seat and then folded her hands, unfolding them immediately to reach for the teapot.

"Thanks." Brian sat down and smiled, rocking the table a little as he hitched his chair forward.

"Tea?" She reached for his cup, and he nodded and gave the saucer a half-turn toward her.

"How are you feeling?" She glanced up from pouring the tea.

"Much better, thank you." He shook his napkin loose and smiled at her again. He waited for her to finish and then lifted his cup.

"There's milk."

"S'all right." He blew gently across his tea, watching her over the cup, and she drew a breath and poured for herself, milk first, then tea, then a single, tiny spoon of sugar from the bowl.

"Listen, I want to apologize for leaving so abruptly last night," Brian began, setting down his cup.

"That's okay." Clare folded her hands around her warm teacup. "I mean, you really looked like you weren't very well." She lifted the cup with both hands, watching the vibrating surface of the tea, and took a sip. It was almost too hot.

The girl appeared again, the kitchen door swinging behind her, to deposit before Brian another bowl of cornflakes, pitcher of milk, pot of tea. Then she was gone again, almost as if she hadn't been there at all.

"So how late did you stay?" Brian lifted his pitcher of milk and meticulously covered his cornflakes.

Clare frowned at her own bowl of cereal, turning it slowly toward her. Last night she'd left nearly right after he had, giving him ten minutes head start, to avoid any further awkwardness in the street or outside their rooms. While she waited she had nursed her warm beer and scowled at the accordion player up on the stage; he left his cigarette in his mouth while he played, dropping ash over his fingers and down the front of his instrument. In spite of her scowl one of the gaunt, hollow-chested young men at the bar had picked up his pint and come over to her booth, approaching her sideways as if presenting a narrower target; all she'd been able to think as she sent him packing was that you never saw any fat people in Ireland. As soon as he retreated she had left, walking back through the empty streets with her scarf wound around her neck, swinging her mittened hands briskly as if she were out for the exercise, a little angry at the lonely Irishman, angrier still at Brian, and angriest of all at herself.

"Not long." She pushed her cornflakes away.

"Well, I apologize again in that case." He lifted a dripping spoonful of cornflakes and milk.

She felt some of the anger coming back now, and she smiled at him across the table and said, "You weren't responsible for me, you know."

"Of course not." He dipped his head, mumbling through a full mouth. He swallowed and said, "It's just that I don't usually abandon good-looking women in bars."

She felt her anger notch a little higher, but she blushed all the same; Brian smiled at her, a drop of milk on his lower lip.

"I'm sorry. Am I embarrassing you?"

Clare looked off across the dining room—what would Jackie say at a moment like this?—and moved her hands across the tablecloth.

"I'm always embarrassed at being called good-looking at eight o'clock in the morning."

"Oh, I meant last night." Brian dipped his spoon into his cornflakes. "I didn't say you were good-looking now."

Clare laughed in spite of herself and felt her cheeks get warm again.

"All right," she warned.

Neither of them said anything for a moment, both of them looking down, Brian at his bowl of cereal, Clare at the teacup between her hands. The clink of his spoon against the bowl seemed too loud to Clare. She wished she could think of something smart-aleck to say, to match him line for line, but it just wasn't in her, she decided ruefully, to stay angry for long. She looked up to say something, finally, anything, and found him looking back, about to speak, and they smiled, each insisting that the other go first.

"I was just going to ask," Brian said at last, catching the stray drop of milk with a corner of his napkin, "if you were heading south today. By any chance."

Clare wanted to hitchhike. She hated buses, she said; the ride made you anxious and irritable with all the stops and detours, and you carried the stale air in your clothes and hair for hours afterward. She looked at Brian as she said this as though she was laying down a challenge, making it a condition for their traveling together. They were walking up the road under a cold gray sky, back toward the center of Donegal Town, and Brian pretended to fuss with the straps and buckles of his pack. He thought he could feel the extra weight of the plastique, five pounds heavier than his sleeping bag had been, but he wasn't sure. Maybe it was just the awareness that it was there that dragged at his shoulders. He glanced at Clare, but she had looked away, walking forward with her chin lifted and her long throat pulled away from her scarf, her thumbs hooked through the straps of her pack. He didn't want to hitch, but he couldn't tell her why. It was probably just as safe, but right now he couldn't face the thought of standing out on the highway with the plastique in his pack and his thumb out. He trusted only the bus, public and anonymous, but he still couldn't think of a reason to give Clare.

As they came across a swollen and sluggish river into town, though, the weather rescued him: massive blocks of glowering cloud glided swiftly off the gray sea, jostling each other like flat-bottomed barges, and one of them dropped a hard shower of rain, the drops dancing like pebbles in the street and rattling the hood of his anorak. Clare trudged alongside him, bare-headed, stubbornly refusing to notice the rain, but by the time they came to the bus station, he had persuaded her of the folly of spending all day in the rain, when they could be in Sligo before noon and spend the rest of the day sightseeing. With water streaming down her cheeks, she scowled up at the turbulent sky and gave in finally with a single brisk nod, as if to let him know that she wasn't really backing down.

Then the weather rescued him again. They were in Sligo by ten, and with one phone call Clare found them a bed and breakfast, a place where the woman would let them leave their packs for the day. Alone in his tiny room, Brian turned completely around in the narrow space between the swaybacked bed and a wardrobe that leaned into the room, wondering if he was obligated to sit in the room with the parcel all day, or if he could leave it and go out. If he left it, should he hide it in a dresser drawer, or under the bed, or on top of the wardrobe? Then Clare was rapping on his door, saying, "C'mon, hurry up, the sun's coming out," and he shrugged convulsively out of the pack, letting it thump to the floor and sag against the wall under the window, pressing against the thin curtain, pulling it tight. Get out of here, he told himself, and he locked the door of the room and followed Clare downstairs, resolved not to think about the parcel all afternoon.

A fresh, blustery wind had driven the clouds away, and the low overcast had lifted to a high, blue haze, lifting Clare's spirits with it. He couldn't even persuade her to have lunch first; instead they stopped to buy some rolls and fruit and cheese and then walked west out of Sligo, following a narrow blacktopped lane that wound between hummocky, irregular pastures. They headed for Knocknarea, an immense, bare hill with a rounded top that dominated the horizon as soon as they were beyond the city limits. There was a bump on top of the dome of the hill, silhouetted against the sky like a nipple, and Clare said it was an ancient cairn, the burial mound of the legendary Queen Maeve.

"How do you know that?" Brian said. "Were you here before?"

"No, but I was reading my guidebook while you were wasting time banging around in your room."

Was I banging? Brian nearly asked, a little alarmed, but he remembered his promise to himself not to think about it, and he let Clare lead the way. She pulled an apple out of her daypack and crunched on it as they negotiated the lanes, trying to find their way to the bottom of the hill. The fields on either side were littered with crumbling megalithic tombs, small, pitted blocks of stone that rose out of grassy mounds like broken teeth. Clare wanted to get a closer look at them, but the fields were private and fenced off, guarded by slow cattle wandering obliviously among the stones. One animal, a great brown cow that had escaped from one of the pastures, appeared broadside in the road ahead of them; it swung its long white face toward them, its liquid eyes filling with terror, and then started running clumsily away in the direction they were going, its hooves thudding into the blacktop, its udder swinging free from side to side between its rear legs. They followed it up a lane under the lee of Knocknarea, looking for a way up the hill, while the frightened cow looked back periodically and trotted even faster when it saw them still coming behind. At last it turned away up a dirt track along a hedge, and Clare and Brian followed the blacktop as it curved along a narrow, rocky beach that lay between the road and the cold blue sea.

"Maybe we should've brought a map," Brian said, but Clare was not discouraged.

"Maps are for sissies," she said. "You can never learn the way from a map."

Finally she led them up a lane that switchbacked up the lower slope of the hill past a long white cottage with a roof of gray slate; a track led clearly from the stony yard of the cottage to the top of the hill. Clare beamed at Brian, vindicated, and they started up, not talking much, only smiling at each other when they paused to catch their breath or pointed out a patch of mud or moist cowflop. At the top of the hill they rested a moment, standing up to their knees in the tall, wind-swept grass, and then Clare led Brian up the rocky side of the cairn.

From behind, Brian admired her coltish, long-legged grace as she stepped from rock to rock, and standing on top of the cairn, her boots balanced on two shifting rocks, she smiled at him, her face flushed with the climb, her hair lifted from her smooth forehead by the wind.

"Thanks," she said, pausing as they both caught their breath, and before he could ask what she was thanking him for, she said, "Thanks for making me take the bus." She lifted her arm and pointed into the distance. "Otherwise we'd still be down there."

In the clear, autumn-angled sunlight Sligo was a tight cluster of white and gray buildings just inside the curve of a long stretch of sand, where a river emptied into Sligo Bay; the yellow crescent of sand cut into the checkered green around it like a slice out of an apple. South of the town a line of red, rounded hills rose like lumpy potatoes half buried in the earth, while north of the town a long, mist-shrouded ridge swept back from the blunt end of Benbulbin. Between the ridge and the red hills lay a long, narrow lake of blue water, gleaming like rolled steel. Clare turned and Brian turned with her, the wind numbing his cheeks and nose and ears. Farther north, beyond the flat land below Benbulbin and across the blue mirror of the sea, they saw a line of distant red cliffs, smooth and high and abrupt, as if a piece of Ireland had been snapped off in a clean, sharp break like a section of milk chocolate. Unexpectedly, Brian thought of his grandfather, and he felt a pang for the old man's loss. It was like losing an arm, his grandfather had said, that's what leaving Ireland forever had been like. It wasn't the pain so much, he always said, it was still getting the itch in your palm when you knew it wasn't there anymore. But at least the old man had all those years to deaden the feeling, the actual pain preempted at last by his stories about it. Brian squinted into the wind at the land rising in a smooth curve to those distant heights across the bay, only to drop away without warning, and he realized that it wasn't his grandfather he felt the pang for, but himself, walking on instinct in a place he didn't know the lay of, following the roll of a hill in the mist or in the dark. One step too far, and all he'd get was a long, windy drop.

"You all right?"

Brian turned and blinked at Clare, who peered at him curiously, her pale skin pulled tight by the wind and burnished red over her cheekbones.

"What's that?" he said.

"You look awful serious."

Brian smiled and looked off in the distance. He wished his grandfather were here now; before his stroke, he could still manage to turn on the charm in the presence of a pretty girl.

"I had his curly hair once," he would say whenever Brian brought a girl to meet him. "Could've been quite the ladies' man myself, if I hadn't loved Ireland more."

Brian would roll his eyes behind the old man's back, but the girl would fix him with an arctic stare, and old Patrick Donovan would be off and running, invoking the sacred names of Pearse and Connolly and MacDonagh, the traitorous names of Collins and de Valera; reciting harrowing stories of Catholic houses looted and burned in Derry, of Catholic workers beaten with sledge hammers and pelted with rivets at the Harland and Wolff shipyards in Belfast, of vicious Protestant policemen, B-Specials who looked the other way while it all went on. Then he would sigh theatrically and move on to his pièce de résistance, the true story of his noble blow struck for Irish freedom, the reason he could never return to the old country.

"I finally killed one of the bastards myself, on a night like this," he would say, no matter what time of year it was. "A B-Special. I shot him off his bicycle from behind a hedge. I've no regrets for it, though; the man had it coming."

By now the girl would be blank-faced and pale, uncertain how to react.

"Word got around that it was me that done it," the old man would go on, taking the girl's arm. "So I went away south, and joined a brigade in Kerry." The girl would let herself be led, half appalled, half fascinated. "Then the truce came, and then their puppet republic, and it looked like the Gardai might pick me up, so it was thought best that I leave the country."

He would stop again and turn to the girl for the kill, leaving Brian behind in grudging admiration.

"It was like cutting off my arm," the old bastard would say in a hushed voice. "I've never been the same man since."

At this point the girl was often shaken and close to tears, and now, on top of Knocknarea, Brian smiled sidelong at Clare, wondering as a purely technical matter if he could pull it off as well as the old man.

"Did I tell you about my grandfather?" he said, and it occurred to him that he and the old man were alike at least in their capacity for bullshit in the presence of women. Except, Brian thought as Clare turned away from the wind to hear him, he's better at it than I am.

They walked back down the hill the same way they had come up, stepping carefully among the stiff tufts of grass at the edge of a muddy cow track, past patches of muck and long pools of greenish water. Brian was beginning to regret having told Clare the old man's story; he'd meant it as a bit of charming blarney, the colorful story of his roguish grandfather, hoping to slide it past the defenses she was still bristling at him. And at first she'd listened quietly, as they ate their rolls and cheese in a hollow out of the wind on top of the cairn. But now, as they picked their way along the track down the hill, she wouldn't let it go, worrying at Brian like a prosecuting attorney. He wondered now if he'd told it wrong, or if he shouldn't have told it at all, if perhaps it simply wasn't his story to tell.

"What do you think of what he did?" she asked, stepping gingerly from stone to stone in a place where the track was nearly flooded over. "Do you think he was right?"

"I won't judge my grandfather, Clare." He recalled Maire trying to bait him in Belfast yesterday, and for an instant he wondered if this girl had ulterior motives as well.

"I'm not asking you to do that." She stopped with her boots

together on a dark rock that glistened with mud, and she gazed across the track at him with an almost pained look of concentration.

"It was sixty years ago." Brian climbed up the embankment to avoid the mud, clutching a wobbly gray fencepost to keep from sliding back down.

"He killed a man."

"I know." He pulled himself along the barbed wire toward the next post, careful to grab the wire between its rusty thorns. "But you and I have no idea what it must have been like for him back then."

"I know that." She danced from stone to stone, her hands raised waist high. "One of my cousins told me some of the same stuff your grandfather told you. Only she used the word pogroms. She said when they used to throw rivets and stuff at Catholics they called it 'Belfast confetti.' So I know it was rough. It's just . . ."

She didn't say anything for a moment, standing hands on hips as she surveyed a possible route through the next patch of mud. Brian waited for her at the next fencepost.

"Just what?"

"Well." She leaped the mud like a deer, landing with barely a splash on the other side. "My cousin the doctor in Cork thinks the whole thing up north is a nuisance. He just wants it to go away. He really doesn't care."

"What do you expect?" Up ahead Brian saw cattle jostling toward them up the track, driven by a man and a boy with sticks. "I'm sure your cousin's a great guy, but he's obviously got a real middle-class view of things." A Malone Road liberal, Maire had said yesterday. Whatever that was.

"Exactly." Clare stopped and looked up at him sternly. "I'd rather he supported the IRA than not care at all. I mean, don't you think that's sort of obscene?"

"You mean not caring?" He pulled himself hand over hand along the embankment toward the next post, the wire cold and gritty in his palms, reddening his fingers with rust.

"I just don't think you can be in the middle." She jumped

143

nimbly across the track, her head down. "I don't necessarily approve of the IRA, I really think that's wrong, but you have to choose. You just can't not give a damn. I mean, either the British have to go or they don't."

"Clare . . ."

"Well, don't they? Isn't that the problem?" She looked up at him with an embarrassed fierceness, her cheeks flushed.

"Clare, the cows." He lifted his chin at the first of the animals slipping and splashing toward her.

"Darn." She turned and blinked up the track at the advancing cattle. Then she leaped the track and started awkwardly up the bank with her arms waving, and Brian reached down with one hand, the other clutching the wire, and pulled her up beside him. The cows trotted heavily past with shivering flanks and wide, frightened eyes. The man and the boy came behind, both in tall rubber boots and dark sweaters. The boy, his hair sticking out like straw at all angles, slogged happily through the mud with the stick in his fist, splashing mucky water halfway up the embankment. The man followed more patiently, his stick tucked under his arm and his hands in the pockets of his jeans. He looked up at the two Americans and nodded, and they smiled back at him. Brian's hand was hooked through Clare's elbow, and he could feel the muscle knotted around her long bones as she let him support her. Then she shrugged him off and slid down the bank to the track again, saying over her shoulder, "Don't you think so?"

"You mean have to choose?" He slid down after her. The track was wider and drier here, and he walked beside her on the other side of a filthy brown stream running down the center of the track from hoofprint to hoofprint. He was irritated at himself, at her, at his colorful grandfather. He wished he could simply enjoy a walk in the country with a pretty girl, but here he was debating Grampa's sixty-year-old crime. Even when he was in college, Grampa Donovan could lead Brian on, relying on his grandson's condescension toward his undimmed Republicanism and his stage Irishisms, and then knock the boy flat with his still pointed Ulster wit. Now he had done it again, and he wasn't even here. Meanwhile Clare watched Brian intently from the other side of the track, waiting for an answer.

"The thing is," he said, refusing to look at her, "is that when you choose, you choose the tactics too, okay? If you want a united Ireland, you support the Provos whether you like it or not."

"Do you really think so?" She tramped now through shallow puddles without watching where she stepped.

"That's what my grandfather says, anyway." Let him get me out of this.

"I don't know," she said. "Isn't that a particularly . . . male way of looking at things?" She frowned at him, as if he had disappointed her. "My cousin's wife was telling me about the peace women. Do you know them?" She didn't give him a chance to reply. "When I was in London I used to go hear some of the Greenham Common women speak. They take it the other way around; they say your tactics should speak for what you're trying to do. They say you should live as if you're already living in the world you want to create."

Brian stopped and laughed, shaking his head and waving his hands.

"You're way over my head," he said. She stopped and turned to him, and he ignored the flash of irritation that crossed her face. They stood where the lane opened out into the yard of the cottage, and she watched him with a pained expression, as if the whole situation in the North was his fault. Behind her the low afternoon sun slanted in under the boughs of a pine wood, making their straight, corrugated trunks shine like redwoods, and through the trees he glimpsed the blunt face of Benbulbin glowing in the red light like iron. He sighed and withdrew his smile, meeting her eyes. What he envied most in his grandfather was that the old man always knew what he was after before he spoke or acted. With Brian it was often the other way around. More than anything else, he wanted to make this girl laugh right now, to crack that look off her face like a plaster mask. But Grampa wasn't here, and Brian couldn't think of a way.

"All I know is this," he heard himself say instead. "There wouldn't be a Republic of Ireland now if it weren't for men like my grandfather. The British would still have the whole island, not just part of it. I don't like to see people killed any more than you do, but it worked in the twenties, Clare, the same kind of guerrilla war they're fighting now. You can't argue with success."

She looked away over his shoulder at the bright halo of the low sun behind the summit of Knocknarea, and she drew in a deep breath and let it slowly out, her knotted brows relaxing as if smoothed by the sunlight.

"You can't always make things work out to fit your best intentions, can you?" To Brian's relief she sounded bemused, if not at the realities of Irish nationalism then at least at her own earnestness. He couldn't resist smiling.

"No, ma'am," he said.

After a long and fruitless day, Tim McGuire returned at dusk to his room off Stranmillis Road; he nosed his little Honda up the entry behind the house, the uneven buzz of the engine thrown back at him from the brick walls on either side. The alley was so narrow that he always had trouble getting the car into the shed where Mrs. Moore let him keep it; there wasn't room enough to turn directly into the shed, so he had to maneuver the Honda back and forth like a trailer truck, grinding into reverse and back again, until the car sat athwart the alley like a roadblock. It was bad enough that the car itself was too small—no matter how far back he moved the seat, his gut still touched the steering wheel—but the narrow alley and the tight fit of the car in the shed drove him nearly wild with frustration every day. It was like having a handicap you never got used to. Once in the shed, with the engine switched off and ticking over, the car door wouldn't open all the way, and he had to roll his paunch around the edge of it and then squeeze himself, grunting and gasping, between the side of the car and the cluttered wall of the shed. He emerged into the alley disheveled and smeared with dust front and back, and more often than not he kicked one of Mrs. Moore's battered dustbins, shaking with rage at a world that was too pinched to accommodate a man of great spirit and large appetites.

This evening he left the dustbins alone; he was tired and his feet hurt from pounding the pavement all day. The frustration was greater than ever, though, and by the time he had limped around to the front of the house he was fuming again. Yesterday, if you'd asked any of the salaried correspondents in the bright bar at the Europa, they'd have told you that the North was calm right now, or as calm as it ever gets. There were the usual penny ante atrocities—that poor bugger up in Ballymena with his hand sawed off, the guy they buried in Milltown yesterday—but these had been balanced out by a couple of dead Protestants in the Shankill Road two nights ago, leaving no deviation from the mean, a zero sum game. White noise, said the guy from the BBC, the background radiation of Ulster, the last echoes of the last big bang. Makes you wonder how the stringers get by, said that asshole from Reuters, sneering down the polished bar at Tim, who sat minding his own business, nursing the one Bushmills he allowed himself every day.

"How about it, McGuire," Reuters had said, already laughing at his own joke. "There's whole families in Belfast who eat less than you do. How do you keep yourself in fish and chips?" He had glanced around the bar to gauge the reaction of his audience. "Perhaps you ought to bribe the Provos to blow up a school bus. That way you can pick up a little pocket change from the *Guardian*, explaining how it was all a tragic mistake."

Now, as he came into the overlit hall of Mrs. Moore's, Tim suppressed an acid belch from his hasty dinner of Indian takeaway and pushed his thick forefinger through the mail on the table under the phone. The only thing for him was a letter from his mother in Boston. No check from *In These Times*, no check from the *Voice*, no answer from *Mother Jones* to his query letter. He scowled and pushed his mother's letter into the pocket of his parka and started heavily up the stairs. What those wire service jerks in the Europa didn't realize—*couldn't* realize, since they never left the fucking bar, did they, didn't have Tim's contacts or years of experience on the ground, Belfast was just another Beirut or Managua to them, with less exotic food—was that there was some kind of unusual seismic activity in the Provos, the tremors before a big quake, and like a nervous draft horse kicking his stall, Tim could smell it coming, had smelled it for weeks. He could feel it in his bones like a change in the weather: his years of fifty dollar articles, of a penny a word, of laying track with Provo leaders, were about to pay off. Then yesterday the Brits had picked up Maire Donovan under the PTA and whisked her off to Castlereagh for seven days, and Tim decided this was it. The BBC guy had dutifully filed a story, but the rest of them didn't even lift their heads from their drinks.

"Steady on, McGuire," Reuters said. "I heard that a British soldier *shouted* at some poor paddy the other day. Stop the bloody presses!" Tim hit the ground running anyway, knocking on doors in the Falls, asking all the right questions. And what he encountered was a silence all out of proportion to a seemingly trivial arrest: nobody was saying anything. Or rather, everybody was saying nothing. The people around Joe Brody, scrambling to prepare for the Ard Fheis in Dublin next week, were apologetic, but wouldn't tell him anything more than Brody had already told the BBC. Brody himself, usually eager for a sympathetic audience, wouldn't even talk to him. Reuters and the others notwithstanding, this time the silence meant something; in normal circumstances Brody would have shouted the councillor's arrest from the rooftops. Something was going to happen, and if he could get in at the start of a faction fight in the Provos, Tim would have it made, get his by-line in the *Times* or the *Post*, jack up his asking price, wipe that smirk off Reuters's face. It couldn't happen to a nicer guy.

But the silence worked both ways: the very thing that told him something was up kept him at arm's length from the story.

Tim stopped on the landing outside his room, a little winded from the climb, and he dug in his pocket for the key. He had to prop his knee against the doorknob and grind the key around with both hands—why didn't she ever oil the fucking lock? He forced back another belch and felt it burn down his gullet like his anger at Reuters: Brody would talk to *him*, wouldn't he; Reuters had leverage, a guaranteed audience of millions. All I've got, Tim thought bitterly, yanking the key out of the lock and pushing the door open, is a thorough and sympathetic understanding of the Republican struggle; that and fifty cents will get you a cup of coffee.

Just inside the dark room Tim stopped and blew out a sigh, and at the edge of his vision the door swung shut on its own. Something rustled in the shadows behind him, but as he started to turn, someone stepped up and pressed the icy barrel of a gun behind Tim's ear, nudging his face forward. Tim stiffened and sucked in his breath; for an instant he had the strange feeling that he was at the doctor's office, and the doctor had just pressed some cold instrument to the back of his head and told him to keep very still. The gun shifted against Tim's skin, and he heard the rusty lock turn. Then a cold hand grasped his wrist and twisted his arm behind him, not painfully, but enough to demonstrate control of the situation, and he was pushed gently forward across the thin carpet.

"Sit," whispered a voice close to his ear, and as they came to the bed at the end of the room Tim's arm was released. A floorboard creaked as the man backed away. Tim turned slowly around, his breath coming short, his hands raised waist high, his eyes crawling warily over the wardrobe and his cluttered desk, his overflowing bookcase and the stacks of *New Statesman*s and *An Phoblacht*s along the wall. His visitor must have climbed up the gardening shed in the back and jimmied the window; it was closed now, but the heap of newspapers under the window had slued to the carpet like a coal tip. Tim averted his eyes from the man still backing away, and he lowered himself by his hands onto the edge of his groaning bed, the waistband of his trousers tightening uncomfortably. He tried to draw a deep breath and wondered if he could loosen his belt without alarming his visitor.

"Hands where I can see them," the man said hoarsely, as if he had just waked from a long sleep. Tim nodded and slid his hands over the taut fabric over his thighs; he dug his fingers into his knees to keep his hands from shaking. Part of his trembling was excitement, though, not fear: after wasting precious time all day knocking on the doors of people who would not talk to him, his story had come to him, and stood breathing quietly now against the door, just out of the fading light from the window. The man switched on the overhead light, and they both turned their faces away from the glare, squinting sidelong at each other across the room. Whatever else Mrs. Moore skimped on, she was a glutton for bright light. Tim had met this guy before: a tall man with a high forehead and a long jaw, unshaven now, with a purplish bruise on his cheek, his eyes hollow and dark from lack of sleep. Last time they'd met, the man had been dressed at the height of Provo fashion, in a hand-me-down field jacket with the rank and badges torn off, faded jeans, and muddy Doctor Martens. He'd been a little heavier then, with hair bristling over his ears. This evening, though, he was thin and pale and dressed like a yuppie, his long body hidden under an expensive raincoat, his hair cut short, his trouser cuffs bunched stylishly over his shoes.

"I know you," Tim said without thinking, and he regretted it instantly, afraid that it was the wrong response. But the man only nodded, scratching the stubble under his jaw. Tim watched the gun—a gleaming, nickel-plated, long-barreled .44—and he counted silently to ten to calm himself; only four months ago, before he'd gotten so thin and stylish, this man had given Tim a deep background interview in an abandoned farmhouse somewhere in the Six Counties. Tim had been blindfolded and driven around in the countryside by two silent men for two hours—time enough to drive from Belfast to Derry and back again—and then led by the hand like a blind man across a muddy field to a dank old house where he and the man with the gun sat across a wobbly table from each other in the buttery light of a gas lantern. They had taken away his tape recorder and his notebook—he wasn't even allowed to write down his own questions—but the man had talked to him for two hours, all about his unhappiness with the direction of the Republican movement, his displeasure at the soft line taken recently by the Army Council, his suspicion over the parliamentary ambitions of Joe Brody. The man didn't leave Tim much opportunity to ask questions, but then he didn't need to: he was a fountain of revelations, the long-pent-up words of an honest, straightforward soldier who'd finally had enough of the inconstancy of his superiors.

"What do you plan to do about it?" Tim remembered asking, and the man's reply had surprised him.

"Nothing, for the moment," he'd said, squinting across the table at Tim. "I just want your readers back in the States to know that their money may not be going to the cause they think it is. They're paying for . . . lapel buttons, when they ought to be paying for armaments. I joined up to run the Brits out of my country, not to run Sinn Fein candidates for Leinster House. I didn't spend two years in the Kesh to further Joe Brody's political career."

"You were in Long Kesh?" Tim interrupted. "When was that?" If he knew when, he might be able to put a name to this man's face.

"That's not important," snapped the man. "Just tell your readers I'm a fighting man."

That the man evidently had only a vague idea of just who Tim's readers were didn't diminish Tim's excitement. All his years of grunt work covering what no one else would cover were about to pay off. Never mind that he had no notes and that he couldn't remember verbatim all of what the man had said, he still had the biggest story since Bloody Sunday. "In an exclusive interview with this reporter at an undisclosed location, a ranking member of the Provisional Irish Republican Army, speaking on the condition of anonymity, revealed his growing dissatisfaction with the direction of the Republican movement." Even the fact that he couldn't sell the story—the goddamn PLO had exhausted every editor's patience with faction fighting that summer—didn't bother him. It was money in the bank, another length of track, *leverage*. When it all came down, he'd be the first one in, leaving all those yin yangs from the Europa in his dust, Reuters begging him for table scraps, his by-line above the words "Special to the New York Times."

Across the room the man lowered his gun and, his eye on the window, moved to the splayed easy chair in the corner. He sank into it with evident relief, his long legs stretched out in front of him, his arm hung over the side of the chair, the gun dangling from his hand.

"I've got a straight proposition for you, Mr. McGuire." The man propped his unbruised cheek against his curled fist. "Do you recall our conversation earlier this year?"

"Shit, yeah." Tim bounced a little on the edge of his bed like an excited child. "Is that what's going on now?"

"That's part of my proposition." Tim thought the man smiled at him, but he wasn't sure, even in the harsh light. "I'm prepared to offer you a unique insight into the situation."

"Has this got something to do with Maire Donovan's arrest?" Tim wished he could move his hands, but he was afraid they would shake uncontrollably if he took them off his knees.

"Not now," the man said sharply. "First you have to do something for me."

Tim considered giving his standard disclaimer about journalistic integrity and then dismissed it. This was too big to play by the rules.

"What do you want me to do?"

The man across the room gathered himself slowly together in the chair as if he were in pain, pulling his legs up and bringing his hands together between his knees with the .44 clutched between them.

"If you agree," he said, pushing his face forward, pale and hollow-eyed in the bright light, "I'll make it all clear to you tomorrow. Let's just say that at the moment I'm a wee bit handicapped in the area of mobility. I need to get across the border into the Twenty-six Counties, and the usual avenues aren't open to me just now. I need someone to drive me to Dublin this time tomorrow evening."

"Why can't you drive yourself?" Tim leaned forward. "Has it got something to do with—"

The man stood up suddenly and crossed the room, and Tim froze, looking up at him. The man's head blocked the overhead light, leaving his face indistinct in its own shadow.

"Look, if you don't want to talk about it now—"

"Another word from you and I'm away." The man's voice had pulled tight as wire with fatigue and, Tim thought, suppressed fear. The .44 hung at his side, his arm as straight and stiff as a length of wood.

"If you can keep your fat bloody mouth shut for twenty-four hours and drive me across the border, I'll give you something nobody else has got. But I need your absolute silence from now until tomorrow night"—his voice was so tight it shook—"or I'm out the window and maybe I'll take your fucking elbow with me." He lifted his gun at arm's length and brushed the sleeve of Tim's parka with the end of the barrel. "Can you take notes left-handed, you soft git?"

Tim gazed up at the man wide-eyed; the light behind the man's head glowed around his dark face like a halo. Tim could feel his heart pounding hard, could feel the sweat coming out on his back and forehead and palms.

"I'll do whatever you say," he said, swallowing hard. "I won't even leave the house tomorrow if you don't want me to. Just tell me what you want me to do."

"All right." The man closed his eyes and let the gun drop to his side; he seemed to sag a little, as if he and not Tim had backed down. Then he opened his eyes again and said, "I'm sorry. Just say nothing to anybody."

"Okay," Tim said hoarsely. He wished he could hide his eyes for a moment, but he didn't dare take them away from his visitor. Instead he tried to smile. "Whatever you say, say nothing," he said, recalling the Provo poster in shop windows all over the Falls.

"That's right." The man lifted the corner of his mouth; it

might have been a smile. Tim felt sweat trickling down his back along his spine.

"Just be here tomorrow evening," the man went on. "I'll come to you."

Tim nodded and the man turned away. In that brief moment out of the man's unbearable gaze, Tim shuddered and silently blew out a sigh. The man stood a few feet away, his back to Tim, and ran his hand over his close-cropped hair. Tim licked his lips and drew himself together again, squaring his shoulders and looking up at the man.

"Listen, do you need a place to hide?" He shifted on the bed as if making room for the man to sit. "You could have the bed. I eat up here all the time, I could bring you something to eat."

The man turned around into the light, and Tim could see his face clearly now. This time the man was smiling, crookedly. He shook his head and stepped to the door, lifting his hand to the light switch.

"I've got to see a man about a dog," he said.

Tim stood up without thinking and said, "Let me check the hall for you, before you go."

The light went out, and the man moved in the sudden dark; Tim started, automatically lifting his sweating hands shoulder high.

"No, I'll go out the way I came in." Tim thought the man gestured with the gun. "Open the window and see if anyone's there."

Tim stepped on the papers the man had knocked over coming in, and he bent, grunting, to lift the window with his sweaty hands, the sash weights ringing like bells. As the cool, damp air flowed over his face he peered into Mrs. Moore's back garden; the blue twilight had gone fully dark now, and he saw the shed where he kept the car, the dark line of the wall along the alley, and, just below the window, the cold, corrugated tin roof of Mrs. Moore's gardening shed. He could smell the turned earth of the backyard, sour with decay and October rain, but he could not see it, only blackness.

"It's okay," he said, pulling his head back in the window, but the man was already standing next to him.

"Tomorrow evening, then." The man trod on the papers, stiff-arming Tim aside like a quarterback, and he bent and slipped out the window, one long leg after the other, his shoes banging dully on the tin roof of the gardening shed. "Thanks for your hospitality."

Then his pale face turned away and was gone, and Tim stooped to the window and saw him leaping off the shed to the damp earth, the skirts of his coat billowing after him in the dark like the cloak of a vampire.

There wasn't supposed to be any music at Mickey's that night, Brian was told, on account of one of the regulars having died, a dear old man who'd been coming in steady for sixty years.

"Any other night of the year, there'd be music," the barman said in his singsong accent. He was a lanky, loose-limbed man with long blond sideburns, and he swung quickly up and down the narrow aisle between the puddled bartop and the ranks of gleaming bottles behind him. He was dressed, Brian thought, like a junior executive who had thrown off his suit coat on a bet to try his hand at bartending, in dark, polished shoes, dress slacks, and a tie he had buttoned into his smooth shirt front. Brian stood wedged in the crowd at the bar, waiting for his beers, and he wondered if the man always worked in his dress clothes, or if he had dressed tonight in honor of the deceased. The barman came back finally, carrying three dripping pints, and he paused for a moment with both hands on the bar, Brian's five pound note folded in his fingers.

"Any other night of the year," he said again. "It's just that since old Pat passed away, we only thought it right, you understand, out of respect . . ."

"Really, it's no problem." Brian pocketed the change and picked up the three pints with both hands. "Don't apologize."

He carried the beers chest high before him, warm Guinness

and a little of Clare's Harp sloshing over his fingers, and he worked through the crowd toward the door. The room with the bar in it was elbow to elbow with old men, their faces weathered like old parchment, their moist eyes swimming in beer, Pat's friends and relations, no doubt, old Irish bachelors whose baggy clothing hung off them as if they weren't even there. The air was stale with the smell of sweat and strong soap.

The air of the next room, though, pulsed around Brian like a warm current. Young couples crowded around long wooden tables under a pall of cigarette smoke, hunched over their beers and talking in low voices. A group of men Brian's age rocked back on their heels with pints in their hands, talking loudly and laughing even louder, and Brian squeezed by them and angled up to a couple of men talking near another doorway. One was a gaunt, unshaven Irishman in jeans and battered running shoes and a threadbare blue pullover; he held a half-empty pint in one hand, foam dripping down its side over his fingers.

"It's what you're doin' here at all that I don't understand," he was saying vehemently. "Don't you know there's a recession on?"

"There's a recession at home," said the other man, an American, a pudgy moon-faced guy in a green-and-orange Hawaiian shirt. His name was Larry, a mailman from San Francisco, and he was staying at the same bed and breakfast in Sligo as Brian and Clare; at the insistence of the proprietress, he had driven them all out into the countryside in his rented car to Mickey's, a celebrated music pub.

"No music," Brian said as he handed Larry his Guinness.

"Of course there's no fuckin' music," said the Irishman, pushing his face at Brian, wide-eyed. "It's a fuckin' funeral. Is that your idea of a good time?"

"Depends on the funeral," Brian said, and Larry snorted, looking down at his beer.

"Jesus, I feel sorry for you fuckin' people," the Irishman said, shaking his head of stiff, tousled hair. "You just don't understand. You're just gonna get ripped off, every fuckin' penny."

Larry rolled his eyes at Brian, and Brian looked past his shoulder through the doorway, into a long, bright, whitewashed room with a high ceiling and a low, bare stage at the far end.

"Who's, um, going to rip us off?" Larry asked mildly.

"Bord Failte!" shouted the Irishman, the light rising for a moment in his moist eyes. "That's what they're for. To rip you poor fuckin' people *off*."

The walls of the next room were lined with separate groups of young men and women, standing slightly apart like differing factions at a caucus; in each group at least one person was sneaking a glance over at the next group, whisking their eyes away quickly if somebody looked back. The men wore jeans and corduroys and their good shoes; some even wore loosely knotted ties. The women had put on make-up and teased their hair, some of them, and they wore bright, baggy trousers or denim miniskirts, surveying the room and the competition from the vantage of low-heeled dancing shoes. Nobody was dressed for a wake, Brian thought, and the center of the dancefloor had been left clear, just in case: Saturday night fever in County Sligo, he decided. Clare stood at the far end of the room in jeans and a white sweater, clutching her elbows and talking with a couple who sat forlornly on the edge of the stage, the man's arm loose around the drooping shoulders of his date, the two of them looking as if they'd come to the beach only to find that the tide had gone out.

"I feel sorry for the lot of ya," the Irishman was saying to Larry. "If I had a pound I'd give it to ya, ya poor fuckin' person."

"I think I hear my mother calling," Brian said, and he slid past Larry into the music room, crossing the empty dancefloor to the stage. He smiled at a girl who glanced at him over her shoulder, and she laughed and looked away. At the end of the room he handed Clare her Harp, and Clare introduced him to the couple, John and Isabel. Brian shook their hands.

"No music, I guess." As he lifted his pint, a look passed among the others, Clare and John and Isabel, as if they knew something Brian didn't. Isabel tugged at John's hand hanging off her shoulder and smiled up at Brian.

"Johnnie's planning an insurrection." She was a small woman with skin as clear as porcelain, her curly hair tied back from her smooth face.

"Sounds like a very Irish thing to do," Brian said.

"Oh, aye." John smiled too, a broad-shouldered man with a bit of a gut squeezed over his belt buckle. "I'm a regular James Connolly."

"More like Brendan Behan." Isabel smiled wryly.

"I love a good time," John allowed.

"Oh yeah?" Brian glanced at Clare over the rim of his pint. "What about dear old what's his name?"

"Christ." John stood up and hitched up his jeans as if getting ready for a dustup. "The wee man's dead. What the hell does he care what we do on a Saturday night?"

John excused himself—to rendezvous with his coconspirators, he said—and when he returned a few minutes later with a pint in each hand, he was followed by a tall young man with a long, serious face, who wore a cardigan with worn patches at the elbows and carried a concertina under one arm, his hands in the pockets of his khaki trousers. John handed Isabel her pint and winked broadly at Brian and Clare, and the young man sat on the edge of the stage behind John and lit a cigarette. Then, with the cigarette suspended between his thin lips and one long leg hooked over the other, he worked his hands through the straps of the concertina and began to play, working his wrists and elbows and shoulders, squeezing out a tune with great energy. John tipped back his beer and swallowed half of it; then he set it on the edge of the stage, took Isabel by the hand, and led her out onto the dancefloor. A few more couples precipitated out of the groups of men and women, and as everybody else moved back along the wall, they began to dance, their feet skipping lightly off the floor, the women's hair lifting off their shoulders, couples wheeling about each other linked at the elbow, or handing each other along to the next dancer like a bucket brigade.

Brian and Clare moved back against the wall, smiling and

avoiding each other's eyes. Brian sipped at his Guinness, and Clare leaned toward him.

"Do you know how to do this?"

"No. I wish I did. Do you?"

"No, I never learned," she said wistfully, her eyes bright as she watched the dancers reeling past them.

Halfway through the first tune the junior executive barman appeared in the doorway at the other end of the room, his sleeves rolled back and his hands on his hips, to make the token remonstrance on behalf of the departed. But when the song ended, John and another dancer, a burly young man, blocked the way, the three of them speaking in low voices as everyone watched. Then the barman shook his head and went away, and John came back to where Isabel was standing with Brian and Clare.

"It's just ridiculous," he said, tugging up his jeans. "The man's already had a proper funeral."

After that the dancing resumed without interruption, the tall boy working the concertina like a bellows, squeezing out jigs and reels and hornpipes, while couples whirled and spun at the center of the room, the men wide-eyed, their mouths hanging open as if they were surprised, the women dancing lightly with their hair flying, smiling as if they knew something that the men did not. Brian went away to get a couple more pints, and when he came back even more people were dancing, couples spinning apart and coming together again, their feet scraping and thumping against floorboards worn smooth and soft as felt. He slid along the wall of the room past leftover men nodding their heads and tapping their feet in time. Brian handed Clare her pint, and she smiled, her eyes following the dancers. He leaned back against the cool, whitewashed wall with his beer, feeling loose, and watched her as she bent toward the dancers with a beer in one hand, her other hand in the back pocket of her jeans, her back arched tight as a bow, her eyes shining, her cheeks flushed with beer and delight. As the song ended with whistles and shouts and applause, she set down her

pint and clapped vigorously, giving Brian a smile over her
shoulder that made him push away from the wall, put down
his own beer, and slip his hand around her wrist.

"C'mon," he said. "Let's dance."

They tried to follow John and Isabel, a half step behind at
first, watching what everyone else was doing and blundering
into each other, but catching up quickly as everyone became
drunker and giddier. John let out a whoop now and then,
answered by whistles and hoots from around the room, and the
floor shook with the stamping of feet. There was laughter at
first when Brian and Clare made a mistake, and then a cheer
and more laughter when they recovered. Between songs they
smiled breathlessly at each other and wiped the sweat from
their eyes, fanning themselves with their hands and taking big
gulps of beer from pints that always seemed to be half full. One
young man who wasn't dancing weaved across the floor to the
stage and bent to whisper in the musician's ear. The tall boy
nodded without smiling and set his cigarette on the edge of the
stage; a long column of ash crumbled to the floor. Then he
pushed his steel-rimmed glasses up his long nose with his
middle finger, slid his hands back into the straps, and began to
play a rousing tune at a blistering pace, his narrow shoulders
hunched forward as if he expected to be hit from behind. The
other man jumped up onto the stage next to him and began to
bellow out the words of the song with hardly a breath in
between, only just keeping up with the reeling, drunken melody:

> Over hillways up and down
> Myrtle green and bracken brown
> Past the sheiling through the town
> All for the sake of Marie

The tall boy joined him on the chorus, harmonizing in a sharp,
nasal voice:

> Step we gaily, on we go
> Heel for heel and toe for toe

Arm in arm and row on row
All for Marie's wedding

Then the room was spinning—or he was, Brian couldn't quite tell—and he kept his eyes on Clare as the only constant in a blur of faces, her face flushed and shining. As John or someone let out a mighty, roof-rattling whoop, Brian found himself in the middle of the floor with her, his arm around her slender waist, her arm around his, and they were wheeling almost out of control, close enough for Brian to smell her hair and feel the heat of her cheek. He heard the rhythmic pulse of their feet and the pounding handclaps all around as the sound of his own heart and hers, until at last, just in time, he and Clare released each other at the same moment and skipped apart, while the crowd roared its unanimous approval. Then the song was over and everyone was laughing and clapping. John slapped Brian on the shoulder and said something Brian couldn't hear, and Brian looked across the space between them at Clare, her hand at her throat while she smiled back at him breathlessly.

On the drive back to Sligo, Brian sat alone in the back seat with a nice buzz on, his temple pressed against the cool window, and watched the hedges and roadside grass flash by, bleached white in the headlights. Larry was driving too fast and talking to Clare in the seat next to him, lifting his hands off the wheel for emphasis. Once they plunged into a milky patch of low mist, and coming out of it Larry threw the car into a skid, shuddering around a narrow corner to avoid a looming hedge. Everybody laughed, and Brian smiled to himself and remembered coming home with Molly on nights like this from some club in Detroit, Molly at the wheel as they drove through all the darkened suburbs along the way, the traffic lights blinking yellow at every intersection—Jesus, did he really just *give* her the Volvo, for Chrissakes, she paid for half of it, but come on . . .

Shit, thought Brian, bad idea. He pulled his temple away

from the window glass and shook his head. Where the fuck did that come from? He sat up straight in his seat like a schoolboy and put it out of his mind, and he watched the back of Clare's head tipped against the headrest up front, the curve of her cheek limned in the green light from the dashboard. Larry had his hands off the wheel again, recounting his conversation with the angry Irishman.

"He asked me where I was going next," he said, "and when I told him the Aran Islands, do you know what he said?"

"No, what?" Clare's voice was plummy with sleepiness and drink, on the verge of laughter.

"He said," Larry went on, talking as fast as he drove, mimicking badly an Irish accent, "he said, 'Jaysus, there's nothing there but rocks. Don't you have rocks in America? Jaysus, take a book, that's my advice!' "

Clare laughed warmly, deep in her throat, and Brian felt his stomach drop at the sound. He thought about his grandfather again and the girl he'd left behind—wasn't that what he'd done?—and he wondered if, under the burden of a violent history and centuries of oppression and the heavy, censorious hand of the church, Grampa had ever danced the way Brian had tonight, if he had ever felt as happy and free as Brian felt right now. Grampa had his responsibilities and so do I, Brian thought in a rush of drunken pride, instantly forgotten. If that's not a reason to dance, what is?

Then they were back in Sligo, the empty streets gleaming in the amber glare of the sodium lights, and Larry, God bless him, dropped them off first at the front door of the bed and breakfast while he skidded off to park the car.

"Shouldn't we wait for him?" Clare whispered outside the door.

"He's got a key, he'll be okay," Brian said, unlocking the door with his own key.

They stumbled up the stairs, laughing and clutching each other's arms in their effort to keep quiet, and without warning he was thinking of Molly again, the two of them giddy and staggering with laughter, stumbling through their darkened apartment toward bed, knocking over Molly's easel in the living room, waltzing up the hallway, their clothes half off before they even hit the mattress, and at the top of the stairs, where their rooms opened off the same landing, Clare started to whisper another joke, turning to Brian and banging into the wall next to her door.

"Whoops!" she laughed, swaying back toward the stairs, and Brian caught her, and together they rolled into the corner between their doors, where he took her hands and kissed her. He closed his eyes, his head spinning, and he felt her start in surprise and try to pull away, but he pressed closer and she began to return the kiss, pulling her hands from his to rest them on the shoulders of his sweater. He tasted the beer on her mouth and felt her tongue just brush against his, and with his eyes shut and her mouth warm against his he felt as if the two of them were weightless in a great, warm space, all alone, miles from everyone and everything. It was wonderful and desperate all at once, as if their very lives depended on this connection right now, and letting go meant spinning away from each other and everything else without hope of rescue. But as he slid his hands up her back to pull her closer, she pushed at him and turned her face away. His eyelids fluttered and he glimpsed her pale face in the dark, her eyes hidden from him, and he bent to kiss her again. But she turned her face the other way, her hands still pressed against his shoulders, her breath warm and damp on his cheek.

"I thought you wanted me to," he murmured. He rubbed her back slowly, felt the bones and tight muscles through her sweater.

Clare pressed her lips together and sighed through her nose, gazing at his chest, her eyes hooded. Now the two of them weren't weightless anymore, but falling, the ground coming up fast. He heard a whining in his ears, like the wind rushing past, and he lifted a hand to her chin and tried to tilt her face to his, but she turned away again, not flinching, but into his hand, firmly, until he moved it away. I'm falling, he wanted to say, don't let me fall.

"Look . . ." He tried to slide his hand along her back again, but down the stairwell they heard Larry banging the front door and thumping up the stairs, whistling "My Wild Irish Rose." She slid her hands back from his shoulders into the crooks of his elbows and pushed him back, turning toward her door, digging in her pocket for the key. Brian's stomach was still dropping; he was afraid he was going to be sick.

"Clare." As the lock turned and the door opened, Brian caught her elbow, but she pulled her arm through his grasp, squeezing his hand at the last moment and making his heart soar like a teen-ager's, making him buoyant an instant longer. Then she was gone, her door closed and the lock turned, and he felt the floor rammed up under his feet as if he'd landed from a great height without a parachute, buckling his knees and making his stomach heave. He grabbed the doorsill with both hands and rolled back against the wall, squeezing his eyes shut and sucking in deep breaths. He heard Larry on the landing below, whistling out of tune and scraping his key all over the faceplate of the lock, everywhere but the keyhole.

There would be rain before morning; Joe Brody could feel it in his wounds. He carried two bullets in his back, the only traces of a botched assassination attempt two years ago, and he felt his back throbbing as he walked up the cul-de-sac past the narrow houses of Turf Lodge. To this day he didn't know for certain who had tried to kill him; nobody had ever issued a communiqué, and by the time it was clear that he would recover, lying face down in bed for six weeks in the Royal Victoria, whoever it was had evidently decided not to make an issue of it. For himself, Brody had always suspected some renegade from the UDA, breaking the unspoken agreement between the Protestant paramilitaries and the movement not to hit each other's leaders. There had been a rumor at the time that it was one of Brody's own, but—until last week, anyway—

he'd never given it any credence. Either way, the bullets were too close to his spine to remove safely, said the doctors, holding his x-ray down next to the mattress where he could see it, two blunt little 9 mm torpedoes floating next to the misty gray shaft of his backbone. Now he carried them everywhere like two new glands that throbbed and ached and even burned with each cold front or high pressure system, telling him hours in advance of the BBC whether he ought to wear a sweater or carry an umbrella.

"I'm a walking barometer," he liked to say in his soft voice, making a wee joke of it.

He had left his bodyguards round the corner in the car, and he walked with his hands in the pockets of his parka, his cap pulled down over his eyes, his beard tucked into his muffler. Most of the houses in the street were unlit at this hour, and he counted the doorways as he passed them, their numbers invisible in the pitch dark. British soldiers had shot out the streetlights as a precaution against snipers, and it had been years since anyone had even tried to replace them. Coming into the cul-de-sac he had glanced once at the Brit listening post at the top of the street, a black tower surrounded by sheet steel, a diamond-wire fence, and concertina wire. By day the slitted pillbox on top of the tower was visibly scarred and battered by everything from rockets and petrol bombs to the odd brick; now it was only a menacing silhouette, but inside, Brody knew, were two bored squaddies, eating out of tins and pissing into plastic bags and watching every movement up and down the street. Peter Egan had been known to shout at listening posts, and even to throw them a jaunty wave like a film star at a world premiere, but after that first glance Brody ignored it all the way up the street to Tommy Flanagan's door.

He lifted a hand out of his pocket and knocked twice. The others should be here by now, having come in the back way at irregular intervals over the last hour or so. The front of the house was dark, and as agreed, Tommy waited a minute before he opened the door, as if he was being roused out of a warm bed. As he waited on the step, Brody rolled his shoulders, trying to ease the unreachable pain in his back. It was no good, though, and he had to force a smile as Tommy opened the door and motioned him in.

"Everyone's here," he said. "In the back."

"Good," Brody said.

The old man helped Brody out of his parka and took his cap and muffler, hanging them all up at the foot of the stair. Brody could smell whiskey on Tommy's breath; Joe insisted that meetings be teetotal, as he was, but this was Tommy's house after all, and the meeting had been called on short notice. And certainly Tommy could do as he pleased: he was an old Forties man and a veteran of the Border Campaign, one of the aging heroes of August '69 who'd saved the Lower Falls from holocaust on a hot summer night, fighting off the drunken mobs from the Shankill Road, firing from the roof of St. Comgall's with four ancient pistols, a Thompson, and an arthritic .303. Unlike other fighters of his generation, Tommy had stuck with the movement as it rose from the ashes, divided, and was at last taken over by younger, more ideologically adept men. At the end of the day, it was simple old age that made Tommy put down his gun. In the meantime, he had lost two sons and three of his fingers but none of his nerve, and now he lived on a pension provided by Belfast Brigade, and if he had a drop taken now and again, that was his hard-earned right.

Now he leaned toward Brody in the dark hall and placed his maimed hand on Joe's arm. Only the thumb and pinkie were left, the others lost years ago in an accident with a jar of gelignite, but Brody never flinched away; instead he leaned toward Tommy, clutching his arm, trying to find his eyes in the dark.

"Are we winning, Joe?" Tommy said.

Brody squeezed the old man's arm and said, "No, but we're not losing either."

Tommy nodded and let go of Brody, motioning him down the hall toward the kitchen.

"Oh, aye," he said, turning toward the stairs, "that'll have to do for now."

*   *   *

Brody had called this meeting of brigade commanders on his own, as Chief of Staff; the rest of the Army Council didn't know about it, not yet, anyway. The Officers Commanding Armagh and Derry brigades were not necessary to this particular discussion, so they were not present, and for obvious reasons, London Brigade was not even to know of this meeting. In fact, only two of the four men around Tommy Flanagan's kitchen table were brigade commanders. Opposite the door, the OC Dublin sat back from the table against the wall as though holding himself aloof, his eyes hooded, the bright light from the overhead gleaming in the taut, pale skin of his high forehead, his hands folded in his lap, his feet set squarely apart on Tommy's worn lino. To the right was the OC Belfast, hunched forward over the table in workman's coveralls, looking at no one, reaming out the undersides of his filthy fingernails with a toothpick; his cover was that of a garage mechanic, and Brody always thought he laid it on a bit thick. Across the table from Belfast was an empty chair where Peter Egan had been sitting; as Brody came in Peter was at the cooker, heating a kettle. He was wearing one of his stiff corduroy suits; Peter fancied that he looked like Inspector Dalgliesh on the television, and he bought his suits off the rack at Marks and Spencer to match the image. Like Brody, he led a double life, a public one and a secret one, and you could tell which one he was leading at the moment by the way he wore his suit: as a member of the Derry city council, he wore a tie and a waistcoat, very Roy Marsden–like, but tonight, as Provo Director of Operations, he wore only the jacket and the trousers, his collar open to his bony neck, as he stood brewing tea for an emergency meeting in Tommy Flanagan's bright, immaculate kitchen.

Brody nodded once to them all and lowered himself carefully into the last chair. Nobody said anything, all of them waiting as Egan turned from the cooker with the steaming kettle and set it on the table. He unhooked four mismatched cups from under Tommy's whitewashed cupboard and pushed three of them into the center of the table; he reached for the kettle and sat, pouring into the fourth cup. Egan pushed the kettle away and leaned back, one hand curled around his cup, his other arm hooked over the back of his chair. He turned to Brody, but Belfast spoke before Peter could.

"Ard Fheis starts in five days," he said in a low voice, without looking up. "Why are we here?"

"Ah, why are any of us here?" Egan rolled his eyes at the ceiling. "That's the question, init?"

No one laughed. Brody placed his hands on the table, one on top of the other, and said in his soft voice, "Got better things to do, have you, Belfast?"

Belfast scowled, but still he didn't look up, tapping a little fingernail dirt from the toothpick onto the table. Brody burned at the sight; Tommy had the fastidious habits of an old soldier, his table clean enough to eat off of.

"I'm doing my bloody job, aren't I?" Belfast said, probing under another nail with the toothpick. "Haven't I got every lad on active duty out looking for the bastard and the fucking Semtex?"

"And what have they found?" Brody said.

Belfast slammed his hands down on the table and scowled at Brody, his eyes red-rimmed.

"They've found fuck all, haven't they," he said, barely controlling his voice.

"Nobody's blaming you—" Peter began.

"Are they not?" Belfast shot back, glaring across the table at Egan. He swung his face toward Brody again, holding up his thick, dirty forefinger. "One. I told you the fucking instant I knew the goods were missing." He held up another finger. "Two. I brought you Billy Fogerty, and didn't he tell you the password and everything you wanted to know?"

Brody said nothing. He knew that Belfast's eyes were red from lack of sleep, but it looked like a sign of weakness nevertheless, as though the man had been weeping uncontrollably.

"Three." Another finger. "I asked you—*I asked you*, Joe—I said do you want Jimmy stiffed, and what did you say? You said no, didn't you? Billy knew the time and the place, it would have been so fucking simple, but you said no, not without talking to him first."

"Not without a trial," Brody corrected him.

"Like Desmond Cusack got?" Belfast put down his hand and pushed his face toward Brody. "I understand that Johnny Boylan was his judge, jury, and executioner."

"That was an emergency situation," Peter interjected.

"Did it work? Did we get the goods back?" Belfast cleared his throat in disgust. "You should've let me put down Jimmy before he got out of the gate. Now you've got one man dead, Billy Fogerty in the Royal with his leg shot off and Special Branch swarming round him like flies, and Jimmy Coogan nowhere to be found."

"It's not my job to find him," Brody said quietly. "I'm not his brigade commander."

"Christ, don't you think I'm trying?" Belfast twisted violently in his seat, the chair squeaking against the floor. "But Jimmy's the best there is, isn't he? He's got his own bloody safe houses and nobody knows where they are. If he don't want to be found, I can't find him. Nobody can."

He sat back in his chair and crossed his arms, defiant, waiting for Brody to impugn his skill as a guerrilla. Brody said nothing, letting him hang. Egan slowly lifted his teacup to his lips, watching Brody over the rim, and at the other end of the table Dublin sat silent and motionless, a piece of the furniture. Brody, mindful of his back, leant carefully back in his chair, his hands still on the table. Egan disagreed with him, but Brody had come to doubt Belfast's sympathies in this matter. Hadn't he come forward as soon as the plastique was stolen, Peter had argued; didn't he bring us Billy? Yes, Brody had allowed, but more to the point, what else had Coogan been up to, and how long had Belfast looked the other way? Something like this didn't come out of nowhere. Coogan had involved London Brigade, or at least some of them. Who else had he been talking to? Brody looked down the table at Belfast, who looked round the table at everyone, breathing hard, his eyes wide, his whole face turning red.

"For Christ's sake," he burst out at last, "what do you want me to do? Borrow some squaddies from the Brits and do a house-to-house? Jimmy knows Belfast like a rat, doesn't he? We'll never catch him here."

"I'm inclined to agree." Dublin spoke up without stirring from his seat against the wall. Everyone turned to him, but he merely lifted his heavy eyelids and gazed down the table at Brody.

"Then where does that leave us?" Peter twisted around to look at Dublin.

"With two possibilities." Dublin's stillness could be eerie sometimes; Brody saw Belfast sweating, even though Dublin had rescued him just now, and even Peter seemed a little tense. Brody frowned; his wound was pressed against the back of the chair and it was beginning to ache.

"Either we intercept the plastique or we don't," Dublin went on, his voice even. "And we won't, since if Coogan has it, we can't find him, and if he doesn't have it, we don't know who does, since we've killed his only known contact."

This could be construed as a criticism of Brody, and Brody could tell that the other two men were tempted to look at him, to gauge his reaction, and he noted their self-conscious effort not to. Brody didn't move, although his back was making him quite uncomfortable. He had known at the time that sending Billy Fogerty out into the blue with a message to Coogan might be a miscalculation, but not as big a miscalculation as killing Coogan outright a week before Ard Fheis. Coogan by himself didn't matter; if Coogan had just gone walkabout with ten pounds of Semtex, Brody would have had him killed without losing a moment's sleep. But there was London Brigade to reckon with, and killing Coogan could force them into doing something rash, splitting the movement open like an overripe peach, setting the struggle back at least fifteen years.

"It's more likely that we'll have to deal with the second possibility," Dublin said, motionless as a statue. "London will get the plastique, and what we do all depends on what they do with it, what the action is, and how hot it makes the Brits."

"It's a damage limitation problem, you're saying." Egan had turned back around in his seat, and he spoke to Dublin over his shoulder.

"Precisely."

And I don't have fifteen years, Brody thought. Ireland doesn't have fifteen years. A simple man like Coogan doesn't have to worry about what sort of Ireland we'll inherit if the struggle lasts beyond the turn of the century. The man can't see beyond the Six Counties, he's got a peasant's idea of what the struggle is all about, a Whiteboy's sense of rough justice. Which was right and true and necessary, Brody was the leader of the armed struggle, for Christ's sake, but Coogan had only the peasant's tunnel vision, the streetfighter's hereditary incapacity to see the big picture, to see it in the context of world historical realities, to see the fundamentally political and economic nature of the struggle. There were a half million unemployed on an island of five million, most of them young. Thousands of them—the best of them—were fleeing to America, the worst exodus since the Famine, and the rest were turning to shiftlessness, petty crime, and heroin, with more junkies per capita in Dublin than in New York City. Brody carried the urgency of this with him every moment of his life, like the pain in his back that never really went away: Ireland was dying, not just the Six Counties under British occupation but the whole desperate country, locked in the stiffening grip of dying monopoly capitalism. And Coogan acted as if merely blowing up Lord Mountbatten would put an end to that! Brody drew in a breath against the pain and sat up straight in his chair. What in Christ's holy name did a sophisticated woman like Maire Donovan see in a *amadán* like that?

"I agree," he said in his soft voice, leaning forward, resting his weight on his elbows on the table, easing the muscles of his back. The others turned to him, free to look at him now; even Dublin lifted his chin to gaze down the table at Brody.

"But in the meantime," he went on, "I still want Coogan, alive if possible. We'll deal with the other situation if and when it arises." He looked at Belfast, who stiffened a little, having thought himself redeemed. "Thank you for coming, Belfast. We'll be in touch with you."

Brody folded his hands, and Belfast straightened up in his chair and looked around at the others as if appealing his abrupt dismissal. But Dublin lowered his gaze again, and Egan scowled into his teacup. There was nothing left for Belfast to do but leave, so he pushed away from the table, clearing his throat, and squeezed past Dublin to Tommy's back door. He paused at the door, licking his lips and glancing back sharply at Brody, but Brody didn't look back, and Belfast went out.

"A cup of tea, Peter. Please," Brody said.

Egan leaned forward and reached for the kettle and a cup, and Dublin shifted slightly in his chair, the barest indication of relaxation now that the source of tension had left the room.

"You want Coogan dead," he said simply.

"Yes," Brody said.

"And you don't trust Belfast to do it."

Egan and Brody exchanged a glance, and Egan rose to set Brody's teacup before him, to save him the reach.

"No, I do not." He lifted his steaming cup. *"Slainte."*

Egan raised his cup and smiled, Brody being the only man he knew who drank the health of his comrades with tea. Dublin didn't stir.

"If Belfast can't find him, what makes you think I can?" He shook his head once when Egan motioned to the teapot. "Unless you think he's not looking very hard."

Brody smiled and sipped his tea; he set down the cup, brushing at his damp mustache with his fingers.

"I think he's looking very hard," he said, folding his hands around the cup, warming his fingers in Tommy's chilly kitchen. "Even if he is with Coogan in this, he doesn't dare do anything else. Not until the bomb goes off."

"That's a knife edge to walk," Peter said.

"No more than what we all walk, every day of our lives," Brody said. "But he won't find him because Coogan isn't in Belfast. I'm certain of it. I think he's in Dublin or on his way, with the parcel. With Cusack out of the picture, he's the only one left to get it over the border. As far as we know."

Egan glanced up at this, and Brody ignored him. Ever since Maire Donovan's arrest yesterday, he'd been watching Brody carefully as if for the first sign of debilitating disease. Egan was the one who had picked up the rumor of Coogan and Maire's marriage and passed it on to Brody, months ago; Brody had sworn him to silence, and neither had spoken of it since. But certainly Egan had made the same inference as Brody after Coogan lost the services of Billy Fogerty, and certainly he couldn't help but wonder about Maire's timely arrest. In a way, it was a bit of luck that she didn't have the Semtex; the Brits would have shouted it from the rooftops by now, and Egan would have known for certain if Brody had given her to them. But there'd not been a peep out of Castlereagh, and all Egan could do was wonder.

"So you want me to watch the ferries and the airports?" Dublin said, ever the man for getting to the point.

"No," Brody said. "He'll take it to Dublin and hand it off to someone else. He knows we'll be watching the points of departure, and anyway, he needs to be back here, in Belfast, when the action takes place. Otherwise, his little"—he hesitated over the word, not actually having said it aloud yet—"his little coup is pointless, and he's wasted ten pounds of the stuff for nothing."

"Who will he give it to?" Dublin asked, leaving unspoken the implication that it couldn't possibly be one of his men. The further implication that Brody thought it was lay heavily on the table between them like an unwanted child, and Brody let it go. Dublin was not yet thirty, but Brody trusted him as much as he trusted anyone.

"It doesn't matter," he said. "You got it right before, it's a damage control situation now. I'm resigned to that. London may be in on this with Coogan, but their motives are different. Coogan's a renegade, but I think London just want my attention, and I'm prepared to deal with them if it comes to that."

He left unsaid the disastrous consequences of a split; Dublin was bright enough to puzzle that one out on his own. We're like cancer patients, Brody thought, talking around the topic, talking about everything under the sun but death.

"You're not overfond of Jimmy Coogan, are you?" Dublin gave one of his rare, bloodless, thin-lipped smiles.

Brody frowned; shrugging was too painful.

"He's undisciplined," he said.

"That's putting it mildly." Egan raised his eyebrows and lifted his cup.

"The man's an atavism," Brody said with unusual vehemence. "He's a faction fighter, not a soldier. A few more like him and we may as well go back to carrying pikes and hamstringing cattle."

Egan smiled but Dublin didn't, having already met his quota for the night.

"I want him out of the picture, but I want it done so that no one outside of this room knows we did it. I don't want the wind put up London Brigade."

Dublin was shrewd as well as tough, but for the first time he looked puzzled. The implication was clear enough, but Dublin balked at it. Brody was on the thinnest ice of his career here, advocating the worst breach of Republican ethics imaginable. Egan got it right away; he glanced up sharply from the contemplation of his teacup, and Brody knew he'd given away the truth about Maire.

"I'm not certain—" Dublin began, and Brody cut him off.

"Every peeler and soldier here and down south and across the water is already looking for him. I've already seen to that. What I want you to do is find him first. He doesn't know Dublin like he does the North. And when you find him, leave him alone and give him to the police. If you do it properly, and Jimmy lives up to his reputation, he won't come out of it alive."

There was a long, silent moment, the tension in the kitchen building like a stormfront. Brody sat rigid, his back throbbing, watching Dublin at the far end of the table, who sat stonefaced with uncertainty. Egan tried to lift his cup but he couldn't, and he sat and stared at it instead, avoiding Brody's gaze.

"You're asking me to tout on him," Dublin said in a thin voice.

"Aye. That's exactly what I'm telling you to do."

Dublin sat silent for another long moment, and Egan looked up at Brody, stricken, as if he'd seen the first sign of the disease he was looking for. Brody moved his own cup aside and leaned suddenly forward over the table, pain spreading across his back in circles, like ripples on the surface of a pond.

"Listen to me, both of you. I've no intention of ending up like Arafat, famous and impotent, forced into moderation by the hotheads on either side of me in my own organization. By God, I'll be the chief hothead in this army. If Jimmy Coogan won't play by the rules, then neither will I. I'm prepared to stop him by any means necessary."

Something was changing in the room; Brody could feel it in the waves of pain in his back. Egan fidgeted, and even Dublin stirred, but there was nothing either of them could say, and they knew it.

"Don't misunderstand me." There was nothing to do but say it outright. "I yield to no man in my dedication to the armed struggle, but unlike those who came before, I intend to win it. I'm no Pearse, I'm not obsessed with my own martyrdom. And I'll tell you something for nothing: without a vigorous political front, the armed struggle is wasted. The last fifteen years have taught us that. Coogan and his ilk would have us fight to the last man, no quarter asked nor given, but there was a time when what we wanted was within our grasp, when a man like Michael Collins could offer the Brits both the carrot and the stick and get results."

Dublin frowned, and Egan, who always dreaded the comparison, murmured, "Perhaps Collins is a bad example."

"I won't make Collins's mistake," Brody snapped. The pain was climbing his spine to his shoulders and neck, and he stiffened himself against it. "But his mistake was one of the head, not of the heart. My point is that if the Brits came to deal with Michael Collins, then they will come to deal with me." He smiled. "And if Jimmy Coogan wants to go out in a blaze of glory in the meantime, then I say we oblige him."

He leaned carefully back in his chair, trying to find a way to sit in the chair that didn't hurt, and at the end of the kitchen Dublin rose slowly from his chair, standing to his full height under the bright overhead light.

"Right," he said.

After Dublin left, Egan reheated the pot as they waited the proper interval before their own separate departures.

"What shall we do about Billy Fogerty, then?" he said, turning around from the cooker with the pot. "Belfast is right, his bed's probably surrounded by Special Branch."

"I wouldn't worry about Billy overmuch," Brody said wearily, stroking his beard. "He's sound. We've got Jimmy Coogan to thank for that."

"All the same, we've got a man in the Royal who could pay him a visit." He topped up his own cup, and then leaned across the table to refill Brody's.

"Only to demonstrate our moral support." He held up his hand to stop Egan pouring. "Let's see about getting him on a pension."

Egan nodded and sat down, setting the pot to one side. Brody reached for his cup and set it down again, rolling his shoulders, the pain passing over his face like a shadow.

"Your back, is it?" Egan said quietly.

"Aye." Brody managed a smile. "We've got some weather coming."

Egan smiled back and said, "What will it be, Joe? Rain or shine?"

"Snow." Brody pushed his teacup away and sighed. "All over Ireland."

Peter laughed, ever the man for a literary joke.

Brian rode across Ireland in the rain, watching his reflection in the window brighten as the gray afternoon light outside faded. He'd had to take the afternoon train to Dublin, having slept through the morning one. His legs were stiff and sore from dancing and hill walking, and his shoulders still ached from carrying his pack. The pack itself was propped in the seat across from him, and he slouched in his own seat with his feet stretched out under the table and the soles of his boots pressed against the plastique in the bottom compartment. He gazed beyond his reflection into the gloom beyond the glass, where the glistening blacktopped lanes and the irregular, tightly hedged fields darkened slowly like an old photograph. He saw the rain itself as a thin, smoky mist, or, when the train stopped at some abandoned-looking station, as a beaded veil falling beyond the edge of the platform roof, the raindrops pocking the dark puddles in the parking lot beyond. Then the train heaved forward again, and as it passed out from under the station roof, picking up speed, the wind threw a handful of drops against the window that crawled across the glass like snails, leaving their wobbly trails behind them.

He was still a bit hung over, his stomach sour, his throat dry, his head muzzy. He tried to sleep, but the rocking of the train only made him more nauseated. Instead he sat numb, watching the landscape roll by as if from a great height, wondering why he wasn't as worried as he should be. He rested his temple against the window and let his eyes unfocus on the blackened blur of the railbed below. Something had changed since yesterday, a threshold had been passed while he slept, but he couldn't figure out what it was. The night before he had passed out fully clothed, sprawled across the soft, creaking bed in his room, only to wake up suddenly in the middle of the night, well before light. He had sat upright in a sweat, the images of some frightening dream receding quickly from his memory, leaving behind only the anxiety.

There's something I was supposed to do, he had told himself, and he pushed himself onto his feet, still light-headed and dizzy from drink, his bladder aching. What was it? he wondered, wobbling from side to side in the dark like a round-bottomed doll, and he almost had it when his stomach rolled over and he slid shaking to the floor to keep from throwing up. He sat with his back against the bed and his knees drawn up to his chest, the night sweat chilling his skin, and he shut his eyes and drew in shuddering breaths of cold air. His hand flopped on its own like a fish out of water across the worn carpet and brushed against his pack, which leaned against the wall under the window. He opened his eyes and lifted his head, pushing at the bulging bottom compartment gingerly, as if it were the belly of a pregnant woman, and he remembered what he was supposed to have done.

"Oh, shit," he said aloud in the dark, squeezing his eyes shut again, thinking, I was supposed to call the Provo at nine tonight. Or would it be last night already? He twisted his wrist to look at his watch, but couldn't read the dial in the dark.

He sat a moment longer to calm his stomach, then he eased down the stairs of the sleeping bed and breakfast, stopping only at the toilet on the landing to empty his aching bladder. There was a telephone at the foot of the stairs, just inside the front door, but he let himself out quietly anyway, and hurried up the cold, empty street in search of a phone booth, keeping close to the wall on his right in case he felt unsteady again. His head still buzzed from the beer, and he felt panicked and ridiculous all at once, his hand curled around the coins in his pocket to keep them from jingling.

Around the corner a pair of green phone boxes stood in the harsh amber light in front of the Sligo post office, and Brian paused on the corner to take a couple of deep breaths of damp air. Inside the box he dialed the Provo's number, and as it rang he dredged the handful of coins out of his pocket, spilling them with a clatter all over the booth. He let the receiver dangle on its short cable while he squatted and scrabbled for the change in the narrow booth, but when he stood again with a handful of coins and nameless grit and jammed the receiver between his shoulder and his chin, the phone was still ringing at the other end. He broke the connection and dialed again, drawing another breath to calm his stomach and steady his reeling head, and he lined the coins up neatly along the steel ledge under the phone. The edge of panic he felt was beginning to sharpen. What if the Provo wasn't there? Shit, what if he'd been arrested or something? The cold air flowing under the door of the booth crept through his clothes to his skin, sobering him inch by inch.

Still no answer. He hung up and dialed one more time, panic tightening his skin as much as the cold, his stomach churning as he wondered if he'd gotten the number wrong. One digit off was as good as forgetting the whole thing. He let it ring twenty times, wondering what he would do if the Provo had been caught or killed. Ditch the plastique somewhere and run like hell was the only option that came to him, and the thought of it warmed him suddenly like a dry summer breeze. Why hadn't he thought of it before? The river was just up the street, there was no one around; he could go back to his room, get the parcel, and dump it in the rushing water like a burlap bag full of unwanted kittens.

"Who is it?" Someone was on the phone, the voice hoarse but urgent, replaced immediately by the pipping of the pay phone. Brian automatically fumbled for a coin from the ledge, but he hesitated with the coin at the lip of the slot. The thought of running was an unexpected relief; the Provo didn't even know where he was. He could get a plane in Dublin and be home by tomorrow—hell, by this evening—out of reach, the whole business out of sight and out of mind, a might-have-been, something to tell his grandchildren about. He leaned slowly to one side and flattened his forehead against the cold glass of the booth, his eyes wide open, washed over with a wave of homesickness. What would Grampa do? he thought, and he let the coin roll into the slot with a click. He dropped in a few more until the pipping stopped.

"It's me," he said, closing his eyes. "Is this Jack?"

"Where the fuck have you been?" the Provo shouted down the line.

"I couldn't get to a phone."

"Bloody hell! What else have you got to do?" The Provo had sputtered wordlessly for a moment, and then asked for Brian's number. Brian stood up straight and read it to him off the phone, and they both hung up. He leaned against the side of the booth clutching the receiver to his chest with one hand, holding down the cutoff button with the other, his mind numb. Quite unexpectedly he recalled his fumbling grab for Clare at the top of the stairs only a few hours before, and he groaned and banged his head against the glass. Smooth, he thought, very smooth. Was he going to spend every breakfast apologizing to this girl? Then the phone buzzed under his hand, rescuing him from his embarrassment, and he released the button, lifting the receiver to his ear.

"I'm here."

"Listen carefully." The Provo's voice was still hoarse, but firm. "Get to Dublin, get a room, and stay in it. Then I want you to go to the General Post Office at eight o'clock. Go inside, go into the room full of phone boxes at the right of the lobby." He paused. "Are you listening?"

"Yes." Brian nodded, as if the man could see him. "I go to the General Post Office in Dublin at eight tonight, go into the phone room."

"Good." Brian could hear the Provo swallow all the way down the line. "Go to the back of the room, the row of phones farthest from the door, and *wait*. When one of them rings, pick it up. That's all. Have you got that?"

"I go to the farthest row and wait for the phone to ring."

"Good. Now ring off."

"Wait." Brian drew a breath. "What if it doesn't?"

There was a silence down the line, leaving only the hiss of long distance.

"What if what doesn't?" said the Provo wearily.

"The phone," Brian said. "What if it doesn't ring?"

"It will." The Provo hung up, and Brian held the phone away from his ear, listening to the buzz of the Irish dial tone. Then he hung up and pushed through the door into the bright light in front of the post office, wide awake and stone cold sober. As he walked quickly back to the bed and breakfast his breath came out in great luminous clouds, like shouts in the empty street giving him away.

Dublin appeared suddenly and unexpectedly alongside the track as the train crept behind dark warehouses and the littered yards of factories and long rows of back gardens. It must have been raining here for days, Brian thought, for the ditch at the foot of the railway embankment was full of dark water that gleamed in the lights of the train; at one point the train slowed to crawl through a wide shallow pool that lay completely over the tracks, the pale reflections of the train's bright windows rippling like flags in the gray water. Then it picked up speed again to rattle quickly past dark rows of houses and dimly lit streets. As the train passed a long cemetery, its headstones glowing faintly in the gray twilight, Brian saw the women in the seat across the aisle cross themselves. He turned and looked out his own window. The train was gliding in a gentle, rocking rhythm high on a trestle around the edge of the city, and beyond his reflection Brian saw Dublin spread out before him like a model made to scale on someone's tabletop, a low, gray expanse of square roofs, with only a few church steeples, a couple of token high rises, and here and there a pale dome rising above the boxy skyline toward the black sky. It was all so dark, Brian thought, almost like a dead city; even the high rises were lightless on a Sunday evening, looking monolithic and funereal. There wasn't the general glow that hung over an American city like the noise of a crowd over a stadium. All he could see amid the gray buildings were a few orange street-lights here and there like distant campfires.

Around the curve Brian saw the canopy of the station approaching, and he pushed himself up out of his seat and jerked his backpack by its straps up onto the table. It occurred to him that for the last two nights he'd relied on Clare to find him a place to stay, and he wondered where she might be tonight. This morning he had nearly slept through breakfast, coming down at nine to find the proprietress of the B&B finishing her own breakfast and reading the paper. Brian came into the dining room, smiling sheepishly, sore and dry-mouthed, his head aching, and she nodded with her mouth full and pushed herself up, starting back to the kitchen without a word. Brian sat at another table and, keeping an eye on the doorway to the kitchen, filched her paper, yesterday's *Irish Times*. He started where the woman had left off, in the middle of the paper, sitting sideways in his chair, ready to put it back when she returned. He lowered it once to survey the tiny breakfast room, but none of the other settings was disturbed. He smiled; in spite of his early morning phone call, he was still the first one down. He settled back in his chair and had read an editorial about unemployment and a couple of book reviews when the woman reappeared with his breakfast on a tray, a pot of tea, a rack of toast, and a plate of fried eggs, potatoes, and sausage. He offered her the paper back, but she shook her head and started to clear her own table. He laid the paper aside and picked up his knife and fork.

"I hope we didn't make too much noise last night," he said, sawing his sausage into sections.

"That's all right," the woman said, balanced over her table on one stout leg. "I'm used to it."

"Am I the first one down?" he said through a mouthful of sausage.

The woman paused from stacking her dirty dishes on the tray and glanced at him.

"Oh, the others have been down and gone already." She turned back to her dishes. "Must've been an hour and a half ago."

"The others?" He swallowed and paused with his knife and fork poised over his plate.

"The young lady and the postal gentleman." She straightened with the tray in her hands.

Larry the mailman, Brian remembered, his heart sinking, his head beginning to throb again. He set down his knife and fork.

"Did they say where they were going?" His throat was dry,

his tongue threatened to cleave to the roof of his mouth. "I mean, are they coming back?"

The woman's eyes were bright above her pale, round cheeks. She looked as though she were keeping herself from smiling.

"I'm sure I don't know where they're going," she said in her soft accent. "But I don't think they're coming back."

"Uh-huh." Brian looked away from her; he lifted his hands to his plate, turning it slowly in place in front of him.

The woman sniffed and turned away, and Brian glanced up from his plate.

"I'm sorry," he said, stopping her again in the kitchen doorway. "One last question. When's the first train to Dublin this morning?"

"Well, you've missed that," she said. "There's another at half one."

"Right." He nodded to her. "Thank you."

"It's the early bird that gets the worm," the woman said, standing in the doorway with the tray in her hands. "Do they have that saying in America?" It was all she could do, he thought, to keep from laughing at him.

"We sure do." He had given her his best smile. "I'll try and remember that."

Now the canopy of the station slid over the train like the lid of a box, and the lights went out in the carriage, leaving only the sickly yellow light of the platform coming through the windows. Brian carried his backpack out into the cool, oily air and followed the thin stream of passengers down the platform, through the gate, and into the echoing station. He stopped in the middle of the station and pulled at the straps of his pack with his thumbs, easing the weight off his shoulders. He watched a man in a dark uniform and a stiff little pillbox hat walk by, and Brian wondered if he should be looking out for the police. The man was only a railway guard, though, wrestling an empty luggage trolley past Brian back down the platform, and Brian realized that he had no idea what to look for, what an Irish cop would look like. He shook his head and started walking toward a brightly lit stairway that led down to the street. The sign over the stair said To Amiens Street, and Brian stopped at the top step, his thumbs still hooked through the straps of his pack, waiting to gather his nerve as if about to enter a maze. Whatever thrill there was in this business was rapidly fading, leaving him merely lonely and afraid in a strange city. He ought to have been as alert as a fighter pilot, drinking in every sight and sound, looking for enemies behind every cloud, but all he could think about was how he was going to find a place to stay without Clare and her guidebook. He sighed and trudged down the stairs, feeling decidedly unheroic. Into the labyrinth, he thought, unceremoniously abandoned by the girl, the Provo waiting for me somewhere in the dark streets ahead like a seedy minotaur, and me without my ball of string.

On his way back to Belfast, just outside of Drogheda in the rain, Tim McGuire's Honda had a blowout, and Tim wrestled the little car to the side of the road. At first, by mistake, he veered automatically to the right, only to be forced back by the howling, head-on bulk of a trailer truck, which blew by Tim wailing its horn and drenching the Honda's windshield with a bowspray of rain water. He made it back to the other side and sat on the verge with his hands tight around the steering wheel, cars hissing by a few feet away. Five years I've lived in this fucking country, he thought, shaking, and I still can't remember which side of the fucking road is which.

He switched on his emergency blinker, tightened his parka around him as best he could in his seat—the zipper had given out long ago, its teeth stripped—and squeezed out of the car into the road. With the rain beating on his bare head and streaming down his collar, he edged around the front of the car and stooped, grunting, to poke at the flaccid left front tire. He cursed and stood up again and slogged through the sodden grass of the verge to the rear of the car for the spare and the jack, cursing again when he stuffed his hand into his pocket and found that he'd left his keys in the ignition.

It could have been worse, he told himself, slipping sideways along the side of the Honda while another truck whipped past his ass, trying to suck him into its wake. At least he hadn't had the flat on the way south a few hours ago, when Coogan was in the car. That would have been an embarrassment, having to reach into the trunk for the spare with Coogan lying there curled in the fetal position. Not to mention dangerous, to be stopped by the side of the road changing the tire as some curious border patrol rolled by.

Tim opened the door and bent in to grab the keys, dripping water all over his seat. The day had been hard enough already without the added nuisance of a flat tire. The Provo had shown up just after sundown, tossing pebbles at Tim's window from Mrs. Moore's back garden like a lovesick teen-ager. Tim had hurried down and snuck out the back way, tiptoeing past his landlady's private parlor, where she was watching television with the volume turned all the way up. Out in the garden the Provo gripped Tim's arm and marched him back toward the shed, hissing instructions in his ear without so much as a good evening.

"Back the car into the entry and open the boot," he said, his fingers sunk into the flesh around Tim's elbow. "I'll ride back there till we're out of Belfast."

Tim nodded to show he understood and wedged himself into his car, easing the Honda out of the shed and into the alley, working it gingerly back and forth. After a couple of passes the Provo banged on Tim's window, motioning him out of the car and sliding behind the wheel himself. He ground the Honda into first and then floored it, bringing the car to a screeching halt back inside the shed. Then, as Tim scrambled out of the way, the Provo jammed into reverse and twisted the car violently into the alley in one go, leaping out with the keys to open the trunk. He lifted the door and bent double, folding himself impossibly into the trunk amid Tim's assorted junk, shoving it all into the corners to make himself as much room as possible, his head tucked down, his knees drawn up to his chest. Tim hovered uselessly about, and the Provo reached up for the door.

"Don't head straight south," the Provo said, "but go out Armagh way, all right?"

Tim nodded. That was bandit country.

"When you're past Lisburn, find a safe place and let me out. I'll show you a way over the border. Now shut the door." He pulled the trunk door halfway down.

"Um, the keys."

"In the bloody lock. Now let's *go*."

Tim pulled the keys out, but he lifted the door a bit and peered at the man curled up in his cluttered trunk.

"Listen, I don't know your name. What should I call you?"

"Jimmy Coogan," the man snapped. "Now shut the bloody door."

After Lisburn Tim pulled into a narrow farm track shielded by trees and let Coogan out, and they drove toward the border southwest of Armagh following Coogan's directions, Tim stealing glances at him in the dashboard light. He'd spent the day keeping to himself, as he'd been instructed, formulating a list of questions in his head for the evening when the two of them would be alone in the car. But Coogan wasn't speaking yet, and Tim was afraid to break the silence. Instead Coogan peered out into the gathering dark, the rolling checkerboard of South Armagh fading beyond the headlights' glare, Coogan glancing nervously around like a cat, speaking only to say "Turn here" or "Go slow." Tim just licked his lips and nodded, guiding the car along a succession of increasingly narrow lanes, until at last they came to an unapproved road, where Coogan made Tim slow to a crawl, his hand on Tim's arm, rolling down his window to peer into the dark hedges along the road. Up ahead a roll of rusty concertina wire gleamed dully in the headlights, and beyond that Tim saw the rubbled lip of a black crater, where the pavement had been blown out by the security forces.

"Stop," Coogan said, squeezing Tim's arm. "Do you have a torch?"

"In the glovebox," Tim said, his mouth dry.

Coogan got the flashlight out and tested it by shining the beam at his feet. Then he got out of the car and stooped to his open window.

"Switch off your lights and follow me slowly. Keep your eyes on this." He flashed the beam at Tim once and then stepped away into the darkness. Tim switched off the headlights and the concertina wire vanished, leaving him alone in the dark without even the glow from the dashboard, his engine idling, the cool, pungent country air pouring through the open window. Then the flashlight appeared, its light swinging, and Tim put the car in first, following the beam through a gap in the hedge where Coogan held aside a section of bare branches. Once through, Tim waited in the dark until Coogan's light appeared ahead of him again, and he followed the light across a rocky field, the car rocking and jouncing as the tires found ruts and holes, its engine whining with the effort. Tim was tossed roughly about in his seat, banging his shoulder against the window, his head against the roof, the steering wheel digging into his gut and twisting roughly of its own accord in his hands. In the dark ahead the yellow light swung across the rough ground, Coogan visible only as a flash of trouser leg or a bright corner of raincoat in the cone of light. He didn't seem to be running, but he must have been, since Tim, wrestling with the willful steering wheel, could hardly keep up with him. Then the light stopped again, swinging from side to side like a railway lantern, and Tim drove through a wide gate onto smooth pavement. He had scarcely stopped the car when the door opened and Coogan slid in, smelling of the field and the night damp, banging the door after him.

"Go," he said, a little winded, tapping the flashlight lightly against the dash.

In the rain outside of Drogheda, Tim dug the jack out first, carrying it forward and testing the ground under the fender with the heel of his shoe to make sure it was firm enough in the wet. He sank heavily to his knees, soaking his pant legs through to the skin, and worked the jack under the car. It took a few tries to get the handle in, and then he slowly ratcheted the car up off the flat. The emergency light blinked a foot or so away from his nose as he worked the handle, and he could feel himself begin to sweat under his sodden parka. I should have brought the flashlight out with me, he thought, and he reminded himself to get it before he went back for the spare. Coming south, Coogan had held onto it, rolling it between his palms as he talked, or holding it up like a baton and rattling the batteries to emphasize a point. Suddenly the man was talkative, as if in crossing the border he had also crossed a threshold beyond which he was free to talk. Like the last time, in the abandoned farmhouse, Tim could scarcely get a word in edgewise. Much of Coogan's talk was the same as before anyway, his rant about the weakening of resolve among the Provo leadership generally, and about Joe Brody's opportunistic backsliding in particular. This time, though, Coogan claimed allies: a few of the lads in London Brigade saw things Jimmy's way, and they were prepared to catch the attention of the entire movement during Ard Fheis in Dublin this week. All he had to do, Coogan said, was provide them with the plastique.

"Couldn't they use their own?" Tim interrupted, watching the road ahead in his headlights. "I mean, shit, London Brigade must have arms dumps all over the place."

Coogan paused at that, a catch in his nervous cheerfulness as he admitted that it wasn't the leadership of London Brigade that was with him and that he'd had to come up with the plastique on his own, borrowing it from an arms dump of Belfast Brigade's, who wouldn't miss it right away. There was another catch here, a significant pause, and Tim saw the opportunity for another question.

"Does all this have anything to do with Maire Donovan's arrest?" he said. The first drops of rain rattled against the windshield, and turning on the wipers Tim sneaked a glance at his passenger. Coogan sat hunched forward with the flashlight clutched between his knees, and he peered past the wipers into the dark, the light from the dash making ghoulish hollows of his cheeks and his eyes. The pause lengthened into silence, and Tim watched the rain flying at him in the headlights, afraid that he had gone too far.

"Brody found out," Coogan began, and what started as a non sequitur became an answer to Tim's question. The whole business had begun to fall apart, and as a last resort Coogan had gotten in touch with Maire Donovan, who, he claimed, was sympathetic to what he was trying to do. Tim listened in silence, afraid of stemming the flow of information. An American cousin was coming to Belfast with money for the movement, Coogan went on, and Maire arranged a meeting, where he persuaded the American to take the parcel across the border for them. Now Coogan needed to get to Dublin to persuade the American to take it all the way to London. As for Maire, Brody had got wind of her involvement and had given her to the RUC.

"Whoa, hang on there a sec," Tim protested, unable to restrain himself. This was incredible: a leading Sinn Fein official involved in a Provo faction dispute and, even more astonishing, the head of Sinn Fein and probable chief of the Army Council turning in one of his own. There's got to be more behind it than that, he protested. How did Brody come to suspect her?

"That's not important," Coogan snapped, his voice hard suddenly. "What's important is that Joe Brody touted on one of his own to save his skin."

Neither of them said anything for a time, leaving only the rhythmic clack of the wipers and the hiss of the tires against the road. Tim didn't say so, but he could see why Brody might react the way he had. Coogan claimed he wanted only to change Provo policy, not to bring Brody down, but he hadn't really left Brody a choice. If Brody wanted to salvage the movement, let alone protect his own position, he needed to react ruthlessly. Tim stole another sidelong glance.

"Why are you telling me this?" he said.

He went back to watching the road, but he could feel Coogan's cadaverous gaze on him.

"Isn't it what you wanted to know?" Coogan said.

"You bet, but it kind of defeats your purpose, doesn't it?"

Tim licked his lips. "I mean, when the action goes down in London, the Brits will go apeshit and blame it on the Provos. Which is what you want, right? To force Joe Brody's hand."

He looked at Coogan again, but Coogan was looking out his own window, the flashlight twisted in his hands. Tim licked his lips again.

"You wouldn't want what you just told me coming out unless"—then he turned and stared openly at Coogan, who leaned back in his seat and turned his dead eyes on Tim— "unless you *want* a split?" Tim said, astonished. "Is that what you want?"

"Not at first I didn't," Coogan said quietly. He leaned forward toward the dash again, wringing the flashlight between his hands, his voice pulling tighter. "But if this is how Joe wants to play the game, then that's how we'll play it. We'll put everything out on the table for the whole world to see and let the lads in the movement make up their own minds who they trust, Brody or me."

For the first time that evening Tim was really frightened; crossing the border was a piece of cake next to this. The man in the seat next to him was talking open civil war; he was perfectly willing to bring down the movement to make a point. Tim opened his mouth to speak, but nothing came. The truth was, this was stunning, priceless, career-making stuff, the sort of thing you usually pieced together afterward, when the smoke had cleared and the bodies had been buried, and even then you only got it second- or thirdhand, never from the lips of one of the protagonists. Reuters and his asshole buddies would have killed to be where Tim was right now, even if it was all on deep background and not a word of it would ever actually see print. But that was the difference, Tim decided, between the yupster careerists in the Europa and a really committed journalist like himself. Here he had the story of a lifetime, and he couldn't print it, not in good conscience, anyway. He *believed* in the Republican movement, he told himself, and if he printed what Jimmy Coogan had just told him, he'd be siding with those who wanted to bring it down. He couldn't be a party to that, could he? Supposing he did print it, supposing he was suddenly flavor of the month, his by-line in every major daily in the States, and then Coogan failed, crushed by Brody. Then I'd be out in the cold forever, he thought, reviled as Jimmy Coogan's publicist, the end of my career in the North, five years down the crapper. I could bend over and kiss my sweet ass good-bye.

They were nearing Dublin now. Coogan put the flashlight back in the glove compartment, and he gazed out intently at the watery glare of oncoming cars. Tim mustered himself to ask a few more questions and was shot down every time. Where was the action going down? He didn't need to know that. What was the American's name? It wasn't important. Apparently the interview was over, and they were back where they had begun, Coogan nervously looking in all directions, tapping his long fingers against the dash, Tim guiding the Honda through the rainy, orange-lit streets of Finglas. Then they were in the rabbit warren of narrow streets between the Royal Canal and the river, Coogan guiding Tim with gestures and monosyllables, until, coming up a street just wide enough for the Honda, Tim was surprised to find himself in Parnell Square, crawling along the pale wall of the Rotunda Hospital. Coogan directed him to stop nearly in front of the darkened cage of Sinn Fein's Dublin offices, closed now on a Sunday evening. Tim pulled up to the curb, the rain rolling down the windshield. The glow of O'Connell Street was behind them, and the street was dark and empty, raindrops dancing like pebbles on the pavement. Tim turned to Coogan, unsure what to say, his journalistic impulses warring with his politics. Should he try to talk him out of it, or should he offer him a lift back to Belfast after his meeting with the nameless American? But Coogan had already opened his door, letting in the sound of the rain pattering against the sidewalk. With one foot out of the car he turned to Tim, his raincoat rustling in the tiny space, and he gripped Tim's wrist, twisting it painfully.

"Jesus," Tim exclaimed, and he tried to pull his arm free. But Coogan merely twisted it tighter; another inch or two, Tim knew, and he could break it.

"Follow me and I'll kill you," Coogan said. "Do you understand?"

"Christ, yes." Tim squirmed in his seat, unable to relieve the pressure on his arm.

"Good. You've got your story, now go back to Belfast and write it."

Coogan let go of Tim and slid out of the car into the rain. He swung the door almost shut, then opened it a crack, stopping to look at Tim, who sat rubbing his outraged flesh and blinking back tears of pain.

"Thanks for the lift." Coogan lifted the corner of his lips; then he slammed the door and was gone.

Now the jack was as high as it would go, and Tim slid back on the wet grass and pushed himself to his feet, slapping the mud off his hands. The skin around his wrist still burned where Coogan had twisted it, and his fingers were getting numb from the cold. He opened the passenger door and got the flashlight out of the glove compartment, careful not to rest any weight on the car; then he padded to the rear of the car again and lifted the door of the trunk. His parka was appreciably heavier with rain water, pulling on his shoulders like his disappointment. The story of a lifetime and he couldn't use it. It was the guys with no convictions at all who got ahead; wasn't that always the way? He stuck the flashlight under his arm and pushed aside the rags and empty oil cans around the spare, and he tugged at the tire with both hands until it came free, nearly tipping himself over backward onto the grass. He hoisted the tire out of the trunk and set it aside; then he flicked the flashlight beam into the corners, looking for the goddamn tire iron. It wasn't in the tire well, and he cursed and bent over the trunk to rummage in the debris Coogan had pushed aside, holding the light in one hand while he pawed through the stuff with the other. The light passed over something smooth and shiny and Tim swung the beam back to it, tossing aside a rag with his other hand.

It was a snapshot, a Polaroid, its smooth, glistening finish scratched and embedded with the grit of the trunk. Tim picked it up gingerly between two fingers as if afraid it might disintegrate, and he held it out of the rain under the door of the trunk, tilting it in the flashlight beam to minimize the shine in the finish. The photo showed two men in the bleached glare of a flashbulb, their arms around each other's shoulders, their eyes glowing red like wolves' in the flash. The background was indistinct; it might have been a café or a pub. One of the men was Coogan, smiling crookedly at the camera. The other man was younger, practically a kid, good-looking in spite of his goofy haircut and his forced grin. He wore an expensive-looking blue anorak, not just a Windbreaker, but the waterproof kind. Tim lifted the photo in the light and flipped it over, but there was nothing on the back. He turned it back and squinted at the coat, some lightweight Gore-Tex confection that must have cost a hundred and fifty, maybe two hundred dollars back in the States, not the sort of thing you saw in West Belfast, more like the sort of thing American hikers wore, like something Maire Donovan's American cousin might walk around in.

Tim lowered the photograph and stood motionless in the rain, his hair plastered to his skull, water streaming down his cheeks. Printing Jimmy Coogan's story would practically make him an accomplice; printing this photograph would guarantee it. What if he didn't print it, though. What if he made use of it another way? What could Joe Brody do with a photograph like this, Tim thought. What would he owe me? But it was probably too late: by the time he got back to Belfast and delivered the picture through intermediaries to Brody, the kid would probably be out of the country already. Not by plane, though; security was too tight. He'd probably be on the boat out of Dún Laoghaire tomorrow morning.

Tim spun about, still clutching the photograph. An idea was climbing his spine, warming him inside his sodden parka like a shot of thirty-year-old Scotch. He shone the flashlight at the picture, raindrops spattering across the finish, blurring the faces of the two men. It was none of his business, it was not his job to get in the middle of this, but Jesus! He bent over the picture to protect it from the rain, studying the smooth face of the American kid; the photo seemed to glow up at him like a holy relic, something fallen from heaven. Bringing Brody the Polaroid would win him a pat on the back and a few tidbits down the road, but what wouldn't Brody owe him if he showed up with the plastique itself, safe and sound! Better still, bring in the plastique *and* the kid, all tied up neatly on Brody's doorstep the opening day of Ard Fheis.

The photograph was glowing even brighter now, the faces washed out and indistinct, the finish shining, and Tim looked up to see the lights of a lorry bearing down on him along the side of the road. He threw up his arm against the glare and stumbled back until he came up against the bumper of his car. The lights grew painfully bright, blotting out everything, flooding his vision with light, and through the glare he heard the screech and hiss of air brakes and the idling growl of the lorry's engine.

"Need a hand, mister?" a voice called out from behind the light.

"I lost my tire iron," Tim called back, lowering his arm and sliding the photograph inside his parka. "I got a flat and I need to get to Dublin tonight."

He heard the thump of the lorry door, and saw an indistinct figure climbing down from the cab.

"Dublin, is it? Well, you're going the wrong bloody way." The man was coming toward him out of the light. "That's one problem solved."

Just before eight o'clock Brian walked through a misting rain toward O'Connell Street, his hands in the pockets of his anorak, the hood pulled up over his head. He had found a room at a bed and breakfast on Gardiner Place, where he'd spent the last two hours stretched out on the bed with the light out, drifting in and out of sleep, watching the orange glow of the streetlight through the thin curtains, a dawn that never ended in sunrise. Fifteen minutes before he had to be at the post office he rolled off the bed and took the parcel of plastique out of his pack; he squatted with it across his knees and stared at the blue nylon cover. Then he shoved it under the bed and reached for his sneakers, leaving the backpack in the corner, slumped over its empty bottom compartment.

Now he came down a hill past newsagent shops and fish-and-chips takeaways, and below him the spotlit and ornate Edwardian façades of O'Connell Street stretched away as if in miniature, a model of a small city with the colored lights of the hotels and cinemas reflected in the wide, wet pavement. The lights gleamed red and blue in the shining metal of cars rolling in packs from traffic light to traffic light, and in the long sides of tall green buses grinding from stop to stop. A median strip ran down the middle of the street with ornate cast-iron streetlights at regular intervals, the white glow of each lamp blurred by a nimbus of drizzling rain. Between the streetlights were the larger-than-life figures of statues, dark glistening silhouettes.

At the foot of the hill Brian walked around a squat, reddish obelisk with a statue of Parnell at its base, and hunching his shoulders he slipped along the sidewalk through a crowd of young couples and skinny adolescents. He passed a long line of bored, cigarette-smoking kids waiting at a multiple cinema for showings of six-month-old American hits, and then stopped before the wide, steamy windows of a Burger King. He peered beyond the edge of his hood and through the misted window at the kids mobbing the counter, and he wondered if he had time to grab a Whopper. But it was too crowded, he decided, and he walked on, thinking that he might as well be in Times Square for all the Irish culture on display on O'Connell Street.

At the curb he waited for a shoal of cars and buses to hiss past him, and he trotted across the pavement to the median strip, where he looked up at one of the statues for a moment, a vigorous-looking man with his mouth open in street-corner oratory, rain water dripping off his upraised arms, the colored lights of the street gleaming in his flying coattails. JIM LARKIN, read the pedestal, and Brian wondered if he ought to recognize the name. Parnell he knew, but Larkin was a new one, and he wondered if this was one of his grandfather's tragic heroes, one of those men who'd made his name by failing to accomplish what he'd set out to do. Brian turned away and looked down the street, past another bright fast food restaurant, its golden arches burning through the rain like a beacon, toward a severe, imperial building of gray stone, its tall pillars spotlit like a movie set. A flagpole rose from the peak of the building's pediment, and a brightly lit tricolor hung limply against the wet black sky.

He started down the median toward the post office. He turned and walked backward a few steps, looking back at the statues of Larkin and Parnell. Could Maire and the Provo's generation boast anyone worthy of a monument? Who were the great spirits of this generation, the Wolfe Tones and the Parnells and the Patrick Pearses? Bobby Sands, for Chrissakes? God bless him, Brian thought guiltily, but where was the heroism in starving yourself to death in your own shit? Margaret Thatcher hardly blinked an eye.

He stopped and lifted his hands out of his pockets and pulled back his hood, letting the drizzle sift across his face and through his hair. On a street lined with heroes, though, only one dominated the view, and he wasn't even Irish. At the head of the street, dwarfing Parnell's obelisk below it, an enormous red-and-white billboard stretched across the front of a pillared theater, and Sylvester Stallone, barechested, hands on hips, his thick black mane held back by a sweaty red headband, glowered down upon the site of the Easter Rebellion, dominating the street with his sullen, heavy-lidded stare, as if defying anyone to do anything about it. So Jim, Brian wanted to ask the passionate orator, was it all worth it? What did you guys accomplish in the end? Maybe there were no romantic revolutionaries anymore, but wasn't that the point? Heroes were for the movies. The methodical Provos got results, while his grandfather's sentimental, self-defeating, hand-me-down nationalism had nothing to show for itself but some heroic statuary and a lot of weepy folk songs. In the end they had lost the war, not to the British or to the Orangemen but to last summer's American blockbusters and the flame-broiled hamburger.

Brian turned away, gauging the traffic for a dash across the street. When there was a lull he ran for it, jumping puddles and pulling up short under the sheer gray wall of the post office. Then he shouldered his way into the steady procession of people under the long, narrow portico, where the murmur of conversation hung like a pall of smoke under the high roof, mingled with the hiss and roar of traffic from the street. He felt light-headed suddenly, almost giddy, as if he were on his way to meet a girl instead of an urban guerrilla. Between the pillars he glimpsed the flash of cars and blunt-ended green buses, and he slipped past gaunt adolescent boys with wispy mustaches who slouched against the gray stone, sullenly smoking cigarettes and watching the parade go by. Up ahead he saw a doorway, and next to it a policeman standing in the manner of cops all around the world, hands clasped behind his back, rocking on his heels. Brian stopped short and touched one of the pillars to steady himself. The cop stood with his cap tipped back and his trouser cuffs piled on top of his shiny black shoes, nodding as he listened to the complaint of a young woman in a miniskirt and sweater, who hunched her thin shoulders and hugged herself against the cold.

Chill out, Brian told himself, and he edged past the cop and the woman into the doorway, clenching and unclenching his fists in the pockets of his anorak. In the vestibule he passed a red-faced, hugely bearded man in a filthy overcoat and fingerless gloves who stared wide-eyed at nothing and sang unintelligibly, and Brian stopped again just inside the next door, in the sickly yellow light of a cavernous marble lobby bounded by massive wooden counters. There were only a few people waiting at the one or two windows that were open, and Brian tried to imagine the place full of rebels and gunsmoke and flying shrapnel. But the light was dreary and the air damp and stale and full of gymnasium echo; the only sign of the Rebellion was another goddamn statue in the middle of the worn floor.

Brian turned to his right, as the Provo had told him to do, and slipped past another cop leaning against the wall, passing through a narrow doorway with a lighted sign above it that read Telephones. He stopped just inside the door, and he pulled his hands out of his pockets and unzipped his anorak. Before him several rows of brown wooden telephone boxes stood on either side of a wide aisle of worn flagstones. The light was dingy, the air cold and damp and sour, like that of a public rest room. Brian wiped the film of rain water off his forehead and started down the aisle toward the last row of booths. In the phone boxes on either side he saw only pieces of other people: a slouching back, a hand gripping the edge of a booth, one foot crossed over the other at the ankle. At the back of the room he moved to one side, out of sight of the cop, and turned his wrist to look at his watch, angling it into the dim light. It was a minute or so after eight, the Provo should be calling right now; maybe he had called already. All the phone boxes in this row were empty, except for one; what if the Provo called a busy line? Brian stepped into the nearest booth and drew a deep breath. The yellowed varnish of the box was gouged with phone numbers and curses. He swallowed against a dry throat and slowly lifted his hand to touch the tacky surface of the varnish, but a phone rang in another booth down the aisle, and Brian started and jerked his hand away. He stepped out of the box, his heart beginning to pound. He resisted the urge to look back at the cop and crossed the aisle down to the ringing phone, pausing in the door of the booth to look at the dull gray receiver and the dense poster of area codes. The phone's ring was a thick burr with none of the crisp bite of an American ring, a phone with an Irish accent. Brian licked his lips and stepped into the booth. The cold, sour smell reminded him for an instant of his junior high school, and he shook off the memory and picked up the phone.

"Hello?"

"Is this Brian?" It was the Provo, sounding close, with none of the long-distance hiss of their previous conversations.

"Yes." Something moved behind Brian and he turned too quickly in the booth, thumping his elbow against the wood as a man hurried past him and around the corner out of sight.

"I want you to meet me at the McDonald's in Grafton Street in fifteen minutes."

Brian rubbed his elbow and said, "Okay. McDonald's. Is that a pub or what?"

There was something like a gasp over the phone and Brian, astonished, realized that the Provo was laughing.

"Don't be an idjit," he said, wheezing down the line. "It's the hamburger place. Surely you know what a McDonald's is."

"Okay, okay, I got it." Brian rolled his eyes at his own obtuseness. "There's one right up the street from where I am. Is that it?"

"No, the one in *Grafton Street*," the Provo said, speaking the name slowly and emphatically, the way you would to a child.

"Okay."

"Fifteen minutes."

The Provo hung up and Brian replaced the buzzing receiver. He stepped away from the phone and glanced up the aisle, half expecting to see faces turning quickly away from him in every booth. But he was alone, and he straightened his anorak and marched past the empty boxes. He turned the corner into the main aisle, and he zipped up his anorak as he came into the yellow light of the lobby. Just outside the door he stopped and smiled at the bored cop leaning against the wall.

"Excuse me, Officer," he said brightly, and the cop pushed himself up with a helpful expression on his face, straightening his cap with a brisk tug on the brim. "Can you tell me how to get to Grafton Street?"

McDonald's shone like an operating room, with chrome trim and mirrors, and it was full of the roar of adolescents, most of whom looked better fed than their sullen peers under the portico of the post office. Brian came in off the crowded pedestrian mall and paused to flip back his hood and open his anorak. He experienced another wrench of cultural displacement, and he wondered if by walking through the door he'd been warped somehow back to the States, to the campus McDonald's in Ann Arbor on a Friday night, full of heavy-metal kids in leather Motorhead jackets, girls with teased and colored hair showing their slender white thighs under miniskirts, and pale aesthetes wearing single earrings and expensive haircuts, not so much the Yeatses of their generation as the Lou Reeds. What was missing, though, were the black and Asian faces he'd have seen back home: here all the faces were thin and pale, whatever their fashion preference, and though he knew there had to be hierarchies and territorial divisions, all he saw were kids crowded around one another in the clusters of green and orange seats, eating and talking and laughing, the din of their conversation syncopated by a boom box playing some tuneless synthopop song.

Brian edged through the crowd toward the mob at the counter in the back, and for a moment he tried to watch for the Provo in the mirrored walls, pleased at his own cleverness in being indirect. But it was hopeless; he saw only pale young faces with dark eyes looking back at him, and as he came to the rear of the mob at the counter he gave up, lifting his eyes instead to the orange menu board over the heads of the crowd. He'll find me, Brian thought, and he slipped into what he hoped was a line, deciding that as long as he was here he might as well get something to eat. As the line crept forward he stiffened every time he was jostled, resisting the urge to turn and find the Provo next to him. When he reached the counter he stammered an order, as though he'd never eaten in a McDonald's before, and a moment later the cashier, a harried, freckled boy with red hair sticking like straw out from under his paper cap, slid a tray of food at him, a Big Mac, fries, and a Coke. Brian took it, unable to recall if that was what he'd ordered, and he pushed slowly back through the crowd with the tray at his waist, his elbows tight at his sides. He kept his eyes down as he moved, watching the dark Coke slosh up against the underside of its plastic lid, and a long-fingered hand plucked the Coke away by the top of the cup. Brian lifted his eyes to see the Provo slipping away through the crowd with the drink, twisting his shoulders as nimbly as a running back. Brian turned as best he could with the tray in his hands and followed in the man's slipstream, excusing himself and elbowing aside kids who scowled and muttered indecipherable slang after him. Up ahead he glimpsed the Provo striding through the fringes of the crowd, the skirts of his raincoat billowing, and Brian followed him into a narrow gallery alongside the kitchen where small, two-seat tables were bolted to the long white wall. The Provo took the farthest seat, facing back down the gallery, stretching his long legs into the aisle. Brian came up the fluorescent-bright aisle and stood next to the table as if working up the nerve to ask for his Coke back.

"So what do I do?" he said, under his breath. "Do I sit or what?"

The Provo popped the lid off the Coke and raised it between the tips of his fingers like a pint of beer. He lifted his pointed chin at the empty seat across from him.

"Don't make a bloody production of it," he murmured. "We're a pair of strangers sharing a table."

Brian slid into the stiff, fixed seat and shrugged off his anorak, draping it over the back of his chair. He cracked the Styrofoam box of his Big Mac, his eyes hooded from the Provo, and stole a glance at him as he lifted the burger in both hands. The Provo took a long, thirsty pull of Coke, his Adam's apple wobbling as he swallowed, and he set the cup back on the table.

"Maire's been lifted," the Provo said, his eyes blank as he gazed back down the gallery at the crowded main dining room.

"Lifted?" Brian raised his eyebrows and bit into his burger.

"Arrested." The ice in the paper cup rattled as the Provo twisted the cup back and forth on the orange tabletop. "The Brits picked her up at a roadblock."

Brian had to force the mouthful of hamburger down a tightening throat. He set the Big Mac in its box, where it sagged to one side, and pushed the box away.

"That's great," he said. "That's just fucking great."

"Don't worry about it." The Provo did not look at Brian, but watched up the bright aisle past Brian's shoulder, his voice just loud enough to be heard over the racket from the main room. "There's several people who know the parcel's coming, but nobody knows who's bringing it except Maire and me. So you've got nothing to worry about."

Brian was unable to speak for a moment, and he stared wide-eyed across the table at the Provo, who lifted the Coke and took another big gulp. Brian looked down in disbelief at his meal, at the Big Mac slued to one side, all its layers exposed, at the stiff French fries tumbled out of their box. Suddenly the food on his plastic tray looked like the site of an accident.

"Jesus," Brian said. He slumped against the narrow seat. "Jesus H. Christ."

"So you're going to have to go all the way to London with the parcel." The Provo set down the paper cup and wiped his mouth on his sleeve, still not looking at Brian. "I'm going to give you a number to ring when you get there."

Brian looked across the table at the Provo, trying to catch his eye. The man needed a shave and some sleep, and probably a bath as well. Finally the Provo glanced across at him, and

Brian started to laugh. He left his hands on the table, afraid that they would start to shake if he moved them.

"Keep your voice down, for Christ's sake." The Provo glanced once more up the aisle and then back at Brian, and Brian hunched over the table, squeezing his lips together, peering at the Provo as if pleading with him. But he couldn't keep it in, and he put his head down on his arms, his shoulders shaking with laughter until tears came to his eyes. At last he sat up, wiping his eyes and drawing deep breaths, and he gave the Provo a killer smile, something he usually reserved for long glances across a smoke-filled room of partygoers.

"No fucking way," he said.

"What?" The Provo leaned forward slightly, as if he hadn't heard properly.

"I said, no fucking way am I going to London for you. I'm out of this thing tonight, as of right now, right this fucking minute."

He felt the urge to laugh coming back, and he picked up a French fry and bit it in half.

"There is no alternative." The Provo watched Brian warily, as if he wasn't sure whether Brian was joking or not. He enunciated each word deep in his throat. "There is no one else who can go. It's you or nobody."

"Then it's nobody, dude." Brian swallowed the half-chewed fry and popped the rest of it in his mouth. "I've already done more than my share."

He smiled again, his mouth pulpy with potato. He felt giddy again, for the second time that evening, but this time it was a different kind of giddiness. Before, walking into the post office, he had been light-headed with anticipation, with the feeling that he'd done it, that he was within minutes of bringing this thing off. Now he felt a kind of vertigo, as if he'd opened the final door and nearly stepped into an empty elevator shaft, a sheer drop into blackness. Across the table the Provo's eyes were furious, the muscles bunching along his jaw, but he made an effort to control himself, pitching his voice low in a vain effort to sound reasonable.

"Maire won't say a word," he said. "She's harder than some lads I know."

"Don't bullshit me." Brian smiled again, teetering at the very edge of the drop, goofy with fear. "You cruise in here as cool as can be and tell me I've got to carry this shit to London for you, and oh, by the way, I almost forgot, one of the people who can nail your ass is in custody. Hope you don't mind." He laughed again, in disbelief. "You're too fucking much. I mean, it's not like they hauled her in for unpaid parking tickets, is it?"

The Provo glared at him, his eyes burning. He came in here hoping to finesse me, Brian thought, but he's no good at it. And even if he ever was, he's too stressed out to pull it off this time.

"Not to mention the fact," Brian went on, "that this is, what, the second arrest in two days? Maybe this shit happens to you all the time, but look at it from my point of view."

"No, you look at it from mine." The Provo crouched suddenly forward over the table, his raincoat hissing against the plastic seat. He leaned on his elbows and ticked points off his fingers, hooking the thumb of one hand over the pinkie of the other.

"One. Your man in Donegal had no idea who he was meeting, so you're well out of that. Two." He hooked another finger. "He had no knowledge of Maire at all, so there's no way to link the two arrests. Three." Another finger. "Maire's arrest is routine harassment; she won't say a word about the parcel."

"She knows my fucking *name*," Brian said. He was wide-eyed and smiling, his nerves singing like plucked piano wire. "I brought your fucking money, they'll trace it back to the reunion."

"I have the money. That's not your problem."

"That's easy for you to say. What if she tells them anyway?"

With a sudden, violent movement, the Provo pinned Brian's wrist to the table with his hand, shaking the ice in the Coke, sending the cantilevered Big Mac sliding over like a stack of poker chips. Instinctively Brian tried to pull away, but he couldn't budge. He stiffened in his chair, resisting the urge to shout, to twist around in his seat.

"In that case you've got no choice but to go through with it."

The Provo's voice was husky, his eyes hard and bright. "The only way out of this for you is forward, *dude*." He tightened his grip, working his long fingers all the way around Brian's wrist. "So the question you want to be asking yourself, old son, is who you want to be answering to, the police or me."

Brian licked his lips, his gaze fixed and unseeing, his face hot.

"Because if you walk out of here tonight without promising me you'll carry on," the Provo said, his voice low and intimate, "I'll give you to Special Branch myself. Believe me, Brian, it's no skin off my back, all you can give them is me, and I was *born* with a price on my head."

Brian was aware of the blood pounding in his ears. The noise of the crowd of kids behind him was muffled, as if through a wall.

"Are you threatening me?" he said in a thin voice.

"I'll do more than that." The Provo pulled on Brian's arm, tugging him across the table. "I'll promise you something." He lowered his voice even further, almost to a whisper. "If I pick up a paper in two days' time and don't read about a bloody great explosion in London, I'll kill you. Not in Ireland, Brian, or across the water, but in America. I'll come to Detroit if I have to and I will find you and I will kill you."

He held Brian's gaze for an endless moment; the edge of the little table dug sharply into Brian's gut. Then he let go of Brian's wrist and settled back into his seat, his breath hissing through his nose. Brian sat back too, rubbing his wrist, the blood throbbing in his hand. His stomach churned painfully, and he looked down at his tray, where the hamburger sat thick and cold and inedible, the fries greasy and limp.

"I'm sorry," the Provo said. He rubbed his hand slowly over his face, squeezing his eyes and nose and stubbled chin. He looked across at Brian and blew out a sigh. "It shouldn't have come to this. I know you'll do your duty, Brian, but I have to be sure you don't abandon us now." He reached out wearily and pulled the Coke toward him. "All you have to do is get on the ferry at Dún Laoghaire in the morning and you'll be in London by tomorrow night. You'll be your own man again by Tuesday morning."

"Why not tonight?" Brian managed to say. "I could get a plane."

"*Christ.*" The Provo heaved himself up in his seat again, and Brian flinched. But the Provo only fixed him with a piercing glare.

"Stay away from the airport," he said. "They search luggage there. Just take the bloody ferry."

Brian opened his mouth to say something, but let it go in silence.

"Here's the number in London." The Provo lifted his elbow to dig in his raincoat pocket, and he pushed a folded slip of notepaper under Brian's tray. "Memorize it and throw it away."

Brian looked up sharply. He almost wanted to laugh. The Provo rolled his eyes.

"Just do it," he said. "Ask for Vincent."

He sat up straight in his seat and drank off the rest of the Coke, wincing as he swallowed the last mouthful.

"Christ, how do you Americans drink this muck. It makes my teeth hurt."

He brought the cup down onto the table with a pop.

"Tell me the time, Brian."

Brian shot his wrist out of the cuff of his sweater, barely able to keep his hand from shaking as he held his watch out for the Provo to read. Their eyes met for a moment, and for the first time Brian saw how bloodshot and bagged the other man's were.

"Nobody's looking for you, Brian, all right? Maire won't say a word to anybody." The Provo gripped the edge of the table, getting ready to stand. "If you do this, you'll be as big a hero as your grandfather."

Brian lifted his eyes as the man stood.

"And if I don't," he said, "I'll be dead."

The Provo looked down at Brian with a blank expression, the corners of his eyes twitching, and Brian's stomach tightened as he realized that the man was trying to smile and couldn't.

"There's heroism for you," the Provo said.

Then he jerked his deadened face away as if he were embarrassed, and he strode quickly down the aisle, the skirts of his raincoat drifting behind him, and slid into the crowd. When he was out of sight Brian lifted his shaking hands off the table and took the folded paper from under the tray. He held it for a moment between two fingers without opening it, and then put it in the pocket of his anorak.

Jimmy Coogan felt numb and distant from himself, as if he were buried alive inside his own head, peering out over his frozen cheeks at the road in the cross-eyed headlamps of his hijacked Volkswagen. He was aware that he was hungry, that he should have eaten something at the McDonald's in Dublin, but it was somebody else's nagging hunger, a child tugging at his sleeve. He knew he was tired as well: every moment was an argument with himself over keeping awake, part of him wanting nothing more than to pull over and close his eyes for a few seconds. But that too was something he merely overheard, distantly, dispassionately, without participating, as if the outcome didn't matter.

Above all, though, he was cold, and as he headed north he felt himself shivering in time with the uneven rattle of the VW's engine. Just his luck, the bloody heater didn't work, and he drove with the passenger window rolled down to keep from fogging up the windscreen with his own breath. The freezing wind blew all around the little car like a dog circling for a spot to lie down, numbing his cheeks and stiffening his fingers on the steering wheel. The electric buzz of the engine came to him through his cold hands as if there were a quarter inch of frost between his palms and the plastic of the wheel. Through the windscreen the road and leafless hedges and the solitary amber lights of silent villages flowed past him like a film, seamless and distant, and he watched them from somewhere far behind his eyes, where the cold had removed him.

He ought to feel scared, he told himself; all the people who wanted him dead, on both sides, were looking for him up ahead, in Belfast. A sensible man would have found a room in Dublin, a hole to hide in where he could pull the ladder in after him. But then a sensible man, he decided, as if he were thinking about someone else, wouldn't have taken the risks he had. A sensible man wouldn't have gotten this far. He should feel hopeful instead; the Semtex was on its way in spite of everything, and Brody would step up to the dais for his opening address in Dublin on Thursday with the action in London still ringing in his ears. Coogan felt himself warm a little at the thought: let Joe hold on to the reins after that, with the proof of Coogan's long reach screaming from every headline and shouted from the BBC. Half of Belfast Brigade will swing my way, he thought, and once they find out Brody shopped Maire to the Brits like a common criminal, the rest will follow.

Jimmy yawned, squeezing his eyes shut and making them water; a moment later he was shaking his head violently from side to side, forcing his fluttering eyelids to open again. He couldn't feel the tears rolling down his numbed cheeks. First order of business, he told himself, once I've got hold of the reins, is engineering Maire's escape from the RUC. Why not? Sooner or later they'd have to move her out of Castlereagh, and by then he'd have a team waiting, a smash-and-grab operation in broad daylight, right out on the street, clean and surgical. Or why not take her out of Castlereagh itself, pluck her straight out of the jaws of the RUC, let them know that somebody else was in charge, that Joe Brody's painstaking caution was a thing of the past. By God, why not!

He banged his palm against the steering wheel and tightened his stiffened fingers around the plastic ridges. But it was a manufactured emotion, performed at several removes from his cold, yawning self. He slowed and shifted down as he came into the high street of Clontibret, silent and empty at this time of night, and he turned off the N2 into the road that would take him to the border crossing. It probably wasn't the best idea to use the same crossing twice in one night, but he was going home, he told himself, back to the battleground he knew better than any man alive. There was safety in that, surely, more safety than in his earlier idea of staying in Dublin. After leaving McDonald's, slipping through the crowd of children in Grafton Street, he'd wondered at first what better place to pop up after the action in London than right under Joe Brody's holy nose, standing up and grinning from the back of the hall as Joe cleared his throat and sipped his water and shuffled the pages of his opening address.

But Dublin was full of Brody's men, any one of whom would just as soon see Jimmy dead. Or worse, coughing up blood at the hands of Special Branch, now that it looked like Brody didn't stop at touting on his comrades these days. And as if to drive the point home, as he had come round the corner toward St. Stephen's Green, a man fell in beside him, a half step back, and murmured Jimmy's name, wishing him a pleasant evening in Irish. Jimmy whirled and stumbled back a step, reaching inside his mac for the gun, but it was only Bill McDermott of Dublin Brigade, standing in the light rain with his palms raised to show he meant no harm, and looking as though he wanted to smile.

"You're a long way from home," he said, still in Irish.

Jimmy, a little tongue-tied with surprise, said nothing, poised in the middle of the pavement with his hand on the grip of the revolver under his coat. Well-dressed young couples hurried obliviously by, arm in arm, on their way to the trendy pubs in Grafton Street.

"The word is you're a wanted man tonight," Bill said a little more warily, the suggestion of a smile fading. He stood out from the passing up-market couples by virtue of his stiff, unfashionable jeans and cheap nylon anorak, and by the laborer's breadth of his neck and shoulders. Only his shoes, a brand-new pair of white Reeboks, were up-market, and Coogan's reflex disdain for ostentation in a guerrilla was immediately tempered by the memory of Maire's opinion of his stolen

Burberry. If only she could see it now, he thought, after a week's hard use.

Bill slowly lowered his hands to his sides, never taking his eyes off Jimmy. A pair of young women, whispering and giggling and clutching each other by the arm, clicked past on their high heels between the two men, trailing the odor of perfume after them through the misting rain. But neither man turned to watch them pass, neither man took his eyes off the other.

"Do you need a place to hide?" Bill had said at last.

Coogan nearly missed the turn into the unapproved lane that ran up to the border. It glided past him in the edge of the headlamps' beam, and he jerked up his chin and blinked furiously, braking and then backing the whining car up to the turnoff. Then he jammed it into first and turned up the lane. Shortly the road narrowed and roughened like a tongue, the bare hedges on either side drawing closer in the bleaching light of the VW's headlamps. The lane dipped into a milky pool of mist, which streamed through the open window and beaded on the inside of the windscreen and on the torn seats and battered dash and, though he couldn't feel it, on his face. But although he couldn't see the road, he refused to downshift, angry now at himself, and he gunned the VW through the mist until the last strands of it parted and the car roared up onto the other side like a horse plunging through a stream. He lifted his arm and wiped the dew off the windscreen with the sleeve of his mac, and then he passed his hand over the cold, wet skin of his forehead, shaking off the drops of water with a flick of his fingers. He guided the car around a narrow curve and a moment later he saw the gate to the stony field come into the headlamps. He slowed and shifted into neutral, coasting to a stop a few feet from the gate.

He switched off the lights and rolled down his own window, and he sat there in the dark drawing in deep breaths of brisk, country air, marshaling himself, trying to wake himself up. He blew into his cupped hands until he felt them again, then he rubbed them furiously along his cheeks and stubbled jaw, trying to bring his cold, doughy face back to life. He rubbed his arms through his coat sleeves and slapped his legs, shuddering in the little car almost as violently as the idling engine. The low growl was probably audible for a long way in the cold air, but he didn't dare switch it off, for fear of not being able to start it again. He would have laughed at himself if he could: the problem with stealing your transportation was that you couldn't try on a car like a coat and put it back if it didn't suit you; you had to stick with your first choice. Bill McDermott had helped him pick it out and start it; worse luck, Bill turned out to be no better judge of automobiles than himself. Standing on the pavement outside St. Stephen's Green with his hand on the gun inside his mackintosh, Jimmy had turned down Bill's offer of a hiding place.

"I need a car," he said instead, in Irish.

After that they had walked up the narrow streets around the green looking for an unlocked car, Bill in front with his hands out where Jimmy could see them, both men uncertain of Bill's status; was he prisoner or samaritan? Bill tried to indicate his trustworthiness with his body language, moving slowly, looking to Jimmy for instructions at every corner. He didn't plead or make excuses, and Jimmy was impressed. After all, if he'd been out to get me, he thought, he'd never have spoken to me in the first place. Even so, he kept his hand on the gun as Bill walked ahead, trying the doors of parked cars.

Finally they had come to a battered VW, its color uncertain in the ghastly sodium light of the streetlights, and together they put their shoulders to it and rolled it around the corner, where Bill started it, crouched across the passenger seat with his bright new shoes poking out the door. Then he backed away, hands in the clear, and came around to the driver's window as Jimmy got in.

"Headed north?" he said, crouched by the side of the car with his fingers on the window sill.

"Thanks for the car," Coogan said, pushing in the clutch and jerking the stick through all its settings.

"Safe home, Jimmy," Bill had said, but Coogan had only nodded his thanks and pulled away from the curb.

Now, with the border a hundred feet away, Jimmy couldn't wait any longer; he was afraid he'd fall asleep right there, sitting up in the car. Wouldn't that be a prize for the Gardai, to find him at dawn in a stalled VW, half frozen through, slumped over the wheel with dew all over him. He shook' himself all over like a dog and opened the door. The hinges squealed alarmingly; he didn't remember their doing that when he'd got in the car. He switched off the little interior light and left the door open, levering himself by both hands like a cripple out of the car. Standing up straight he arched his back, rolling his shoulders and spreading his arms wide behind him. He walked stiff-legged toward the gate, his body tingling all over like a limb that had fallen asleep. Never mind the bloody heater; next time he'd hijack a bigger car. He straightened his mackintosh around him as he went, pausing to fumble with thick fingers at the belt, buckling it snugly around his waist. He unlatched the gate and walked it slowly and noiselessly to one side, pausing to glance once around the field at the dark silhouettes of trees and hedges. He was coming awake again, and about bloody time, his stomach aching with hunger.

Back at the VW, he bent into it like an old man, wincing at the squealing hinges as he pulled the door to, just enough to hook it but not latch it. He put the car in first and crept through the gate without lights, his breathing shallow, his eyes widening at the gloom beyond the windscreen. He was beginning to ache all over now, from hunger, from fatigue, from the sting of the cold, and he wished for an instant that he could retreat into numbness again. There'd been a little rain, he could feel the tires slipping a bit, but not enough to turn the field to muck, thank God. He yawned again and smiled to think of Maire, of what she would say of him riding to her rescue in a noisy, bashed-in, twenty-year-old Volkswagen, and for the first time in hours he felt a surge of heat, nearly erotic, at the picture of her sharp features, at the memory of her precise and graceful movements, at the sound of her voice. My hero, she'd say dryly, twisting her lip, but even she wouldn't be able to withhold her gratitude this time, and for a moment the heat he felt within his mackintosh was almost that of Maire herself, her arms around him, pulling him close.

The car jounced against stones and slipped in the thin film of mud, shuddering into a rut. He gave it some petrol, and the engine whined and sputtered and stalled. "Shit," Jimmy said aloud, and he banged the wheel with the heel of his hand. This time he really felt it, the anger close to the surface, and he shoved the stick into neutral and sat fuming for an instant. Leave the car, he thought, get out and walk, that'll bloody wake you up. But it was a long way to the nearest town yet, where he'd just have to hijack another one. So he drew a breath and reached through the wheel, feeling gingerly along the steering column for the ignition wires Bill had twined together, peering uselessly down into the dark where his hands were. When he found the plastic sheathing he let out his breath and fumbled stiffly at the wires. Outside the car the night was nearly perfectly dark and perfectly silent, no birds this time of night. The silence poured in the window with the cold, coating his skin like frost, numbing him again, pushing his mind deeper once more, away from what he was trying to do. He twisted in his seat and squinted uselessly down into the blackness, his eyes searching for information even as his hands fumbled at the ignition wires. He blinked, his eyelids fluttered, his head dipping loosely toward his chest, and from outside, through the clear night air, he heard a single, sharp, metallic click, the only sound in all that darkness, and he lifted his chin in time to see the windscreen fill with brilliant white light, first from one powerful source, then in sudden bursts, pairs of headlamps all around him, one right after another. He sat stunned for a moment, completely blinded; then he began to move, abruptly, still numb, still distant from what was going on, his limbs moving under the force of a cold electricity. He jerked his hands back through the wheel, banging his knuckles, and he toppled over across the passenger seat, his legs drawn up, his left arm pinned under him, the gearshift jammed in his ribs.

He twisted his head and looked up: the space above him was full of harsh white light like a photoflash, but unlike a flash it didn't fade, it didn't go away, but only brightened like the glare of oncoming cars, the interior of the VW bleached out like an old snapshot, the strips and knobs of metal and plastic shining like steel. He heard shouts now, heard the electric crackle of somebody's amplified voice, but he couldn't make out what they were saying, his ears ringing with the cold, his mind refusing to catch and start. He was watching himself from a distance again, furious at himself, but impotent, unable to move. It was as if he were going into shock already, before anything had happened, as if he had been flattened by the overpressure of a bomb blast, his limbs weak, his nerves ringing, his head thick and slow.

Then he heard the rhythmic, industrial percussion of a machine gun, like something rapid and hydraulic stamping out tin, and above him the windscreen puckered and cracked and burst in, filling the car with shining fragments like stars, coating him with a brittle blanket of glass. From somewhere he managed to drag up a shout, and almost without willing it he twisted onto his back, pressing the soles of his shoes against the driver's door, tensing his knees, all of it automatic as if this were some kind of drill. There were more shouts and the pop of automatic fire, and he felt the car shake under the impact of bullets, settling one corner at a time as the tires burst. The mackintosh was rucked around his middle, the belt drawn tight, binding him; he held his hands curled close to his chest like a spastic, listening to himself scream. Then he was brushing at the glass on his coat, tearing at the buttons of the mac to get to his gun, but it was no good, his hands were shaking too hard, the buttons sewn too tight, the gun too far away.

The firing stopped, the last few shots dribbling out, and somebody was calling his name, a loud metallic voice, the voice of God or a vast machine, and Jimmy ignored it, it was no concern of his, and he lifted his hands over his head and gripped the sill of the open window, drawing up his knees, kicking out at the driver's door, banging it open on its shrieking hinges. The gunfire erupted again, the bullets singing through the driver's door, and he tightened his grip and heaved himself up and back through the passenger window. But he was caught; the gearshift knob was hooked in a pocket of the mac, and he hauled harder at the window, felt ligaments in his shoulder stretch and tear. He screamed again, but it was somebody else's shoulder, it wasn't him, and he kept pulling blindly. The pocket tore free, and he heaved back through the window and slid onto his shoulders in the mud, broken glass cascading down the front of his coat into his face.

He twisted onto his stomach and kicked free of the car, writhing in the mud like a snake. He knew that the pocket had slowed him, that he'd already lost the moment he'd gained kicking open the driver's door; in the floodlit glare the dirt was roiling all around him like water. There were lights ahead of him and on either side and behind, the glare of headlamps and spotlights punctuated all around with muzzle flashes. I've got to move, he told himself, this matters, and from far off he felt the searing pain in his shoulder, somebody else's pain, but he gathered it to him anyway, as something they had given him that he could cling to. Then he was crouching like a sprinter at the block, breathing hard already, but all set to go, alert, awake, *alive*, by God, for the first time in days. And he took off, bent over like a footballer, weaving in the light like a star for All Ireland, unable to hear the crowd over the rasp of his own misting breath and the thunder of his heart, pounding down the field toward the goal he couldn't see in the ring of lights all around, but easy on his feet and steady as a locomotive. They say Jimmy's playing with an injury, lads, but you wouldn't know it to *look at him go*, we hear his wife is in the stands today, would I be wrong in suggesting that she might have a wee bit to do with this *magnificent performance* . . .

A series of blunt impacts, a line of hammer blows across his chest, picked him up and spun him around, the skirts of his mackintosh swirling, his legs pedaling uselessly in midair. For a long, silent moment he floated weightlessly in a cloud of light, and he thought of a number of things, thought of his wife standing up alone in the crowd just to watch him fail, thought of the act of contrition, a brief one under the circumstances, Jesus, Mary, and Joseph be with me in my hour of death, and finally he thought ruefully of the ruin of his beautiful mackintosh, pungent with his own sweat, rumpled and creased in the boot of Tim McGuire's car, its pocket ripped out, the front of it embedded with broken glass and smeared with mud and stitched through with holes.

Then the light faded and he began to fall, and in the last moment of his life Jimmy Coogan heard the sweet, sharp voice of his wife scolding him, turning the air blue all around him with her scorn, letting him know in no uncertain terms that at the end of the day it was that goddamned coat that got him killed.

In the cool, underwater light of the Sealink terminus at Dún Laoghaire, Tim McGuire paced the old railway platform, as if waiting for a train that would never come. The tracks alongside the platform had long since been torn up, the railbed covered over with white gravel and littered with crumpled soda cans and stray sheets of newspaper. As he walked, he clutched the stitch in his side with one hand, still breathing hard from the run across Crofton Road into the cavernous open end of the terminus. In his other hand he curled his fingers around the snapshot he'd found in the trunk of his car, waiting to compare the face of the American in the picture to one of the groggy, early-morning faces of the passengers trudging up the platform toward the glassed-in ticket office behind him. But so far all he saw were shapeless, middle-aged Irishwomen traveling in pairs, and a handful of small, gaunt, solitary men in cheap windbreakers and stained overcoats, shabby men of no fixed abode who shuffled between the dole at home and day labor in London. The only American he'd seen this morning was a breathless girl carrying a backpack, and Tim, his hasty breakfast churning in his stomach, began to worry that the boy in the picture had taken the wrong boat, the ferry out of Rosslare to Fishguard, or out of Dublin to Liverpool. Tim lifted his hand, glancing at the palmed photo, and looked at his watch. In a few minutes he'd have to make a decision, whether to get on the ferry here in the hope that the American had already boarded, run back to his car to make a mad dash for the terminus in Dublin, or even to run out to Shannon and hopelessly watch the boarding gates.

For the moment, though, he put off the decision, forcing himself to think of some approach he might make to the kid on the outside chance he showed up. Tim looked like hell, he knew that: he'd spent the night in the Honda in a carpark just outside of town, crammed in the narrow back seat with his knees up and the car full of the wet dog smell of his soaking parka. His watch had awakened him at six thirty, and he'd groaned and reached between the front seats to switch on the radio, just in time to hear Radio Eireann announce the death by gunfire of a suspected Provo at the border last night. They didn't have the name yet, but Tim sat up suddenly in the back seat, grinding the little Honda down to the roots of its suspension, and he lunged between the seats to turn up the volume. Acting on information, the bland announcer said, which meant that somebody touted, a British army unit was waiting for the man, which meant the trigger fucking happy SAS. By now Tim was wide awake, his pulse racing, his head pushed between the seats like an ox's through a harness. The suspect was armed and driving a stolen car, which could only mean Jimmy Coogan, and he was killed at a clandestine border crossing near Clontibret, which could only be the same fucking crossing I took him through twelve hours ago. By now Tim was shaking, and he banged the driver's seat forward and shoved open the door, bumping the horn with his elbow as he heaved out of the car into the colorless, predawn light of the parking lot, cursing out loud the bastard Brits who'd murdered Jimmy Coogan and screwed everything up.

He found an all-night transport café in Santry where he

splashed some cold water on his face in the gents' and wolfed down some beans and toast, propping the Polaroid of Coogan and the American against the salt shaker before him. No way the kid would catch a plane out of Shannon, he decided; Coogan would have told him not to fly. He'd almost certainly have told the kid to take the ferry out of Dún Laoghaire to Holyhead; it was the most direct route to London and the most crowded. Tim snatched up the photograph and left the café, racing to Dún Laoghaire in his Honda.

But he parked the car on a side street a block from the terminal, rather than driving it up into the ferry, hedging his bets, leaving himself a back door if the kid didn't show up. The ferry loomed across the road, the white decks gleaming in the slanting light off the Irish Sea, the twin stacks rising on either side, the radio masts skeletal against the deepening blue of the morning sky. He'd hoped he was early yet, but coming around the corner he'd seen the great doors below the afterdeck hinged aside like wings, the last of a line of cars whining up the ramp into the maw of the car deck. He'd put on some speed then, huffing across the road and the dewy lawn into the vast barn of the terminal.

But the platform there was nearly empty, and none of the people who showed up as he waited was the one he wanted. Tim looked at his watch and began to worry again. The connecting bus from Connolly Station had yet to arrive, a guard assured him, but what if the boy wasn't on it? If he drove like hell, Tim might make the nine o'clock ferry from Rosslare, but what if the American wasn't there either? What if the boy had heard the radio this morning and put it all together? He might already be sweating in some Special Branch interrogation room. With every step down the platform Tim silently cursed the Brits and his rotten luck. The boy had probably heard the news and taken off like a greyhound.

Then another possibility came to him that made him stop dead on the bare concrete: what if the kid had rented a car and had already driven it on board? All this time Tim should have been standing out on the lawn beyond the roof of the terminus, where he could watch the driver of each car as well as the passengers arriving on foot.

"Shit," he said aloud, and he jammed the snapshot into his pocket and jogged up the platform toward the open end of the terminus. He came out into the salt breeze and the cool shadow of the building as the tall green bus from Connolly hissed to a stop just across the narrow strip of grass from him.

"Shit," Tim said again, his breath coming short, and he started walking backward down the lawn, leaving his footprints in the dew, glancing over his shoulder at the dark opening of the car deck as it came into view beyond the end of the terminus wall, glancing ahead at the passengers streaming off the bus, mostly women again, more shabby men, and a mother dragging two sleepy children by the hand. Behind him he heard a single car coming up the drive toward the ramp, and he backed toward it, nearly losing his balance, afraid to turn around, afraid not to, tears of frustration squeezing into the corners of his eyes. In a sudden rage he spun on his heel, but the car thumped up the ramp too quickly for him to see the driver, and he spun again to face the bus, aware of what he must look like to the puzzled guard on the platform, a fat man doing pirouettes on the lawn early on a Monday morning, and he nearly shouted as he saw a backpacker step down out of the bus, a man in a blue anorak carrying a blue backpack. Off balance, Tim caught himself from toppling over backward, pausing to squeeze the tears out of his eyes with his thumbs, peering down the lawn at the backpacker as he walked into the shadow of the terminus. Tim couldn't tell at this distance if it was the boy from the photo, and he started after him, checking his stride, forcing himself not to run, clawing the snapshot out of his pocket.

Down the platform he nudged obliviously through the stream of people from the bus, watching the blue backpack up ahead. But the pack obscured the guy's head, and Tim still couldn't be sure. Then he found himself at the end of the line just outside the ticket office, the backpacker five or six people ahead of him. Tim bit his lip and lifted himself up on tiptoe, but it didn't

help. Sinking back onto his heels he risked a look at the snapshot trembling in his hand, wondering if he dared slip alongside the outside of the office to peer through the glass at the
guy from the front. The line slipped forward, though, and he
found himself caught in the doorway of the office, five people
back from the clerk. Ahead the backpacker turned away from
the counter, and Tim's heart leaped at a glimpse of curly blond
hair. But then the guy was out the far door and carrying his
pack around the end of the railbed toward the stairs to the
gangway, his face partially blocked by the pack, lost in the
sheen of fluorescent light in the office window. Tim wanted to
manhandle the people ahead of him, to lift them out of the
way. He wanted to stamp his feet and shout, swing his fists,
break glass.

"Single or return?" said the ticket clerk, and Tim spun away
from the window, turning to find himself at the ticket counter
trembling and flushed. He caught his breath and pocketed the
snapshot again, charging a ticket on his Access card, smiling
unsteadily across the counter in the hope that the clerk didn't
call in his number and find out the truth about Tim's balance.

Ticket in hand, Tim heaved up the stairs behind the young
mother and her two poky children, one interminable step at a
time, rolling his eyes and silently mouthing obscenities as the
mother hauled first one kid up a step and then the other.
Finally he scooped up one of the brats, lifting the little boy
under the arms, and with a queasy smile back at the dumb-
struck mother, the boy turning rigid and wide-eyed with terror
in his hands, Tim took the rest of the stairs two at a time,
charging down the gangway child and all, swinging the kid to
the floor like a duffel bag just inside the door of the crowded
vestibule. Red-faced with fear and outrage, the mother appeared a moment later, dragging a screaming little girl, and
she snatched her son's hand and let fly at Tim with a stream of
sharp, uniquely Irish invective. But Tim didn't hear a word,
pressed up against the wall to one side of the door, his heart
pounding, raptly watching the kid from the photo sling his
backpack with both hands like a battering ram through the

crush around the luggage racks. The mother gave up and dragged her kids away, and Tim slid his hand into his pocket, touching the snapshot there lightly with the tips of his fingers like a talisman.

A crewman in blue coveralls elbowed Tim aside, pulling the door shut as the gangway rattled back from the ship. He wanted to look at the photo, just to be sure, but he was afraid of dropping it in the crowd. Then the kid edged away from the luggage racks, leading with his shoulder, and Tim wanted to shout for joy, he swore he could hear angels singing. It had to be him: same blue anorak, his face pale and unshaven, his hair curling over his forehead like a wave. Tim held his breath as the kid squeezed through the crowd up a narrow stairway.

He counted to ten, then to twenty, waiting for the crowd to thin out and for his heart to slow down. The boat had already begun to move; he felt the motion in his gut, a gentle, rocking glide that set his center of gravity swaying from side to side like a plumb line. He crossed to the luggage racks and saw the backpack wedged between a leather suitcase and a cardboard one, bulging under the pressure. The end of the pack with the boy's ID, a scratched plastic window framed in leather on the top flap, stuck out of the rack, and Tim squatted, grunting, to read it, pulling himself up again with both hands on the rack above.

Brian Donovan of Ann Arbor, Michigan, he thought, smiling, come on *down*. He laid his hand on the pack, and just for an instant, he let himself think about stealing the plastique. He could buy a nylon carryall in the duty-free shop, hustle the pack into a stall in the gents' when no one was looking, and make the switch. What could the kid do, call the cops?

But there was more to it than that. Now that Coogan was dead, Brody would want the whole package, the plastique and the delivery boy, all wrapped up together. That's where the story is, Tim decided at last, pulling himself up the forward stairs after Brian: YOUNG AMERICAN CAUGHT IN IRA FACTION FIGHT, it was a nice sidebar to the main event, maybe a long feature in the *Voice* or, hell, even the *Times* Sunday magazine.

Tim stopped at the top of the stairs to catch his breath. Up
ahead, at the other end of the paneled lounge, Brian stepped up
to the bar, the first customer of the morning. As Tim watched,
the blank-faced barman came down the bar, nodded, and drew
him a pint, and Brian leaned on the bar and hoicked his wallet
out of the hip pocket of his jeans. Tim drew a breath and pulled
the photograph out of his parka for the final test, and it was
him, the kid next to Coogan in the picture. As if I needed any
other proof, Tim thought, stuffing the photograph out of sight.
Who else, when all the other passengers were crowding the
breakfast buffet on the deck below, would need a drink at eight
o'clock on a bright Irish morning?

Come to think of it, Tim had to admit, it wasn't the worst
idea he'd ever heard, not after the night he'd had. He started
across the lounge, but after a few steps ducked his head and
circled nervously back to the top of the stairs again, his hand
squeezing his stubbled chin. This was a delicate moment,
he couldn't just barge right in, it required a little finesse.
But then he pushed out his chest and sailed out across the
lounge again, his gut swaying like a balloon before him with
the motion of the boat. Bluff it out, he told himself. It's now
or never.

Tim stepped up to the bar an arm's length from the kid and
slapped his palm down on the counter.

"A Bushmills, if you please, my man," he called out, giving
only fleeting thought to the likely reaction of beans and toast
with his favorite whiskey. Jesus, it was early, but Brian had a
pint in front of him, standing with one hand on the bar to
steady himself against the rocking of the boat and the other
curled around his glass, staring straight ahead at nothing, his
eyes red and bagged. Tim turned and smiled at Brian, reaching
for his wallet as the barman came back with his glass.

"Hope they got the doors shut down on the car deck, don't
you?" The barman narrowed his eyes at Tim's remark, but he
palmed Tim's money and walked away to the end of the bar.
Tim lifted his glass and kept smiling, but Brian only stared
ahead at the bottles lined up behind the bar. Tim took a sip,

and the Bushmills, usually the smoothest of whiskeys, burned down his dry throat all the way to his breakfast.

"It'd be a real bitch if this baby rolled over," he gasped, licking his lips. "Specially at this hour of the morning."

He leaned a bit forward into Brian's line of sight, unsure if the boy was ignoring him or just didn't know he was being spoken to. Roll with it, Tim thought. Take advantage of the situation.

"God, it's early," he said, mustering his barroom bonhomie as best he could at eight in the morning. He smiled knowingly at Brian. "Hair of the dog, huh?" He lifted his glass for another burning sip.

At last the kid moved, blinking and slowly lifting his pint as if he'd only just awakened. But he drank without speaking or looking at Tim, setting the glass back down slowly and staring straight ahead.

Tim looked away from Brian and repressed a sigh. At the end of the bar the barman was sitting on a stool, reading a Fleet Street tabloid. All right, Tim thought, I wouldn't want to talk to some asshole at this hour either. Try another tack. Be direct.

"I'll bet you're an American," he said. "Wanna know how I can tell?"

There was no answer, but Tim twisted closer to the bar, angling toward Brian.

" 'Cause I'm a Yankee myself. A real one, from Boston." He exaggerated his vowels a bit. "I pahk my cah in the yahd." He smiled. "That's how we talk in Southie."

He took another quick, wincing sip of Bushmills.

"My name's Tim," he said. Keep it friendly no matter what, he told himself, just the two of us having a belt. "You might say I live over here now."

He paused, thinking he'd seen a flicker of response in Brian's eye.

"I'm a journalist," he said, hunching another inch forward. "Free lance. I do odd jobs, stringer shit, all over Europe, but the Six Counties are my specialty." He licked his lips. Keep it rolling, don't stop. "You know, Northern Ireland." He lifted a hand and nearly touched Brian's shoulder. "Hey, you've probably read some of my stuff."

"I never discuss politics or religion," Brian said, raising his glass to his lips. His eyes slid toward Tim and away again, and he breathed hard through his nose after he swallowed.

"You're telling me?" Tim said. He half raised his hand to Brian again, nearly putting it around the kid's shoulders. "That's all I ever get over here, is politics and religion." He forced a laugh, wagging his head. "Sometimes I wish I could just go back home and cover, I dunno, dog shows or something."

Brian set down his pint, his hand tight around the glass, twisting it against the bartop.

"Look, I'm sorry," he said, still refusing to look at Tim, his eyes wide and unfocused. "But it's early and I'm in a shitty mood, okay?"

"Hey, partner, I understand." Tim touched Brian's shoulder, but Brian twitched it off.

"I don't think you do, asshole," Brian snapped, turning to face Tim at last. "Fuck off."

He started to turn away, leaving his half-drunk pint on the bar, but Tim gripped Brian firmly by the arm, hooking his hand through the kid's elbow and leaning forward to whisper in his ear, "Brian."

He felt the boy stiffen, his elbow still in Tim's grip, his eyes bright suddenly with surprise and maybe even a little fear.

"I can't fart around with you any longer, Brian," Tim said, keeping his voice low. He glanced down the bar at the barman, lost in his paper. "We gotta talk."

"My name's not Brian," the kid said unsteadily. "My name is Jack."

He wrenched his arm out of Tim's grasp and walked quickly away from the bar, nearly running between the padded empty booths of the lounge. Tim started after him, leaving half his Bushmills on the bar behind him, his own heart pounding again, thrilled to know he was on the right track, but terrified that he'd blown it already. Come on, come on, come on, he told himself, twisting this way and that between the booths, play it light, play it easy, don't fuck it up. Brian didn't look back, pushing through a door onto the open deck, and Tim hustled a little faster, squeezing through the aisle toward the door, watching through the bright windows as the boy pushed against the wind toward the front of the ship, his hair blown back, the shoulders of his anorak bulging in the wind. At the door Tim paused a moment to catch his breath; then he pushed past the heavy door into the wind.

"Hey, Brian, wait." Out on the deck he was nearly blinded by the sudden light, the early morning sun shining straight into his eyes, and he ducked his head away from it and hurried forward into the stiff, salty wind, his eyes squeezed half shut, his fists balled up in the pockets of his parka. For a frightening instant he thought he'd lost the kid, and then, squinting against the light he saw Brian, a few steps back from the rail ahead. Tim felt a rush of relief: Brian was as far forward as he could go. There were no stairs; the only way off the slice of deck was over the cold, white rail onto the foredeck below, over the side into the sea, or back the way he had come. Brian turned around, and Tim saw him brace his legs against the weight of the wind hurled suddenly against his back. Tim himself struggled up the deck as if uphill, against the wind and the roll of the ship. He thanked his luck again; only a few people sat on the plastic benches under the lifeboats, well out of earshot, their hands in their pockets and their heads sunk into their collars like sleeping ducks.

At the rail the two of them wheeled slowly about each other. Tim made sure to keep between Brian and the rest of the deck, and he held up his palm, silently begging Brian for a moment to catch his breath.

"Listen, Brian," he said finally. "I know what you're thinking, and you've got nothing to worry about. Honest to God. I'm on your side." He held out his hand. "Tim McGuire." He mustered a smile. "From Boston."

Brian kept his hands at his sides and backed up against the cabin wall behind him, out of the wind, his weight shifting from leg to leg with the heaving of the sea.

"What makes you think my name is Brian?"

Tim lowered his hand to the rail but kept smiling.

"From the tag on your backpack, partner." He blew out a puff of air. "If you're not Brian Donovan of Six Forty-eight South Fifth Avenue, Ann Arbor, Michigan, then by God you've got his backpack." He grinned a little wider. "I didn't catch the zip code."

Brian stared at Tim, and Tim kept smiling, trying to slow his heart, drawing deep, salty breaths to clear his head.

"Hey, Brian, relax, boy." Tim leaned forward and tapped Brian matily on the shoulder. "I'm just a free-lance scribbler, no shit. I know what's going on and I'm here to help."

"So what's going on?" The kid looked scared, a small animal caught in the headlights of an oncoming car.

"What's going on," Tim sang, à la Marvin Gaye, rolling his shoulders. "It's okay. Jimmy Coogan put me in the picture. I know all about it."

"Who's Jimmy Coogan?"

"Okay, right, I understand." Tim winked, a coconspirator. "Hey, probably he didn't even tell you his name, right? Jimmy was a pro, no doubt about it, one of the best."

"I don't know anyone named Jimmy," Brian said. "I don't know what you're talking about."

Tim moved an inch forward along the rail. The kid was talking, that was the main thing.

"You're wary, and that's okay, Brian. I would be too." He smiled again. "I know what I must look like. I mean, I slept in my car last night."

He laughed, waiting for a reply, but Brian said nothing. Tim swallowed, his smile stiffening.

"Semtex, Brian. That ring a bell?" He kept his eyes steadily on the boy. "Ten pounds of it, which is a fuck of a lot, partner. Jimmy gave it to you to take to the lads in London, am I right? A big, and I mean big surprise for the Brits." He chuckled deep in his throat. "Ba-*boom!*"

He slammed his palm on the railing, making it ring dully, and Brian turned away from him, scraping his anorak against the grainy paint of the cabin wall. He leaned forward beyond the corner of the cabin, and after a moment Tim leaned on the rail next to him. The wind hit them full in the face, cold and salt-smelling and heavy with damp, and Tim let the boy be for a second, let him have a moment to collect his thoughts. The sky ahead was no longer blue; a whitish film of cloud had drawn itself across the sun like a veil, blurring it. The sea no longer glittered but only heaved, oily planes of cold green water tipping up and down. Up ahead the bow of the ship rose and fell against the gray horizon, clouds of white spray floating weightlessly over it to hiss upon the deck below.

"I'm a journalist, Brian." Tim leaned toward Brian, his hand on the boy's elbow. "I'm a bearer of tidings, okay, and I've got some good news and some bad news. The good news is I'm on your side, one hundred percent. When you met with Jimmy last night? In Dublin? I'm the guy who brought him across the border. If I were Special Branch, you think I'd be up here talking to you? Hell, you'd be down in the engine room, hand-cuffed to the boiler." He squeezed Brian's arm. "Like the man says, partner, your secret is safe with me."

He paused again, but Brian said nothing, gazing beyond the rail at nothing, his hair blown back from his forehead, his cheeks burnished by the wind.

"Now the bad news, Brian, is that Jimmy is dead." Tim shifted his grip on Brian's elbow and leaned forward over the rail to catch Brian's eye. "After he left you, he tried to get back across the border without my help, and the fucking SAS were waiting for him. They blew him away, Brian. He's got more holes in him now than a cheese grater. You with me so far, partner?"

Brian nodded, and Tim's heart soared.

"Fantastic!" He lifted his hand to Brian's shoulder and kneaded it through his anorak and his sweater. "Now here's the thing. On the way down last night, Jimmy told me that if anything happened to him, I was supposed to help Brian get the goods to London. He said to me, make sure Brian gets across okay. Everything depends on Brian."

Brian wrenched his shoulder out of Tim's grasp and pushed himself violently back from the rail, wide-eyed and trembling.

"You said you got my name from my pack, asshole." He glared at Tim, nearly smiling, and Tim heaved back from the rail, his heart hammering again, cursing himself silently for an idiot, a moron, a fuck-up. He blinked and stammered, trying to smile without success.

"I don't know what the fuck you're talking about, jerkoff." Brian pedaled back, away from the rail. "Stay away from me. Fuck *off.*"

He started to turn away, but Tim lunged forward and pinned him to the cabin wall by his shoulders. Suddenly the deck was unsteady, the roll of the ship threatening to unbalance him. He pushed his face at Brian, narrowing his eyes.

"You're in a world of shit, son," he said, his voice suddenly a register lower, "and you don't even know it."

Brian jerked his hands up to bat Tim's arms away, but just as abruptly Tim let go of Brian's shoulders and backed off, lifting his palms in a gesture of placation.

"Lemme show you something," he said, and he reached into the pocket of his parka and pulled out the snapshot, holding it up cupped in his palm. The blood was thumping in his ears, but to his relief his hand was steady. "Know what this is, partner?"

Brian, tensed to flee or strike out, settled back on his heels. His eyes gave him away; he couldn't hide the recognition in them. Tim licked his lips.

"That's a picture of you with a known terrorist, okay?" Tim waggled the photo in his palm, his voice low and insinuating. "That's seven days in the slammer right there, all by itself. That's all they need, Brian, to lock you up for a week so that Special Branch and MI5 and anybody else who wants to play can bounce you off the walls and ceiling like a fucking basketball."

Tim lowered the picture and leaned forward with his hand on the wall next to Brian's head, like an overfriendly drunk trying to pick up a girl at a party. He knew he stank just now, he knew his breath reeked of whiskey, but he pushed his face closer.

"And they're not the only ones, either." Tim let his voice drop to nearly a whisper. "There's something Jimmy forgot to tell you, there's a piece of the puzzle you haven't got, partner, and that is that before the fucking SAS nailed him last night, Jimmy had gone renegade. He ever tell you that? The stuff you're carrying is stolen from the Provos, and they're real pissed off about it. In fact, they're so pissed off that I wouldn't be surprised if they gave Jimmy to the Brits last night. The fucking SAS pulled the trigger, but his own guys dropped the dime on him, if you catch my drift. Still with me, partner?"

"I don't know what you're talking about."

"Goddamnit!" Tim banged the wall next to Brian's head, surprised and pleased by his own anger, at the way the boy jumped. "Don't fuck with me, boy! I'm the only friend you've got right now!" He drew a deep breath and lowered his voice. "You've got both the Brits and the Provos looking for you, and for your sake you better hope the Brits find you first."

He paused again, his eyes searching Brian's face, afraid of pushing too far. He looked away over the rail at the bow plunging against the sea, then back at Brian.

"I'm the only one who can get you out of this scot-free, Brian," he said. "Jimmy's people in London are screwed, any way you look at it. They sided with the wrong guy and they lost, so fuck 'em. They're history. You don't owe 'em a god-damn thing." He swallowed and lowered his voice. "So the smart thing for you to do is let me take you to the Provos, not Jimmy's guys, okay, but the regular guys, the mainstream guys, the winners. We'll return the stuff to them, I'll explain the situation vis-à-vis you and Jimmy, and you walk out with-out a scratch, guaranteed."

There was another long pause, and Brian looked away over Tim's shoulder.

"And if I don't go with you?" he said quietly.

"This is news, Brian." Tim lifted the photograph between the tips of his fingers again. "I gotta print it. I'd be a fool not to."

It was a threat, and there was no way to make it sound as if it wasn't, but even so Tim looked pleadingly at Brian, tipping the snapshot toward him as if he were offering it for sale.

"It's not a good likeness," he started to say, turning his head a little to look down at the photo, his weight still propped at arm's length against the cabin wall, and Brian snatched it and ducked around him. Tim roared and pushed away from the wall, nearly losing his balance, whirling around in time to see the Polaroid spinning like a Frisbee over the side. It soared up and then began to fall, and as Brian stood back and put his hands back in his pockets Tim heaved up against the rail next to him, the two of them breathlessly watching it fall, a pair of enraptured spectators at a skeet shoot. Tim stood shaking with rage, clutching the rail desperately, his stomach dropping as fast as the photograph. A sea gull dived for the picture, and Tim's heart stopped, but then the wind caught the snapshot broadside and flipped it away, and it fell twisting over and over, light side, dark side, light side, until it sliced into the green water and vanished. Tim turned to Brian, afraid to let go of the rail.

"Now you got shit," Brian said, giving Tim a smirk that made the reporter pry his hands off the rail and grab the boy's arm again, in a tight, angry grip. Brian tried to pull free, but he couldn't, and Tim hauled him around until they faced each other, squeezing Brian's arm until the boy's face twisted with pain.

"I don't know where Jimmy dredged you up," he said huskily, just loud enough to be heard over the wind, "but you got amateur written all over you. Jimmy only used you 'cause he was desperate. When the lads get hold of you they're going to rip your lungs out through your teeth and float you out to sea on the tide."

Brian tried again to pull away, but Tim hung on, digging his fingers through the anorak, his eyes brightening.

"So go wherever you want, punk, but remember: I'll be right behind you, watching every mistake you make and loving every minute of it." He made himself smile. "I'm going to stick to you like shit sticks to a shingle."

He let go of Brian, and Brian danced back, nearly stumbling on the slick deck. Tim took a step toward him, and the boy fled, jogging down the deck and back through the door into the lounge bar. The wind pushed Tim's back as if urging him after the boy, but he stood where he was, his lips pressed together, breathing hard through his nose, letting his pulse slow down.

"Round one," he promised himself, and he started down the deck.

On the ferry to Holyhead, Clare Delaney carried her hangover with her across the Irish Sea. She sat cross-legged on a wide seat in the aft lounge as if she were meditating, her hands on her knees, her eyes closed behind her sunglasses, her aching head tilted against one of the wings of the seat. She ignored the whining of bored children and the chatter of the television, playing some offensively chipper British morning show. She tried to sleep and couldn't, and she opened her eyes every few minutes or so, the light flooding in from around the edges of her sunglasses. To her dismay, on the one morning of her life when she would have been more than happy with a gloomy, overcast sky, the cold air around the ferry glittered painfully in every direction like broken glass, the rising sun flaring in the rippled surface of the Irish Sea like burning magnesium. Even behind the dark glasses the light tightened her headache like a band around her temples, making her squint everywhere she looked.

It didn't seem fair: after all, she and Eileen had not had that much to drink last night, certainly no more than the night before last with that guy in Sligo. What was his name? Larry, she thought, and immediately the band tightened. No, she corrected herself, Larry was the guy you dumped in Athlone. The guy you dumped in Sligo was the cute one, the one with the haircut, the one you danced with. Brian. The one who kissed you.

She groaned quietly at the memory. It serves me right, she decided, and she thought with miserable self-satisfaction that her hangover this morning had more to do with guilt than with Guinness. Somehow, in the last twenty-four hours she had managed to abandon three people, at least one of whom she was fond of. All right, be honest, she thought. Two of them. Maybe.

She'd never done anything like it before, never stood up anyone in her life, and now she'd done it three times in one day. The first time had been out of sheer embarrassment, although even now she couldn't decide exactly what she was embarrassed about, or even if she should be embarrassed at all. She'd lain awake in bed for nearly an hour on Saturday night, her heart racing, wondering every second if she'd missed an opportunity, if it was too late to change her mind. He's right next door, she thought, vacillating between the two poles of what she knew was a particularly self-defeating dialectic: was she a tease for letting him kiss her, or just a bitch for pushing him away? Finally she twisted violently over onto her side in the creaking bed and squeezed the pillow over her head to shut out the sound of her own voice, and she woke up early the next morning angry at him but also at herself. Why did she always blame herself for embarrassing situations, she wondered, shoving yesterday's clothes roughly into her pack. Maybe it was *his* goddamn fault! She thumped down the stairs dragging her pack like Christopher Robin petulantly trailing Winnie-the-Pooh by one leg, determined not to care about waking anybody, only to find herself all alone in the dining room, up even before the cook. Then, when she finally heard footsteps on the stair, her anger vanished like smoke up a chimney, and she found herself poised on the edge of her seat, ready to flee, her face hot, her hands unsteady, her heart hammering like a teenager's. But it was only the frowning proprietress, and the second time she heard steps, nearly upsetting her teacup into her lap, it was only Larry, the moon-faced postman from San Francisco. By then it made no difference why she was embarrassed —because she had or because she hadn't—she knew she'd rather die than face Brian again, and when Larry offered her a ride— without offering to wait for Brian, to her relief—she wanted to hug him.

Within an hour and a half she had dumped Larry too. This time she fled because the first time made it easy to do. Poor garrulous Larry had the unfortunate gift of talking in ever-increasing spirals, his conversation becoming somehow more general and less detailed the longer he went on. Leaving Sligo he was from North Beach, but by Athlone he was from the Bay Area, and Clare began to worry that by Dublin his address would have ballooned out like a fifth grader's to the solar system and the Milky Way. They stopped at the train station in Athlone so that Larry could use the bathroom, and while he was in the gents' Clare discovered the Dublin train idling at the platform. Within thirty seconds she had charmed the conductor into holding the train, dashed out to the car for her stuff, and hustled back to sling her pack into a seat and collapse next to it as the train lurched out of the station, inordinately pleased at her own cleverness: Nancy Drew, girl detective, escapes from the kidnappers, disguised behind her designer sunglasses.

Now, however, she sat sweating in the overheated lounge of the ferry, clutching her knees, trying to ignore the glide of the boat, a debauched Nancy Drew in need of a long, hot bath and a couple of Tylenol. Somebody, probably one of the restless children prowling the lounge, shook her shoulder, and she jerked the shoulder away, irritated but still too listless to open her eyes and bark at the kid. Instead she kept her eyes tightly shut behind her glasses and withdrew as far as she could, thinking of her worst betrayal, her third unannounced flight, only a few hours ago. Clare had arrived in Dublin yesterday at twelve thirty, and she splurged on a taxi all the way from Heuston Station to University College. Her cousin saw her first, shouting Clare's name all the way across a wide lawn, flinging her arms around Clare's neck, and generally acting as if she was honestly thrilled to have her American cousin drop in unannounced. She blew off her plans for the day with a tall young man with a head of stylishly unkempt red hair—he shrugged it off, trying to make it look as if he didn't care one way or the other—and led Clare off arm in arm, assuring her sotto voce that Clare's visit was a godsend, rescuing her from what promised to be one of the worst Sunday afternoons of her life.

"He's a jerk," she said of the tall boy. Eileen affected an American style of epithet.

At her flat she fed Clare chicken curry and rice, and then they took the bus to Killiney Hill, where they sat on a bench carved out of a squat obelisk of cracked and water-stained cement, gazing over the stunted, windblown pines at the long curve of pale sand enclosing Killiney Bay below. The water looked cold, the color of gun metal, and the peaks of the black mountains beyond were lost in the lowering gray sky. Eileen wanted to hear everything Clare had done since she'd left Cork, and Clare started out talking about the landscape and ended up talking about Brian, which, she realized with relief, was what she'd come to her cousin to do. She found herself building the suspense right up to the clinch at the top of the stairs, the two of them, Clare and Eileen, huddled together on the bench, their faces numbed and reddened by the wind. And when Clare finished, her cousin laughed out loud and shoved Clare by the shoulder.

"Christ, girl, you blew it," she laughed, and when Clare protested that she had not, Eileen jumped up and pulled Clare by the arm off the bench.

"Come on, then," she said, leading the way down the hill. "Let's go out tonight and break some hearts."

Back at Eileen's flat they opened a bottle of Spanish wine and dressed each other up, Eileen in a leather miniskirt and mismatched stockings, one white and one black, Clare in her jeans, but with Eileen's silk blouse, a pair of her earrings, and Eileen's high heeled black pumps, which made her ankles wobble. Together they ventured out to the bus stop, where they waited giddily for the 64A to take them to the center of town.

"We'll knock them over like skittles," Eileen declared out loud, aiming to scandalize the beshawled old women at the stop.

In the vicinity of St. Stephen's Green they teetered in the rain from pub to pub, the two of them becoming steadier on their high heels as the night wore on, clutching each other not for balance but for solidarity, or to emphasize a point, or for one to steer the other out of danger. Near the end of the evening they found themselves in a dimly lit cellar, where a folk group sang gamely in one room while Clare and Eileen sat at a table against the sweating stone wall in another, whispering loudly and stifling laughter over a guttering candle set in a jar. At a lull in the conversation Eileen reached across and clutched Clare's hand across the sticky tabletop, her eyes bright and liquid.

"I'd have had him," she said in a low voice, as if she were giving away a secret.

Clare pinched her lips together to keep from laughing and said, "Had who?"

"Your lad in Sligo, that's who." Eileen's eyes shone, and she fixed Clare's gaze with her own, tightening her grip on Clare's hand. "I'd have fucked him right there, at the top of the stairs, right up against the wall. Christ, why not?"

Clare wanted to laugh, but even so she felt her face get hot, and she wished Eileen would let go of her.

"I dunno," she said, gulping back a random hiccup. "AIDS?"

"Oh, fuck." Eileen let go of Clare and leaned back in her chair, rolling her eyes. "Any God who'd give you a fatal disease for a harmless night like that," she said, with a young Irishwoman's gift for blasphemy, "doesn't deserve the name."

They made big plans coming home in the taxi: Eileen was going to drop her classes and together they were going to run off to Spain in the morning. They'd rent a villa on Eileen's fee money—was it a villa or a hacienda, they couldn't decide—and they'd eat figs all day and drink wine out of goatskins and take lithe, beardless goatherds as lovers. This morning, though, with Eileen sprawled senseless next to her, her face buried in her pillow with her long black hair hiding every trace of pale Irish skin, Clare rolled out of bed, staggered to the sink, and threw up. Even running the water out of the clanking pipes for ten minutes to wash it all away didn't rouse Eileen an inch, and finally, in a panic, her head an aching riot of recrimination, self and otherwise, Clare pulled on yesterday's clothes with shaking hands, stuffed the rest into her pack, and crept out into the hall with the pack and her hiking boots clutched to her chest. She composed first one note for Eileen in her diary, then another, crumpling up each one, and finally shoved the third one back under the door.

"Gone to the Continent without you," she wrote blandly, not knowing what else to say. "See you at Christmas." Then she tiptoed down the stairs in her stocking feet, laced up her boots on the curb in the pearly predawn light, and fled on foot for the eight o'clock ferry to Holyhead.

It took her an hour and a half, marching along Rock Road between the sea and some sleeping Dublin suburb whose name she didn't know, the sun glaring over the horizon beyond the littered strand to her left, the new light picking out every brick and flashing from every blank window of the terraced houses on her right. In spite of the morning chill and the penetrating salt air she felt awful, her hair lank, her mouth gummy and sour, her eyes gritty behind her dark glasses. Squat Martello towers passed like milestones, too slowly, and ahead the long pier at Dún Laoghaire shone in the morning air like brass, impossibly far away, never getting any closer. Little two-car commuter trains ratcheted by noisily on a track between the sidewalk and the sea, making her wince, and watching one pass she saw a huge spraypainted graffito on the sea wall revealed in reverse, one word at a time, reading the whole thing only after the train had gone. PROVOS ARE BOORISH, it said, and then in what might have been the same hand—it was hard to tell when the letters were so big—AND BESIDES THEY DRESS BADLY.

With the ferry at last in sight, massive and gleaming, she heard the sharp cries of gulls hovering about the decks, and she started to jog down the sidewalk, hooking her thumbs through the straps of her pack and pulling it tight against her back. For the first time this morning she felt a little less sluggish, the band loosening around her temples, her stomach lifting weightlessly in the pleasant anxiety of departure. But once on board the sight of the terminus gliding away beyond the window of the lounge had startled her into nausea, and now, halfway to Holyhead, she sat clutching herself, enduring the gentle rise and fall of the ship, reluctant to move, unable to sleep.

She felt the hand on her shoulder again, and heard a voice close by that may or may not have been addressing her. Her irritation growing, she opened her eyes behind her sunglasses without moving her head. Across the lounge, on the seats under a long, bright window showing only high, white clouds, she saw a whole family asleep on each other's shoulders, huddled together like birds on a telephone wire. None of them was saying anything to her.

"Hey, Clare."

The hand pushed gently but insistently at her shoulder and she lifted her head, giving herself away, turning to see Brian leaning forward in the seat next to hers. Without meaning to she caught her breath, and she straightened up in the seat and turned a little to face him, pulling her shoulder out of his reach.

"Hi," she said, pushing her sunglasses more firmly up the bridge of her nose with a long finger. Some clever disguise: Nancy Drew, girl detective, asleep at the switch.

"How are you?" he said. He was smiling, but it didn't have quite the same effect as it had had a couple of nights ago, not when he looked as pale and stubbly as he did now. This morning, in fact, he looked as scruffy and tired as she felt, as if he was hung over too.

"I'm okay." She tried to smile back at him. "How are you?"

"Tired." He leaned his elbows on his knees and smiled at her sidelong. "Really tired. Been on the road too long."

"Uh-huh." She nodded, watching him from behind the safety of her glasses. There was a long pause while they both nodded at each other, and Clare shifted slowly in her seat, uncrossing her legs and pinching her knees together as she turned toward Brian. Finally they both spoke at once, and he deferred to her.

"Um, I was just going to ask where you were headed."

"London." He clasped his hands between his knees. "I'm going back to London. Yourself?"

"Me too." She pulled her knees up to her chest and wrapped her arms around them. "Then maybe on to Paris. I don't know."

"Right."

They sat nodding again, and Brian turned to look over his shoulder, twisting around with a hand on his knee to look across the lounge.

"So anyway," he said, still facing away from her, "I was just pacing around the deck the last couple of hours and I thought I'd come in out of the wind and I saw you sitting here." As he talked he slowly untwisted himself, turning back to her. "And I thought I'd come over and wake you rudely out of a sound sleep and apologize for the other night."

"Oh." Clare felt her face heat up.

"Because I was way out of line and I wanted to say I'm sorry." He lifted his blue eyes to her. "I was drunk, but that's no excuse. I acted like a jerk and I apologize."

"That's okay." Clare hugged her knees and felt her face burning like a neon sign.

"Because I like you, Clare." He kept his eyes on her and smiled again, and this time, fatigue and stubble notwithstanding, it had some of its old charm. "I've had sort of a crush on you ever since we met on the bus, and when I saw you sitting here I thought, this is, like, my second chance, so don't blow it."

She found herself smiling back at him, and she lifted her shoulders and let them drop.

"I'm sorry too," she said. "I mean for ditching you like that."

Brian shrugged and said, "Forget it. I understand."

"No, I won't forget it." She dropped her arms and clutched the ankles of her boots, leaning forward and giving him a smile that would make her mother proud, a little angry at herself and at him, but flattered all the same. "Because I like you too," she said, still protected by her sunglasses, "that's sort of why I ran like that, 'cause, you know . . . you know?"

"I know." Brian laughed and sat up straight, leaning back expansively in his seat, and Clare felt her stomach tighten.

"Friends?" she said, offering her hand in two hesitant jerks.

"Friends," he said, taking her hand. "So I can sit next to you on the train and you won't jump out the window or anything?"

She jerked her hand away, pleased behind her glasses at his surprise.

"No funny business?" she said, lifting a finger.

He laughed again and raised his hand with the first three fingers pressed together, his pinkie hooked by his thumb.

"Scout's honor," he said.

Coming into Holyhead Clare and Brian stood as far forward as passengers were allowed, huddled in the wind nearly shoulder to shoulder at the rail. The sky, which had been clear when she'd boarded the ferry, was now a featureless gray, and beyond the plunging bow a parabolic hump of dark Welsh cliff climbed slowly out of the haze at the horizon. As they talked the cliffs rose higher to become a long headland, undulating like a sine curve, tiny white puffs of waves crashing soundlessly against the rocks below, the dim outline of the peaks of Snowdonia rising beyond like a painted backdrop.

The two of them had reached the point of joking about the day before, and when Brian asked her about what's his name, the mailman from San Francisco, Clare buried her face in her hands, groaning and laughing at the same time.

"You don't want to know," she said, lowering her hands and giving him a smile like a warning.

As the ship rounded the headland they heard at last the hollow rumble of the waves against the rocks, and straight ahead a pale green checkerboard of farmland was tipped gently toward the sea, as though presented for their approval. She told him selected highlights of her night out with Eileen, and he nodded periodically and said "uh-huh" to show he was paying attention. But he was still a little nervous around her, she decided, turning his bright eyes away from her as other people crowded up on deck to see the landfall, kids hoisting themselves up on the rail, pale teen-agers craning over each other's shoulders, pairs of middle-aged women in cloth coats leaning together with their headscarves rippling in the wind like flags. Once when he was gazing down the deck away from her she stopped talking and waited to see what he'd do, and he turned back to her with a corner of his lips lifted and repeated what she'd just said.

"Just checking," she said.

The town of Holyhead came into view, red and gray houses spread up the hillside and punctuated with steeples, above a long breakwater protecting the placid water of the harbor. Clare tugged Brian away from the rail and led him back along the deck to beat the rush at the luggage rack.

"This way we can get a good seat on the train," she said as they hauled their packs out of the racks, but Brian was looking about the already crowded room as if he'd lost something.

"Uh, what about customs?" he said as he squeezed up next to her near the door.

"Forget customs." She leaned near him and lowered her voice, the silence of the vestibule like that of a crowded elevator. "They just sort of look at you as you go by."

She watched him from behind her sunglasses, and he seemed a little seasick as the ferry drifted weightlessly up to the terminus, his skin even paler than before, a little sweat coming out along his forehead in the heat of the quiet vestibule.

A moment later, though, they were free of the crowd, Clare leading the way down the wide, switchbacked ramp, leaning backward to compensate for the weight of her pack. Near the bottom she looked back and saw Brian stopped near the wall, tugging busily at the straps of his pack as people brushed past him carrying luggage and plastic bags bulging with duty-free liquor. She rolled her eyes and trudged back up the ramp against the stream of people, and she hovered behind him, tightening a strap behind his back.

"Is that better?" she said, and he mumbled something, his head down while he fumbled at his waist. Up ahead the first of the crowd passed two bobbies who rocked on their heels outside a doorway. A couple of the passengers began to run, through the waiting room and out onto the train platform. A customs man in a dark blue jacket came out of a doorway behind the bobbies and peered over his glasses at the crowd trotting past.

"Brian, we're going to miss the train," Clare said, tugging at another strap.

"Uh-huh." He suddenly started down the ramp again, jerking the strap out of Clare's hand. At the foot of the ramp the customs man and the bobbies conferred with their heads together, and Clare jogged past them to catch up with Brian in the cold, diesel-smelling air of the train station. A yellow-and-blue Inter-City sat humming at the platform, doors opening all along the train as a couple of Britrail guards shouted "London Euston!" and languidly waved people aboard. Brian stopped short again, and Clare nearly ran into him, while other people veered around them and hustled onto the cars. He turned abruptly, swinging his backpack around heedlessly, and glanced back up the ramp into the advancing crowd.

"Is this the only train?" he said in a remote voice, as if he was thinking of something else entirely.

"Yes," Clare laughed, and she grabbed him by the wrist and dragged him across the platform, over the white line, and into the rear car.

"It's nicer at the back of the train," she said over her shoulder as Brian followed her up the aisle of the empty car. "They're usually the last to fill up. Everybody wants to sit up by the snack bar."

She slung her pack behind two seats and slid in to the window, facing forward, but Brian dumped his pack into the window seat across from her and leaned around it to watch out the window as the last of the passengers from the ferry ran for the train. Outside the window she heard the indecipherable electronic blare of some announcement, and the clack and thump of doors slamming shut all down the platform.

"Did you bring any food?" she said. She took off her glasses, squinting a bit in the bright light.

"What's that?" Brian leaned back in his seat and blinked at her.

"I said," Clare went on, raising her voice as if he were hard of hearing, "did you bring any food? The stuff on the train is really awful."

"Uh, no." He leaned forward again to look out the window at the empty platform. From somewhere out of sight came the rising shriek of a guard's whistle, and the train began to move almost imperceptibly, the clock and the schedule boards creeping by.

"Hold it!" came a shout from the platform, loud enough for Clare to turn and see a fat man running alongside the train at a speed that belied his bulk, his parka flying behind him, his potbelly wobbling, his face red.

"Look at that guy," Clare laughed, glancing at Brian, but he was bent over into the aisle, nearly out of sight under the table, fussing with his bootlaces. He cocked an eye up over the rim of the table at Clare.

"Do you know him?" he said.

"Who?"

Brian lifted his eyebrows toward the window without raising his head.

"The guy you were laughing at."

"No." She laughed again, thinking it a strange question, and she pressed her temple to the cool glass as the train lurched to a stop and the fat man huffed out of sight. The sound of a door banging shut reverberated down the platform, and the train strained forward again. Clare pulled her head away from the window and sat back, and she watched Brian, still bent over, glance up and down the aisle and then sit slowly up, leaning back in his seat and drawing a deep breath.

"Are you okay?" she said, tugging her sunglasses between her hands. "You look, I don't know, seasick or something."

"Did he get on?" Brian tipped his head back against the seat and peered down his nose at her.

"Who?" Clare began to feel queasy again herself, and she wasn't sure why.

"The fat guy. Did he get on?"

"Yeah, I think so." She glanced out the window at the last of the platform girders gliding by, as if the man might still be running alongside. "Do *you* know him?"

"He's following me." Brian sat very still, his head rocking gently with the acceleration of the train. His gaze was a little frightening, as if he were passing judgment on her.

"He's following you?" Clare winced at her own voice, sounding high and inane, and she shook her head once and said, "Why is he following you?"

"Listen, Clare." Brian leaned forward suddenly, clasping his hands on the table. "Maybe you should ditch me again. Or maybe I should ditch you. Or something." He turned his face away to look out the window across the car. The back gardens of Holyhead drifted by, an accelerating succession of weathered sheds and white laundry and battered, rusty bicycles.

"Why is he following you?" Clare dipped her head over the table and lowered her voice.

"This has got nothing to do with you, okay?" He swung his gaze past her to look out their window. He lifted his hand to the top of the pack in the seat next to him.

"Brian," she said, gritting her teeth and glaring at him. "Why is he following you?"

He met her gaze, and he lowered his hand from the pack and drew a breath. He looked down at his hands.

"Remember I told you about my grandfather?" he said.

"Yes." She sat very still and did not take her eyes off him. She remembered their walk two days ago, standing in the wind on top of Knocknarea.

"He was in the IRA, did I tell you that?"

"Yes."

"Well, I brought some money over for him." He lifted his eyes to her; they were bright now, and he was nearly smiling. "On his behalf, I mean. Ten thousand dollars. For their pension fund."

"What pension fund?" Her hands twisted the sunglasses between them.

"The Provos." Brian tapped the table with his clasped hands.

"The IRA." He swiveled his eyes away, out the window and back to her again. "He sends money over for the families of guys who got killed or caught. This time I brought it over and gave it to this cousin of mine who's in Sinn Fein, which is—"

"I know." Clare made herself keep her eyes on him. She felt her pulse racing.

"You know?" His eyes widened.

"I mean, I know what Sinn Fein is."

"Oh." Brian licked his lips and pushed himself back, his hands on the edge of the table. "Anyway, I gave it to her, and she got caught. With the money, I mean."

"Is that, like, illegal?" Stupid question, Clare, she thought, blushing at her own stumbling naïveté.

"Yes." Brian nearly smiled. "I could go to jail, too, for bringing it."

"And this guy . . ."

"This guy came up to me on the ferry, Clare," Brian said, leaning forward again, peering up at her from under the lock of curly hair over his forehead, "and he said he was an American, a journalist. He knew my name, he knew about my cousin, and he knew that I brought the money." Brian searched her face, trying to capture her gaze again. "He threatened me, Clare. He said he'd turn me in if I didn't give him information."

Clare scowled down at the glasses between her hands as if they were broken.

"That doesn't sound like a journalist," she said.

"I know." She could feel Brian's eyes on her, searching for a reaction, but she didn't look up. "But it doesn't sound like a cop either, or he would have arrested me by now, right?"

"I guess." Clare nodded, her chin tucked into her throat. "That makes sense."

Her heart was pounding now, nearly louder than the rhythm of the train. As carefully as her hands would allow, she folded the sunglasses and centered them on the table, leaning back and pulling her hands away to her lap. She drew a breath and said, "So what do you think he is?"

"I don't know," Brian said, and behind him the door at the

front of the car slid open and the fat guy swayed through it as
though drunk, wedging himself in the narrow aisle between the
toilets with a hand on either wall. He was still flushed and
breathless, his face glistening with sweat in the bright fluorescent light of the car, his ginger hair pushed up along one side of
his head where he'd slept on it.

"Is it him?" Brian whispered.

"Yes."

The man stared down the car at her, his chest heaving under
the tight buttons of his shirt. His eyes hooded, Brian slowly sat
up straight in his chair, until his blond curls were visible over
the top of his seat. Then the fat man pushed himself into the
aisle, handing himself along the backs of seats until he was
four or five rows back from Brian, and he sagged back into a
window seat, his gut squeezed up against the edge of the table.

"Is he watching us?" Brian said in a low voice, his eyes
focused like a sleepwalker's on nothing at all.

"No, he's looking out his window."

The man was mopping his face with a huge red handkerchief,
watching out the window with nearly the same dead light in
his eyes as Brian, seeing nothing, ostentatiously not looking in
their direction. The man clutched his handkerchief on the table
and pushed his thick fingers back into his ginger hair, and even
at a distance she saw that he needed a shower and clean
clothes. He vividly reminded her of the kind of gross Philadelphia
Irishman who had terrified her as a girl every St. Patrick's
Day, boisterously drunk at eleven o'clock in the morning, staggering alongside the parade in a green hat and puking in the
gutter as she cowered behind her father, and suddenly she
hated him, hated his thick, florid features and his piggy little
eyes, hated how he'd pushed his gut ahead of him as he ran
down the platform a few minutes ago, hated the way he had
lurched down the aisle just now.

Brian was leaning forward again across the table and saying
something to her, but she didn't hear what it was. Instead she
watched his wide blue eyes, which for the first time in the
three days she'd known him looked vulnerable and beseeching.

This wasn't the cocky guy playing at vulnerability on top of Knocknarea, charming her with colorful tales of his grandfather, nor was it the guy she'd danced with, and half wanted at the top of the stairs, the night before last. Today his eyes were wide and scared and nearly out of control, and she wondered what Eileen would do now. Have him up against the wall? Or, more likely, run like hell, especially from someone whose need was as great right now as Brian's?

Up the aisle the ginger man blew his nose into his handkerchief. Partly she was afraid for Brian, afraid that this was something his smile and blue eyes couldn't get him out of, but mostly she just hated the man. Hatred was a feeling that she'd never allowed herself before, that she'd never felt was wholesome or useful, but now she let it wash over her like heat, a heat that calmed her stomach and steadied her hands. She smiled to herself, at the thought of baffling Eileen, her mother, and Brian all at the same time.

"Listen," she said suddenly, reaching out to lay her hand on Brian's wrist. "Do you want to ditch this guy?"

She'd interrupted him in mid-sentence, and he blinked back at her open-mouthed as if she'd spoken to him in a foreign language.

" 'Cause it would be really easy to do." She smiled at him, letting herself go, her heart racing, a smile to make Eileen proud and astonish her mother.

Brian stammered something. She lifted a finger to her lips to quiet him, and she picked up the sunglasses, snapped them open with a flick of her wrist, and put them on. Then she smiled again and leaned back in her seat.

"Trust me," she said. "I'm good at this."

Brian rode backward all the way into England, the train rocketing along the Welsh coast like a carnival ride designed to keep him from facing forward, carrying him toward a destination he couldn't see. Everything about the ride made him feel queasy and weak: the unpleasantly bright orange seats and cream-colored walls of the nearly empty car. The uneven rhythm of the train rocking over points, the sour horn of the engine up ahead. The sight through the window across the car of mountains rising in dim blue ramparts, the taller peaks lost in the overcast. The sight out his own window of the sea, as gray and wrinkled as elephant hide, slow breakers rolling up to give out on the dull mud flats. His peripheral vision was startled again and again by the shabby caravan parks flashing between the train and the beach, by the rusted derricks of abandoned factories, by the skeletons of dead, off-season amusement parks, the bare girders of roller coasters hunched over the littered beach like the steel ribs of shipwrecks.

Until the ferry, Brian had managed to maintain a comfortable numbness, rising out of a fitful sleep to coast unthinking through the bus ride to Dún Laoghaire, gliding up the stairs to the ferry like a sleepwalker. Coming up into the lounge and seeing the barman behind the bar, it had come to him with the fractured but convincing logic of a dream that he might as well have beer for breakfast. A few minutes later, though, his ears had rung with the sound of his own name spoken by a stranger, his stomach had clenched like a fist at the sight of Maire's Polaroid, he and the Provo pale and pink-eyed in the bleaching light of the flash. His reptile brain had taken over, pumping him full of adrenaline and hissing at him to run like hell, and he'd managed to snatch the photograph and pitch it over the side. Then he'd prowled the decks of the ferry for an hour, almost managing to convince himself that the fat guy was a hallucination brought on by lack of sleep and Guinness on an empty stomach, but the man waited around every corner like a ghost, watching Brian with his dead eyes. Finding Clare asleep in the aft lounge was almost as much of a relief as finding Molly, and for a moment, sitting across from her on the train at Holyhead, waiting for it to start, he'd thought he'd done it, that he'd pulled it off, that it was a downhill ride to London.

But now he couldn't even turn around, because McGuire was there. Brian could hear him every few minutes, like a foghorn,

announcing his presence. He coughed, he belched, he cleared
his throat, and once he issued a long fart in descending pitch
like a sigh, as if he were squeezing every last pocket of gas out
of his body. Brian wished he could laugh. But with each little
noise Brian was certain that McGuire had moved closer, until
he was in the seat behind Brian, or across the aisle, or finally
leaning against the back of Brian's seat, close enough for Brian
to smell the man's whiskey breath again. He closed his eyes,
waiting for a whisper in his ear, waiting for a hand on his
shoulder, but opening his eyes again all he saw was Clare
sitting across from him, her head rocking against the headrest
of her seat, smiling to herself as if she were the one with the
secret.

She wouldn't let him talk. If he started to say something the
corners of her mouth drew down and she raised a finger to her
lips; when he couldn't stand it anymore and put his palms on
the table to push himself up out of his seat, she tightened her
thin lips and slowly shook her head until he settled back in his
seat again. He'd no idea what she had in mind, but he clung to
the idea of trusting her like a man dangling from a cliff, afraid
to look down. In fact, when he couldn't take looking at the
gloomy sea any longer, he watched her across the table, wondering if she had fallen asleep, or if she was watching him back
from behind her dark glasses. Just when he had decided that
she had accomplished the impossible, that she had managed to
fall asleep with McGuire only a few seats away, she yawned or
scratched her elbow or pushed her long fingers back through
her hair.

"I need a shower," she murmured, but when he started to
answer her she frowned theatrically at him to keep quiet.

"Yes, ma'am," he said, smiling weakly, and she shushed him
like an angry librarian.

Behind him the door at the front of the car slid open and a
conductor called out, "Tickets, please." Then Clare stirred,
sliding into the aisle to get into her pack, and Brian peered into
his wallet. He heard the man transact his business with McGuire
without hearing what they said, and then he was standing at

the end of Clare and Brian's table, swaying from side to side with the rocking of the train.

"Tickets?" he said.

"How much to London?" Clare said, smiling brightly. She had pushed the sunglasses up into her hair. Her wallet and a small black leather notebook lay on the table before her.

"Twenty-three pounds," the conductor said, rubbing his nose. As Brian offered him Irish money he dropped his hand and said, "We don't take that."

Brian heard himself stammering uselessly, but Clare touched his hand to silence him and filled out a traveler's check for two tickets.

"You can owe me," she said, as the conductor sighed and raised his eyes to the strip of fluorescent lights above, puzzling out the exchange rate in his head. As he made change Clare asked him how long it was to London.

"The ferry was late," he said sternly, as if it had been their fault. "We'll be getting into Euston at half six."

"When's the next stop?" Clare said.

"Chester." He glanced dourly down the length of the car, then looked at his watch. "In fifteen and a half minutes."

Clare reached across the table and took Brian's wrist to look at his watch.

"Will we be stopping long enough for me to get a newspaper?" she said sweetly.

The conductor looked severely at Brian, as if he were to blame for Clare, and for an instant Brian was unreasonably afraid that the man was going to speak to him by name.

"I doubt it very much, miss," he said, turning back to Clare, shaking his head like a reproving schoolmaster. "We're trying to make up time."

"Well, thank you." Clare gave him a brilliant smile and tipped her glasses back onto her nose.

"Ta."

As the conductor went forward and left the car, Clare reached across the table and slid Brian's watch off his wrist, placing it on the table where they could both see it. Brian narrowed his eyes at her and spread his hands, instead of saying out loud, "What now?" Clare shook her head and leaned her elbows on the table. She opened the notebook, slid a pen out of the binding, and began to write. Brian recognized his own name upside down, but it was too hard to follow the rest, so he sat back and closed his eyes, trying to keep himself from turning around to look at McGuire, trying to pretend that he wasn't even there. But everything seemed magnified with his eyes closed: the rocking of the train shaking him from side to side in his seat, the hum of the lights overhead, the scratch of Clare's pen against the page, the rhythm of the wheels against the track. Behind him McGuire cleared his throat again, a long, drawn-out process that worked its way up and down in pitch like a bagpiper playing scales. Brian screwed his eyes tighter as if that would shut out the sound, and at last McGuire gave up with a few, final percussive coughs.

Finally Brian opened his eyes and saw by his watch on the table that only a couple of minutes had passed. Beyond the window across the car the mountains had dwindled to low, green hills; out his own window he saw the sea as a gray line beyond marshy green fields and wide blond tidal flats. Clare reached across the table and touched his hand, and she tore a page out of her notebook and slid it across the table to him. He picked it up and read through the note once without understanding a word of it; then he drew a breath, shook his head, and read it again. He looked across at Clare, who watched him solemnly, her mouth a straight line under the insect gaze of her glasses. She lifted her eyebrows at him.

"Eleven minutes," she said.

"Okay," he said.

Five minutes out of the station the outskirts of Chester had appeared outside the train, abandoned-looking warehouses and long lines of redbrick terraces, some of them snaking alongside the track, others flashing by on end like rows of corn. Clare gazed at Brian's watch with her elbow on the table, her cheek propped against her knuckles, her glasses pushed slightly askew. Brian stared hard out the window at the narrow houses gliding by shoulder to shoulder. His mouth was dry, his stomach tight, his heart beating slow and hard. Don't think, he told himself.

With four minutes to go Brian could feel the train slowing, pressing his back more firmly against his seat, dislocating his gut as if it floated free inside him like a gyroscope. Clare lifted her head from her half-curled fist, the bloodless white imprint of her knuckles still in her cheek, and she said quietly, "Take off your boots."

"What?" He started at the sound of her voice.

"Take . . . off . . . your . . . boots," she said slowly. She smiled. "It's a great touch. Trust me."

Brian swung his legs into the aisle and bent over, unlacing both boots simultaneously, one with each hand. He risked a glance at McGuire and looked down again; McGuire was staring at him. Brian tugged off one boot, wriggling his toes against the thin carpet, and he made himself look back down the aisle at McGuire, meeting his eyes and nodding. McGuire's expression didn't change, but he didn't look away. Brian pulled off the other boot and pushed them both under the table, and he sat up and looked at Clare.

"It's time," she murmured, her cheek pressed against her knuckles again. "Three minutes."

Brian drew a breath and slid his watch onto his wrist. He pushed himself halfway up out of his seat.

"Don't forget my boots," he said.

"*Go*," Clare said under her breath, not looking up.

Brian stood and walked up the aisle in his stocking feet to McGuire's seat. McGuire looked up and watched him come; Brian could feel his heart beating faster even as the rhythmic clacking of the rails got slower and slower. As McGuire's eyes followed him, Brian slid into the seat across from him and slouched down with his hands in the pockets of his anorak. McGuire gazed blankly across the table, his blunt features set like wax.

Brian turned his face toward the window, watching McGuire sidelong.

"I'm sorry," he said.

McGuire said nothing. Brian licked his dry lips and said, "Look, I acted like a jerk, and I apologize." He turned to McGuire, waited a moment for him to speak, and then went on. "I just didn't know what to think, is all. You came out of nowhere, okay, and I got scared."

He waited again, watching McGuire.

"It's Tim, right?" he said, and this time, after an endless moment, McGuire nodded.

"Like you said, Tim, we're on the same side." Brian smiled as best he could. "I guess we should act like it, huh?" He balled his fists in his pockets, felt the pulse beating in his wrists.

"Yeah." McGuire nodded again, still refusing to smile.

"So I thought, what the hell, it's a long way to London yet." Brian pulled his hand out of his pocket, praying for it not to shake, and looked at his watch. Two minutes to Chester. "So how about we cut this little charade and I'll buy you a beer?"

McGuire watched him for a long moment, and Brian felt waves of heat rippling under his skin. He looked out the window at a trainyard, at long lines of battered blue cars crawling by. The train was at half speed now, he could feel it. He turned back to McGuire.

"It's the least I could do, right?" His lips were still dry, but he would not let himself lick them again. "I mean, I owe you one."

"You got that right." McGuire nodded with self-conscious dignity, his eyes narrow.

"So how's a beer sound?" In his pocket, Brian dug his fingers deeper into his palms.

At last McGuire gave a thin smile, and he said, "A beer sounds just about right."

"Great." Brian breathed deep and smiled back; he slid out of the seat as McGuire sucked in his belly and pushed himself out into the aisle. Brian stepped toward the front of the car, but McGuire stood in his way. Brian froze and caught his breath.

McGuire rocked from side to side with the train; he lifted his chin over Brian's shoulder.

"Your lady friend?"

"Ah, she doesn't drink this early." He moved to start forward, but McGuire stood a moment longer gazing down the car at Clare. Brian was on the verge of turning to look at her himself when McGuire swung his gut around and started forward, grabbing the back of each seat as he went. Brian followed him, afraid to glance back, and at the end of the car McGuire held the door for him.

"After you, partner," he said, smiling like a cat.

"Right." Brian smiled tightly and edged past McGuire's gut.

In his stocking feet Brian felt almost naked, his feet sliding alarmingly on the metal flooring between the cars, the wind there piercing straight through the wool to his toes. He felt every bump and corrugation in the floor as he led the way up the next car. Tim huffed along behind him, the pale faces of the other passengers turning toward them like flowers as they passed. Brian's stomach fluttered with each dazed glance; he half expected one of them to speak to him, to call him by name, to reach out into the aisle and catch his arm. The cars were more crowded farther forward, full of conversation and cigarette smoke, and they had to stop two or three times to let people go by the other way carrying drinks and sandwiches on plastic trays. Brian grinned stupidly at them as they nudged by. Through the windows he saw the littered tracks and grimy walls of the trainyard gliding by slower than before. He resisted the urge to look at his watch again.

"Long way to the bar car," he said as he held the door for McGuire between cars.

"Hey, you chose the last car to sit in, son, not me." He slapped Brian's shoulder and laughed deep in his throat. He paused in the vestibule to let Brian get ahead of him again.

Halfway through the next car Brian saw the adjacent track dead-end against a pile of cinders, and then, rising from the gravel, the bare concrete ramp at the end of a station platform. His heart began to pound, and he thought of Clare, wondering if he'd read the note right, wondering if she'd decided not to go through with it, if she'd decided to ditch him again after all.

Behind him he heard Tim's labored breath over the clatter of the train and the noise of conversation, and through the window he saw a post glide by bearing a black-and-white sign that said Chester. He drew a deep breath and stopped suddenly in the aisle to pat the pockets of his anorak. McGuire bumped into him from behind, stopping with his hands on Brian's shoulders.

"Shit," Brian said, and he turned around out of McGuire's grasp to face him. "I forgot my cigarettes."

McGuire frowned and looked about the car, as if a stray pack might be lying around.

"You go on ahead," Brian said, patting the breast pocket of his shirt through his sweater. "I'm going to run back to get them."

For an instant McGuire hesitated, frowning at Brian. Brian felt light-headed and weak, as if he was about to pass out, and he smiled and rolled his eyes, miming disgust at his own absent-mindedness. Through the window he heard the metallic voice of the public address on the station platform, saw people crowding up toward the train.

"Gotcha." McGuire winked and squeezed past Brian with his hands on Brian's shoulders, nearly forcing him into the lap of the woman seated behind him. Brian waited as McGuire moved away up the aisle, and he felt the gentle lurch of a complete stop, saw a man outside pulling a suitcase on casters past the window.

"Tim, wait," he called out. McGuire stopped and turned, and Brian fumbled for his wallet and pulled out a couple of pound notes. I'm capable of a nice touch or two myself, he thought, and he jogged up the aisle to McGuire.

"Get a couple of Guinness if they got 'em, okay?" He pushed the bills into McGuire's hand, but the fat man smiled down at the money, bemused.

"They don't take these, partner." He looked as though he were about to wink at Brian, waggling the green bank notes between his thumb and forefinger. "Irish money."

"Oh." Brian felt his pulse leaping out of control. He let his mouth hang open, speechless.

"I got it covered, man." Tim laughed, insufferably familiar, and he banged Brian on the shoulder. "Go get your cigs."

Brian wheeled around, queasy with relief, and walked briskly back the way they had come, into a line of new passengers pushing up the aisle with bags and children held before them, scowling from side to side for empty seats. He lowered his shoulder and forced his way past them until he reached the end of the car, where he looked back. The door at the front of the car was shut; McGuire was gone.

A couple of women barked at him as he shoved his way into the vestibule, and he knocked back a man as he pushed out into the cold air of the platform. The man shouted at him, but Brian was already running, vaulting suitcases and side-stepping children, weaving like a wide receiver through the people moving in slow motion down the platform. The concrete under his feet was cold and hard, and he felt the shock of every footfall through his bones all the way up to the top of his head. But it didn't matter, it was a crisp autumn afternoon and the kid was hot today, the kid was almost there, and he felt he could almost lift his feet and soar the last ten, fifteen, twenty yards to the goal line, all the pressures of the last three days released in him like a giant spring. A teen-aged boy froze wide-eyed in Brian's path, and Brian spun him aside and skipped around a woman pushing a stroller. Somebody yelled and clutched at his arm, and Brian slipped free without breaking stride, already beginning to laugh. All he heard were the incomprehensible echo of the public address, the thud of his own feet on the concrete, the pounding of the blood in his ears—all of it like a crowd cheering him on, screaming his name.

Then for a sickening moment his gut seized up. The platform at the end of the train was empty, there was no one there, and he nearly stumbled and fell as if he had been blindsided. Where was Clare? Where was his pack? He kept running, but he felt his heart twisting painfully, felt his legs giving way under him.

"No," he moaned aloud, beginning to stagger to a stop, and up ahead the forward door of the last car swung open and Clare's red backpack sailed out the door and landed with a thump on the platform. Brian nearly fainted with relief, and he pushed himself faster again, running along the train and swinging into the open door. He collided with the wall and wrenched aside the sliding door to see Clare trotting up the aisle with both arms wrapped around his backpack. He stood breathlessly aside, trying to laugh, and held the door for her.

"I thought," he gasped, rolling light-headed toward the open door behind her, "I thought . . ."

"Come *on!*" she called over her shoulder from the platform, dropping his pack next to hers. He swung out the door after her, stumbling against her and spinning her around by the shoulders. Clare laughed and sat down on the packs, pulling off her sunglasses. He danced a few steps past her, watching down the train as the last little puddles of people at the car doors emptied into the train. He wanted to shout but he didn't have the breath to do it.

He spun back to her suddenly and said, "My boots!"

"Oh, shit!" Her face fell, wide-eyed and slack-jawed, and she struggled to push herself up. But Brian whooped and ran for the car again as doors began to thump shut down the length of the train.

"Brian!" He heard her laughing as he skidded through the vestibule and jerked open the sliding door. He ran down the aisle to their seat, ducking under the table and grabbing his boots in one hand. The car jerked forward and stopped again as he stood and bolted up the aisle. Then he was out of the car, flipping the door shut behind him, twisting himself nearly off balance. Clare was laughing, and a red-faced guard was advancing on them both from across the platform.

"Clare, catch!" He tossed the boots toward her, the two of them tumbling slowly apart, their laces flying, and she gave a little yelp and caught one of them. The train had begun to move, and he ran alongside it past bright windows full of dulled faces. He could almost hear the adrenaline thundering in his veins, and he laughed to think that he could run all day if he had to. He came abreast of the bar car just as the train began to move as fast as he could run, and he saw Tim sitting next to the window, sipping beer out of a plastic cup, two dark bottles and another cup on the table before him. Brian pounded on the window with his fist, and Tim looked up and choked on his mouthful of beer, spraying it everywhere, jumping to his feet and upsetting the bottles. He splayed his beefy hand against the glass, his face red and constricted, and Brian ran gulping for breath alongside, jerking his arm up and cocking his middle finger up out of his fist. Then the train began to pull away, and Brian slowed to a walk, gasping and shaking and laughing. Touchdown, he thought, wishing he had a football to spike against the platform. Instead he bent over with his hands on his knees while the end of the train rumbled past him, and he drew great, ragged breaths as he watched the last car dwindle up the track.

This time there were three other people across the table from Maire in the interrogation room, and one of them was a woman. The two men were Glassie, looking no worse than he usually did for having kept the same hours as Maire for the past three or four days, and a tall, long-faced man in a tailored suit whom Glassie introduced as the Director of Public Prosecutions. He was here, Glassie said, to offer a deal, a chance for her to go free in exchange for certain information pertaining to the location of ten pounds of Czechoslovakian plastic explosive. All other charges pertaining to the PTA would be dropped, added the DPP himself, in a country accent that belied his sophisticated suit. In spite of his importance, the DPP stood, leaning in the corner under the video camera with his hands clasped behind his back and his expensive suit coat hanging open to reveal his red braces and the full length of his green silk tie. There were only three chairs in the room, and the DPP had given his up to the other woman. She sat next to Glassie in a stylish, tailored suit of her own, her chin supported between her thumb and forefinger, her thick black hair, newly washed, threatening to topple forward over her forehead. She watched Maire across the table with her bright eyes narrowed and her small mouth pursed, as if she were about to share a laugh with Maire that these men couldn't understand. When Glassie had introduced her only by name as "Miss Pulleine," the woman had corrected him, pushing back her rebellious hair with her free hand and saying "*Ms.* Pulleine" in a Whitehall drawl, and the accent and lack of announced affiliation convinced Maire that Ms. Pulleine was MI5. In that moment Maire transferred her contempt from the DPP and his misplaced chivalry to Ms. MI5, the sort of Age of Thatcher woman who saw her rise through the ranks of a secret police as a step toward liberation. For her, Maire thought, feminism no doubt meant earnest discussions with her husband over who did the washing up, who drove their blazered children to their expensive school, and whether to hyphenate their name.

"This is your last chance, Mary," Glassie was saying, his thick fingers wedged together over her file in its buff folder. "We're at the end of our patience. We're only going to ask you these questions once more."

For Maire, commitment meant that she slouched in her chair in the same clothes she'd been wearing since her arrest, refusing to wear the prison clothes she'd been offered. By now, after however many days it had been, she could smell her own sour odor, but even that was a source of satisfaction, as she watched the DPP and the whore from MI5 restrain the urge to wrinkle their noses when she was brought into the room. Glassie, on the other hand, was used to it now.

"Going on the blanket already, are we?" he'd said in one of their earlier sessions. "Very patriotic, Mary, I'm sure."

Maire no longer knew what day it was. She had seen neither daylight nor a clock since she'd been arrested, and Glassie never wore a watch. Just to keep her off balance, they liked to wake her in the middle of a sound sleep and march her off to the interrogation room for another session. God only knew what time it was. Then it was back to her overheated cell, where she lay on top of the thin blanket on the bed, baking in her own clothes, refusing to give them the satisfaction of finding her in her underwear. Sometimes when she wanted to sleep they left the light burning, and sometimes they switched it off, leaving her wide-eyed and wide awake in pitch darkness, listening to her own breathing.

"Are you Mary Cathleen Donovan?" Glassie said. The DPP shifted his weight from one long leg to the other and Ms. Pulleine watched Maire across the table, radiating her inconsequential sisterhood.

They always took her to the same interrogation room—she knew that by counting the doors—but once inside they did what they could to disorient her, rearranging the furniture every time or even replacing some of it, to make it look like a different room. Sometimes the rough wooden table was there, sometimes it was not; sometimes the chairs were contoured chrome and plastic, sometimes wooden and stiff like a convent school's. One time Maire caught herself wondering whether the video camera with its unblinking red light had always been over the door or not, and the fact of her doubt frightened her more than Glassie ever had. After that she made it an article of faith that it was always the same room, whether it really was or not.

"Are you a Sinn Fein city councillor for West Belfast?" Glassie said, his eyes down on the open file, and for only the second time Ms. Pulleine spoke, lowering her hand from her chin and laying it halfway across the table toward Maire, a gesture of stern sympathy.

"Surely you can tell us that," she said, all headmistressly compassion.

And all this time, whether it was three or four or five days, Glassie had worked at her, asking her the same questions over and over: where was the money, where was the plastique, where was Jimmy Coogan? Who brought the money, we know there was money in the money belt, don't fuck me about, Mary, where did it go? Who's got the plastique, Mary, where is he taking it, what's it for? Glassie played himself like a harp, he shouted and banged the table, he pleaded and clasped his hands together like a tender country priest, he wheedled and threatened and begged. She knew he was just the front man, part of a game they were playing: the erratic lights, the abrupt awakenings, the cold food they served her at odd hours, the rearranged furniture, Glassie's threats—though he never touched her—of violence. All of it danced right up to the edge of the law and probably over; if it hadn't been for the camera and her minor celebrity as a city councillor, they wouldn't have messed about: they would have stripped her and beaten her senseless, the European Commission and Amnesty International be damned. But given who she was and given that they had caught her with nothing except the flimsy evidence of an empty money belt, all they could do was hold her for the full seven days and lock her in a room to be shouted at by a florid, sclerotic Orangeman, the terror of nineteen-year-old ghetto lads. And that, Maire thought with some satisfaction, was not nearly good enough, not by half. All the while Glassie raged and blustered, she kept her silence, practicing the only form of resistance left to her, a refusal to answer, a refusal to speak at all except to protest her illegal arrest and ask for a lawyer. A man would have broken by now, would have spoken just to hear the sound of his own voice, would have sought Glassie's worthless fatherly approval. For all she knew her seven days were up, but she refused to give him the satisfaction of asking. She refused to shout when they shut out the lights. When Glassie called her Mary, she refused to correct him, even though she was unsure whether that was his victory or hers. It wasn't those who could inflict the most, she reminded herself, but those who could suffer the most who would conquer.

"What can you tell us about ten pounds of Semtex plastique," Glassie was saying, "taken from a Belfast Brigade arms dump sometime last week, without the approval of the Provo Army Council?"

Maire crossed her legs and leaned forward to lace her fingers over her knee, a chat-show pose, herself the coy starlet flogging her latest film. She looked back at Glassie with a bored, blank expression, as if waiting for the cameras to start rolling. In fact the camera was on, the silent image watched somewhere by some bored peeler swilling tea, but by this point Glassie was reading through the list only by rote, hardly pausing between questions for an answer. Maire almost felt sorry for him, for his failure in front of two higher-ups. He looked unusually shabby by comparison, his clothes off the rack in the company of two tailored suits. She was tempted to answer one of his questions with a joke—"You'll never get me to talk, copper," something like that—if only to let him know that she knew the difference between him and the other two, almost as if she and Glassie had a bit of shared history together, something they might laugh over like a private joke just to puzzle the DPP and Ms. Pulleine.

"When did you last see Jimmy Coogan?" Glassie said, and this time he waited for an answer, looking up across the table. She let the silence drag on, as she'd let it drag on before, but it was different when there were two other people listening, as if the room were hotter than before.

"Yes, tell us about Jimmy, Maire," said Ms. Pulleine, leaning forward with the tips of her fingers pressed together, her eyes brightening. Maire noted the correct use of her name and the confidential tone, just us wee girls together, and she nearly smiled, knowing that it was planned, that Glassie had promised to soften her up so that the expensive bitch from MI5 could come in and pluck her like an apple with an act of compassion.

"Surely it can't matter now," said the DPP from his corner, shifting legs again.

Across the table both Glassie and Ms. Pulleine stiffened, and instinctively Maire stiffened too, locking her fingers tighter around her knee. Ms. Pulleine languorously swung a look of irritation at the DPP, a great lady's disdain for some idiot hanger-on, while Glassie blew out a long sigh and scowled down at the dossier.

"Oh, dear, hasn't she been told?" The DPP leaned slightly forward out of his corner.

"Did you know Jimmy Coogan, Mary?" Glassie said in a loud voice, and the DPP shut up and pressed himself back into his corner like a chastened schoolboy.

Maire felt her fingers squeezing tighter around her kneecap, felt her muscles tighten all along her arms and legs, but she forced herself to smile, just a little, at the transparency of the DPP's slip, at Ms. Pulleine's theatrical irritation, at Glassie's sudden use of the past tense. It was all planned, she knew, right down to the last gesture and glance.

Glassie smiled back at her, a canny peasant.

"Butter wouldn't melt in your mouth, would it, lass?"

She caught herself glaring at him and looked away, at the woman, at the tall man in the corner, at the wall.

"You might as well tell her, Inspector," said Ms. Pulleine quietly.

Maire squeezed her knee even tighter, to the point of pain. This was another part of the game, something they had rehearsed laughing up in Glassie's office over cups of tea.

"Did you know Jimmy Coogan?" Glassie said again.

"Never heard of him." Christ, how did that slip out, that was a mistake, keep your mouth shut, give them *nothing*.

"Then it probably won't concern you to know that he's dead, Mary." Glassie licked his thumb and started leafing through her file.

Her heart began to pound, she felt nauseated on an empty stomach.

"Perhaps you ought to show her the photograph, Inspector," murmured Ms. Pulleine, pushing her fingers back through her hair, lifting it from her face.

This was it, this was their last act of desperation, they had no photograph, Glassie wouldn't find it in the file, if she could just hang on white-knuckled and qualmish a moment longer they'd have to back down, admit that they had no photograph, that it was all rehearsed, a bluff, a bluff, a bluff.

Glassie pushed something across the table from the dossier, slid it around with his blunt forefinger so that it was right side up to Maire. Then without meaning to she was looking at it, and saw her husband in glossy color, nude, his eyes wide open and blank, his cheeks sunken and unshaven, his mouth hanging slack, his pale, hairless chest puckered with purplish holes, bloodless and dry like punctures in the photograph itself. Maire's breath was gone, she sat in an airless void, her blood pounding in her ears. Jimmy lay on a wheeled table on a bright tile floor, his penis shriveled and his feet splayed, and in the corner of the photo, standing on the shining tiles, was a pair of legs in camouflage trousers and muddy black jump boots. Whose feet are those, Maire thought, breathless, who is that man?

"It's a nice likeness, but of course you wouldn't know," Glassie was saying. "Very Che Guevara, though, wouldn't you say? Myself, I can see it splashed nicely across the front of *An Phoblacht.*"

Maire gasped, it just escaped, there was nothing she could do to hold it in, all her energy devoted to holding herself together, to keep from fainting in front of her enemies, to keep her blood from pounding her to pieces.

"I know how you feel, dear," the whore was saying. "I know what you must be going through."

She had clutched herself too tight, she was going to snap in two like a stick, and she twisted abruptly in her seat, both feet on the floor, her hands pried apart and clutching the edge of the table. It was a lie, the picture was a fake, Jimmy was alive and more than anything else right now he needed her strength, her refusal, her silence.

"Someone touted on him, Mary," Glassie said, tapping the photograph, "told us where he was crossing the border, and all we had to do was wait for him."

God, she was going to be sick, the pain of it was too great to hold in, but they hadn't fed her in so long there was nothing to heave up, only torn and bloody pieces of herself. If she held it in a moment longer, just one more instant, she would die, she would cave in on herself, a kind of self-immolation by implosion.

"He was armed, you know," the DPP said. "We had no choice."

She couldn't stand it, the time for silence was over, he was gone and they had brought her his head the way they brought Cuchulainn's to Eimher, and now she would clutch it to her breast and kiss his lips and drink his blood and drape a silken shroud about him. What he deserved was no longer silence, but her wild keening, he deserved to be sung over in the ancient fashion of all her mothers before her, century after century of wailing Irishwomen, and she heard her own cry before she willed it, rising unbidden from years of buried memory, filling the room and frightening her enemies around her, making them wide-eyed and pale with fear at the depth of her grief.

"Let her be for a moment," Ms. Pulleine said, touching Glassie's sleeve.

This was her weapon now, she would blast their souls with her grief, she would wither their hearts where they stood, down to their roots, like an arctic wind. The English whore stood and came around the table and crouched on her high heels next to Maire's chair, and Maire struck her backhand across her pale, porcelain face, knocking her back into the corner onto her arse. Glassie heaved himself to his feet and the tall man sprang away from the wall, but Maire was on her feet now and knocked her chair away, stepping back from the woman gasping in the corner.

"*Tá fhios ag Íosa Críost!*" she cried, throwing out her hand. "*Ná beidh caidhp ar bhaitheas mo chinn, ná léine chnis lem thaoibh . . .*"

Glassie and the DPP stood dumbfounded, as if bewitched at the clear and unwavering sound of her voice, as if it was a curse and not a lamentation.

"*Ná bróg ar thrácht mo bhoinn, ná trioscán ar fuaid mo thí*"— the words came unbidden after all these years, dryly memorized in convent school and nearly forgotten, and sprung to life now in her rage as if they were her own—"*ná srian leis an láir ndoinn, ná caithfidh mé le dlí . . .*"

"For God's sake, what's she saying?" The whore's voice shook; she tried to push herself up out of her corner, red-faced and hair awry, tucking her knees together under her tailored skirt.

"Damned if I know," Glassie said, itching to come around the table.

"It's Irish, isn't it?" ventured the DPP.

"... 's go raghad anonn thar toinn ag comhrá leis an rí"—the words rang around the hard walls—"'s mura gcuirfidh ionam aon tsuim go dtiocfad ar ais arís ..."

"Well, translate it!" Ms. Pulleine's heels scrabbled on the lino.

"I don't know the fucking language!" Glassie roared.

"Are we getting this on tape?" whispered the DPP.

"... go bodach na fola duibhe"—she dropped her voice and was here again, alone in a room with her enemies, her back against the wall, her eyes shut, her heart forever broken—"a bhain díom féin mo mhaoin."

She stopped and opened her eyes, the room still ringing in the sudden silence like the fading tone of a bell. The other three gazed at her as if they were the ones backed into a corner.

" 'Tis known to Jesus Christ," she began in a low voice, her eyes wide and bright and dry, "no cap upon my head, no shift upon my back, no shoe upon my foot, no gear in all my house, no bridle for the mare, but I will spend at law."

No one moved but Glassie, who dropped into his chair, picked up his pen, and began to write, holding up his other hand, whether for Maire to slow down or the others to be silent, she could not tell. But she did not slow or stop or wait for him, but only closed her eyes again and said the words, feeling her way through them in the dark as if into a room she didn't think she knew, but turned out to know after all.

"And I'll go oversea to plead before the King," she sang, her voice rising, the words harder and louder with each one, until at last she was hurling them like stones, "and if the King be deaf, I'll settle things alone with the black-blooded rogue that killed my man on me."

"**D**id I ever tell you about my mother?" Clare said. She folded her hands on top of the stone windbreak and rested one scuffed boot on the narrow bench, and she gazed east, where the mountains fell away into a wide green valley full of blue haze. The long spine of the Pennines was just visible at the far edge of the valley, like a low, blue wall.

"Your mother?" Brian stood up next to her, squinting into the wind, the curl of hair at his forehead blown back. "What about her?"

"Well, it's nothing like your grandfather." She smiled at him sidelong, aware of the pose she was striking—chin lifted, back erect—but pleased at the effect.

"I hope not." He glanced away, solemn suddenly, his cheeks polished red by the wind.

Above the haze at the horizon, stately, flat-bottomed clouds floated south like an armada against the bright blue sky, dragging their shadows after them. The nearer mountains were rounded and old, their green slopes mottled with gray boulders like scattered chips of old bone, their sides cut away in wide brown scallops of scree. The closest peaks were strung together with the windbreak on Helvellyn by blunt, narrow ridges slung low like rope bridges, distant hikers in bright nylon inching along them like beads in a groove, red and green and blue.

"She used to give money to the IRA," Clare said, watching as a cloud shadow glided up one sway-backed ridge, flowed over the hikers, and rolled down the other side like a regiment on the move.

"You mean she gave to Noraid or something."

"No, I mean she gave money to the IRA." She turned to Brian, resisting the urge to smile. "For guns and stuff."

"Guns and stuff." Brian smiled and propped his chin against the heel of his hand.

"You know what I mean."

"Sorry."

She drew a breath and gazed down between the two arms of Helvellyn below, into a wide, green hollow nearly at their feet, its steep walls edged with low ramparts of rock and littered with boulders. Getting him to talk about this was like pulling teeth, and it was making her angry. At the center of the hollow below lay a dark tarn reflecting the clouds and the sky, its surface wrinkled by sudden gusts of wind.

"My mom and dad used to argue about it," she went on, ignoring him. "This man from the city used to come around a couple of times a year and my mom would talk to him and my dad wouldn't." She glanced at Brian. "My dad said he didn't want anything to do with it."

"With what?"

"With what the guy was collecting for." He was doing this on purpose, she could tell, and if she'd known him better she would have punched him in the shoulder.

"So what did your mother say?" He turned to her, rolling his cheek into his palm.

All around the windbreak the grass was worn down to dirt by hikers, and sharp little lines of rock were exposed, set into the mountaintop like china plates on edge, a midden of ancient crockery exposed by wind and rain and boottreads. A line of hikers appeared one at a time over the sharp east side of the mountain, climbing up from Striding Edge red-faced and winded.

"We never really talked about it much," Clare said. "She stopped when I was in high school, when the peace women won the Nobel Prize." She had his attention now at least, but he was making her self-conscious, watching her like that. "She sent me a long letter in London this summer, after the bombings. She wanted to let me know that she hadn't given them money in years, not even during the hunger strike."

The hikers, five of them, came up to the windbreak talking to each other in breathless spurts about the climb, and they sank out of sight on the other side of the wall, lining up together on the bench there, their voices and laughter rising over the wall toward Clare with the wind.

"Anyway," she said, looking down at her hands, "my dad told her that after Regent's Park, if the guy ever showed up again, he'd beat the shit out of him."

"What guy?" Brian said.

"The guy who collected the money," Clare said, and this time she did punch him in the shoulder, and he backed away, startled but still smiling.

"Are you listening to me?" she said. "I'm trying to take this seriously." She stepped back from the wall and turned to face him, and even in the wind she could feel her face get hot. "I mean, don't you think we ought to talk about yesterday?"

He lifted a hand to calm her, but she batted it away.

"Because I stuck my neck out for you, buster."

Somebody yelped on the other side of the windbreak, and as the others hooted at him one of the hikers appeared beyond the wall, lunging for a crumpled piece of wax paper caught by the wind.

"Watch it, mate," somebody called, out of sight. "One gust and you're over the edge."

But the hiker tramped on the piece of paper with his boot and bent grinning to retrieve it, and Brian lifted a finger to his lips, nodding toward the hikers behind the wall.

"Not here," he said. "Why don't we keep walking?"

Clare nodded abruptly and started to collect the leftovers from their lunch, stuffing cheese and rolls and wastepaper into her daypack while Brian stood off a few paces and wrapped his scarf tighter under his anorak. She saw his point, but it still made her mad, and they started south along the spur of the mountain, following a wide trail marked by small cairns, not speaking to each other.

It had been Clare's idea to come here, a sudden decision on the platform at Chester. Brian had still been strutting up and down and grinning like a teen-age football hero, but as soon as they were on the train north he fell asleep like an overexcited child, his head on her shoulder while Clare gazed out the window at the railway yards and dingy redbrick houses of Warrington and Wigan and Preston, and wondered what on earth she had just done. She wanted to shake him awake and make him explain, frightened at the thought of her complicity in something illegal, but she let him sleep, and let her own adrenaline high subside into something like disappointment, into the restless melancholy of train travel. She'd even slept for a while herself, thinking idly that she could ditch him again if she had to, dozing to the rhythm of the wheels against the track, It's not too late, it's not too late, it's not too late.

She took him to the Lake District, where she had first gotten to know Ian, her English lover, and she hoped a long tramp in the hills would have a similar effect on Brian, that it would loosen him up and get him to talk. But he wouldn't talk on the paytrain from Oxenholme, not with other passengers all around, nor on the bus from Windermere, and by the time she and Brian got to Ambleside it was after dark and the hostel was full; they had to walk into town and book overpriced rooms at a bed and breakfast. Inside, he wouldn't talk in the parlor, where a couple of other guests sat, and then upstairs, on the carpet outside their rooms, the memory of Saturday night came to her, and in spite of everything she asked if they could talk the next day instead, backing toward her door like a nervous sorority girl.

"You're not going to disappear in the morning again, are you?" He smiled, his hands safely in his pockets, and she hesitated in the doorway.

"No," she said, and kissed him. Then she stepped back into her room and shut the door.

In the morning there were other guests at breakfast, and climbing up Helvellyn from the northwest they were both too breathless to talk until they reached the windbreak at the top, hungry and aching and cold. Now, on the way down, she led the way, walking briskly a step ahead like a governess. To her left the wind gusted up from the cliff, while to her right the mountain fell in rolling curves to the narrow lake valley below, where the water glittered through the pines. Above the lake to the west, against the afternoon glare of the sun, the mountains were dark ranks of blue silhouette, pushing up against each other like waves against a headland. At the edge of her vision she was conscious of Brian just behind her, and she was aware of striking a pose again, with long strides and her chin lifted.

"You pissed off or what?" she heard him say.

"No," she said, without stopping.

"Clare, I'm sorry."

"Me too." She kept walking, and behind her she heard the crunch of his boots as he stopped on the trail.

"I said I'm sorry!" he shouted, but it sounded thin and weak up here in the wind. She stopped and turned around, and with his smooth cheeks and windblown hair he looked like a child, more petulant than apologetic.

"I've got a lot on my mind, is all," he said, coming toward her.

"So do I."

"I know." He stopped a few steps away, squinting at her in the wind and cold sunlight, the gusts over the edge of the mountain pressing his anorak against his back.

"It's just that I've been thinking," she began, and looked away.

"About what?"

She shrugged, unsure how to begin. She remembered their walk to the top of Knocknarea three days ago; it seemed they were right back where they started.

"About last night?" He started to smile.

"About *yesterday*." She opened her eyes wide and tightened her mouth, one of her mother's expressions.

Now it was his turn to look away, and she stepped to the side to stay in his line of sight.

"Do you want to hear this?" she said.

"Sure."

"Because I've been thinking about what you said the other day about tactics."

"Tactics?" He turned his head as if to hear her better.

"You remember. You said when you choose the goal, you choose the tactics, that if you wanted a united Ireland . . ."

"Yeah, all right." He twisted his head the other way, looking past her again, and once more she stepped sideways to stay in front of him.

"So maybe that works the other way around," she said, pushing her hair back against the wind. "Maybe the horribleness of the tactics outweighs the outcome. Maybe a united Ireland isn't worth it."

Brian blew out a sigh, and Clare took a step toward him.

"I hate the way my cousins don't care, but maybe bringing money for, you know, isn't the answer either."

"This isn't about that," he said, still avoiding her eye. "Your cousins have nothing to do with it."

"Brian, they have everything to do with it."

"Look, Clare, this isn't your problem."

"Yes, it is!" Now she was shouting. "If that guy on the train goes to the police, it sure as heck is my problem."

Brian looked cornered, and for a moment she was afraid that he was going to swing at her. There was no one else in sight, beyond Brian only the blunt, brown mountain against the hard blue of the sky, but she felt as if she were locked in a room alone with him.

"Look," he said, his voice low and urgent, as if he had only a moment, as if he didn't want anyone to overhear. "There's more to this than you want to know."

"Try me."

He twisted his face away and tried to step around her, but she caught his arm. He wrenched free, shouting at her.

"I have a right to know," she said, her voice sounding thin and shrill to her.

"I didn't just bring the money, okay?" He backed away from her, shouting back. "When I got there, they wanted me to do something else, okay?"

He pulled his hands out of his pockets and lifted them into the air, a gesture of helplessness that made Clare feel cold and defenseless herself, made her heart contract in her chest.

"What do you mean?" she said.

"I *mean*, I'm taking some of it to London for them, all right?" He stopped backing away and let his arms drop, looking past her over the edge of the mountain into empty space. "Is that what you wanted to know? Are you happy now?"

"Some of what?"

"The money, Clare." He lifted his hand, rubbing his thumb and forefinger together. "Five thousand bucks."

"Where is it?" Her heart squeezed tighter still, like a fist.

"Right here." He patted his waist. "Christ, I shouldn't even be here. I was supposed to be in London yesterday. I'm in deeper shit right now than you can imagine."

"Did the guy on the train know?"

"Yeah."

"How did he know?"

"Christ, I don't know." He sounded as if he wanted to laugh. "Why do you think I was so scared on the train?" He sighed again and gave her the ghost of a smile. "I shouldn't be telling you this."

She watched him for a moment, speechless, as the wind blew between them and the cold shadow of a cloud glided over them.

"What's it for?" she said at last, her mouth dry.

"What?"

"The money." She laughed, in spite of herself.

"What I told you before." He lifted his shoulders and slid his hands back into his pockets. "Widows and orphans. Pension money."

"In London?"

"There's a lot of Irish in London, Clare."

They watched each other for another moment, meeting each other's eye and glancing away again, two teen-agers contemplating a first kiss.

"Is it, like, illegal?" she said.

He smiled and said, "Like, yeah."

She smiled back and said, "It's a good thing my dad isn't here."

"He'd beat the shit out of me, huh?"

"You bet."

Not knowing where else to look, they both stared down at their boots.

"So why'd you come up here with me?" she said. "Why didn't you just catch the next train to London?"

"I dunno. Scared shitless, I guess." He lifted his head just enough to look at her. "I wasn't sure I wanted to go through with it or not."

"Well, that's really stupid."

"Pardon me?" He lifted his eyebrows.

"Don't you think you'd be in deeper shit if you don't show up at all?"

He drew a breath and nodded.

"I guess," he said.

"So come on." She took his arm and turned him around, walking him down the path against the wind.

"No way are you coming with me," he said, but he let himself be led.

"Oh, right, like you can make it all the way to London on your own. That's a laugh."

He started to protest, tried to shake her off, but she only held on tighter.

"Brian," she said, "shut up."

What's your name?

Somebody was speaking to Tim again in the dark, and he tried to answer, but his tongue was swollen and his mouth full of blood. His shoulders ached where his arms were pulled back, though his wrists didn't hurt anymore. In fact, he couldn't feel his hands at all. The waistband of his trousers cut into his gut. He tried to say his name, and they hit him again.

Tell me your name.

He tried again, he opened his mouth and tried to push the blood past his tongue, but it just dribbled out, down his bare chest, warm and thick like his mother's maple syrup.

Give him a drink.

A pair of warm hands lifted his head from behind and something touched his lips, he felt it from a distance, and then his mouth was full of cold, bitter water, and he nearly gagged. A lot of it went down the wrong way and he coughed it up, and somebody rested a hand on the back of his neck. The cup was held to his lips again and they told him to sip and spit it out. He shook his head. Take this cup from me, Father.

Tim McGuire, he said through thick lips.

But the hands tipped his head back and he was at the dentist's in some clammy cellar, and the jerk had given him way too much Novocaine. His head was full of it, stuffed up to his aching eyeballs with cotton. Then his mouth was full of water again, but this time he didn't gag, he knew what to do, he swirled it all around his gums and teeth, squirted it through the space between his gums and his lower lip to get the crud out, and turned his head to the side.

Rinse and spit.

In between blows there were moments of blackness, little losses of consciousness, and if it wasn't for the pain and the iron taste of his own blood, he might almost have been dozing on the train, rocking in and out of a hot, restless sleep, watching the scenery glide by in between cat naps, thinking of the Irish pub he knew in Kilburn, in North London, where he knew a guy who knew a guy who could put him in touch with the lads of London Brigade. He slept. Then they hit him again and he woke up.

Tim.

Somebody was rubbing his shoulders from behind while his head lolled from one side to the other like a boxer's after the fifteenth round, his head as big as a basketball, his skin as taut as a wineskin full of his own blood.

Where is the plastique now?

I don't know.

They hit him again.

I don't know.

They hit him again.

I don't know. He wept, he squeezed his turgid eyelids together, waiting for another blow, but it didn't come.

Who has it now?

Brian.

Brian who?

Strong fingers kneaded his shoulders, one more round, champ, a winner never quits and a quitter never wins, says Father Charlie Curran, the Fighting Priest of Southie, Cardinal Cushing's Bantamweight Contender.

Donovan.

What was that? says Father Charlie. Say that again.

He'll need stitches, Father, says Mrs. Cavanaugh, the housekeeper. The lad's dripping blood all over my clean kitchen floor.

Brian Donovan.

Say it slowly, says Mrs. Cavanaugh. She sponges off the blood. Enunciate clearly so the Father can understand.

Brian Donovan, Tim said thickly, 648 South Fifth Avenue, Ann Arbor, Michigan.

Where is he now?

He ran. With the girl.

What girl? says Father Charlie.

I don't know, Father. He cringes, but the fingers lift his head, knead the back of his neck.

What happened?

Oh, God, Father, the niggers beat me up! cries Tim, and Father Curran clouts him on the side of the head, a ringing open-palmed blow to the ear, the first step in Tim's political education.

Jesus, Mary, and Joseph! cries Mrs. Cavanaugh.

I'll have no bigots in God's house! shouts Father Curran.

Where did they run?

I ran all the way back from Roxbury, Father. Tim starts to cry, tries to hold back the tears because they sting too much through the cuts on his face. They're burning their own stores, Father.

Dr. King was a great man, says Father Curran. The O'Connell of his people.

Well, I didn't shoot him, weeps Tim. I only went into some spade store on Blue Hill Avenue to call my mom.

They hit him again. Step number two.

I'm sorry, Father.

Where did they run?

All the way back! Tim cries, and they hit him again.

When he woke again he was in daylight, lying on his back in a lumpy bed with his trousers on and a blanket pulled up to his chin. The room was cold and smelled of mildew, and the blanket was thin and scratchy. It didn't do him much good. He ached all over, but especially his face. His throat was dry. Someone touched his hand and he turned his head on the thin pillow, wincing. The man who touched him sat on a wooden chair by the bed, a balding man with a monkish fringe of brown hair. Behind him, by the bright window, stood a man and a woman.

"Do you know where you are?" said the monk. He was Irish.

Tim opened his cracked lips and moved his tongue. It was still thick.

"Kilburn," he said. "North London." He was cold all over. His bare arm lay on top of the blanket in the cold.

"You were in Kilburn," the monk said. "Now you're someplace else."

Tim's tongue cleaved to the roof of his mouth.

"Bring him some water," the monk said over his shoulder, and the woman left the room.

"You came into the Harp of Erin," the monk went on, squeezing Tim's hand on the blanket. "You said you wanted to speak to the head of London Brigade. Do you remember?"

"Yes."

The woman came back and the monk, who was very strong, lifted Tim up with an arm around his shoulders and held the glass to his lips. The water was cold and made his teeth ache.

"Well, this does not concern the head of London Brigade," the monk said, settling Tim carefully back onto the bed. "You'll have to talk to me."

There were cracks in the ceiling above Tim's head. He shivered under the blanket.

"Do you understand why we beat you?" The monk took Tim's hand again.

"No?" Tim suggested. He held tightly onto the monk's hand, so that the monk wouldn't hit him with it.

"There were three reasons, Tim. Shall I tell you what they were?"

Tim nodded and closed his eyes against the cracks above him.

"Don't fall asleep, Tim." The monk let go of Tim's hand and laid his own hand on Tim's bare shoulder. "Stay with me, this is important to you."

In Tim's private, painful dark, the monk's voice was a balm, filling the dank room with heat. He nodded to show he was still listening.

"The first reason we beat you, Tim, is because you knew something we didn't, which is the name of the American lad bringing the parcel from Jimmy Coogan. We wanted to make sure you weren't keeping anything back. Were you?"

"No," Tim said.

"Can you tell me the name of the girl with the American?"

"No."

"Did you shop Jimmy to the Brits?"

"*No.*" Tim felt his throat tighten and tears come to his eyes, and he rolled his head against the pillow and opened his eyes.

"Easy, Tim. I believe you now." The monk rubbed Tim's shoulder with his powerful hand. "The second reason is that we wanted to ensure your silence. We don't want Special Branch to know our business, let alone the general public. Do you agree?"

Tim nodded, his eyes full of salt tears.

"Good, Tim. That's a good lad." The monk smiled. His teeth were blunt and yellow, like a dog's. "The third reason we beat you is because Jimmy was a friend of mine and it made me very angry that anybody would betray his trust. You helped him in his hour of need, and for that reason we didn't kill you, but after he was dead you tried to shop him to his enemies in the movement, and that makes me very angry indeed. Because his enemies are my enemies. Do you understand what I'm saying to you?"

"Yes."

"I forgive you now." The monk's hand slipped to the back of Tim's neck and gave him a squeeze like an absolution. "I think you understand the situation. Now pay close attention. I'm going to tell you what's going to happen next."

The monk slid his chair closer to the bed. He clasped Tim's hand between both of his. His hands were warm.

"We're going to let you rest here for a few days. Then this gentleman here"—he turned and glanced back at the man by the window, who stepped forward into the cold light, a hazy silhouette—"this gentleman here will take you to Heathrow and put you on a plane to the States. Are you following me so far?"

Tim nodded, his eyes overflowing, his nose stopped up.

"We're letting you go this time, but you have to promise me two things. Will you do that?"

Tim's vision was watery, but the monk's dark eyes found him through the blur and held him.

"Here are the two things. You must promise never to reveal any of this to anyone, and you must promise to never come back to Ireland. If you break either of these promises, we will kill you. Do you understand?"

Tim nodded. He heard himself sob. His whole body shuddered under the blanket.

"Do you promise?"

"Yes." The tears poured down his cheeks onto the pillow.

"There's a good lad." The monk smiled and reached into his coat pocket. He pulled out a clean white handkerchief and wiped the tears from Tim's face, mindful of his bruises. He held the damp cloth gently to Tim's tender nose.

"Blow," he said.

Brian leaned forward against his pack like a moonwalker, and he came off the platform into Euston Station as if onto the surface of another planet, his heart beating harder against the pull of a stronger gravity. Just inside the arch he stopped, overwhelmed; the station was too big and too bright, the ceiling too high, the lights harsh, the vast room ringed around with bright newsstands and cafés. Even the air was strange, an acrid compound of diesel fumes and body odors and London damp. Businessmen and schoolchildren streamed past him to cross each other's paths and disappear through the doors onto the street or down a bright stair marked To the Underground. The tap and scrape of their feet receded into the fundamental, echoing roar, out of which arose the bang of car doors, the hollow incoherence of the public address, and the monkeyhouse cries of children.

"So what do you have to do now?" Clare appeared at his elbow, startling him.

"I've got a number I'm supposed to call."

She touched his elbow and pointed toward a row of half-shell phone stalls near the entrance to the Underground, and she led the way across, Brian following with a wary glance at the high ceiling, as if somebody watched them from above.

At the phones she started to unbuckle her pack, but he touched her arm.

"Um, maybe you should wait over there someplace." He looked across the station toward a line of plastic seats against the wall of the Travellers-Fare café. She rolled her eyes, but he grasped her hand tightly and caught her eye.

"Clare," he said, and she sighed and rebuckled her pack. He watched her walk away, and then unbuckled his own pack and slung it to the floor. There was no place to lean it, so he propped it against his leg and pulled the slip of paper the Provo had given him in Dublin out of his pocket.

Coogan, he thought, his name is Jimmy Coogan. Or was.

He turned to the phone and plugged in a coin, and as the phone burred flatulently in his ear he arranged the rest of his change on the little metal shelf in descending order of size, fat little English coins like chocolates wrapped in tin foil.

"Hullo?"

Brian looked up sharply, and a handspan away from his face he saw a typewritten notice on an oblong sticker, pasted to the side of the stall:

BAD HABITS CURED THE OLD FASHIONED WAY!
REPORT TO MADAME DEBBIE AT ONCE!
7248300

"Hullo?" It was a woman's voice on the phone, and Brian stammered and nearly said, Madame Debbie? "Uh, hello," he said instead, his throat tightening. "Could I speak to Vincent, please?"

"May I ask who's calling, please?" It was a young woman, and she sounded English, not Irish. I've got the wrong fucking number, he thought. Hang up.

"Brian." He choked off the word, swallowing it more than speaking it aloud. *Hang up.* He drew a breath and said a little more steadily, "It's Brian calling."

"Please hold the line."

The phone clunked against something as she put it down. Against what? Brian wondered. A table, a counter, a wall? He held his other hand out over the coins on the shelf and watched it tremble.

"Brian, hullo." A man's voice. "Where the hell have you been?"

Brian shifted the phone from one hand to the other.

"I got held up." How's he know my name? he thought, and answered himself, squeezing his eyes shut. I just told them. "Everything's okay, though."

"Imagine my relief." The man was very soft-spoken, and it was hard to tell if he was Irish or not. Brian could hardly hear him over the racket of the station.

"Look, can we get together?"

"Oh, aye. What would be a good time for you?" Was this guy being sarcastic? Brian sighed and leaned out of the stall; there was no one near him.

"Listen, Vincent," he said, leaning into the stall and lowering his voice. "I don't know what your problem is, but I'm the one standing out here all alone."

The line was cut off, replaced by a high-pitched beeping. Brian jumped back and the phone was nearly jerked out of his hand by the short cable. He twisted around and his pack toppled over onto the floor. The police had cut him off, they had traced the call, they were closing in. He clutched his palm over the mouthpiece and looked around. The station was nearly empty now, a solitary man in a trench coat trudging across the wide floor far under the lights, as if crossing a desert. On the other side of the station Clare was slouched in her seat with her long legs stretched in front of her and crossed at the ankles, her pack on the seat next to her. She lifted a hand to him. Brian gave a tight smile and waved back, and he turned around and tried to peel another coin off the metal shelf. But his fingers were too unsteady and he finally had to slide it off the edge with his thumb.

"You're nervous, Brian, it's plain to see," Vincent said when the beeping stopped. He was Irish. Or something. It was hard to tell over the phone. "I'm sorry if I was short with you, but we expected you several days ago, and we're a wee bit anxious."

"Okay." He pressed his temple against the cool side of the stall. "What do you want me to do?"

"Do you have a carryall or something?"

"A what?"

"Something to put it in."

It, Brian thought, drawing a breath.

"I have a daypack," he said.

"All right, then, put it in your daypack. Can you be at Paddington Station in half an hour?"

He glanced uselessly around him and said, "Yes," without knowing if he could or not.

"Good. Wait by the phones across from the Underground entrance and I'll call you there. Don't bring anyone with you."

Vincent hung up, and Brian caught his breath, afraid of having lost an important detail. And what was that last thing, why had he said that? The phone buzzed angrily in his ear, and Brian banged it down too hard, stepping back and drawing a deep breath. He swept the rest of his change off the shelf into his palm and stooped to pick up his pack.

Clare stood up as he approached.

"So?"

"I've got to go meet this guy." Brian tightened his hands around his shoulder straps. He didn't want her to see how his hands shook. "Right now."

She nodded, arching her back and sliding her hands into the hip pockets of her jeans.

"Can I come?" she said.

"No." He looked past her at the steamy window of the café, avoiding her eye. The people within were only dark blurs with pale, indistinct faces.

"Okay." Clare nodded again and lifted her shoulders as if trying to shake something off. Over their heads the public address echoed like distant thunder, an indecipherable list of place-names.

"I'll meet you later," Brian said. "Where do you want to meet?"

"Okay." She looked down at her boots and then up at him. "How long . . ."

He shrugged. He had no idea, but he said, "Two hours?"

"Okay." She lifted a corner of her mouth. "Victoria Station. In front of W. H. Smith's."

"What's that?"

"Bookshop," she said, pointing to the brightly lit bookstall across the station. She turned to jerk her pack out of the seat.

"All right." He nodded and looked at his watch. "Victoria Station at six thirty."

She smiled brilliantly and slipped into the straps of her pack, dipping one shoulder and then the other like a dancer. His blood pounded in his throat, and he wanted her to wish him luck, wanted her to talk him out of it, wanted her to take his hand and show him the way.

"So I guess I have to go first, huh." She buckled the belt of her pack. "I'm not supposed to see which way you go, right?"

He shrugged and smiled, his tongue thick in his throat. They stood watching each other as if across a crevasse, and she pushed her fingers back through her hair.

"I could cover my eyes and count to a hundred," she said, and Brian leaned forward against his pack, against the leaden weight of the plastique dragging at his shoulders, and he laid his hand along her cheek and kissed her. She kissed him back and then pulled away. She walked backward a few steps, her thumbs hooked in the straps of her pack.

"Olly olly in free," she sang, and she spun on the ball of her foot, her own pack as light as a balloon on her back, and walked away.

He put the bundle in his daypack and deposited his backpack in the left luggage at Euston Station. He made it to Paddington with only a minute or two to spare, jogging up out of the Underground with the strap of his daypack digging into his shoulder. He paced along the row of dingy, battered phones, sick with anticipation, his bowels loose, his stomach tight. For the first time since Belfast he was directly aware of the weight of the plastique itself, ten pounds of it stuffed into the fraying canvas daypack, and he shifted it from one shoulder to the other until one of the phones rang and he jumped forward, letting the pack slide down his arm, catching it by the strap, the pack swinging inches from the grimy floor.

"Check it at the left luggage," said Vincent on the phone. "Bring me the ticket."

He gave Brian directions that got more and more specific as they went along, circling in tighter like a spiral, and he made Brian repeat them. Circle Line to Gloucester Road, then change to the westbound District Line. Make you sure you get the Broadway or Richmond train; don't get on the Wimbledon. Get off at Turnham Green, down the steps, left under the bridge, right across the road at the zebra crossing, down the path into the common, along the fence.

"How will I know you?" It was a stupid question, a blind-date question, but Brian felt giddy, and Vincent gave a gasp that could have been laughter.

"I'll wear a fatigue jacket and a woman's stocking over my face," he said. "That'll be me with my nose flattened like a boxer's."

Great, Brian thought, hanging up. Terrorist humor.

In a tunnel between Earl's Court and West Kensington the lights in the car flickered, went out, and came back, and the train stalled beside another train on the next track. Brian wanted to scream. In the hot press of commuters, he hung onto a pole near the door, inches away from a plump young man in a frayed suit who smelled of sweat and fading deodorant. No one spoke, no one looked at the train alongside except Brian, and he felt as if he was the only one who knew it was there. The heads of the standees in the next car were cut off by the window frame, and the people in the seats stared at points in the air just beyond their noses. It was all Brian could do in the oppressive, sweating silence to keep from pounding on the window, just to get one of those people to look back at him. Instead he closed his eyes tightly and wished he had the plastique with him, he could blast his way out of here, awaken those pale, blank faces, fill the grimy tunnel with blinding light, crumble the walls like shortbread. He slipped his free hand into his anorak pocket and rubbed the little left luggage ticket like a rabbit's foot, and the train lurched forward, the pitch of the engine rising to a whine. Brian swayed against the plump man.

Station by station the car emptied out, and Brian took a seat, stretching his legs into the aisle. The train ran on an elevated track now, and beyond his own reflection in the window he saw roofs and chimney pots silhouetted against a purple, twilight sky, caught sudden glimpses down cross streets full of gleaming cars and buses in the amber streetlights. He tipped his head back against the vibrating window and matched the name of each station with the map of the line above the window opposite, digging his fingers into his palm and counting his pulsebeats between stops. At Hammersmith he saw a poster that asked IS THERE HOPE IN THE AGE OF AIDS? and as the train started to move again he laughed out loud, causing the woman a few seats away to look up from her paperback in numbed alarm.

At Turnham Green he swung onto the bright platform as soon as the door hissed open, and he thumped down the steps two at a time, bovine commuters looking up dully as he passed. He slapped his ticket into the palm of the black man in the exit booth and jogged past the newsstand, turning left under the bridge as the train whined away overhead. A car splashed through a puddle alongside him, and up ahead he saw bright shops and streetlights framed in the arch. Just beyond the bridge two yellow lights blinked in sync with each other at either end of the zebra crossing, and Brian and a van waited for each other in a series of false starts until the driver rolled down his window and shouted at Brian to bloody well cross if he was going to. Brian stopped on the other side to feel in his pocket for the ticket. Ahead of him the dark common was bounded by a semicircle of houses in black silhouette, the bare branches of trees latticed against the luminous sky. Overhead a jet outlined in flashing lights dragged its roar after it.

Brian started down a paved path, light-headed, short of breath. On his right were empty tennis courts behind a chain link fence, and on his left was a row of trees behind a fence of black iron spikes. The dim yellow globes of lampposts lit only the pavement at their feet and the lowest limbs of the trees; a cold wind rattled a few dead leaves on the bare branches. Brian shoved both hands deeper in his pockets, and somebody touched his elbow. Brian jerked his arm away and whirled, wrenching his hands free of his pockets.

"Brian?" A short, compact man stood a step or two back, one hand raised, the other hooked around the strap of a pack over his shoulder. He was bald, with a square, skull-like face and a fringe of dark hair around the edge of his high, domed head. He wore a sleeveless parka over a sweater, and a pair of loose, worn jeans over a pair of scuffed black work boots.

"I'm Vincent," he said, lowering his hand, offering it to Brian. "I'm sorry if I startled you."

His eyes were deep and bright, and with the corner of his mouth lifted he looked as though he were about to laugh.

"Hi," Brian said, his breath short, and he took the man's hand. His grip was strong, his hand even more callused than Brian's, and he released Brian and put his hand on the American's shoulder.

"Let's sit down for a moment," Vincent said, and he guided Brian by the shoulder toward a bench across from one of the streetlights, on a square of pavement in an indentation in the iron fence. Brian sat with his hands in his pockets, and Vincent sat twisted toward him on the seat, one leg tucked under him. Vincent slid the pack he carried down his arm and set it on the bench between them.

"This is for you," he said, and in the yellow light Brian's heart twisted painfully. The green nylon pack was new, its price tag still clipped to a strap, and it was bulging with something. It wasn't over. They wanted him to carry something else.

"It's a new sleeping bag," Vincent said in his soft accent. He looked as if he wanted to laugh again. "To replace the one you lost. The rucksack's yours as well. Jimmy insisted."

He pushed it toward Brian with the tips of his fingers, and Brian hoped that the light was dim enough so that Vincent couldn't see him blush with relief.

"Thanks." He pulled the pack against his leg and rested his hand on it.

They sat in silence for a moment as a woman passed pushing a stroller, the baby wrapped up out of sight. Vincent urged her on with a smile and a nod, but Brian stared hard across the path at the dead leaves caught along the bottom of the chain link fence. Beyond the tennis courts the stained white concrete of the railway embankment rose like a fortress wall, and with an ascending whine a silver train crawled out of the bright glare of the station and over the bridge, throwing sparks off into the darkness.

"We've talked to your man Tim," Vincent said. "The man who accosted you on the ferry."

The gleaming train clacked rhythmically along the top of the embankment against the deep velvet of the sky, the windows full of white light, the backs of heads like cardboard cutouts against the glass.

"He came to us by mistake," Vincent said, "which was a bit of luck for us."

Brian turned to him, but the man's eyes were hooded in shadow, the dome of his head gleaming in the yellow light of the lamp behind him.

"What do you mean, by mistake?" Brian said.

"What did Tim tell you? About us, I mean."

"He said Jimmy stole the, you know." He paused, unused to calling the Provo by name. "He said you were renegades."

"An unfortunate choice of words, that." Vincent smiled. "We're all on the same side. We're just prodding the leadership on a wee bit."

Brian's heart beat slow and hard. It was none of his business, he decided.

"Jimmy's dead," Vincent said. "Did you know that?"

"Yes."

"It doesn't change anything, though. You were right to come to us. Jimmy's gone, but his work goes on."

Brian nodded. He didn't want to go into this, he didn't want to know.

"Do you want the ticket now?" he said.

"In a moment." Vincent lifted his bony hand from the back of the bench and let it drop. "I want to ask you something first."

Brian shrugged and said, "Sure."

"Where were you yesterday?" Vincent said, his eyes in shadow. "Tim lost you Monday afternoon and I didn't hear from you until today."

Brian was suddenly aware of himself all alone with this man, in a vast, dark space, the whole circle of the world far away in the cold evening air, ringed around by the skeletal trees, the cresent of dark houses, the hiss of traffic in the distance. His mouth was very dry.

"I was scared," he said. "I took off, I guess. I wanted to kind of hide out for a day."

"You needn't worry about Tim, Brian," Vincent said. "It took us twenty minutes to convince him that our affairs are none of his business. Now I want you to tell me where you went."

Brian breathed deep through his nostrils to keep himself calm.

"The Lake District," he said.

"Ah." Vincent's eyes widened, filling up with shadow. "It's very scenic, I'm told. Tell me, what was the name of the girl who went with you?"

"The girl." Brian gazed back wide-eyed. He sat very still, his heart racing, as if the slightest movement would give him away.

"Yes. Tim said she was quite attractive."

"Um, she's just a girl I met on the ferry. She's not important."

"I'll decide what's important, Brian." He lifted his hand off the back of the bench. "I want you to tell me her name."

Brian shrugged and tried to smile. He felt as though he were caught in a searchlight, surrounded by people he could not see.

"I don't know," he said. "I forget."

"I don't believe you," Vincent said, still smiling, his voice still quiet, but with something taut in it. "You practically jumped off a moving train with her. You must have told her something."

"I didn't." He squinted at Vincent as if he really were looking into a bright light.

"Put yourself in my position, Brian." Vincent touched Brian's hand on the daypack, and Brian felt the man's cold touch all the way up his arm to his spine.

"I don't know you, so I've no reason to believe you," Vincent said. "If your girl goes to the police, you've put us all in danger, not just yourself."

"She won't," Brian insisted.

"Ah, then she does know." Vincent's hard fingers closed around Brian's hand, and Brian tightened his arm without trying to pull it away.

"Jesus Christ," he said, trying to laugh. "I mean, come on."

"Because if anything goes wrong," Vincent said, "it'll go very hard with the both of you."

"Just leave her out of it, okay?" Brian's voice shook. "She's innocent."

Vincent seized his wrist and twisted it painfully.

"Nobody's innocent," he said, his voice tight as wire. "What is her name?"

Brian tried to twist free, but only felt the burn of his skin in Vincent's grip.

"Jesus," he gasped, and Vincent jerked his arm over the back of the bench, twisting Brian's shoulder.

"I'll break it in a moment," he said. "Tell me her name."

"Clare," Brian said, and he squeezed his eyes shut against the tears. He wanted to cry out, he wanted to disappear.

"Clare what?" Vincent pressed Brian's arm back an inch farther, and Brian choked back a groan.

"Delaney," he heard himself say, and then the pain was gone, his arm released, and he turned away on the bench, opening his eyes and rubbing his wrist, his heart pounding, his breath coming hard. I could have lied, he thought. I could have lied.

"Is she Irish, Brian?" Vincent's voice was calm again.

"American." His voice trembled. "From Philadelphia."

I could have lied.

"If your girlfriend goes to the police," Vincent began, and he paused. Brian felt a hand on his shoulder and he stiffened, but Vincent eased him back against the bench, waiting until Brian turned to look at him.

"If Clare goes to the police," he said gently, "I can't guarantee her safety. It was very foolish to tell her anything."

Brian tried to speak, but his breath came short. The three blunt cars of a train glided along the top of the embankment, their wheels click-clicking over the same point in the track.

"You can trust me," he said, and he felt Vincent's hand squeezing his shoulder.

"I know I can." Vincent's voice was warm, and without looking at him Brian knew he was smiling, the disappointed but understanding father.

"Let's go now," Vincent said, and he stood, his hands balled in the pockets of his jeans. Brian blinked up at him a moment before he stood, still rubbing his wrist.

"Don't forget your rucksack." Vincent lifted his chin.

Brian picked up the daypack by a strap and slid it over his shoulder. They started to walk back toward the road without speaking, and Brian breathed hard through his mouth as if he'd just been running, his heart still racing, and he thought, It's not supposed to be like this. He wanted to stop Vincent with a touch on the elbow and say, It's not supposed to be like this, it's supposed to be over and instead everything's scarier than it was before and that's not the way it's supposed to be.

"I'll have the ticket now," Vincent said, his hands still in his pockets. He stopped, well back from the light from the road ahead, and Brian stopped without looking at him.

"What about Clare?" he said.

"What about her?" Vincent's face was blank, his eyes still pools of shadow.

"I mean, what about leaving her out of it?" He turned to Vincent, but kept looking ahead, beyond Vincent's shoulder toward the road.

Vincent smiled, searching Brian's face like a lover looking for a sign of infidelity.

"Are you going to tell me about innocence again?" he said. "I've no more time to waste, Brian. You're in no position to negotiate."

Brian tried to meet his gaze but he couldn't do it, and he stared numbly up the path where the two yellow lights blinked on opposite sides of the zebra crossing. A truck rumbled suddenly out from under the bridge and through the crossing, and Brian felt Vincent's hand on his arm, and he looked down to find the left luggage ticket between his own fingers. The truck ground into a higher gear, and Brian scowled down at the ticket as if someone else were holding it. Then Vincent took it and stepped back, glancing at the ticket and slipping it into his pocket. The truck whined away into the fundamental roar of the city, and Brian watched it go, until it disappeared behind a building and he realized Vincent was speaking to him.

"What?" Brian turned to the Irishman slowly, as if in a dream.

"I said," Vincent went on, the corner of his lip twitching, "stay away from the National Gallery tomorrow."

"The National Gallery," Brian repeated, and then he understood. He caught his breath.

"They'll be rearranging the paintings." He smiled. "There won't be anything to see."

"Right." Brian found himself laughing. "I mean, okay."

"Thank you, Brian." Vincent took Brian's hand in both of his and squeezed it. "Wish us luck."

"Good luck," Brian said, but Vincent was already gone.

Brian walked slower than the crowd, carrying his backpack up out of the Underground a leaden step at a time, while the people around him clattered up the steps into the cold, bright air of Victoria Station. He stopped at the top of the stairs and let them brush by him, and then walked slowly forward into the echoing roar of the station, a single, sluggish mote in the eddying currents of commuters. Up ahead he saw the wide, bright frontage of W. H. Smith's, its aisles crowded with browsers, heads bent over paperbacks and magazines. He drifted toward the bookstall, watching for Clare, but he didn't see her. He was half an hour late: she would be gone, she had ditched him again. He had almost not come himself; retrieving his pack from the left luggage at Euston Station, stuffing the new sleeping bag into the bottom compartment where the plastique had been, he thought of running, of taking the tube back out to Heathrow and buying his way onto the first plane home. But he was bone weary of lies and threats and deceptions, bone weary of running on somebody else's business. From now on, he thought, drifting to a stop under Victoria's high, latticed ceiling, my time belongs to me.

"How did it go?"

He turned to see Clare standing next to him, her eyes bright. For a moment he could not speak. She'd changed her clothes; she had on a blue sweater and scarf and mittens. She was wearing earrings now, he saw.

"Um, fine," he said.

"What did he say?" Her face was scrubbed and bright, her cheeks red in the cold.

"Who?"

"The guy." She pushed back her hair with a mittened hand.

"Thanks." Brian shrugged, the whole weight of his pack tugging at his shoulders. "He said thanks."

She drew a breath and let it out slowly.

"Are you hungry?" she said.

"Not really."

Another moment passed while they nodded at each other, and then she said, "Come on. I found us a place to stay."

She touched his elbow and they started forward, her hand hovering at his side until at last she took his arm.

They walked without talking past the rows of narrow hotels on Belgrave Road, their white breath trailing after them in the streetlit air. Pressing his arm she led him across the road into a hotel called the Liffey, through the hall past the lobby, where Brian glimpsed a red-headed woman watching a Fred Astaire movie on television, and then up a narrow, listing stairway. Clare let go of him to lead the way, the carpet rods clinking with every step, and she waited flushed at each landing as he came up with his pack.

On the third floor she pulled off her mittens and unlocked a door, opening it into a high-ceilinged room with two narrow, swaybacked iron beds, a sink in the corner, a huge wardrobe, and a dresser with an age-spotted mirror. Brian stepped past her into the middle of the room; it was overheated and smelled of old paint and disinfectant, lit only by two tall windows at the front overlooking the street, the amber light of the road glowing through the flimsy curtains. Clare's pack and some of her things—her boots, a notebook, a hairbrush—lay on one of the beds. Brian unbuckled his pack and unzipped his anorak; he turned around. Clare closed the door and leaned against it, her hand on the light switch. But she did not turn it on, and in the light from the street Brian slid out of the straps of his pack and lowered it to the floor, leaning it against the wall.

"Where's the bathroom?" The sound of his voice seemed too loud to him, even over the racket of taxis in the street below. He took off his anorak.

"Down the hall," Clare said, her hand still on the switch. "There's a bathtub too."

"A bath." He stood with his anorak crushed in his hand.

"Do you want one?"

"Not really."

He looked around for a place to hang the anorak, and she left the door and came across the room and took it from him, opening the rattling door of the wardrobe to hang it up on a hook. She closed the door and turned to him in the half-light, still clutching her mittens in her hand. Brian took them and tossed them on the bed with her other things, and he unwrapped her scarf and pulled her to him by the ends of it. He kissed her and tasted toothpaste, and he pulled her close, his face in her hair.

"You smell good," he said.

He felt her laugh against his chest, and she said, "You smell like the Underground."

"Do you want me to take a bath?"

"Not really," she said.

In the narrow, creaking bed, Brian felt as though he could not move. He had come back, he thought, to protect her, to keep her from harm, but instead Clare knelt over him in the glow from the window next to the bed, and she gazed down at him with a look of terrible patience, as if she knew what he was thinking, his whole history, everything he had ever done. She took his hand in hers and lifted it until it was full of her warm breast, pulling him up to her until he was kissing the smooth skin of her throat. Together they rolled, the bed whining under them, her legs tight around his waist, and he felt dizzy, vertiginous, as if he had dived into deep, unfamiliar water and could not tell which way was up. She had taken him by surprise, overwhelmed him. He was drowning. It was hard to breath. He pushed himself away from her, onto his side.

"Clare," he said, his throat tight, his hand on his forehead.

They lay half tangled still, Clare propped up on one arm watching him, one earring resting against her jaw while the other dangled in the light from the window. There were beads of sweat on her forehead.

"Are you okay?" She rubbed his chest, and Brian folded his hand over hers. He watched her without speaking for a long time, listening to the two of them breathe, sliding his hand slowly up her hip and ribs and across her shoulder and along her neck to brush her face with the tips of his fingers. He pulled her to him and kissed her between her breasts. He could feel her heart beating.

"You scare me to death," he murmured into her.

The first time inside her Brian moved slowly, carefully, as if he were afraid of hurting not her but himself, as if he were uncertain what to do. She held on to him tightly with her knees and rubbed his shoulders hard as he moved above her, her breasts shuddering as she breathed, her eyebrows drawn together as she looked up at him, concentrating on something just out of her reach. Brian was lost, he hadn't expected her to want him this much, he hadn't expected her fierceness in love. He pulled out of her suddenly and sank back on his knees between her legs, gasping for breath, wanting to cry, his back chilled with sweat. Clare breathed deep and pushed her fingers back through her hair, and she reached up to him with her other hand. Brian took it and bent to kiss her palm, then slowly he slid back and bent all the way down to bring his mouth between her legs. She twined her long fingers through his hair, and he closed his eyes and lapped at her desperately, as if he were drinking from her out of great need, and he did not stop even when she cried out and arched back into the bed and clutched at the back of his head, did not stop until she pressed her palms against his temples and pulled him away, up to her. She rolled him onto his back, covering his face and neck and chest with kisses, pushing him back into the bed with her smooth, warm hands. She straddled him and started to move against him with her eyes closed, until Brian grasped her by her shoulders and pulled himself up and cried out, "Clare, do you love me?"

She opened her eyes and steadied him back into the bed with her hands on his chest.

"Yes." She smiled and closed her eyes again, drawing him all the way up into her with the ancient rhythm, her breasts swaying, the bed creaking softly beneath them. He started to move with her and she bent down to him, her breasts warm against his chest, her breath warm on his throat, the two of them moving easily together as if this was the way they had always been.

On the morning of the seventh day they let Maire go. There was a final session in the interrogation room, where a furious Detective Inspector Glassie roared at her one last time from across the table, but she sat numbed and silent, buried alive in her own flesh by fatigue and grief, scarcely able to think of her own name, let alone say it aloud. In between his bluff threats, even Glassie admitted that they didn't have enough to charge her, only the microscopic threads from American currency that they'd vacuumed from the inside of the money belt, and even in the Six Counties, even under the PTA, it wasn't against the law to have a money belt that used to have money in it. Still, they kept the belt; there was no mention of it at all as they returned her coat, her watch, her purse, and a large plastic evidence bag full of assorted rubbish from the inside of her car. They were keeping the car a bit longer too, they said, she could come for it next week, and she said nothing, only signed the receipt for her possessions and let a constable in a bulletproof vest march her out into the street, his hand curled around her elbow.

"Maire."

When the hand was gone and the constable had gone back through the slitted blockhouse, she walked a few unsteady steps in the cold morning air and stopped on the pavement, her coat hanging open, her filthy hair lank against her neck, the evidence bag sagging from her hand at her side. Inside it had been bright all the time, a shadowless, fluorescent glare; outside it was just as shadowless, but dim and gray and overcast, as if she had a greasy film over her eyes. I'm free, she thought. She wondered what time it was, and slowly slid her hand into her purse for her watch.

"Maire."

The watch had stopped. Either the battery had died, or the buggers had taken the watch apart and killed it. She set the evidence bag down on the pavement and held the watch in one hand, tapping the crystal with a fingernail of the other. I can smell myself, she thought.

"*Maire.*"

She looked up from the watch and saw a blue car creeping along the street toward her. It stopped in front of her, its tires crunching against the curb, and Peter Egan watched her hopefully from behind the wheel, his eyebrows lifted, his face pale, his arms hanging out his open window, half lifted toward her.

"I've come to fetch you, Maire." He made as if to open his door, but Maire pocketed her watch, scooped up the plastic bag, and walked on her own around the front of the car. Peter leaned across and unlatched the passenger door, and she slid heavily in and sat with her knees pinched together, her purse and the bag clutched on her lap.

"All right." Peter put the car in gear and wheeled sharply around in the street, driving back through the roundabout and up Mount Merrion Road.

"Joe's opening the Ard Fheis this evening, else he'd be here himself." He glanced at her. "He left me behind to wait for you. I've been hanging about the gate like a lovesick schoolboy, asking after you every couple of hours or so, and all of a sudden there you are."

He laughed nervously, but she kept her eyes straight ahead, not seeing the houses and shops gliding by beyond the windscreen.

"What time is it?"

"Ah, it's half eight." He was watching her again. "Thursday morning. Ard Fheis starts tonight. We didn't think you'd make it." He was smiling at her, she could feel it. "So were they hard on you, then?"

She tightened her arms around the bundles in her lap. To look at him was to want to kill him.

"Listen, I thought I'd drop you at my flat, so you could shower and have a wee bite if you want it. Your flat's pretty well torn up so. Looks like the Brits played rugby in there." He cleared his throat, ponderously shifting gears. "I know you're only just out, but there's things we need to discuss."

He fell silent as he came to the corner of Ormeau Road, waiting for an Ulster Defense Regiment Land Rover to pass before he turned right toward the center of town. There were cars and buses out, and people on their way to work, those who had jobs.

"Maire, I need to know what they asked you," Peter said, not looking at her, his voice low. "There's been some things gone on since last Friday that you need to know about."

"Left here."

"What?"

"Turn left here." She tapped on the windscreen, and he braked suddenly, following the Land Rover into Sunnyside Street.

"It's the long way around, init?"

Another glance, but she said nothing. He licked his lips.

"Maire, Jimmy Coogan's dead." His voice was nearly inaudible over the hum of the car. "The Brits got him Sunday last, crossing the border."

The Rover paused at the gate of its base, waiting for those inside to open the double doors. The base was all corrugated iron and concertina wire, garnished with a few bold graffiti. FORT APACHE, somebody had spraypainted.

"We know about the Semtex." Peter drew breath as if he were about to plunge underwater. "We know what Jimmy had in mind, but now he's gone surely you can see there's no point in going through with it."

He paused again to turn left toward the bridge. The silence in the car reverberated; her arms ached around the bags on her lap. Given half a chance she'd tear his eyes right out of his head.

"Joe's willing to hear your input," Peter was saying. "Now that Jimmy's gone, none of us wants a split, do we?"

They were crossing the bridge over the river, the water swift and gray below. Now that Jimmy's gone, she thought. That's where you lose me, Peter.

"Stop the car," she said.

"Maire, listen to me. We need to think about unity now."

"You fucking bastard," she screamed, "don't you think I know who killed Jimmy? Stop the fucking car!"

When Peter did not stop, Maire began to hammer his face and shoulder and arm with her fist. He shouted and tried to fend her off with one hand, trying to steer with the other, weaving all over the road like a drunk. He grabbed for her wrist and missed, and she hit him and hit him and hit him.

"Stop the car!" she shouted, dry-eyed and furious. "Stop the car! Stop the car!"

On the far side of the bridge Peter veered for the side of the road. He tramped on the brake and heaved them both forward toward the windscreen; the car lurched to a stop and stalled, one tire up over the curb. She left off hitting him and clutched the sleeve of his thick corduroy jacket, digging her fingers in tight and twisting the fabric.

"Here's a message for Joe," she hissed. "Are you listening?"

"Maire." He turned his face to her, his eyes guilty and solicitous all at once, his hair disheveled. "I don't know what the Brits told you, but it's not so." He tried to reach for her.

"*Listen to me.*" She shook his arm violently by the sleeve, tearing the seam a bit at the shoulder, and he held up his hands to ward her off again. "Tell Joe I learned the hard way just how right Jimmy turned out to be. Tell him I learned how low a man can stoop to save his own arse. Tell him I learned what a lying, touting Judas he turned out to be."

Her voice had begun to tremble, and she stopped, flinging Peter's arm at him. He sat all in a heap in the corner of door and seat, glaring white-faced at her.

"Tell him Jimmy's gone, but if he thinks that's the end of it, he's bloody mistaken."

She reached past him and jerked the keys from the ignition, fumbling behind her for the door latch. Peter sat up from his petulant slouch and grappled for the keys, his eyes wild suddenly, but she battered him with her fists and pushed back out of the car, climbing from the open door with the purse and the evidence bag pressed under her arm, the keys in her other hand.

"Maire, don't be daft," Peter said out the door, his eyes pleading, and she flung the keys overarm, away over the car. Peter shouted, and she watched the keys tumble brightly over the road, watched them with something approaching release as they sailed over the rail and into the river. Peter scrambled out of his side of the car, florid and speechless, glancing at her, then toward the river in disbelief, then back at her. She gave a bark of a laugh.

"Tell him," she laughed, dancing back along the pavement in a rage, "tell him he's nowhere near the bloody end of it. Tell Joe his problems are just beginning."

Then she turned and ran, giddy and free like a wee girl again, chasing up the street for all she was worth, her purse bouncing at her side, the plastic bag swinging from her hand like a weapon. She glanced back once to see Peter Egan paralyzed in the middle of the street, cars swerving round him and blaring their horns; he rocked from one foot to the other, trying to decide which way to go, after Maire or after the keys. But I already know which way to go, said Maire to herself, clutching her new freedom under her coat, and she dashed around the corner and was gone.

At midday a man and a pregnant woman came out of the Underground in Trafalgar Square, the woman leaning on the man's arm as they came up the last few steps into the roar of traffic, the squeal of children, and the moan and chirrup of pigeons. The man was short and compact, with deepset eyes and gaunt cheeks, an old gray-checked cloth cap pulled down low across his forehead. He wore a green nylon Windbreaker zipped halfway up, while the woman on his arm let her cloth coat hang open, her enormous belly pushing her frock out past the lapels. Even in her flat shoes she was as tall as the man, waddling alongside with one hand tightly clutching the crook of his arm, her other hand in the pocket of her coat. A pair of round, black sunglasses rested on her nose, and her black hair hung like a helmet all around her head, bangs across her forehead, the straight sides like curtains over her cheeks.

The vault of gray cloud overhead was held up in the middle by Nelson's Column, newly cleaned and gleaming even in the overcast, and by the spire of the church of St. Martin-in-the-Fields, while in the street below black taxis and tall red buses raced each other around the square. Just outside the Underground, under the statue of Sir Henry Havelock, K.C.B. —his dark green head and shoulders smeared with white droppings—a crowd of thrilled and terrified children fed the birds out of little plastic cups. One boy stood grinning frantically with his head sunk between his shoulders and his arms rigidly outstretched, while fat gray pigeons prinked along the sleeves of his school blazer, picking at the feed in his shivering hands. The man and the woman walked straight through the strutting birds on the pavement, and the pigeons suddenly rose as one, thumping their wings to the shrill cries of the children. The pregnant woman clutched the man's arm more tightly, waving her other hand weakly about her face to ward off the thundering birds.

The woman set the stately pace, but the man led the way, through the chill, sifting spray from the fountain, up the wide steps under the equestrian statue of George IV—his head and shoulders likewise mantled with droppings—and slowly up to the curb at the corner of the square. They waited a minute or two until the traffic thinned out sufficiently, and then the man started across, holding up his hand to the oncoming wall of buses and taxis until he and the woman made the other side. They walked a little less stiffly along the front of the National Gallery, the woman's hand only resting now in the man's elbow. Coming up the steps under the portico of the gallery they waited for a mob of students to pass through the revolving door ahead of them, young men and women in dark overcoats and torn jeans and teased hair, all of them carrying sketch pads of various sizes. The last of the students, his dark hair artfully greased and tangled, stood back and motioned the couple ahead of him. The man smiled and nodded to the student and ushered the woman into a compartment of the door, where she held up her hands without touching the glass and walked forward with tiny steps.

At the cloakroom the man plucked a map of the gallery off the counter from under the dulled eyes of the attendant, and then returned to the woman, who leaned with one hand against the marble side of the first stair. She took his arm again, tightly, and climbed slowly through the vestibule, keeping to the side, out of the way of faster traffic, inching through the crosscurrents of people on the landing. Another flight up, in the bright, crowded museum shop, the man fell behind the woman and gently pushed her through the crowd of idling patrons, her belly clearing the way before them like the bow of an ocean liner through a crowded harbor. At the far end of the shop they stood near a sales counter, the woman surveying the racks of bright postcards from behind her sunglasses, resting her weight back on her heels, her hands pressed against her belly, while the man scowled down at the map spread between his broad hands.

"We'll improvise," Vincent had said the night before, in an upstairs room of a Kilburn pub, peremptorily ending a debate conducted over a brand-new, stiff-spined copy of a National Gallery guidebook. Passed around a rough table coated with rings of dried Guinness, the book was a little the worse for wear, the foldout map at the back half torn out. The British rooms were the obvious target, they all agreed, until Ann, who knew the museum from childhood, pointed out on the ground plan how much traffic was liable to pass through, people on their way to other galleries. Not to mention, interrupted Martin, who much to Vincent's dismay imagined himself an intellectual, what if one of the painters in the Brit gallery is Irish?

"I beg your pardon?" said Ann, who was never able to disguise her posh English upbringing.

"I mean," said Martin, who fancied Ann hopelessly, "half

your bloody English literature was written by Irishmen. Maybe some of the painters are Irish too. Somebody should check it out."

"Constable?" said Ann, her voice rising in disbelief. "Turner? *Gainsborough?*"

The others joined in, and Vincent was forced to take the conversation in hand.

"There's no more time," he said. "Brody opens the Ard Fheis tomorrow night, so there's no time for a trip to the library. We'll improvise. Once we're inside, Ann and I will find a quiet room and plant the device."

"You shouldn't risk yourself," said Martin, trying a different tack. "You're too important to the struggle." He drew himself up heroically. "I'll go with Ann."

Across the table Vincent saw Ann roll her eyes and open her mouth to cut the lad dead, and he held up an intervening hand.

"It's all right," he said, giving Martin's shoulder a comradely squeeze. "I'm a bit more experienced at this."

Martin pressed his lips together and nodded gravely to hide his disappointment, but even after the meeting was adjourned and Vincent was on his way down the stairs, Martin caught his sleeve and whispered a last bit of unsolicited advice.

"Try and find a room where the pictures are really expensive," he said, unable to restrain his own cleverness. "Money, that's something the Brits understand."

Arm in arm again, the man and woman walked slowly through the British rooms, and they passed under a rotunda in the chilly light of a skylight, surrounded by cool marble walls and tall archways leading off to other rooms at each point of the compass. A pair of guards, a black woman and an Asian man, nodded to each other from separate doorways, while well-dressed white women, singly and in pairs, circled slowly about, murmuring in the cavernous echo, pausing in front of tall, aristocratic portraits or cloudy landscapes to lean back on one spike heel each and lift their narrow chins. But the flat-footed woman urged her companion straight through the room with a squeeze of her hand, and they turned slowly like a double star through galleries of eighteenth-century French and Italian paintings, the man glancing at the pictures in passing, touching the brim of his cap as they glided past the guard in each doorway, while the woman only looked straight ahead through her sunglasses, as if she were blind as well as pregnant.

They came to a doorway without a guard and paused there, at the end of a long, wide, high-ceilinged room with white arches above and dark blue fabric covering the marble walls below, the paintings vivid against the fabric even in the diffuse underwater light from the skylight. The man pulled his arm free of the woman to look at his map—room 32, it said, French seventeenth century—and the woman watched as the only other patron, a pudgy, balding man in jeans and running shoes, drifted slowly past the guard in the doorway at the far end. Down the center of the room were a pair of wide, padded benches of black vinyl, with low backrests down the middle, a small gray dehumidifier between them.

The man pocketed his map and the woman took his arm, and without looking at each other they walked down the room, the only sounds the soft tread of their feet against the carpet and the cool hum of the dehumidifier. They passed a white statue of a nude, armless man and stopped at the first bench, where the man helped the woman lower herself onto the seat; she hung onto him with one hand and groped behind her with the other. Once she was settled, the vinyl creaking under her, the man glanced down the room at the guard in the far doorway, a tall Sikh with a pale turban above his trim blue uniform. When he turned back to the woman she was smiling up at him.

"Cardinal Richelieu," she said in a low voice.

"What's that?" The man widened his eyes, still clutching her hand.

"Behind you. It's Cardinal Richelieu."

He turned to see a huge, full-length portrait across the carpet from him, taller than life-size, of a man in rich, flowing red robes, holding his little hat out in front of him in one hand, his eyes drooping mournfully, on either side of his thin nose, with the burdens of power. The man turned again to the woman, glancing back the way they had come in. There was no one else in the room.

"An easy delivery," he wished her, squeezing her hand. She smiled again, and he let go of her and walked slowly down the room to the far door, past the guard. Halfway into the next room he stopped, turned, and walked back to the guard, who turned away from room 32 and lifted his eyebrows at the approach of the man in the cap.

"Pardon me," the man began, and behind the guard the woman pressed her shoulders against the low backrest and spread her legs out in front of her, flattening herself as much as possible. She pushed her hands through the pockets of her frock, which had been slit open on the inside, and felt with both hands for the tabs of the zip she had sewn under her false belly. Under her frock and over her rolled-up jeans she wore a tight muslin bodice with a large pouch stitched to the front of it, which she had made herself, following a pattern from a book of theatrical costumery. The zip was her own modification— plastic instead of metal, because it was quieter—and she found the twin tabs and pulled them apart under her frock, up the sides of the pouch near the seam. She glanced once over her shoulder, her black hair swinging, to see the man in the cap nodding at something the guard was saying, and then, her hands still pushed through her pockets, reached up into her belly and tugged the device free of the padding sewn into the pouch, until it rested between her thighs. She jerked her hands free of the pouch and bent over, hair falling past her cheeks, the sunglasses threatening to slide off to the carpet. Reaching under her skirt she let the device, wrapped in twine and dark muslin, drop into her hands, and she lowered it to the floor, leaning back with her hands on her knees to push it back with her feet into the shadowy overhang of the seat.

She stood up immediately, tossing her hair back, pushing the sunglasses up her nose with her middle finger. The skirt of her frock dropped down and she began to button her coat over her diminished but still rounded belly. She heard voices and turned to see a boy and girl, two of the students she and the man had met under the portico, whispering to each other as they came in the nearer door. The woman drew a breath and stepped forward away from the bench, stopping just under the doleful gaze of Cardinal Richelieu. The boy and girl dropped heavily to the bench behind her, the air whooshing out of the cushions. They whispered to each other, laughing and opening their sketchbooks with a rattle of paper. The woman smiled up at the cardinal.

"It's a girl," she said under her breath, and turned away.

"I want an outrage," Jimmy had said a week ago, shouting down the crackle of long distance to Vincent, pay phone to pay phone. "I want blood on Brody's hands, something that will shake him down to his toes and turn his beard white."

Vincent had nodded, though Jimmy couldn't see him from Belfast. He stood in the echoing roar of King's Cross, with both hands in the pockets of his jeans, the handset of the phone wedged between his jaw and his shoulder.

"The Underground?" he suggested, his hooded eyes following every passer-by.

"No," Jimmy said. "Not the general public. I want something to outrage the elite. I want the Tories to scream bloody murder."

"Something scientific?" Vincent said. "Jodrell Bank?"

"Christ," Jimmy burst out. "Who cares about astronomy?"

They were interrupted by the angry pipping of the phone, and while Jimmy plugged more coins into the slot his end, Vincent turned round, pulling a hand from a pocket and shifting the handset from one shoulder to the other.

"Art," Jimmy said when he came back. "Thatcher's a woman, women like art. The elite go to art galleries."

"Which one? The Tate?"

There was another burst of disdain from Jimmy.

"Nobody minds if you blow up modern art," he said. "The Tories'd stand up in Parliament and cheer."

Vincent rolled his eyes toward the blackened girders over his head. Jesus, but Jimmy was hard to please.

"How about the National Gallery?" It was the only other art gallery he knew.

"That sounds good." Jimmy's voice changed suddenly, sounding almost enthusiastic. "I like the sound of that. What's that like?"

"I don't know, I've never been. It's big, though. It's in Trafalgar Square."

"That's the one!" Jimmy shouted like an excited football fan. "Right at the heart of the beast!"

"We'd lose some support," Vincent felt constrained to mention. "Art lovers, the trendy Left, like that."

"Ah, that's Brody's constituency." Jimmy had laughed. "Fuck 'em."

In the ladies' toilet downstairs, the woman perched on the edge of the seat in a narrow stall, her legs crossed, her shoulders hunched, the false belly still thick around her middle. The cloth coat hung a foot away on a hook inside the door. Her frock was tucked up around her waist, the legs of her jeans rolled down, a fashionable inch or two of her bare calf still showing. She propped her elbow on her knee, her chin on the heel of her hand, and smoked a cigarette as she waited for the elderly woman she'd come in with to have her pee and leave. The sunglasses were already in one pocket of the hanging coat, the black wig folded flat in the other. She lifted her chin and blew smoke up over the top of the stall, and listened at last to the toilet flush in the next stall, listened to the click of the old woman's heels against the floor, the rush of water, and the whine of the electric dryer. The woman pushed her fingers back through her cropped blond hair, and she took another drag on the cigarette. The click of the old woman's heels came closer and stopped just outside the stall. The woman held herself very still, her lungs full of smoke, and the old woman outside tapped timorously on the door of the stall.

"Pardon me?" came her voice.

The woman exhaled and dropped the cigarette behind her into the bowl, freeing her hands.

"Yes?"

"I say, I couldn't help noticing that you're a bit pregnant," came the old woman's voice, deferential and insinuating all at once.

The woman said nothing; she silently uncrossed her legs, both feet flat on the floor.

"Of course, it's not my place to say anything," the old woman went on, pitching her voice higher and louder, "but you shouldn't smoke, dear. It's very bad for baby."

"Yes, of course," the woman said, unclenching her hands. "My husband says the same thing."

"Well, he's right, my dear." Her heels clicked away. "He's only thinking of what's best."

The door thumped shut after her, and the woman stood. Reaching under the frock, she wrenched the bodice around until the padding was against the small of her back. She tucked the frock securely up, and then lifted the coat off the hook. She pulled both sleeves all the way through, flipped the collar over, and put it on, buttoning it all the way up. Outside the stall she stopped and regarded herself sideways in the mirror, throwing her shoulders back enough so that the hang of the coat fell straight and smooth past the padding. Her hands in her pockets, her eyes wide and blank, she walked out of the ladies' and up the steps into the vestibule, shouldering through the door and out under the portico. It was raining now, the cars and buses hissing through the gleaming street below. The children were gone from the square, the birds hidden in the trees out of the rain, but Nelson's Column still gleamed, Nelson himself standing high above, one foot forward, his back to the woman on the portico. She stood in the shadow of a pillar to light another cigarette and then stepped out into the rain, coming down the steps trailing smoke, her shoulders back, her chin lifted, the rain beating through her hair to her scalp.

At the same time a balding, compact man, his blue nylon Windbreaker zipped halfway up, pushed through the door at the north end of the gallery into Orange Street. Out on the pavement he paused a moment in the rain, rubbing the high dome of his head. Orange Street was empty except for a woman struggling with an umbrella, but up ahead he saw people hurrying by the corner into St. Martin's Place, clutching the collars of their coats, holding newspapers over their heads, running for cover. He made as if to reach inside the Windbreaker for the checked cap tucked in his belt, but instead he tugged the zip all the way up, shoved his hands in his pockets, and ducked out into the rain. He jogged with his shoulders hunched up around his ears until he came into Charing Cross Road; then he slowed to a brisk walk, twisting his shoulders this way and that through the crowd. In Leicester Square he dashed across the street into the entrance of the Underground, where he paused for a moment to brush the water off his head. He waited by a phone as a shoal of people climbed up the steps from the latest train and stepped out into the rain. Then he picked up the handset, dialed 999, and waited for the emergency operator.

"This is the IRA," he said when she came on the line. "Listen carefully."

When Clare awoke she was alone in bed, and she rolled over in the tangled sheets to see Brian standing naked on the thin carpet, folding last night's scattered clothing in the cold, gray light. His butt was smooth and pale, set off by the summer's fading tan, and he held her sweater up to his chest by its shoulders and folded it shut, flinging it up with one hand and expertly doubling it over his other forearm. She felt like applauding, and she pushed herself up on her elbow. Brian stooped to pick up her jeans, and he saw her watching him and smiled.

"Are you going to bring me my breakfast too?" she said, stretching out under the sheet, still sticky with sweat, her legs pleasantly aching, the taste of him still in her mouth.

"Depends." He held her jeans up by the waistband and shook the legs loose.

"On what?" Through the window next to her she heard the traffic from Belgrave Road, and a small but determined draft through the window chilled her between her shoulder blades.

"On what you want."

"Well, whaddaya got?" She waggled her shoulders, vamping a bit.

"Jesus." Brian shook his head, and he bent nearer the bed to pick up his shirt. Clare lunged for him and caught his wrist, pulling him off balance into the bed, kicking the bedclothes away. He protested, laughing, and they grappled with each other, the bed shaking noisily under them.

"Clare," he said as she pinned him back, "it's ten o'clock already."

"Yeah," she said, throwing a leg over him just to be sure, "and I'm *starving*."

She wouldn't tell him where they were going, she said, because she wanted it to be a surprise, but the truth was she didn't know herself. After last night it didn't really matter where they went today, it was just good to be out walking in the roar of the city, last night's love-making trapped like a flame under their sweaters. Even the gray clouds overhead seemed fulsome and bright, and the fine, misting rain that fell across their faces seemed to Clare cold and bracing for once, like the thrilling, ecstatic shock of a mountain stream.

Later, maybe tonight, she'd take him around to see some of her English friends, maybe even display him to Ian, but right now she wanted him all to herself. She led him past Bucking-ham Palace because she knew he'd grumble about it, but there was nothing going on, just red-coated guards parading use-lessly up and down the forecourt for the benefit of sodden tourists huddled against the railing. To her surprise, Brian scarcely noticed, and walking under the bare, black trees along the Mall, through the fine spray thrown up by passing taxis, he seemed silent and withdrawn. She was afraid to look at him, afraid that he was beginning to regret last night. Coming under the Admiralty Arch, she drew a deep breath and took his hand, and he held on to her tightly, his hand strong and callused, the heat of his touch shooting all the way up her arm and down her spine.

At the edge of Trafalgar Square they waited for a break in the traffic, their hands swinging between them. The rain had stopped and the overcast lifted a little, Nelson's Column shin-ing against the backlit clouds; the broad-shouldered buses were bright red against the dirty white façades of the imperial build-ings all around, punctuated by the black taxis scuttling be-tween them.

"How 'bout finding a place to eat?" Brian shouted over the traffic.

"All right," she said and dashed forward, dragging him after her, the two of them holding on to each other all the way across. On the other side he hauled her to a stop, and folded her hand in his arm.

"Slow down," he said, but she led the way across the square under the lee of the Column, the pigeons in their path strutting obliviously out of the way.

"I know a good place," she said, turning to him.

"Is it far?" he said. He hung back a little, dragging his steps, pulling on her arm. "I, I don't know if I can make it. I'm too weak."

She punched him in the arm and pulled him forward be-tween the fountains.

"Don't be a baby." She pointed up at the National Gallery with her free hand. "It's right there."

She let go of him to start up the steps, and Brian came a step or two behind her.

"That's a place to eat?" he said. "What, it's like a really big McDonald's, or what?"

At the corner she took his hand again.

"No, it's the National Gallery. It's an art museum. Come on."

She pulled him into the traffic again, and they jogged across in stops and starts. On the other side, he pulled her to a stop again and let go of her hand.

"Wait a second," he said.

She turned and kept walking, backward. "Hurry up," she said. "There's always a crowd at lunch."

They stood several paces apart on the sidewalk, and Clare smiled back at him. He wasn't looking at her, though, but stared up at the museum, his eyes searching out details as if he recognized them, his tongue pushing at his cheek. He opened his mouth and closed it again without saying anything.

"What?" Clare started back to him, still smiling, but she was beginning to feel anxious again.

"Museum food." He pushed his fingers back through his hair, still not looking at her.

"Well, yeah." The smile was getting harder to maintain. Brian didn't look as though he was joking anymore.

"A lot of soup and salads, right?" He lowered his eyes and looked at her sidelong. "Little dinky sandwiches with sprouts and shit."

"Brian, it's not that bad."

He lifted his hands as if he was trying to calm her down, and the gesture annoyed her.

"All right." He nodded, looking past her again. "All right. It's just that I'm really hungry, okay?"

"Okay." She gave up trying to smile. "Where would *you* like to eat?"

Her stomach was tightening. He was watching her now with that look Ian had given her in the last weeks, the look that said

"I'm being straightforward" when he wasn't, the way he looked as he jerked the rug out from under her smaller enthusiasms in order to postpone breaking her heart outright.

"You see what I'm saying, Clare?" He gave her a crooked, charmless smile, the light gone from his eyes, hidden out of sight.

"All right, I'll take you to Pizza Hut."

She brushed past him and started around the corner toward Charing Cross Road. He caught her arm but she kept walking.

"Clare, wait." He trotted alongside her. "Are you pissed? Clare, hang on, I'm sorry."

She stopped abruptly and he caught himself a few steps past her, turning back with his hands raised again. The gesture annoyed her even more this time.

"Is this about food?" she said, peering at him as if into a bright light.

"Clare." He came up to her, gingerly touching her shoulders. She watched him search her face, watched his eyes plead with her while he fumbled for something to say.

"Come on." She took his arm and led him away to keep from having to meet his eyes, and they walked without talking up Charing Cross Road. She felt him glancing at her, and she tried to smile but couldn't. He isn't Ian, she told herself, that was a month and a half, two months ago. She drew a breath and blew it out. Count to ten, her mother always said. Life's too short.

"Clare, are you still mad?" They stood on the curb in Cambridge Circus, and she shrugged, trying to think of a way to say that she wasn't without appearing to back down. They crossed the road without touching each other, and as they came out from under the huge, unlit marquee of the Palace Theatre, it began to rain again, fat drops bouncing in the street between the taxis. They ducked their heads, and Brian grabbed her hand and pulled her into the dull doorway between a picture framer and an all-day café. He pressed her shoulders up against the door of the Town and Country Language School and kissed her.

"I'm sorry," he said. "I didn't mean to start an argument."

She watched him, hanging fire a moment longer, but his eyes were shining now, as brightly as the night before.

"Was last night a mistake?" she said, astonishing herself.

"No." He kissed her again, and this time she lifted her hands and laced her fingers behind his neck.

The blast wave of an explosion moves faster than the speed of sound. The detonation wave, the chemical reaction that spreads in a front through the explosive itself from the spark of detonation, moves even faster, up to 30,000 feet per second, so that all of the explosive appears to ignite simultaneously, interlocking rings of carbon, hydrogen, nitrogen, and oxygen violently releasing their binding energies as heat and as huge volumes of gas. The gases released are all simple end products— carbon monoxide, carbon dioxide, nitrogen, steam—but they expand at an enormous rate, driving the ordinary air around the device outward, the heat of their release converted to a thick wall of pressure, much higher than that of the surrounding atmosphere. This wave front, the blast wave itself, lasts in passing for only a few thousandths of a second; although it moves faster than sound, all that energy is expended to heat the surrounding air, to put it under pressure, so that the intensity of the wave decreases rapidly, becoming a few rooms away a strong, hot wind blowing dust and fragments before it, becoming at last only sound itself, a hollow, percussive boom accompanied a moment later by the concussion, shivering the floor and walls like a tuning fork, rattling your bones and the teeth in your head.

But that is still rooms away, just enough to tighten your stomach and make you look around frantically at the other patrons looking frantically back over their shoulders. The hot wind is gritty and smells of dust, and a moment later it blows back the other way, the air around the center of the explosion rushing back to fill the hollow space of low pressure behind the shock wave. As you stand shaking and anxious, you can hear in the distance, down the long, cool halls, the tinkle of glass and the shrilling of alarm bells and screams for help. Guards in blue uniforms, moving slowly at first like dream walkers, begin to shout at one another, some running in the direction of the blast, some shepherding frightened patrons in the other direction, arms wide and voices sharp and loud.

Closer to the blast, in the adjoining rooms—where it is possible to experience the blast wave itself and not its fading echoes, but far enough away to pass through the shock wave and still survive—you feel the concussion before you hear anything. Or see anything, for that matter, for there is no flash. Instead, the advancing wall of air carries you right off your feet and hurls you away like wadded paper, stinging you with needles of dust and splinters of wood, metal, marble, and bone. And for one brief, endless moment, as the wall of overpressure engulfs you, you feel the insufferable weight of it all around you like the hot weight of miles of seawater, twisting your limbs in all directions, crushing the air out of your lungs, driving your eardrums in. Then it passes, leaving you to fall breathless in what is called a region of decaying pressure, and you lie among the debris, insensible and uncomprehending, as the wind rushes back where it came from, the vast indrawing of breath after the enormous sigh of the explosion.

In the room itself, the effects are the most severe. When the blast wave strikes the walls, the air comes abruptly to a complete stop, the rest of the expanding gases piling up behind it. This arrested velocity is instantly converted to heat, which in this case is the same thing as pressure, sometimes as high as eight times the pressure of the original wave. In other words, although there is no one left alive to see it, the walls crack and bow outward and groan, the floor beneath the device is blown out completely, hurling fragments and chunks of marble into the basement room below. Statues, one of them already missing its arms, crack and break apart like plaster and spin away in pieces. Farther away, where the heat of the arrested blast wave is not enough to ignite canvas and ancient oils and wood, the paintings are only blackened and torn, their frames splintered and wrenched apart. Closer in, though, just across the room from the device, the devious aristocrat Cardinal Richelieu flashes instantly into flame and crumbles away, the black smoke of his ignition flattened into an expanding ring of molecules against the wall around the portrait. The dehumidifier is rent into tangled pieces of metal; the bench itself evaporates into fragments of wood and shreds of black vinyl and plastic foam. Finally, at the epicenter of the blast, the boy and girl on the bench, young enough to believe still in their own immortality, cynical and glib and foolish with the easy nihilism of students, and utterly innocent of all but the pettiest cruelties and betrayals, have no consciousness of being blown to pieces, because it is over before sensation is possible. They are literally reified, converted instantly to by-products, more complicated than carbon dioxide and nitrogen and steam, but nearly as inert.

Overhead the iron frame and the roof slates of the skylight detach and rise straight up into the air, the aged glass blown outward in brilliant greenish fragments. Then, having hung impossibly motionless at the apex of its rise, the skylight falls back through toward the ruined floor below, the iron twisted and warped, the slates loose and cracked, pulled through by gravity and the inrush of cold, damp air, crashing at last against the cratered marble like a final chord, a last dissonant crescendo.

In the British Museum, in the slow-moving line for the coffee shop, Brian let go of Clare's hand, afraid that she would notice how his heart was pounding. He was hot as well, and he stripped off his anorak and folded it over his arm. Clare smiled at him and then mercifully looked away, and he leaned against the pale wall and silently let out a deep breath. Neither of them had said much on the walk from Cambridge Circus, but it had been raining, and by now Clare seemed to have put their argument behind her, resurrecting it only when Brian had insisted they eat first, before they toured the museum.

"I thought you hated museum food," she'd said with a light in her eye.

"Art museum food," he'd said, trying to smile, trying to bring them back to where they had been that morning, in the hotel. "I meant art museum food."

Something was lost, though, her guard was up again, and perhaps that was just as well. Her silence on the way over had given him time to think of an approach, of a way to explain, his knitted brow and shortness of breath hidden by the hood of his anorak, pulled up over his head against the rain. But the time had been wasted: everything he thought to say seemed feeble and useless.

Clare, we need to talk, he'd thought, staring down at the raindrops spattering against the sidewalk, his lips working behind the edge of his hood. There's something I need to tell you.

In the cafeteria line Claire pushed the tray, and Brian followed at her elbow. He picked up a plastic-wrapped sandwich without noticing what it was and put it on the tray, and she caught his eye and said, "I thought you were hungry." So he picked up another one and nodded for her to keep going, certain that he wouldn't be able to eat a bite of either.

"Oh, look, somebody's leaving."

She clutched his arm, and he looked across the square room, full of diners at square black booths. A couple of men were leaving a booth, shrugging into their coats and clearing away their trash.

"I'm going to grab their seat," Clare said. "Have you got enough money?"

She slipped away down the line without waiting for an answer, and Brian slid the tray along, fumbling slowly for his change at the cash register. He carried the tray high through the crowded aisle, and he set it on the table Clare had claimed, slipping into the narrow booth across from her. She lifted her salad and her cup of tea off the tray, and peeled the plastic wrap from the salad with two precise fingers.

"Clare."

She lifted her eyes to him, her eyebrows raised, and she stabbed a forkful of lettuce.

"Are you still mad at me about the art gallery?"

It was feebler than anything he'd thought of on the way here, but he watched her across the table, his hands tightly clutching either end of the tray.

"No." She looked at him and closed her mouth over the salad.

"Are you mad about something else?" His throat was dry. He was afraid that if he let go of the tray his hands would flop all over the table like landed fish.

Clare put down her fork and looked away, forcing down the mouthful of salad.

"I'm sorry," he said. "It's just that I feel like something's wrong."

She sighed and swung her gaze to him. "It's nothing," she said, fingering her fork. "I've never done anything like this before, that's all."

"Like what?"

"Like us." She blushed and looked away again, lifting her hand to gesture at the space between them. "I mean, I've only known you for a week. It's all been so fast, you know?"

She looked tentatively back in his direction and smiled, and for a moment he felt an unbearable tenderness toward her, passing over him like heat, almost as if they were alone together again, back in bed in each other's arms, with nothing at all between them.

"But like, this isn't the place to talk." With two hesitant jerks she laid her cool fingers on his hand.

"Clare, it's not just us." He let go of the tray and grasped her hand, tightly.

"What do you mean?" She watched him, her eyes narrowed, sweetly puzzled, breaking his heart. He tried to speak, but his throat tightened as if someone—Jimmy Coogan, perhaps—were closing his hand around Brian's neck.

"The money?" The light rose in Clare's eyes and she let go of him, looking down and smiling to herself. She picked up her fork again. "This is definitely not the place to talk about *that*."

"Clare."

She poked at one of his wrapped sandwiches with her fork.

"Aren't you going to eat?" she said, spearing a tomato slice from her salad.

He started to reach across the table for her hand again, and a couple of students, a boy and a girl in bulky sweaters and teased orange hair, brushed against their table, and Clare glanced up at them. Above their drawling apology the public address pinged, and a voice began to make an announcement in a droning voice.

"There wasn't any money," Brian said, trying to catch Clare's eye.

"Hm?" She raised her eyebrows at him again, her mouth full. The students slid into the booth behind her.

"Clare, there isn't any money. There never was."

He wanted to reach for her again, and Clare watched him, her eyes narrowing, the fork poised in midair. The public address was a bit louder now, repeating what it had said before, and the orange-haired girl in the next booth hushed her companion and twisted around in her seat to touch Clare's shoulder.

"I beg your pardon," said the girl, "but did you hear what they just said?"

Brian glared past Clare at the girl, and the boy with her said, "Listen."

The public address cleared its throat again with a ringing tone, and all around the room people looked up. Conversations dwindled away. Across the table Clare sat straight-backed with her head nearly touching the girl's over the back of the booth. Brian tried to speak again, but Clare lifted her hand for him to be quiet. He could hear only snatches of the announcement, like a radio station fading in and out.

"The British Museum regrets," it said, a thin, nasal, feminine drone. "Absolutely no cause for alarm."

"They're closing the museum," whispered the girl, exchanging a glance with Clare.

"They can't be," snapped the boy. "It's only one o'clock."

"Appreciates your cooperation," droned the public address. "Regrets the inconvenience."

"What's going on?" someone said loudly, over the silence of the other diners.

Clare turned to Brian, her face blank, as if she couldn't see him, as if he wasn't even there, and he sat unable to move, his nerves ringing like an alarm.

"Look, I'm sorry, but you all heard the announcement."

Brian twisted around and saw a guard in a blue uniform, a ruddy, black-haired man, lift his hands and march halfway into the dining room.

"You'll just have to leave your tea where it is and go." The guard stopped and patted the air with his hands. "Nobody's in any danger, but you all must leave immediately."

The room began to rustle with movement, the murmur of anxious conversation rising again like a tide.

"Please gather your things quickly," the guard shouted. "Quickly and in an orderly manner."

Clare passed Brian in the aisle before he realized she'd gotten up, and he snatched his anorak out of the seat next to him and pushed out to follow her against the stream of people. Up ahead he saw her touch the guard's arm, saw the man nod to her and answer her with a shrug and a lift of his hands and a few words that Brian could not hear. Brian stood numb and enervated; nervous, whispering people brushed past him, stepping on his feet. He watched Clare drift back to him with the crowd.

"What's he say?" He turned as she passed him and reached into the booth for her scarf.

"He doesn't know anything." She jerked the scarf around her

neck without looking at him. "He says they have orders from the police to evacuate the building."

"Clare . . ."

She turned away and was carried by the crowd toward the door, the two heads of orange hair bobbing ahead of her like flowers. Brian couldn't move, his feet were fixed to the floor, and then he was pushing through the crowd, watching the back of Clare's head flash in and out of view up ahead.

"Clare," he said sharply, and she glanced back without seeing him, her face as dark and still as if she were asleep.

The crowd pressed through the doorway, crushing him, and Brian popped through like a cork into the stairway. The crowd was thinner and faster here, feet scuffing down the steps, and he pulled his anorak around him, jamming his hands through his sleeves. He dashed down the stairs just behind Clare, weaving through the crowd after her into a long room of masonry and fragments of statues, the tap and scrape of footsteps echoing around the long, white hall. Clare seemed to move no faster than the others, but somehow he couldn't keep up. At the far end, in the doorway of the museum bookshop, she stopped in front of two guards, and Brian shot past her, turning to beat back to her against the tide. He pressed against the wall across the doorway as the crowd streamed between him and Clare.

"It's a precautionary measure, miss," the guard was saying, and Brian saw that the man wasn't a guard at all, but a policeman no older than he was, with a youthful wisp of mustache. He wore a long black overcoat and a checked band around his cap.

"There's been a bombing in another museum, and sometimes these things come in series." The cop's eyes flickered across to Brian and returned to Clare, while his partner stood by with his hand pressed to his ear, listening to an earphone and watching the crowd slip by.

"Which museum?"

He couldn't see her face, but Clare's voice was steady and controlled and hard. He started across to her and was buffeted back by the crowd, his hand half raised to her.

"National Gallery, miss," the young policeman said, and he dipped his head toward the diminishing stream of people behind her. "Best to move along now."

Brian slipped across to her and tried to steer her away from the cop, but she was immobile in his grasp, rocklike.

"Who did it?"

"The bombing, miss?" The cop lifted his eyebrows.

"Yes."

Brian smiled frantically at the cop with the earphone, who frowned and jerked his head toward the far door.

"It's much too early to say, miss." The young cop lifted himself up on his toes.

"Fuckin' Irish, probably," snapped the cop with his hand to his ear. "Now pack it in and move along."

Clare twisted away from Brian and bolted through the door, and he started after her, his legs shaking under him, his heart banging in his chest. He couldn't catch up, though, and she began to run, down the long room past the displays of books and bright postcards, dodging through the last of the crowd toward the far door.

"Clare!" Brian cried, turning several heads but not hers. He jogged through the door and came into the lobby, where anxious voices echoed like a waterfall and shoes squeaked against the floor. Two lines of guards formed a wide V funneling people toward the bank of glass doors, and ahead Brian saw the back of Clare's head slipping in and out of sight as the crowd thickened near the doors. He waded in after her, his chin lifted to keep her in sight, his blood pounding in his throat. Somebody barged into him from behind, and Brian was forced to the side, carried by the crowd toward the bright doors, unable to see Clare in front of him.

Outside the doors he squeezed through the stream of people between the tall pillars until he saw the steps falling away before him, bright sunlight pouring through a ragged gap in the clouds. Clare walked down them slowly as the crowd clattered past her, her back erect, her head dipping with each step as if she were too tired to hold it up. Brian jumped down two steps at a time, squinting in the unexpected glare, and coming alongside he grabbed her wrist and jerked her to a stop. She whirled and twisted her arm to free it, but he did not let go.

"Clare," he said hoarsely, "I didn't know."

She wrenched her arm free, and he saw that her face was white, the blood drained out of it, her lips squeezed bloodlessly together, her breath coming slow and hard.

"What have you done to me?" she hissed.

Her eyes burned at him, but Brian could not look away. He searched her face as if for a wound, trying to speak.

"You said it wasn't money," she whispered, her voice tight with pain.

"It was money," Brian said, choking. "It was just money."

"Liar!" she cried, and she hit him with her closed fist beneath his eye, hit him hard enough to knock him down. He fell against the steps, his eyes squeezed shut. He heard the thud of pigeon wings. He pushed himself blind up off the cold stone and she hit him again, and he fell back and slid with a bump to the next step down. Someone hooked a hand under his elbow, and he lifted his arm to ward off another blow, squeezing his eyes even tighter. But the hand tugged him to his feet, and a woman's voice said, "Easy. It's all right." He opened his eyes. A thin woman with black hair pulled straight back from her brow held his arm and peered into his face.

"Are you all right?" she said, and Brian, speechless, pulled away and started uneasily down the steps. Clare was halfway across the gleaming courtyard in the bright light, the crowd spread out all around her. The chain had been pulled aside at the main gate, and people poured onto the sidewalk and into the street. Clare sailed among them without looking back, splashing heedlessly through a shining puddle, her chin up, her back straight.

"I don't think that young woman wants to talk to you," the thin woman called after him, but Brian stumbled across the courtyard like a sleepwalker, his legs stiff and slow. Ahead he saw people peering back at the museum through the black bars of the railing, and beyond them a single black taxi creeping slowly up the street through the crowd. The dim lights of a zebra crossing flashed uselessly, ignored by everyone. A policeman at the gate waved Brian through, and over the heads of the crowd he saw Clare climbing into the taxi, a bright red Coke advertisement on its door.

"Please move along," someone said behind him, but Brian was already running through the crowd toward the taxi, pushing people aside and shouting Clare's name. The taxi rolled away even as she pulled the door shut, the driver leaning on the horn as he bulled his way through the people milling in the street. Brian saw the dark of her hair in the rear window, and he ran faster, thinking he was catching up, yelling her name again. He collided with someone and spun against the low wall beneath the museum railing, and as he pushed himself away the cab broke free of the crowd and charged ahead. It leaned heavily to one side as it took the corner, and he saw Clare's arm through the gleam of the side window, her hand clutching the strap. He ran, breathing her name. At the corner he stopped, shaking, watching as the cab disappeared around the next corner, at the far end of the museum.

Brian was running, looking for cabs or buses or even an entrance to the Underground. There had been no more taxis in front of the museum, so he ran down narrow, dark streets, their filthy gutters smelling of garbage, trying to find his way back to where he'd been before. Above him the torn edges of gray clouds cut off the light again, and in a thin drizzle he came into a street full of black taxis and tall red buses. But all the taxis were taken and virtually immobile, ticking loudly fender to fender, the buses shouldering their way among them. So he ran, his throat dry, his side stitched with pain. He couldn't think; he didn't know where he was, glancing in vain up every side street for a sign or a landmark. Everyone else on the sidewalk seemed to be going the other way, or stopped in the open doorway of a shop or a cinema, and he charged through them, pushing them aside, clutching them by the shoulders and spinning them around. They cursed after him, but he kept running, past bright boutiques full of pounding pop music, past shabby men on street corners selling windup toys and digital watches and Christmas wrap, past McDonald's and Burger King and Benetton. Alongside him taxis squealed and ticked, crawling up the jammed street inch by inch.

He veered into the traffic suddenly, slipping between cabs as they heaved forward against their brakes and their drivers shouted through windshields, pushing off the side of a bus and vaulting the rain-slick railing on the opposite sidewalk. He grabbed the arm of a man trying to light his pipe in the damp.

"Underground station," he blurted.

The man blinked and stammered something with the pipe clenched between his teeth, the lit match poised over the bowl. Brian danced backward breathlessly, begging the man with his eyes.

"Ah, ah, Oxford Circus," the man gasped, jerking the pipe out of his mouth and pointing up the street.

He shouted something else, but Brian was gone, running through the odors of greasy food and automobile exhaust, through the pulse of loud music and the grind of buses. He could run all day, run forever if he had to, but he needed a clear, open stretch, he couldn't do it stopping and starting, pushing and weaving against the bovine stream of people. He dropped off the curb and ran slack-mouthed in the gutter alongside the taxis, and ahead, above the heads of the crowd, he saw the red-and-blue sign of an Underground station, and he jumped another pedestrian barrier, shoving his way through to the entrance and plunging two steps at a time past the people on the stairs into the bright, dank corridor below.

In the station he pushed through the sluggish lines at the dull gray ticket machines and swung over the turnstile on one hand, hammering down the metal steps of the escalator to the Victoria Line, the people riding below glancing back at the sound and squeezing to the side at the last minute to let him pass. The doors of the train were sliding shut as he came onto the platform, and he shouted "Wait!" his voice echoing up and down the platform, turning heads. He slipped through sideways just in time and fell into a seat.

He rode with his breath coming hard and his eyes closed, opening them only when the train stopped at Green Park, squeezing them shut again as the train glided forward, trying to convince himself that Clare's cab was caught in traffic someplace, that if he could only talk to her for five minutes he could make her understand. But his ears were full of the clatter of the train, and all he saw behind his eyelids was the rage and hurt in her eyes when she knew; he felt impaled by that look as if upon a spear, and no matter how he twisted and writhed he could not push himself off.

At Victoria Station he bolted onto the platform, shoving through the crowd and up the escalator. He vaulted the gate again on one hand, the woman in the booth shouting after him, and charged up the stairs into the train station. He made himself walk, his heart pounding, until he was out of the station, and then he started to run again. It was raining harder now, and the people on Belgrave Road walked quickly with their hands in their pockets and their shoulders hunched. As he ran the rain fell against his face and trickled through his hair to chill his scalp.

He banged the door of the Liffey against the wall as he came in, and he entered the lobby with his chest heaving, dripping water all over the worn blue carpet. A broad-chested man in a sweater stood behind the desk watching the television across the lounge, his mouth set, his eyebrows drawn together. Brian unzipped his anorak and rested his hands on the counter. He gasped for breath, his eyes wide.

"Number eleven," he managed to say, but the man behind the counter didn't move, didn't even turn away from the television. Light-headed, Brian swung around to look, dragging his hands off the counter. The red-headed woman from the night before leaned forward in an armchair, her hands on her knees. On the television a man in a cream-colored raincoat stood holding a BBC microphone.

"We've still no word yet on casualties, Peter," he said, "but as you can see, there are still ambulances arriving here in Trafalgar Square, over an hour after the explosion."

"Bastards," said the man behind the counter. He was Irish.

Brian turned back to the counter, where the man was slowly shaking his head.

"Number eleven," Brian said, and the man turned to him.

"What room?" he said, and Brian closed his eyes.

"Eleven," he breathed. "Number eleven."

As the man turned for the key he called out to the lounge, "Isn't number eleven the young American couple?"

"Aye, it is," said the woman in the armchair, without looking away from the screen.

"Well, here's the lad, then."

The man held the key in his hand, but close to his chest, out of Brian's reach. Brian nearly lunged across the counter for it, but he turned and saw the red-headed woman pushing herself up out of the chair.

"What did you do to that girl?" The woman stood before Brian with her thick arms crossed and her feet set apart on the carpet.

"Was she here?" Brian said.

"Oh, aye, she was here, and practically in tears." The woman lifted her chin and rocked back on her heels. Brian felt trapped between her and the man behind the counter. "Long enough to fetch her rucksack and check out."

"How long ago?" Brian twisted back to the counter, and the man closed his fist over the key.

"And checking out's hardly what I'd call it," the woman went on. "Didn't she just leave the key and head for the door, and I say are yez leaving us, then? You've paid for the next night, and she says yes, keep the money, I'm goin'."

"When?" Brian pleaded.

"So I say what about your young man, and she just waves her hand and says not a word, all the time backing for the door and blinking back the tears." The woman waved her hand abruptly. "I could see the wee girl was in distress, so I say, darlin', is there anything the matter?"

"For Christ's sake, when?" Brian banged the counter with his palm, tears coming into his eyes. On the television the correspondent was gone, and an ambulance sped by, the shaky camera panning to follow it, the blue light flashing as the ambulance splashed around a corner.

"Well, she could hardly hold back the tears, and she says tell him I left him a note." The woman pointed her chin at Brian. "And off she goes. By time I get to the door she's in the taxi and it's off down the street."

"Where did she go?" Brian pushed his fingers back through his wet hair.

"So I'll ask you again," the woman went on, ignoring him, "what did you do to that girl?"

He said nothing. It was hard to breathe. He turned and gestured weakly to the man.

"Please could I have the key?"

The man let his fist wobble back and forth on his thick wrist, and he looked from Brian to the woman.

"We run a decent place here," he said.

"I think it'd be best if you took your rucksack and stayed somewhere else," the woman said, and Brian heard the click as the man pushed the key at him across the formica. "If I thought that poor girl was getting any of it, I'd think about refunding your money," the woman went on, but Brian had already snatched the key and pushed past her to the stairs.

"You bring that key right back!" the man behind the counter called out.

At the third floor Brian fumbled at the lock in the dim light and dropped the key. Finally he pushed the door open and let it slam behind him, looking around the room as he caught his breath. In the gray light he saw his own backpack leaning against the bed next to the window, where both backpacks had been that morning. The curtains next to the bed shivered in the draft, and he crossed the room slowly, as if afraid of giving himself away. On the worn blanket on the bed he saw a page from a notebook folded in half. He picked it up and sat carefully on the mattress, holding the note unopened against his leg. His name was written in clear script across the top, neatly centered. He covered the note with his hand, and sat rigidly, listening to the noises from the street, horns and brakes and the hiss of rain. Then without thinking he spread the note in his fingers, pressing it against his thigh.

"I won't tell anybody," it said in the same graceful handwriting. "Please please please leave me alone." It was not signed.

He folded the note again and slid it into the pocket of his anorak. His hand shook as he pulled it out of the pocket, and his breath came in gasps, as if he had just broken surface. He gripped both his legs just above the knees, and bent all the way forward as if he were about to throw up, holding himself tightly, squeezing his eyes shut in pain, afraid that if he let himself go he might start to weep and never stop. Finally he sat up and tipped his head back. He opened his eyes to the stained ceiling and let out a single sob. He pushed himself unsteadily up off the bed and yanked the backpack off the floor, stumbling as he slipped it on.

In the lounge the red-headed woman had returned to her chair by the television. The man at the counter looked up at Brian.

"Can you just tell me where she went?" Brian slid the key across the counter.

"Even if I knew, which I don't, I wouldn't tell you." The woman spoke from the chair without looking away from the correspondent on the screen. "You leave that girl well alone."

"A police spokesman has been unable to provide a casualty count as yet," the newsman was saying. "Witnesses at the scene say that there were fatalities, and that, quote, dozens of people, close quote, were injured."

"Please." Brian stepped back from the counter, looking from the man to the woman. "It's an emergency."

"You'd best just leave," the man said behind him.

Brian swallowed against a thickening throat.

"I'll pay you," he said. He unbuckled the belt of his pack to get at his wallet.

The Irishwoman shot straight up out of her chair.

"Get out!" She flung her arm toward the door, and Brian froze with his hands on the open ends of his belt.

"Thomas, throw this lad out," the woman barked, and the man behind the counter blew out a sigh and started around the counter. Brian snapped the belt shut and fled toward the door, his face hot.

He rode the Underground all afternoon, not caring where he went, his pack on the seat next to him. Sometimes he closed his eyes, thinking of what he would say to her, what would make her sit and listen for five minutes. But all he could do was watch as Clare reeled with him across the dancefloor of an Irish pub, as she turned her burnished face to him on top of a mountain, as she folded herself around him in bed the night before. Then his breath came hard and he opened his eyes and stood; he dragged his pack off the seat and marched out of the train in the crush of people to find another platform and wait for the first train to come along. He would stand there immobile, waiting, the pack dragging at his shoulders, and finally a train would come, pushing its oily breath before it, leaning out of the tunnel, dipping one shoulder.

It seemed to Brian that he saw the same people over and over again, the same skinheads and housewives and tramps. He looked at all their faces, though, and at all the faces of the people on every platform. He was afraid he would pass her without seeing her, afraid that he would look up from his seat to see her on the platform as the train pulled away, or that he would glimpse her averted face on a train that was leaving him behind. On one platform, looking up at the blackened back walls of the houses above the railway trench, he felt sick, thinking that she might be up there while he was looking for her down here. I can't look for you everywhere, he thought, pleading silently, it isn't fair.

When he came up out of the Underground it was dark, as though he had been trapped below for days. The bright lights of shops and theaters gleamed red and blue and green in the wet streets, and he followed the stream of people alongside a wide street full of traffic. He thought once that he ought to pull up the hood of his anorak, but he didn't, letting the rain tap against his head. He was hungry in spite of himself, and he went into a Burger King, where he stood in line with rain water dripping off his pack to the floor. When he sat with his meal, though, he saw an evening newspaper on the next table, its headline turned toward him: IRA BLAST AT NATIONAL GALLERY. Below that, next to a photograph of a man with rivulets of blood down his face, it said, 11 KILLED. He stared at the words until they no longer made sense, his Whopper cooling untouched before him, and at last he got up and left.

On the sidewalk again he tugged the hood of his anorak over his head. Up ahead he saw a bright glow where the crowded buildings opened up into a bright square, a giant rotunda of light, the ceiling of low clouds lit from below by the hellish orange light of the city, the wall of massive buildings all around brilliantly lit, all white pillars and arched windows. Traffic rushed in a bright, headlit stream around one edge of the square, the other two sides having been cut off by police barricades. Brian crossed the empty street to the square, wading through the fringes of the murmuring crowd at the foot of Nelson's Column. He walked around a fountain, its mist sifting through the rain, and climbed the steps until he came up against a vivid white tape reading POLICE LINE: DO NOT CROSS. Across the street uniformed men with bright, lime green vests moved quickly among vans and trucks and police cars, the vehicles crowded at all angles against the opposite curb under the brightly lit portico of the museum. Radios hissed and spit, men in black moved up and down the steps in parallel opposing streams as if on an escalator. Directly across from Brian, before an embankment of grass, unnaturally green in the harsh light all around, several television correspondents stood microphone in hand before their respective cameras, each surrounded by a nimbus of light, a Renaissance angel.

It's all theater, Brian thought. It's a lie. Nothing happened here; there's not a mark on the place. He felt something like relief: all the pillars were intact and perfect, there were no halos of soot over the windows, there was not so much as a broken pane of glass, nothing that even approached the ruin of any single shop on the Falls Road. He almost laughed at the sight of the uniformed men, scurrying like ants repairing their nest, but he couldn't make the laughter come. I don't feel a thing, he thought, not even where she hit me, it doesn't even hurt. A couple of policemen standing at one of the nearer cars were looking in his direction now, and he thought, It's all because the blast was deep inside, where it could kill without leaving a mark. One of the cops nodded to the other and came around the car toward Brian, walking slowly in his long, gleaming raincoat, his feet reflected in the empty, rain-wet lanes of the street, and Brian knew that the inside of the museum was hollowed out and ruined and full of smoke, that he could put his shoulder to a pillar and push the wall over, that the whole building would crumble in on itself, like a corpse with its organs all turned to dust, like the aching, paper-thin walls of his heart.

The policeman lifted a pale hand against the black of his coat.

"Lost your way, have you, sir?" he said.

Coming up the narrow lane behind Mansion House, Brody walked alone in the middle of four bodyguards, boxed in like a film star at a premiere. They were not his usual lads, who instead of minding him were managing security for the whole party conference, sweeping the hall for bombs, manning the doors, and checking credentials. The press alone this evening were enough for anybody to handle; they were waiting for him as he walked the few cold paces from the car to the back door of the hall, crushing around him between the walls of the lane. He ducked his head through a cacophony of shouted questions about the day's events in London; then he was up the steps and through the doors that one of his escorts held open for him.

The four lads with him now were just boys, really, Dublin ghetto youths hand-picked for him this afternoon by the head of Dublin Brigade, four lads without a record, who had yet to join an Active Service Unit but who had demonstrated steadfastness and loyalty in some other important way. They had waited for Brody all day in the house where he was staying in North Dublin, watching out the windows and answering the door and the phone. In the car on the way to Mansion House they had hemmed him in, one on either side in the back seat, without saying a word, and now they walked him slowly up the carpeted corridor toward the waiting delegates, the murmur of six hundred men and women growing louder as they approached the door.

"Are they necessary?" Brody had asked when Dublin arrived at the house with the boys.

"Yes," Dublin had said, laconic and cadaverous as ever.

Brody reached inside his coat pocket and pulled out his opening address, folded over once, lengthwise. At his own insistence it was the same speech he had been working on for the past month; there were no new pages, no handwritten marginal inserts. The paramount role of a leader at a time like this, Brody had concluded, ending a hastily called and near hysterical meeting of the party leadership only an hour or so before, was to provide continuity and the appearance, at least, of his imperturbable control of the situation.

"Postpone it a day," Peter Egan had suggested, trying as usual to walk the middle way. "Give us a day to find out what Coogan's people want."

"No," Brody had said, sitting stiffly upright on a couch, his back giving him hell. "We know what they want. I won't let renegades set the agenda for this movement." He had looked once around the parlor, gauging everyone's backbone. "Don't forget, Coogan is gone. They haven't got a leader any longer. Give it a few days and they'll throw in the sponge."

"They haven't a leader at the moment," Peter had warned,

verging on anger. "But they will by the morrow, I'll tell you that for nothing."

It was a clear reference to Peter's failure that morning with Maire Donovan, though Brody was, as far as he knew, the only one in the room Peter had told. He had yet to doubt Peter's loyalty, but it was clear that Egan disapproved of Brody's handling of the situation so far. Some of his discontent could be put down to his embarrassing misadventure in Belfast that morning. Peter had spent the better part of an hour arguing with a UDR captain who had cordoned off the area and wanted to impound Peter's car as an abandoned vehicle, all the while the lone remaining staffer at the Falls Road offices tore the place apart looking for the spare set of keys. Peter himself had been on the brink of arrest, for refusing to say what had happened to the first set, when the staffer breathlessly showed up with the spare. Peter had arrived in Dublin at last at midday, still furious, and Brody would have laughed it off had not the OC Dublin arrived a short time later with four somber lads and news of a phone call from London, a good half hour before the first radio bulletin.

"OC London called," he said. "Coogan's lads got the parcel and set it off in the National Gallery."

It had been just the two of them in the kitchen at that point, Dublin standing away from the window, his hands curled at his sides, Brody standing near the cooker, his back erect against the pain.

"Who's responsible?" Brody had said.

"The police received a call five minutes before, claiming it was a Provo action. London says it's the first he'd heard of it."

"What's he think?"

"Vincent Brennan and his ASU have vanished."

"What's the situation?"

"Special Branch are in a frenzy. They're kicking in Irish doors all over London."

Dublin stopped, having said what he needed to say, and waited while Brody walked slowly along the kitchen, rolling his shoulders to ease the unreachable pain between them. A moment later, though, Dublin spoke again without prompting, offering a rare unsolicited comment.

"We'll have to deal with them now," he said, his voice still the same taut monotone. "It's gone beyond Coogan."

But Brody had said nothing more to Dublin, and he did not back down later in the day, in the emergency meeting in the parlor.

"Today's not the day to argue the importance of the political front," Peter said. "Taking your seat in the Dail is not the issue any longer."

"Today's as good as any other," Brody replied, and then Peter played his trump, a flat remark accompanied by a hard stare that Brody could only interpret as a veiled threat.

"They've got a martyr already in Coogan, Joe," Peter said. "The Brits have seen to that."

Peter's insinuation that he'd reveal who was really responsible for Coogan's death stung almost as much as Brody's unhealed wounds. Peter was a good man, but he was not indispensable to the movement. Brody ajourned the meeting without further comment, saying only that they would issue a communiqué later in the day.

Now he stood at the door of the conference hall, the Round Room in the Mansion House, where the Dail itself used to meet. He waited patiently in the corridor with three silent young men while the fourth conferred just inside the door with the security man there. Through the glass in the double doors Brody saw bright lights around the rim of the rotunda, and below, under the crests of the Lord Mayors of Dublin, the faces of the people crowding the balcony. What had been a murmur in the corridor was a roar here, six hundred anxious voices all talking at once, analyzing Brody's position from every possible angle and then some. His speech, important in any case, was now almost painfully anticipated, his words liable to be parsed down to their bones by every man and woman in the room even as he spoke them aloud. But Brody knew that at the end of the day what he said was not nearly as important as his demeanor, his carriage, the set of his shoulders. The entire Republican movement lay at this moment like an egg in the palm of his hand, and something as simple as a cough in the wrong place, a mispronounced word, a stumble as he stepped up to the lectern could shatter it irrevocably. Without smiling he drew a breath and wondered if Arafat ever had days like these.

Then he was on. One of the Dublin lads took his coat. The door pulled open and one of his regular bodyguards, a burly Belfast lad, beckoned him in, and Brody stepped through the door into the light. The roar of conversation fell away from the back of the hall to the front as he walked up the central aisle into a deafening silence. In spite of all the delegates on the floor and the observers in the gallery, the room was chilly, smelling of varnished oak and musty drapery. A rustle came from the balcony as people edged forward against the rail, their faces white against the ornate cornices. The delegates seated on the floor turned to watch him pass, their seats creaking in a rolling wave that followed him toward the dais. Brody ignored their eyes, though, gazing steadily ahead at the black lectern, at the words Ard Fheis in old Gaelic lettering enclosed by gold piping. Behind the lectern a huge, dark green banner hung without stirring from the balcony, with more old Gaelic lettering proclaiming SINN FEIN: ONE PEOPLE ONE NATION.

He stepped up onto the dais with just a nod to those at the tables on either side, and he edged along behind their chairs, his back stiff and numb. Some he could depend upon; others, like Peter, he was not certain of; Coogan had not left him time to marshal his support. At the lectern he lifted the speech to the polished wood and smoothed it flat, frowning at the thicket of microphones before him, red and gold and black. Collins and de Valera had stood here and looked out on this room, at faces like these, pale and indistinct and expectant; but others had refused to enter this place, preferring to spill their own blood and the blood of others in the pursuit of an ingrown and autistic idealism, vicious and blind with frustration, unable or unwilling to participate in the difficult and unspectacular bricklaying of a modern nation. Brody stood before the delegates like a man at the very edge of the precipice, ignoring the long, fatal drop at his feet, and he paused a moment longer to pour himself a glass of water from the carafe at his elbow. Then he curled his hands around the edges of the lectern and, clinging for dear life, lifted his face to the light and began to speak.

Brian woke up under a bridge, stiff and aching and covered over with a beaded net of dew. He opened his gummy eyes and saw above him the black girders of the bridge arching away. Below, starting just beyond his numbed cheek, the cracked gray stones of the embankment sloped down to the river. The leaden water glided sluggishly by, pale mist curling off it, and Brian stared hard, trying to decide if it was moving or he was. Something passed inches over his head with a deafening thunder that made the embankment shake under him, and he started wide awake, frantically pressing himself flat against the gritty ledge, his heart pounding, listening to each thump of the wheels against the joint above as if it were inside his head. When it was gone he pushed himself stiffly up from the ledge, scraping against the dirt and sending a cascade of pebbles bounding down the embankment to plunk into the water. He leaned back against a girder, his anorak crackling, his legs draped over the edge of the embankment. His head still pounded to the hollow rhythm of the wheels against the bridge, and after a moment he felt the cold of the girder through all his layers of clothing. He drew a deep breath to hold back a climbing nausea.

He had tried calling Vincent's number twice last night and had gotten no answer, and at last he had taken the Underground all the way out to Turnham Green again. The park was vaulted over by the same orange glow he had seen in Trafalgar Square, and he sat on the same bench as before with his pack beside him in the yellow light from the lamp, watching the trains glide along the railway embankment. Finally he went back to the station under the railway bridge and called the number one more time, impatiently, as if Vincent had stood him up. This time someone picked up the phone on the first ring.

"Hallo?" A man's voice, tentative.

Brian's heart hammered, and he couldn't find his voice. There was a rustle on the line, as of a hand slid over the mouthpiece.

"Hallo?" The man again, more sure of himself.

"Vincent, please," Brian whispered.

"Come again?" The man's voice, an Englishman, then a taut silence.

"Vincent?" Brian held the phone slightly away from him.

"This is Vincent," said the Englishman pleasantly. "Who is this, please?"

Brian bobbled the receiver like a clumsy center fielder, and he banged it down on its hook and walked as fast as he could out of the station and up the street past the dark shops to a brighter, busier street, glancing back every few steps, each glance an awkward turn to see around his backpack. He caught a bus and rode the top section all alone for a few minutes, jumping up again when the bus started across a bridge over the Thames. He ran down the little spiral staircase, the pack scraping the wall, and he pulled the cord, the conductor turning around at the front of the bus and thrusting two fingers at him as the bus stopped in the middle of the bridge. On the sidewalk Brian had shouted back at the conductor and given him the finger as the bus ground away.

Now he winced as another bus thumped over his head, its wheels drumming against the bridge, and he swallowed against a sour throat and tried to remember where he was. Last night he had carried his pack over the bridge, cars hissing past in parallel streams of advancing white lights and receding red ones. It was this bridge, he thought, feeling a little balm of satisfaction in the dull throb of his head, but then he started violently, panicking. Where's my pack, he thought. What if somebody finds it? If they find the plastique I'm fucked. He pulled his stiff legs under him, but the nausea climbed higher and he slid back onto his ass, turning his head to one side and retching dryly. He closed his eyes and remembered the bright pub at the far end of the bridge, its long bank of bright windows overlooking an empty brick veranda and a dark, grassy common. He remembered sitting in a corner away from the crowd of laughing, well-dressed people, all his own age or younger, his head tipped back against the wallpaper, a small round table between his knees; he remembered alternating between pints of beer and shots of Scotch, remembered staring at the shining glasses hung upside down over the bar. Once he had closed his eyes, and opening them again there had been a round-faced girl in a yellow sweater sitting across the little table from him. He'd moved his head too suddenly from the wall, his brains sloshing up against his forehead, and the girl had smiled and said something. She'd said her name eventually, but now all he remembered were the yellow bangs across her forehead and the swell of her breasts under her sweater, and he twisted his face away from the memory as if averting his eyes. He opened his eyes and saw his pack ten feet away from him on the ledge, lying in a heap and covered with droplets of dew like another sleeping drunk.

He grunted with relief and crawled toward the pack, digging his fingers around a strap and dragging it back after him with a hiss. He remembered laughing and whispering with the girl in the corner of the pub, remembered the beads of sweat on her forehead and the liquid shine of her eyes as they agreed to meet outside in five minutes.

"I gotta get my pack," he'd said, swaying on his feet over the wobbly little table. "But like, don't tell anybody, okay?"

He remembered pissing against a wall and then scrambling in the dark up the gritty embankment to the ledge where he'd stashed the pack before going into the pub. There was nothing after that, until now. Rattling pebbles, he slid with his backpack down the enbankment in the thin gray light to the little path above the water, his fingers tight around the straps of the pack. He knelt for a moment with his eyes closed and his head doing circles around his shoulders, and then he slowly stood, pulling the pack up with him, pushing his arms stiffly through the straps one at a time. Before he buckled the belt he felt for his wallet and looked at his watch. It was six o'clock.

He walked out from under the bridge, uncertain of his legs, and found himself behind the pub, dark now, looking abandoned in the gray morning. He went into a dank gents' against the side of the bridge, its light smashed by vandals, and in the acrid dark he pissed and splashed freezing water from the tap against his face, all without taking off his pack. Outside again he heard the hollow rumble of a jet, and he looked up, wiping the water off his face with his numbed palm. A plane hung in the gray clouds, seemingly just out of reach. He started up a flight of steps alongside the bridge, clutching the wet handrail all the way up, stopping once to look back at the jet gliding away overhead. He had to find an Underground station, he decided. He couldn't be far from Turnham Green, but he couldn't go back there. The way his luck was going he'd be certain to find the police waiting for him, or worse yet, Vincent.

At the top of the steps he paused to let his stomach settle; then he started over the hump of the bridge. He needed to get on a plane; the longer he stayed in England, the deeper the shit he was likely to find himself in. He managed to walk a little faster, putting his head down and pulling at the railing of the bridge as if struggling against a stiff wind. His head was beginning to clear at last, and he shook it and told himself to just keep walking, don't think. But by then it was too late, and yesterday came back to him, a pain he had forgotten while he slept. He walked a little faster, his only consolation that Clare was probably as far from him as if he had never known her, beyond his or anybody else's reach, safe.

He sat alone in the bright interior of the car, the backpack rocking in the seat next to him as the train carried him sideways through a thickening mist. Across from him, in the curve of the car's roof, was a sign in red, black, and white that said BOMBS! BE ALERT! and he averted his eyes, watching out the window instead. Empty suburban platforms slid out of the mist and paused for a moment before sliding away again; leafless trees alongside the track faded into the fog like shadows. The contrast between the indistinct light outside and the glare of the light in the car reminded him of school when he was a child, when everything inside the classroom seemed brighter and newer than the overcast autumn sky outside. He felt the same queasy eagerness now, and he looked forward to the long monotony of the plane. If he closed his eyes, he could make the rattle of the train become the low, seamless roar of jet engines. He would refuse the food offered him and tip his seat all the way back; he would look out the tiny window for a while at the milky clouds, and then he would close the plastic shade and sleep suspended as far above himself as the plane floated above the Atlantic.

The track plunged underground, and the roar of the train doubled, its clatter thrown back by the sides of the tunnel. Brian opened his eyes and concentrated on the grainy streak of wall beyond the window, struggling not to think of Clare. At last the Heathrow station glided into view, bright and empty. He wrestled the pack on and stepped onto the platform, where the air felt damp and sticky, clinging to his face and hands like a wet tissue. At the top of the escalator he saw two policemen walking toward him down the concourse, their black coats soaking up the gray light, and he felt nothing as they passed, not because he no longer had the plastique, he decided, nor because he was clever or lucky but because he was invisible. Nobody's looking for me, he thought, because I don't matter now. No one can see me anymore.

In the crowded international terminal he bought a stand-by ticket to Detroit, and the dapper Indian clerk told him there was a seat available on the next flight. He took off his pack and propped it against his leg as he waited in line at the check-in desk, and a handsome Asian, the top buttons of his white shirt undone, came up to him and said, "Good morning, sir. I'm with Pan Am security. May I see your ticket and your passport, please?"

Brian handed them over, and the man held them between his hands.

"You are checking your rucksack onto the plane, sir?"

"Yes." He wished he had left it under the bridge, or heaved it over the side into the Thames.

"This is your own personal luggage, packed only by you?"

"Yes."

"It contains only your personal belongings?"

"Yes."

"And it has not been out of your sight, sir, since you packed it last night?"

"No." He wanted to laugh, but he didn't think he could manage it. The security man handed back Brian's ticket and passport.

"Thank you, sir. Have a pleasant flight."

He put the passport in his pocket, and upstairs, when he pulled it out again for the man at the passport control desk, there was a piece of paper stuck in it. He pulled the paper out and read it while the officer looked over his passport. "I won't tell anybody," it said. "Please please please leave me alone."

A surge of blood through his chest cleared everything before it like a wave, and Brian felt tears squeeze unwanted into the corners of his eyes. He blinked them back as he walked through the metal detector into the boarding lounge, thinking, It doesn't matter, Coogan's dead, Maire's already under arrest, no one knows about me, I am invisible. Clare's all right if she doesn't say a word.

Someone jostled him in passing and Brian shuddered, shoving his passport into his pocket, crushing Clare's note in his hand. He looked around, blinking at the rows of orange checked seats, to see if anyone had noticed his distress, but he was still invisible. He started walking, certain of his anonymity as he slipped past black men in expensive, stylish clothes, past plump Indian women in saris, past jowly white men in turtlenecks and tweed jackets and checked tweed caps. A group of dusky men in turbans and dark, baggy suits squatted on the orange carpet around a wailing tape player, and coming around them Brian stopped short as three girls in sweaters and jeans and hiking boots walked by, one of them with a single tight braid of blond hair swaying across her back. None of them looked like Clare, but his heart stopped a moment anyway, and he followed a stream of people to a newsstand, where he found himself staring down at the neat stacks of papers, all them broadcasting a single story like a drumbeat: 15 DEAD. PROVOS STRIKE. THATCHER VOWS JUSTICE. The front page of one tabloid was filled with a single word in black:

OUT-

RAGE

Brian squatted to read one of the papers without touching it. Legs brushed against him, arms reaching past him to peel papers off the tops of the stacks. He read a little black bordered sidebar between the main story and a photograph of a ruined gallery at the museum. BOMBING UNAUTHORIZED, IRA CLAIMS, read the headline, and Brian felt the blood beating in his knees and throat.

"In a communiqué issued late last night in Dublin," the article said, "the Provisional Irish Republican Army announced that, although carried out by some of its members, the bombing yesterday at the National Gallery in London was not authorized by its ruling Army Council. The communiqué went on to express the IRA's regret at the loss of life, and promised that those responsible would be disciplined."

The rest of the article disappeared under the fold of the page, and Brian's knees began to wobble under the strain of squatting. He pushed himself suddenly to his feet, staggering back, his head light, pinpricks of black floating before his eyes. The journalist on the ferry was telling the truth, he thought, breathing deep. I'm not just in trouble with the police, I'm in trouble with the IRA.

He found an empty seat at the end of a row, next to a blue girder and facing the sliding glass doors of the corridor that led to the boarding gates. Across from him sat a fortyish, thickening man in a sportcoat with a fat Robert Ludlum hard-cover propped open on his lap. Next to him was a young boy with his feet dangling over the edge of his seat, reading a tabloid with a picture of the blast damage on the front page, listening to the tinny crackle of a Walkman. Brian stared first at the man, then at the boy, but neither looked back at him. He looked away across the lounge, and it came to him that if he was invisible it was because Clare was not, because she had carried off the risk along with the secret, like a contagion. She knew only by accident, but that wouldn't cut any ice with someone like Vincent, or with the rest of the IRA for that matter. The police certainly would not believe her innocence. If Tim had found him, so could the police, and if the police were looking for him, chances were they were looking as well for the girl who had traveled with him. And Vincent, Brian thought, he only trusts me because he knows I know that he'll kill me if I talk. Why should he trust Clare?

Brian felt sick, and he leaned forward in his seat, propping his forehead against the heels of his hands. And now Vincent knows her name, doesn't he, he asked himself. What asshole told him that? He closed his eyes. She's all right if she doesn't tell, and she promised, she said she loved me, she won't tell. He rubbed his head, unable to keep from asking himself, But what if she does? She's gone back to the States by now, but they know her name; how hard can it be to find where she lives?

His heart beat hard, as if he had been running, and he lifted his head and opened his eyes. Beyond the glass doors across the lounge he saw two policemen walk by down the corridor, their hands behind their backs, and in the tall windows beyond them the mist pressed up to the glass, as if the lounge sat high up in a cloud. Brian pushed himself back and drew a deep breath. If she's that easily traced, then she's safe, as long as she keeps quiet. The Provos know that if they hurt her, that would lead the police back to me, she's a loose thread, and the slight-est tug would unravel everything. All they can do is trust her, Brian told himself, and he nearly chanted aloud, like an invo-cation, She's safe, she's safe, she's safe.

A rapid mechanical clicking made Brian glance up, and he saw the blur of letters and numbers on the flight departure marquee. Over the whirr of the marquee and susurrus of talk he heard the public address announce an Air India flight to New York.

"May we take this opportunity," the voice went on, "to remind passengers not to leave their baggage unattended. All unattended baggage will be removed by the police."

Brian stood up, clammy with sweat, and he wiped his forehead with his palm. The man reading the Ludlum glanced up, and then looked back to his book. Brian slipped past his knees down the aisle and walked until he found a bar, where he ordered a Bass. He leaned against the bar and took a long pull of the beer, and setting the glass down he wiped his lip and saw a billboard across the lounge that said:

WE'RE THE YOUNG EUROPEANS
THE REPUBLIC OF IRELAND

The billboard showed four fresh-faced, well-dressed young students clutching their books and laughing. Brian thought of Clare's face and pushed the memory away, and he left the rest of the beer and went back to the lounge, where he found another seat, away from anyone else, a stand-up metal ashtray between his knees. He wished he had a cigarette.

I shouldn't worry about her, he thought, I should be worrying about myself. The beer in his empty stomach made him want to retch, and he bent over again, face in hands. If she talks, I could go to prison. Or worse. But she won't say a word; she loves me. He sighed, his breath coming hard. What if she lets it slip by accident? I hardly know this girl, he started to tell himself, but then he thought, That's bullshit, I know her well enough to know that she will let this eat at her from inside until she tells somebody or somebody reads it off her knotted face. Then they'll kill both of us. They'll hold me responsible if she talks, but they'll kill both of us.

He lifted his head, nauseated and sweating. I'll find her. If they can find her, I can too. I can protect her. Grampa can make a deal with the Provos; he can buy her safety and mine. If I could talk to her for five minutes, I could make her understand.

He twisted in his seat, covering his mouth with his hand. Across the lounge the wide red sign of the duty-free shop and the doorway below it were surrounded already by tiny white Christmas lights. I can't do it, he thought, I can't bully her like that, even if it saves her life. He almost wished she would tell, because if she didn't she would drag at him for the rest of his life; thinking of her, he would always see her face at the moment she knew the truth. Every woman he would ever touch would look at him with those eyes.

It came to him after a moment that he had been staring so hard at the sign across the lounge that the words "duty" and "free" no longer made any sense, and he shifted in his seat, uncomfortable no matter how he sat. The worst possibility of all was that she would keep his secret, carrying it forever like a malignancy. All she would have to show for loving him would be guilt for something she hadn't done, and he couldn't bear to think of Clare bent under the weight of the risk he'd taken on so casually. It was worse than unfair. He'd rather she hated him and informed on him than that.

The public address was broadcasting again, announcing his flight, the first boarding call for Detroit. He sat up straight in the chair, exhausted. He put his hands on the armrests and pushed himself wearily up, and he started down the rows of orange seats toward the glass corridor. The door ahead hissed open and he stopped abruptly in the aisle, and though his eyes were wide open all he saw was a brilliant white flash behind his eyes, all he felt was the thump of a concussion against his ears. He heard the flat tinkle of glass and the crack of masonry, heard screams and the singsong wail of a siren. And he saw Clare lying limp, her limbs twisted unnaturally, her face a sheet of blood. The blast killed her, or worse, he thought. If she tells, she dies, but if she doesn't, I have crippled her. He blinked and stepped back, the door hissing shut, and he stood for a moment, still trembling. The only way to save her life and relieve her of the burden was to make her telling or not telling irrelevant.

He turned down the aisle, away from the doors, and walked back to the seat, sitting forward with the ashtray between his knees. He held his hands out in front of him until they stopped shaking, and he felt quite giddy as he saw how simple it was, his head clear for the first time all morning. Across the lounge people passed in ones and twos through the sliding door into the corridor and turned right against the mist, toward the gate. He took Clare's note out of his pocket, along with the piece of paper with Vincent's number on it, and he thought, The only question is, am I up to it? He tore the two pieces of paper into smaller and smaller pieces, and lighting them in the ashtray he found himself laughing. If I'd thought this hard about taking the parcel in the first place, I wouldn't be here right now.

He bent over and blew out the last of the tiny flames, and he started up the aisle again. His hands were steady now and his head light, and he wanted to laugh again at the thought of his backpack flying home without him. The doors hissed open, and Brian stepped through and looked both ways. It was cold in the corridor, the mist scratching silently at the outside wall. He was no longer so anxious, though it sobered him to think that the best he could hope for was to be alive this time next year. He would try not to tell them about Clare, but even if they found out there would be no harm done now. It would be harder not to tell them about his cousin, but he'd do his best. I'll go on hunger strike, he thought, I'll tell them I got the plastique from the fucking leprechauns, that I found it under a toadstool, at the end of the fucking rainbow.

From somewhere out of the gray beyond the glass he heard the rising whine of jet engines, and he started down the corridor to the left, away from the boarding gate, toward the two policemen coming back his way. He smiled to himself, thinking, God knows I look the part, unshaven and unwashed, wearing yesterday's clothes. One of the policemen walked with his hands behind his back, the other with his arms crossed over his chest, and they talked to each other in low voices. The one with his arms behind his back saw Brian coming and murmured something to his partner. They both stopped, and Brian came up to them, smiling and apologetic.

"Sir," said the first policeman, raising his eyebrows politely.

Brian couldn't speak for a moment, and he let out a laugh like a long sigh and looked out the window into the mist. Somewhere the unseen engines screamed, and he had to raise his voice, the policemen inclining their heads toward him to hear.

Detective Inspector Angus Glassie stood bareheaded in the middle of the M1 motorway, wrapped in his heavy brown woolen overcoat and muffler, out in plain view of God and everybody. An old, heavy pair of army binoculars hung by a leather strap around his neck, and he kept his gloves in his pockets so that he could finger the focus of the glasses if he had to. He slapped his hands together to keep the feeling in them, but it wasn't doing much good. His circulation wasn't what it used to be.

The little bitch from MI5, who was working under the delusion that she was supervising this operation, sat in her posh quilted coat inside the warm van behind Glassie, watching it all on video and listening through her padded headset to the pickup from the long-range microphone. That wasn't Glassie's idea of intelligence gathering, by God, not by half. All she was liable to hear in there was a lot of Fenian rubbish, the usual hysterical and sanguinary funeral oratory. The real intelligence this morning was to be gathered out here, under the cold, gray sky, by a man's own eyes and ears.

The motorway was blocked off a quarter mile in either direction from Glassie, with British squaddies in full combat gear and his own men in bulletproof vests and riot helmets strolling up and down, showing the flag as it were. Beyond the waste ground on the other side of the road every bloody taig in Belfast was spread across the low hill of Milltown Cemetery, crowded among the gray tombstones for Jimmy Coogan's funeral. Glassie could only glimpse the coffin, draped in the tricolor—no doubt "Miz" Pulleine had a clear shot of it from the Brit helicopter angling noisily over the crowd—but then he didn't need to see it clearly. Jimmy Coogan was the least of his worries now, just another bloody name for the taigs to spraypaint all over town, this year's martyr, the Fenian flavor of the month.

Rather, it was that wretched bloody woman of Coogan's that Glassie wanted to have a word with. Thanks to an unusually stupid cock-up on the part of the UDR yesterday, she had vanished already, probably into the rabbit warren of West Belfast. Hadn't been seen near her flat, though, nor anywhere near the Sinn Fein offices in the Falls, and for all he knew she could be across the border into the Republic by now, rubbing her hands in unholy glee at the outrage in London yesterday. At first, before the news from London arrived, Glassie had been willing to let her disappearance go for the time being; she'd show her face soon enough, he'd thought, if only to let the press know what a freedom-loving hero her man had been. Now, of course, she was a suspect, and under his breath Glassie cursed the UDR for losing her, cursed the PTA for not allowing him to keep her another six hours, cursed his own rotten bloody luck. All he wished for now was her alone in a room without a camera, a pair of close-mouthed lads, and twenty minutes, and he'd clear up this business about the National Gallery before they had the glass swept up.

But instead of looking for her, he was playing nursemaid to Ms. MI5 at this sodding funeral. He banged his hands together and then lifted the binoculars, slowly scanning the hillside. There were perhaps a couple of thousand mourners, clustered among the foreshortened ranks of white and gray and black tombstones, with tall Celtic crosses rising here and there above the crowd, or a gleaming white Madonna, or even the dangling Y of a crucified Christ, hanging in the glasses against the bleak heights of Divis Mountain. Many of the mourners were women old and young in headscarves, and old men in caps, all of them hunched into their coats against the wind. There were a lot of teen-age boys who should have been in school, and the usual large number of men of employable age. Glassie worked the focus with his numbed middle finger and wondered at a race of men who had nothing better to do with their time than drink up their dole money, watch the telly all afternoon, and go to terrorist funerals of a workday morning.

He found the center of the funeral, the balding priest with his fringe of white hair blowing, holding his little black book in one hand, holding down his surplice in the wind with the other. Forget the Provos, Glassie always said, let me round up every bloody priest in Belfast and the troubles would end tomorrow. The Provos, in fact, he understood, and sometimes even grudgingly respected, but it was the priests, the ostensible men of God, for whom he saved his special contempt, and he'd said as much to Ms. Pulleine on the way here this morning.

"I don't think God takes sides in the matter, Inspector," she'd said in her infuriating drawl. "I think that in this particular instance God is a Buddhist." She'd smiled. This evidently was her idea of wit.

"Not in Ulster, ma'am," Glassie had said in return, crossing his arms. "Here you're either a Catholic Buddhist or a Protestant Buddhist."

Now, as Glassie watched, the priest closed his book, bowed his head, and turned away. The inspector lowered the glasses, turned around, and jogged to the van, where he opened the door on Ms. Pulleine and one of his own men seated on swiveled stools, surrounded by banks of blinking lights and video screens and revolving reels of tape; she'd tied her expensive hair back this morning, the better to wear headphones. They squinted down the van at him, cave creatures exposed to a sudden light.

"This is it," Glassie said to them, and he slammed the door

and stepped back to the middle of the road, beckoning over a British squaddie with a radio on his back.

"Tell your captain to keep sharp," Glassie said to the boy, gesturing up the hill. "The same goes for the lads in the copter. If anybody interesting shows up, it'll be now."

The boy nodded and trotted away, his radio crackling, and Glassie lifted the binoculars again in time to see five men file out of a gap in the crowd at the gravesite, each one in a field jacket and a black balaclava. They ranged themselves neatly across Glassie's field of vision, and he tightened his grip on the glasses. Frankly, he was surprised to see them; until now, the hallmark of this funeral had been not who had shown up but who had not. None of the Sinn Fein leadership had seen fit to drive up from their party conference in Dublin, even for the morning. In light of what the anonymous caller had told them a week ago about Coogan's standing with the Provos, and given the contents of the Provo Army Council's communiqué last evening—not our fault, they said, but we apologize—Joe Brody's uncharacteristic absence from a Fenian funeral spoke volumes.

But now there was an honor guard, and as Glassie watched they raised their mismatched pistols at arm's length over their heads and fired in unison, the thin cracks blowing down the hill over the heads of the crowd. Glassie looked away from the binoculars and glanced down the motorway to either side, making sure that the soldiers and the police all held their positions; a charge up the hill into that lot would be a public relations disaster and, judging from past experience, wouldn't yield them a bloody thing anyway. The honor guard always managed to melt away like smoke, and the crowd, feeling its collective strength, always regarded even the gentlest intrusion of the security forces as an excuse for aggro.

But they were all good lads along the motorway, nobody budged an inch, and Glassie looked through the binoculars as the honor guard fired their third and final volley. They lowered their guns, and the man on the end, shorter than the others, stepped forward, closer to the grave that Glassie could not see, and lifted his pistol one more time. What's this, Glassie wondered, and the lone figure lifted his other hand to his throat and peeled off the balaclava with a twist of his head. Glassie's heart thudded painfully to a stop, and he squeezed the binoculars so tightly that they shook in his hands, bouncing Maire Donovan's pale face all over his field of vision. He mastered his shaking hands and watching as she fired three more shots into the air, her face a stiff mask of rage, her hair newly cropped down to her skull, shorter than that of the men around her. Then she turned away and the honor guard was gone in the crowd, the women around them hoisting umbrellas to hide them from the copter, and Glassie was shouting down the motorway at the soldiers and policemen who were loping across the waste ground up the hill.

"Nobody move!" he bellowed, on the run himself. "Everybody stay where they are!"

He grabbed the radioman again by the arm and shouted in his face.

"Tell your commander to recall his men! Now!"

"But the lady in the van—"

"To hell with her!" Glassie pounded on the boy's arm. "Do as I tell you!"

Up and down the road men hesitated, looking in Glassie's direction. One line of men was creeping along the diamond-wire fence to the left, their weapons at the ready, while the fringes of the crowd were turning to them already, their shouts carrying down the hill. Glassie ran down the middle of the motorway, waving the men back from the fence, the binoculars thumping against his chest. He heard cries from farther up the hill; it was too late to stop the soldiers moving in from the Falls Road side.

"Inspector!" The van door banged open, and Glassie whirled to see Ms. bloody Pulleine stumbling awkwardly to the pavement. "What the hell do you think you're doing?"

"My fucking job!" Glassie thundered.

"I beg your pardon? What makes you think you're in charge here?" She was stalking forward, her coat flying behind her, hands on her hips. "I want those men moved in, Inspector, *now*."

Christ, the woman was worse than the harlot up the hill.

"Not unless you want a bloody riot, ma'am," Glassie shouted back, nearly in her face. "You're guaranteed to lose her this way."

She stopped, glaring up at him, and he brushed past her and flung open the other door of the van, heaving himself up into the dim, cluttered interior, the whole vehicle rocking under him. Behind him he heard the Englishwoman shrieking at the men along the road, trying to get them to move up.

"Where's the Donovan woman now?" Glassie said to the constable. He was flushed and breathless, and he had to bend half over under the low roof.

"We've lost her, sir." The constable watched the video screen above him, touching a finger to one of his earphones.

"The copter too?" Glassie wheezed.

"Sir." The constable nodded, still not looking at Glassie. "When the first troops met the fringes of the crowd from the Falls Road, all hell broke loose." He gestured at the screen. "She could be anywhere by now."

"*Christ!*" Glassie pounded the side of the van. Then he drew a deep breath and said, "Call them back."

"Sir?" The constable turned toward Glassie for the first time, glancing past him out the door toward Ms. Pulleine.

"Do it. It's my responsibility," Glassie added wearily, backing out of the van to the pavement. "Tell them all to pack it in. Gas the lot of them and back off."

On the motorway he found the men standing about looking at each other while Ms. Pulleine yelled red-faced at the British captain, who looked pleadingly over her head at Glassie. Up the hill Glassie heard the useless rattle of the helicopter and the unmistakable cries of a riot in progress, and he didn't even bother to look. The gas would blow down the hill in a minute or two; it was time to go. Ms. Pulleine turned away from the relieved captain, and she marched past Glassie without looking at him.

"I'll have your job, Inspector," she called out in passing, her voice shaking.

"You wouldn't want it, lass," Glassie muttered. "Too many idjits telling you what to do."

He waved his arm at the captain.

"It's over," he shouted. "Send 'em home, Captain."

The captain shouted the order down the road to his men, and Glassie heard the van doors slam behind him. The captain came up to him and said in a low voice, "Can she do you any harm?"

"Not likely." Glassie sighed, pushing his hands into his pockets. "She's on her way back to the typing pool, even as we speak."

The captain laughed, and beyond him Glassie saw British troops and his own lads falling back to their vans and Saracens.

"What about the one up the hill?" the captain said.

Glassie looked back, saw the people in the cemetery fleeing from the crest of the hill, which was lost in a gray cloud of CS gas. He turned back and took the captain's arm, father and son walking up the motorway.

"Ah, well, she's another story," he said.

When the sky was clear she thought she could see both shores from the ferry nearly all the way across. Her friends and her Irish cousins laughed at her, but she was sure of it all the same, look back and see Wales, look ahead and see Ireland. But today the sky hung low over the sea, and the coast ahead and behind was hidden by the rain and the steely waves that rose up to meet the clouds. Standing under the bridge Clare could feel the rise and fall of the ship, and she watched the white spray rising in slow motion over the bow to crash against the deck. The light was failing already, and it seemed to her that everything about this day was futile, that it was over before it had begun. There was no point in waiting to see land, the boat wasn't moving anyway, all its effort served only to keep it in the same place while the waves battered it back and forth.

At first she had thought of calling Eileen. Eileen would understand. But Eileen couldn't keep a secret to save her life, and that's just about what it amounted to. Another drunk wasn't going to do the trick this time. So instead she had called the family in Cork, and asked her cousin Rose, Eileen's mother, if she could come back. Well of course you can come back, Rose had said, sounding almost irritated at the question. Is there anything the matter? Clare had started to cry over the phone, slow, deep, suffocating sobs. She could tell them that she'd had a fight with a boyfriend, and if they didn't ask too many questions she wouldn't have to lie. Then the phone had begun to pip, infuriating her, and she'd banged it down and marched up and down the pier until she'd finished sobbing. Then she'd called Rose back long enough to say she'd be on the next ferry, and could Rose meet her at Rosslare? She'd hung up again, unable to say anything more, standing in the phone box with her hand over her face until the crying stopped.

She was far from tears now, snuffling only to keep her nose from running, crossing her arms against the cold. She stood as far forward on the boat as passengers were allowed, her face numb and her ears burning, ignoring the raindrops that blew in under the bridge against her cheeks. Once someone else ventured forward against the wind, a woman who held the high collars of her raincoat together with one hand and pressed down on her headscarf with the other. She turned her face out of the wind and squinted at Clare, saying something that Clare did not hear. After a moment she went away.

Unable to sleep, Clare had bought all the newspapers at Fishguard and read them in the lounge. They all had the same photographs, or nearly so, pictures taken at the same time by photographers standing only a few feet from one another. There were the same quotes from bystanders and survivors, the same statements from the police and the Home Office and Buckingham Palace, the same condemnations by M.P.'s and Mrs. Thatcher and the Irish Taoiseach. All the papers printed the communiqué from the Provos; by now they all gave the same death toll. None of them mentioned Brian.

Now Clare no longer felt the cold or the unsteady roll of the ship, or heard the boom of the waves against the hull. She was the lifeless figurehead of St. Clare, all the sweetness hollowed out of her in a single instant, the explosion severing her from everything that had ever happened to her before yesterday, extinguishing her life before that, leaving her with only a single, unlivable day with which to proceed. She could divide her life now into before and after, and everything before was lost to her, the memory of it useless and frustrating like the false sensation of an amputated limb.

Her mind couldn't function any longer; the pain had penetrated all the way through and numbed her. Still, she began to feel the cold in her cheeks again, and she wondered if she shouldn't go back to the humid warmth of the lounge. It wouldn't hurt to have some tea, or a beer. But as she shifted on her feet and moved her shoulder away from the cold metal wall, she thought she saw through the dull veils of rain something of an outline, a darker shade of gray between the leaping waves and the lowering sky, and she decided to wait it out, until the hills of Ireland stood out clearly above the sea.